THE JUDGE'S DAUGHTER

THE JUDGE'S DAUGHTER

A Novel

Thomas T. Thomas

THE JUDGE'S DAUGHTER

Cover photo by Greg Henry via iStockphoto®
Cover design by Kimberly Killion

ISBN: 978-0-9849658-9-2

Contents

Summer 1938

To see a world in a grain of sand
And a heaven in a wild flower,
Hold infinity in the palm of your hand
And eternity in an hour.

—William Blake

OCTOBER 1948

1. JANE DOBRAY

LOOKING OUT THE window of the Greyhound bus as it followed Route 6 into Pennsylvania, Jane amused herself by counting cows in the fields until she lost count. Next, she counted barns. Then, only the barns painted with Mail Pouch Tobacco signs. Finally, as the two-lane blacktop road climbed into the mountains and the forest closed in on both sides, she was left with nothing to count but the trees. And they were just plain uncountable.

Jane pulled the envelope out of her purse, just to hold it in her hand again and make sure it was real.

The letter had come from Pennsylvania three weeks after her mother died. From the outside it looked like a letter, anyway, but when Jane opened it, the only thing inside was a check. A check for two hundred dollars. It was drawn on the Bank of Roulette, which Jane Dobray had found irresistibly funny. Like the Bank of Craps. Or Black Jack's Bank. The date was just three days past, the first of the month. And the signature was that of a man named Robert W. Wheelock, which didn't ring any bells. His name was embossed on the check, too, with an "Esquire" after it. Like the magazine.

Two hundred dollars! Couldn't she use that!

Then Jane had realized she would not be able to cash the check, because it was made out to Margot. She briefly considered forging her mother's name and what the hell. It was not like stealing from anybody. But for that much money, the banks in Brooklyn would hold up the cash long enough to check out her identity. And Margot was officially dead, with a certificate from the New York Department of Health and everything.

The years since the war had been hard for her mother. After getting laid off at the Navy Yard, she had tried to go back on stage. But a lot of girls, younger girls, were now looking for work, too, and nobody seemed to be hiring. And, as Margot would admit after her second whiskey sour, she never had that much of a career, even in the good times. When Jane searched her childhood memories, she finally figured out the closest her mother

3

ever came to working in the theater was six months as a cashier at the Radio City Music Hall.

Then the cough that Margot had, from working around the asbestos dust and paint fumes in the shipyard, started bringing up masses of bloody foam, and that was the end of the line. The kind of jobs Margot could get, mostly as a typist because she wasn't strong enough to wait tables, had kept them in a two-room flat with a narrow view of the East River and an occasional meal out at the Italian place around the corner. Money for a year at an upstate sanitarium didn't exist. Margot worked until she couldn't get out of bed and then died in the other room.

Even with her high school diploma, the best work Jane could find was sales clerk at the five and dime. On those wages, and after paying for her mother's medicines and the funeral, she could keep the apartment only by playing games with the rent money. Although the grocery bill was supposedly cut in half, Jane found more potatoes than meat on the table each day, and the Italians didn't see her anymore. So it was worth a couple of days and an eighteen-dollar bus ticket to someplace in Pennsylvania that she had never heard of to get her hands on two hundred dollars. Jane had called in sick and started this journey the next day.

When she turned to the window again, Jane could see the shadow-image of her mother's face reflected in her own. She certainly had Margot's lustrous, thick hair, which glowed like satin right after being washed, except that Jane's was an in-between reddish brown, rather than Margot's raven black. And Jane had her mother's strong, somewhat pointed chin, always set and ready for a fight. What she lacked were the shelving cheekbones, which had given Margot's face and flashing black eyes their bold definition. Jane had the dark eyes but, set in a flatter face, they merely looked somber, not vibrant like her mother's. And she didn't have Margot's wide mouth, her lips curving with the arch and sweep of a bird's wing. By comparison with her mother, Jane believed her face was as plain and humdrum as a flour dumpling.

And then there was her jawbone. The defect was concealed at most angles, but when she turned full face to the window, as now, it became obvious. The lower part of her face was out of alignment, lopsided. The corner of her jawbone on the right stuck out an inch further and an inch higher than the corner on the left. It pulled out her cheek on one side and gave her face a tough look, like a prize fighter or a hoodlum.

When she first noticed the defect, at age fourteen, when girls start looking in mirrors, she had asked Margot about it. At first, her mother couldn't see the problem, and then she dismissed it. "You were a difficult birth, you know," she said at last. "I guess in his grappling the doctor pulled your face kind of sideways. Nobody will notice."

But Jane noticed. And ever since, she had been conscious that she carried only odd fractions of her mother's perfect looks.

Well, it was too late to go back and ask for anything better.

Eventually, the bus pulled up at Jane's destination. She was disappointed to find that Roulette was just like every other little town out here: a crossroads with a diner, stuck between the Burma-Shave signs. Except that Roulette, being the county seat, also had a two-story courthouse built out of big, square blocks of gray stone. And, gee, she'd only passed through three, maybe four, other county seats like this one on her trip to nowhere.

Halfway down a side street she found the Bank of Roulette. It was another substantial building, although only one story and the stonework was much whiter than on the courthouse. Maybe limestone, Jane guessed. Nothing like the marble you saw on buildings in New York—not as sparkling and translucent. The door was a heavy thing made of solid bronze, with the pull polished bright by hundreds of rough hands. Inside, a long counter flanked one whole side of the lobby, decorated with intricate brass tellers' cages. In the back, a big steel vault door was visible above the line of cages. It must have made the money feel very safe.

Jane approached the first cage and waited until the teller noticed her. Then she smiled, put down her suitcase, and took Robert Wheelock's check out of her purse.

"I have a check drawn on this bank that I want to cash."

"Certainly, ma'am," he said. "Of course, your own bank should be able to¾"

"Well, there's a problem," Jane said. "You see, this check was made out to my mother, Margaret Dobray. But she's dead. So I wondered if you could give me the money instead." She slid the check through under the bars.

The teller studied it with a frown. "If she has died," he said at last, "her estate can cash this check. Then, after probate, if you are the rightful heir, the estate will pay you."

"My mother didn't have—" Jane stopped, not knowing how much to tell this stranger. "Sir, we are not rich people. Estates and probate are things beyond our means. Mother always said they were lawyer's tricks to get hold of your money. When she died, I just took her clothes and gave away what didn't fit. But this check is—"

"It's a legal matter," the teller finished for her. "The bank can't just make the check over to you. But ... I tell you what, why don't you go see the judge? He can decide what to do."

"The judge?" Jane was confused. Was this some special procedure they had in small towns? Apply in person for a legal shortcut?

"Over at the courthouse," the teller prompted. He leaned against the bars of his cage to point the way back up the street. "The bank will abide by his decision in the matter."

"I see." She took back the check and picked up her suitcase. "Thank you."

She cut across the courthouse lawn, which also seemed to be the town square, and climbed the wide, gray steps. The two facing doors were solid wood, weathered almost as dark as walnut, and bound with strips and studs of a green metal that might once have been red copper or bronze but now was badly discolored. On either side of the doorway were big oil lamps made of the same greenish metal and fitted with round globes of clear glass. Their design was more industrial—like great hurricane lamps with flat, conical shades—than the gothic style Jane would have expected to go along with the bleak stone and timber. She stood on tiptoe, to look inside these lamps, and saw that the oil wicks had been replaced with light bulbs. So they were fakes, too.

Jane pulled open one of the doors and stepped into a vestibule of frosted glass. Beyond was a foyer of checkerboard tiles, with stairs leading up to the second-floor landing. The woodwork in here was lighter colored than outside and had been recently varnished. She walked over to the nearest door, the only open door, under a sign that read "County Clerk's Offices - Records." She stuck her head inside.

The room was maybe fifteen feet by ten, taking up a corner of the building. Deep shelves lined each of the walls and framed the room's two windows, one in each outer wall, with the backs of leather-bound folios. From the short tags on their spines, Jane guessed they were the County Records, arranged by month and year. She tried to imagine birth certificates, death certificates, property deeds, and tax notices all jumbled together under this system. The only furniture was a roll-top desk, freestanding in the middle of the room, with a swivel chair behind it. A man was sitting there, apparently asleep, with his feet up on the desk, the chair tipped back as far as it would go, and his chin sunk on his breastbone. What she could see of him—the bald spot on top of his head, one ear and the side of his face, part of his neck—was brown and evenly creased, like a farmer's skin. Presumably, this was the County Clerk … of Records.

"Excuse me?" she said.

He lifted his head and peered at her with dull eyes. "Yes?"

"I'm looking for the judge."

"Well …" He yawned. "The judge's busy with a case."

"I can wait." Jane turned back toward the bench in the hallway. It was the same blond wood, with a dark patch where the varnish had rubbed off the seat.

"Be a while," the clerk called after her.

"Oh? How long do you think?"

The man squinted, as if calculating. "Trial's in the middle of testimony. He won't normally recess until four-thirty. After that, he may have to confer with counsel. Then he likes to write up his notes while they're still fresh. Could be six, seven o'clock before he comes down."

"I'll wait," she repeated.

"Courthouse closes to the public at five."

"Oh. Then … could you … interrupt him?"

"Not and keep my job."

Jane suddenly felt tired. She suspected she had come all this way on a fool's errand.

"Look," the man said, seeming to relent. "Why don't you tell me what you need? I'll see to it the judge sets aside some time on his calendar. Say, in the next day or two?"

"I wasn't going to be in town that long," Jane said.

He looked at the suitcase in her hand. "Well … whatever."

"No, I should thank you. Probably not another bus today—is there?"

He looked at his watch. "Not until tomorrow morning."

She put the suitcase down. "You see, it's about this check …" She took it out of her purse again and explained about her mother being dead and all.

The man squinted at the check. "Margot Dobray," he said. "Be damned!"

"You knew her?" Jane asked, because the check said "Margaret," her mother's given name.

"Knew *of* her. She was a bit before my time."

"She lived here?" Of all her mother's stories, Jane had never heard this one.

"Twenty years ago, just about."

"How did she—what did she do?" Jane didn't know quite where to begin. "Tell me everything about her."

"Not much to tell. She wasn't here long. She used to work for the judge, back before he *was* judge. Then she went away. No one knew where. … Sorry to hear she's passed on."

"Thanks." Jane had a sudden idea. "If Mother worked for the judge, then maybe he will know this Wheelock fellow."

" 'Course he does." The man seemed perplexed. "Judge Wheelock must of wrote that check himself."

"Oh! Then I definitely want to meet him. Tomorrow, you say?"

"I'll tell him you're looking for him, first chance I get." Then he gave Jane the once-over. "You got a place to stay?"

"No, not really."

"The Allegheny Hotel is very good."

"I don't have the money for anything so grand as a hotel!" Jane said.

"Well then, my missus runs a boardinghouse, nothing expensive but a nice clean place all the same. Second house on your left, just a ways down Water Street. Normally, she'll only take a single woman with a letter of reference. But I'll vouch for you, seeing as you're Margot's kid."

"Thank you, Mr.—?"

"Burke. Harold Burke."

"Thank you again," she said.

He just nodded. "See you later."

2. THE JUDGE

ROBERT WHEELOCK TURNED off the lights and locked up his courtroom. As he was coming down the stairs, Burke called out, "Evening, Judge!"

"You still here?" Wheelock asked, surprised. Usually, the county clerk was gone by the time Wheelock himself had disrobed, written up his personal notes on the day's cases, looked over the mail, and taken one drink of whiskey, for his health.

"Cold out there," Burke said, nodding at the evening dark outside.

"It is that," Wheelock agreed.

"Warm in here."

The Sylvan County Courthouse was a product of the Federal architecture programs of the 1930s, built of thick sandstone blocks and paneled in a rich red oak that Alfreda Burke waxed every spring until it shone like the sunrise. All that stone might have been cold and dank, except for the gas-fired furnace in the basement. Wheelock's courtroom as cozy enough to make the jurors nod off in the afternoon. But then, jury duty was popular in Sylvan County—at least once the snow started to fly.

"Remember to turn down the furnace."

"Aw, Judge! Don't I always?"

"Just checking."

"That reminds me." Burke snapped his fingers. "There was a girl here, looking for you. Said she was Margot Dobray's daughter."

"Really?" Wheelock's heart fluttered in his chest. "Did she say what she wanted?"

"Something about a check you had written—to her mother."

"I'll take care of it." He paused. "Anything else?"

"Just that Margot's died, so she said."

"I see. Too bad about that."

"Yes," Burke grinned.

"Well, good night."

10

Wheelock let himself out onto the wide steps and looked for his car. From the other side of the square, only the twinkle of its chrome showed in the shadows between the street lamps. It was more car than Wheelock needed, really, a new Chrysler Crown Imperial sedan. Wheelock's son had made him a good deal on the car—only insisting that he buy a black one, as befitting a judge's dignity. It ran smoothly enough and reliably took him the four blocks from his home to the courthouse and back.

Margot Dobray—dead. The thought came back at Robert as he was fishing for his keys. She had been young, in her twenties, when he knew her. So she would have to be—have been—at least forty by now. *Dead how?* he wondered. *Natural causes? Or misadventure?* Robert would bet on the latter.

Arriving at home, he turned into the driveway, drove down to park in the garage, and walked back up to the house, entering through the kitchen. From the sharp yeast smell, faint as it was this late in the evening, he knew that his wife had baked bread that afternoon. He took off his overcoat, hung it in the back hall, and called out, "I'm home!"

"Up here!" floated down from the second floor. "Dinner's in the oven."

Was Libby in bed already? Robert pulled out his watch: half past eight. Later than he thought. And he knew his son Willie would be out with friends—or maybe with that girl of his.

Robert went back into the kitchen and tested the heat of the oven door with the back of his hand. Just warm from the gas pilot light. He opened it and took out a napkin-wrapped plate. He lifted a corner of the napkin: glazed pork chop, fried apples, and a fresh roll, crusty now, cut and buttered so that the butter had melted into a glistening sheen on the bread's surface. He set the plate down and got himself silverware and a glass of water.

And now the daughter is in town. That thought gave Robert pause. She was probably using the Dobray name, too. How many people in Roulette would remember Margot? *Burke had remembered.* But then, how many would know, or even suspect, that there had been a daughter. *Well, the fact hadn't surprised Burke.*

Robert sat at the kitchen table and started eating.

Of course, Libby would remember the Dobray name.

He stopped with his mouth open, fork hanging in mid-flight.

Could the daughter possibly have stopped here—at the house—before going to the courthouse? That was an ominous thought, but it might explain Libby's going to bed early.

Robert tried to remember how he usually sent the checks. In a plain envelope, always, and not his personal stationery. And he did not use a return address. But could he, just once, have forgotten these precautions? It was possible. And, certainly, there would be a postmark, but that alone would not lead Margot's daughter to the house.

Next he tried to interpret the tone of Libby's voice, when she had called down a few minutes ago. Had she sounded angry? Not really. Upset? Hurt? Perhaps. And perhaps she was just tired, from baking, and so had turned in early.

Well, one way to find out how she was feeling would be to go upstairs and talk it out with her. But that would require a pretext, and Robert did not have one. Or none that he could use with Libby. And, after thirty years of marriage, he had learned that some questions were better left unasked. Time and a judicious amount of watching usually took better care of them. The morning would either bring its own confrontation and a dustup, or it would not.

When he had finished eating, he washed up his plate and silverware and set them in the rack on the drainboard. To his glass of water, he added a splash of whiskey from the bottle in the cupboard. Then he went out, down to the garage, where years ago he had built a windowed ell with a workshop and potting shed. The light of his work lamp reflected brightly off his tools, then lost itself among the burlap bags of peat moss and bushel baskets full of flower bulbs.

Robert turned up the gas stove until it made a cheerful red glow on the asbestos backboard. From his stock bin he pulled out a roll of six-gauge copper sheet and felt the weight of it. It was thin enough for his project tonight. With a pair of tin snips he cut a strip seven inches long and an inch wide. He flattened the piece with his hands, traced the diagonals from two directions to find its center, and made a tiny prick with one point of his metal-working compass to mark it. Then he measured off and made two more prick marks on either side, evenly spaced on one-inch centers.

During the past couple of months Robert had started collecting silver dimes of the type known as Winged Liberty Heads, pretty things with a face that reminded him of his wife's. He now had three of them: one dated to the year that he and Libby had been married, and one for each of the succeeding decades through 1938. He would have liked to collect the current year, too, but they had stopped minting these dimes right after the war. He was going to braze the three coins onto the copper as a bracelet for her. Polished up, they would make a fine piece of jewelry. But first he had to prepare the metal surface.

He started working with his ball-peen hammer on the center of the copper strip. *Tap, tap, tap* … light blows, spaced side by side, always hitting the same spot on the anvil, but moving the work, so the blows fell about a sixteenth of an inch apart, the dimples just overlapping. Each one bent the copper a little bit, curving it, thinning it, hardening it. *Tap, tap, tap* … a rhythm to the blows, the hammer song that let his mind drift.

A bracelet for Libby.

Three Liberty Head dimes.

Three decades of marriage.

The years of his life with Libby.

How had it all begun?

Tap, tap, tap, tap …

WINTER 1918

1. ROBERT

… *TING-TING-TING-TING*. AT five o'clock on a January morning, Robert Wheelock's alarm clock went off. He reached out and cupped the steel bells to muffle them. Even though no one else slept up here on the third floor—except the cook, and she could sleep through Sunday morning in a church belfry—he instinctively wanted to keep peace in the darkened house, on this day of all days. With his palm damping the bells, his fingers found and pushed down on the lever that stopped the mechanism. But by then the cold air and the colder metal had chilled his hand like an icy glove. He drew it back into his nest of warmth under the rough white percale sheets, which still smelled faintly from the scorch of a hot iron.

When he started to drift off, Robert roused himself with a jerk. He had too much to do today. He slipped sideways out of bed, so as not to disturb the layering of sheets, woolen blanket, and homemade quilt. That way he could make the bed more quickly, just by pulling the layers taut, without the complications of stripping it back and starting over. Robert had a methodical mind.

His leather slippers were at the bedside, right under his feet. Before sliding into them, however, he lifted his neatly folded trousers off the back of the desk chair and pulled them up over his knitted cotton union suit. Then he put on the slippers—minus his stockings, as he meant to take a bath this morning. His white shirt from yesterday was wrinkled and stained beyond possible repair with kettle and sponge, but it would do for now. He buttoned it without a collar, stood up to fasten his fly, and left the suspenders dangling about his knees. He wasn't dressed, exactly, not to appear in public, but his nakedness was covered enough to get about his morning chores.

All of this dressing was without benefit of a candle, his hands and feet working in the dark from memory. Robert's father, William Henry, had installed the new electric light throughout the house when it was built in 1900—after all, he owned the town's generating station and had started the electric company. But his

17

second wife, Lydia, who maintained the household accounts, promptly pulled the fuses on the circuits leading to the third floor. Candles were good enough for the servants and her grown stepson, she had declared, and she rationed them at two per month. So one learned to do without. Robert saved his stubs and melted them down to have more light for reading.

He went out into the upper hallway, which was even colder than his room, and down the front stairs. As he crossed the second floor landing, the beveled glass in the upper casement broke the stars into tiny rainbow spectra as they slid past the corner of his eye. He turned his head and looked out at the moon, three days shy of full and hanging just above the ridgeline to the west. Its cold light etched the hunched forms of his father's little orchard—eight black walnut trees in two parallel lines—into the snow.

Robert continued down the stairs. At the bottom he paused, his fingertips dragging across the carved acanthus leaves of the newel post. He listened to the house's quiet—and for any sound coming from the parlor. It was irrational, of course, because the thing in there, resting on draped sawhorses in front of the fireplace, could no longer make sounds. Not any more. But still Robert listened.

Nothing.

After a minute, he went down the back hallway to the cellar steps. Here the electricity did work, lighting the wood-plank risers and bare wall studs with a hard glare. Robert's first job on a winter's morning was to stoke the furnace. He went up to it and held his palm six inches from its iron side, then slowly moved in to touch it. Warm but not hot. He took the shovel and used its edge to unlatch the door and swing it open, stepping aside in case the clinkers inside shifted and rolled out.

Robert looked in at the mottled gray bed of ash. Unless he could find a live coal in there, this was going to be a hard, messy business. He stuck the corner of the shovel blade between the bars of the grate and shook it gently, holding his breath. A cloud of fine, white particles flew up as the surface dissolved in cinders and fell through into the ash pit. Only half a dozen dark lumps remained intact. One had a dull yet faintly rosy cast to it, like molten copper.

Robert planned his attack like a stone mason buttressing a sagging wall. From the nearby bin he selected three of the brightest pieces of anthracite, pawing them out onto the basement floor with his shovel. He scooped them one at a time and laid them on three sides of that live coal, nudging them in close. He put down the shovel, took the leather bellows off the hook, and began blowing on the ember. Little sparks flew off, revealing patches of brightness. After it was shining redly, and the surrounding masses of anthracite were smoldering, Robert selected more coal from the bin and laid it gently across his fire. More bellows work, followed by more coal, and soon he had a fine bed. Three more shovelful, and the house above would start to heat up. He added a fourth for good measure—though he knew who might have complained, if she had known—and the job was done.

Upstairs in the kitchen Rosemary Cobb, the family cook, was awake now and feeding the stove with kindling. "Morning, Master Robert," she said as he came back up from the cellar.

"Good morning, Mrs. Cobb." He went to the wood box and lifted the lid. It held enough split oak to last another day, given that no one would be expecting Rosie to cook dinner. Chopping wood for her was another of Robert's morning chores.

"My, that's a nice sound." She nodded toward the back hall, where the radiator had started gurgling. After a pause to acknowledge his work with the furnace, she ventured, "Big day today, sir."

"You could say that." Robert sat down at the table.

She bustled around and served him a cup of black coffee, a glass of water with a slice of lemon—from a basket sent fresh from Florida by train for his father—and a bowl of oatmeal porridge which had steeped on the stove overnight. Robert poured the cream she had set out for his coffee over the porridge and ate in silence. When he was done, he patted his lips with the linen napkin she had folded for him.

Rosie turned from the stove to look at the wall clock, a big Regulator from his father's long involvement with the railroad business. It filled the kitchen with a solemn tick, like slowly cooling metal. Six twenty-six, it said. "Shouldn't you be getting on, sir?"

"The train doesn't come until eight."

"But you can't go dressed like *that*, sir," she said with a sniff. "You want to be looking your best for your cousin."

"She's not my cousin, Rosie," he said mildly.

"Miss Lydia's niece, then. That still makes her family."

"But I've never met her. I don't even know what she looks like."

"Just take the prettiest girl who gets off the train. That will be Miss Libby."

Robert made a face. He could well imagine what Rosie Cobb's standards for "pretty" must be, having been in service with the family of Lydia Wheelock, formerly one of the Bracketts of Binghamton, across the border in New York State.

Rosie caught a glimpse of that face. "Oh, you'll see," was all she said.

Feeling he had somehow lost in the exchange, Robert went back upstairs. It was still dark, of course, so he lit one of his precious candles on the table just inside the door.

His apartment was at the front of the house, which faced north. He had one large room which served for his bedroom, sitting room, and study. Its single window, eight feet wide and bordered at top and sides with leaded glass, looked over the trees in the front yard to the fragment of Main Street that fronted the property and the mountain spur that defined the north side of the valley. At the room's west end was a cozy little fireplace, but its brickwork was swept bare, the lion-headed andirons polished and cold. Lydia would not pay for the wood Robert might have burned there nor let him carry it up three flights of stairs, strewing chips and bark throughout the house.

A connecting doorway beside the fireplace opened into a curious round room, just ten feet across, with diamond-shaped windows that looked north and west. This was one of two turrets built into the front corners of the house. Lydia had thought this room would make an excellent walk-in closet, and installed hooks and plank shelves at odd angles around the curved wall. Robert, however, preferred to keep his suits and small clothes in the tall cherrywood armoire—which he suspected she had secretly wanted for her own bedroom. He made the turret room into a library and filled its shelves with his law books and novels.

At the other end of the main room was the opposite turret, with oval windows facing north and east and paned in frosted glass. This was Robert's convenience. The floor and the walls, to waist height, were covered with alternating black and white tiles no bigger than his thumb. The room was fitted out with a basin, a flush commode, and—because the space was not large enough for a tub—a glazed metal stall with a spray nozzle overhead. If Robert wanted a good honest soak, he had to go down and use the communal facilities on the second floor.

He set the candleholder on the edge of the basin, and tested the hot water tap. The furnace had done its work, and the water was just warm enough to shave with. He took out his brush and mug, stirred up a thin lather, and painted his face with it. The stubble on his jaw was not long enough to poke through, but he proceeded with the shave anyway—for his father's sake, if not for Lydia's niece.

He stropped his razor on a horsehide belt and began the first downward pull from a point just in front of his ear. On the dark side of his face, away from the candle's flickering light, shaving was an adventure if not a positive danger. He used the fingers of his free hand to smooth the lather and draw the skin taut over the difficult angles of chin and jawbone. On this day, of all days, he did not want to look like he had lost a battle with Barbary pirates. But the trick to shaving with a straight razor was to move quickly and decisively: slow strokes and hesitant stabs were the surest way to get cut.

When his face was smooth to satisfaction, he stripped to the skin and stepped into the shower stall. The hot water was still more tepid than hot, but he soaped up quickly and rinsed off before it went completely cold. If he drained the tank in the basement for a while, no matter; the rest of the household would not rise for another hour yet, plenty of time for it to refill.

Robert dried himself next to the radiator, one of life's great pleasures on a cold morning. Too bad he had to use the thin, scratchy towels that Lydia favored throughout the house, like things stolen from a cheap hotel. At law school in Cambridge, Robert had grown accustomed to the thick Turkish towels supplied by the local French laundry. But Lydia would never stand for anything as luxurious and foreign—not to say costly and heathen.

When his hair was pomaded and combed, Robert dressed with some care. He put on his long johns again, on account of the cold. His best suit was a navy-blue worsted instead of black, but it would be dark enough, especially against a clean white shirt. (They were not following the old custom of dying the family's wardrobe black, thank God.) His best celluloid collar was only slightly frayed, and the gray cravat held with his onyx pin would cover the worn spot. He fingered a thick pair of argyle socks. Because the snow was deep in the yard, he would be wearing boots rather than shoes. Still, even though their lively pattern would be hidden from all eyes, he deemed the socks inappropriate. Instead, he chose a pair of black knitted silk, and never mind snags from the rawhide lining of his boots. He finished by putting his room key and coins in one trousers pocket; a clasp knife, comb, and handkerchief in the other. His wallet went into the left breast pocket; watch, chain, and fob through the middle buttonhole of his vest.

Ready to face the world—or at least Lydia's niece from Binghamton—he walked out of his apartment, locked the door, and started down the stairs whistling. Then he remembered, stopped, and went on more somberly. None of the family was stirring yet.

As Robert passed through the kitchen again, Rosie took her nose out of her coffee cup and looked pointedly at the clock. "What? Are you still here?"

He waved her off. "I'm already on my way."

The snow hung in soft scallops on the balustrade along the back porch. It was a foot deep for most of the driveway. There was a drift three feet tall around the barn, which sat exposed on the creek bank at the rear of the property, away from the spruces that surrounded the house. Robert kicked his way through the drift and found that the wind overnight had carved its inner surface into a hard-packed curl. He pulled the barn door back and went in. The two carriage horses and the five sheep that William Henry kept to clear the lawns in summer made the air inside warm and slightly moist.

Robert looked longingly at his father's hunter-green Pierce Arrow. How dandy it would be to drive up in the automobile, its brass gleaming and its paintwork shining in the low morning sunlight, to pick up Miss Libby. Then she would see what quality of people her aunt had married into with the Wheelock family. But he would make a poor impression arriving an hour late due to the snow, or perhaps breaking an axle in a ditch somewhere and never showing up at all. With a sigh, Robert decided the sleigh would have to do. He hitched up the bigger and stronger of the horses, named Jack Wax because he would eat the thin splashes of unthickened maple syrup thrown out on the snow during the sugaring off.

The horse walked up to the drift just beyond the barn door, broke through it in one long-legged plunge, hauled the sleigh over on a wave of white crumbles, and trotted up the drive. By the time they turned the corner into the lane, Jack Wax was in stride and the runners were squealing over the rutted snow.

2. LIBBY

IT WAS STILL mostly dark when Elizabeth Brackett stepped from the train onto the ice-crusted concrete platform that served for a station in Roulette, Pennsylvania.

With a death in the family, her mother had lost no time in sending Libby down to Emporium by the afternoon train and paid for her to spend the night in a hotel there so she could catch the early morning "mixed train daily"—for that was what the Pennsylvania Railroad's station master in Emporium had called it—up to Roulette. Or "*Raw*-lette," as Libby's mother had coached her. The locals would be suspicious of *Rue*-lette, she said, as a nasty game played on a slotted wheel spun by a Frenchman with the croup, or something. It was a game fit for the carnival midway and not honest gambling like dice or cards, where the players could get their hands on the mechanics of fate once in a while.

The tiny Emporium & Roulette Railroad was the principal claim to fame of William Henry Wheelock. That was Aunt Lydia's husband—her first marriage, but his second. Anyway, outside the confines of Sylvan County, where the E&RR mostly ran, Wheelock was known mostly as a railroad man. Within the county, he was also the local judge—practically the sole paid magistrate, as Aunt Lydia would always add with a touch of Binghamton scorn—as well as reputedly being the county's largest landowner. That was if you counted up all the acreage under his railroad's right-of-way, Aunt Lydia would have reminded you. Libby herself had seen most of that right-of-way this morning.

She had been the only passenger to board the train at Emporium. The conductor was a pot-bellied man in farmer's overalls and a gray sweater, the only sign of his authority being a blue peaked cap with a silver badge. He took her ticket, asked if she was riding through to "the terminus" at Roulette, and punched it. Then he tossed three chunks of coal into the round iron stove at the front of the passenger car and settled down for a nap. At each of the towns along the line—Wharton, Costello, and Austin— he roused enough to see that no other passengers were wait-

24

ing to get on. Then he just watched as the fireman wrestled the freight—mostly milk cans from the surrounding dairy farms—into the boxcar to join the single wooden crate and two black steel drums of kerosene put aboard at Emporium. Freight and passengers together, that's what the station master had meant by "mixed."

East of Emporium, the E&RR's line crossed a branch of the Sinnemahoning River and then followed it almost due north, deep into the mountains. It was heading toward the place her mother once called "the triple watershed of the Eastern Seaboard." She went on to describe how a drop of rain that fell into Sylvan County had a three-way chance of finding its way back to the Atlantic Ocean. First, it could go north into the Genesee River, flow through Upstate New York, empty into Lake Ontario at Rochester, and from there pass through Canada to the Gulf of Saint Lawrence. Or that drop could go west, down the Allegheny River to Pittsburgh, join up with the Ohio River, eventually flow into the mighty Mississippi, and reach the Gulf of Mexico at New Orleans. Or, lastly, it could come back down the Sinnemahoning to the Susquehanna River, pass through Harrisburg, Pennsylvania, and empty into Chesapeake Bay.

It was this last bit of water that Libby had traced back nearly to its head. In the early morning dark she had watched from her train window for the moonlight glinting off its slick, black surface in the fields of white snow. Or she spotted gray-flecked patches where it tumbled over rocks in the woods below the railroad cut. At some point the rail line must have crossed from one valley system into another, because Libby knew from Aunt Lydia's letters that Roulette was situated on the Allegheny River, not the Sinnemahoning. As the smoky little engine burrowed deeper into the mountains, it seemed to her that the winter's dawn drew further and further away to the east. Now, in Roulette, it was almost eight o'clock by Libby's little gold pocket watch. Up on the ridgeline to the west she could see a dazzle of sunlight and count the shadows of the trees, but down here, in the valley bottom, the morning had not yet been born.

Of the town itself, Libby could see only the bare brick wall and plank doors of a warehouse that crowded the station platform. More of William Henry Wheelock's property, no doubt. As soon as the train stopped, the conductor and engine crew had jumped down and disappeared around this building's western end, where there was a paved street wide enough for two cars to pass. The snow in the street was faintly rutted, as if from last night's traffic. Across the street Libby could glimpse the corner of a low, barnlike building made up as a store, its window advertising animal feeds and machinery parts, a reminder that Roulette's economy was mainly agriculture, which supported and reached market by Wheelock's railroad.

At the other end of the warehouse, a snowy lane humped across the tracks and passed into the woods beyond. This forest of spruce or fir or some other kind of evergreen was laid like a dark fleece on the mountainside. A single light, maybe on a householder's front porch, glowed a dozen yards inside the trees. A hanging column of wood smoke came from a chimney further in.

Above the quiet panting of the steam engine and distant chuckle of water running in the river, she suddenly caught the clop-*plop* of heavy hooves moving at a smart pace, the creak of harness, and squeal of steel runners on ice and cinders. Libby craned her neck toward the street end of the platform, and so missed her first sight of the horse cutting in from the lane and coming up the tracks behind the train. She turned just as the sun crested the ridge to the east. The light caught in the mane of a huge white horse, turning it into liquid silver. The animal's snorting breath and the steam rising off its back cast their own shadows on the air.

"Whoa, Jack."

At first, as the driver climbed down out of the sleigh and came around the horse, he was just another shadow: a hulking outline, broad shoulders, thick arms, gloved hands, and a wide-brimmed hat. Coming nearer, a pale face materialized in the darkness under the hat. It was a wide face with a straight mouth, long jaw, and a rounded chin with a dimple like the seam of a peach. His eyes were large and gray and seemed to take in everything, reminding her of an owl's prudent stare. What she could see of his hair, because of the hat, was light brown and brushed back around his ears. When he was within a few paces, Libby saw that her first impression of size was due mainly to his bulky coat, which puffed him up like an owl's feathers. Inside it, his body was thin, if not actually scrawny.

"Hello?" he said uncertainly. He took off his hat, which pulled up a lick of hair on the back of his head. He smoothed it down with a gloved hand. "Are you Miss Brackett?"

"You must be Cousin Robert," Libby replied with a smile.

"How did you know that?" he asked. He seemed confused.

"Mother said you would be meeting me. And here you are."

"Oh, of course." Robert nodded. "Um, then …"

He took two hesitant steps backward, blinked at her, then turned and went to the horse. He seemed dismayed by her presence, and Libby guessed Robert felt more comfortable dealing with a dumb brute or machinery than with a woman. Still, she had to admire the ease with which he grasped the reins up close to the bit, urged the animal left and sideways, and rotated the sleigh in a half circle on the tracks for the drive back out to the lane. When one of the runners caught up on the rails, he steadied the horse, then went back and threw his shoulder against the sleigh to free it. He settled the runners off-center on the tracks, then arranged the reins on the horse again. Finally, he came back to where Libby was standing, picked up the bag at her feet, and put it in the sleigh against the dashboard.

Facing her again, he asked, "Is there anything else?"

"Just me." She moved beside him and tucked her hand under his elbow.

Robert walked her over to the sleigh and helped her up onto the seat.

"A sleigh is so romantic," she said as he went around the other side.

"Well, with all this snow … the car …"

Libby arranged her skirts under her knees. "I understand."

He got in and gave the reins a shake. "Go, Jack!"

The big horse started and they flew down the tracks. Where they crossed the lane, the horse turned off and the sleigh wobbled as it slid down from the roadbed, throwing Libby against Robert's arm. "Sorry!" he said automatically.

"It's all right," she replied.

They crossed the river on a spindly bridge of black-iron trusses, passed a street of small white houses on widely spaced lots, and immediately entered the town of Roulette proper: two blocks of red-brick store fronts on the south and west sides of the courthouse square. The courthouse itself was built of clapboards, painted creamy white with narrow windows trimmed in black and an arched doorway in the center, looking more like a church without a steeple. In a dash of snow they were past it and heading east, over another iron bridge, and up the county road, which was lined on either side with dark stands of evergreen.

Robert pulled right on the reins and steered the horse into a gap between the trees that concealed a snow-crusted driveway. Just off to one side stood a tiny house, truncated as if it had been cut off from something larger. The wooden siding and jigsaw-cut porch decoration were gray weathered wood with barely a fleck of the paint that must have peeled away years ago. It could hardly be the residence of a railroad tycoon and was too shabby even for his gatehouse.

Libby blinked. "The house is … charming," she tried to say graciously.

"Oh, we don't live here," Robert said. "The house is up ahead."

The evergreens were no thicker than two or three deep, a screen protecting an open, park-like property: dormant lawns deep in unbroken snow, ornamental fruit trees pruned back to globes of bare branches, and low hedges with their own white mantles, around formal gardens laid out in domed beds under tents of burlap sacking. Alongside the driveway was the only discordant note: a triple row of dead cornstalks, standing uncut, withered gray-black and weighed down with ice.

"You have a farm, too?" Libby asked.

"It's a liberty garden," Robert replied.

"I take it corn didn't grow well here?"

"Well enough. Lydia didn't like corn."

Ahead now was an inner screen of trees, shielding the Wheelock mansion. Libby's first sight of it was the two round brick towers which, along with the peak of the roof, were all that the local people might see from the main road. The tower on the right she decided to call Rapunzel, because its conical top of lapped black slates reminded her of a medieval lady's headdress. The one on the left was the Crusader tower, because its top was cut with wide, square crenellations lipped with blocks of pale sandstone, the perfect place from which to shoot Saracens. The rest of the house, as it came into view, was the same dull-red brick, with stone lintels and mitered woodwork which had been painted bright white the summer before and was now only a little dulled by a dusting of coal soot.

The driveway passed through an elegant porte-cochere, supported by twelve Ionic-scrolled columns arranged in four groups of three at the corners. Under its roof the horse's hooves clopped loudly on the solid ice that overlay the paving stones.

"Whoa, Jack," Robert said again, drawing in the reins expertly. The sleigh stopped just abreast of three thick sandstone steps that came down from a raised walkway that was at the level of their heads. The last step was still several feet above the pavement and must once have been a convenient height for entering or leaving a carriage. It was too high for the sleigh, however.

"That's kind of a stretch," Libby said doubtfully, wondering how she would manage the climb in her heavy skirt.

Robert stood up, planted a boot firmly, and levered himself up onto the step. Then he turned and offered her both hands.

Libby stood up and crossed the width of the sleigh, then paused. "We can go in the back door, can't we?" she suggested.

"It's all right," he said. "Take my hands."

She gripped his palms, which were solid, like iron bands beneath his gloves. All she had to do then was brace her arms, because Cousin Robert lifted her out of the vehicle and set her on the step. It was a narrow step, and she had to lean in quite close to him. Surprised at herself, she drew back. Suddenly she was falling backwards.

"Whoa there," Robert said easily, whipping his arm around her shoulders and pulling her to him. Then he retreated up the steps to give her room to ascend.

They were standing on a stone platform that was overlooked by the deep windows of the formal dining room.

"You go on," he said huskily. "I'll tend to the horse and bring your bag along."

Libby turned toward the back of the house, the direction they had been heading, and found herself confronting a glassed-in conservatory at the southeast corner, adjoining the dining room. Veils of moisture shrouded its wide windows, but she could discern the spikes of green fronds pressed against the insides of the panes. There was no door into it from the landing.

"Why don't you show me in?" she said. "Surely Jack can wait."

"But I have to—" He seemed to catch himself being disagreeable and forced a smile. "This way, please."

Robert led her off along the walkway in the other direction, following the side of the house to the curving base of the Crusader Tower. A wide railing supported by fat, white balusters lined the outer edge of the walk. The wind coming around the corner of house had cleared the snow from both the top of the railing and the pavement, except for a thin scimitar of drift and a few icy patches in the shape of footprints. The windows in the brick wall along this stretch were high up, filled with diamond-shaped leaded panes, and the windows set into the tower itself were heavily curtained, so Libby had no idea what room was inside. Under the front portico Robert waited for her to admire the door's ornately carved pattern of vines and leaves. Then he opened it for her and, as she passed through into the vestibule, squeezed by to open the inner door for her as well.

The main hall stretched away in the dim light through half of the house's length. Libby was aware of darkly silvered wallpaper embossed with a lacy design, varnished mahogany columns carved to resemble the white-painted Greek copies outside, and oriental rugs laid edge to edge over a finely parqueted floor. To her immediate left and right were formal archways closed off with sliding doors.

"What's behind the doors?" she asked out of curiosity.

"The parlor," Robert said, pointing to the right. "And the library," pointing left.

"And where is your father …?" She tried to think of a polite way to phrase it.

"Let's go find your aunt first, shall we?" he replied with forced cheerfulness.

Robert took her down the pillared front hall, made a turn at the foot of the grand staircase, went through a door, and took her down the back hall, which was crowded with cupboards and coat hooks.

They emerged into the kitchen. Its wide windows and the big glass pane in the back door let in a flood of snow-reflected sunlight. As her eyes adjusted, Libby saw they looked out on a broad porch—with more of those squat balustrades—above a high terrace of swept flagstones. The back of the property was more open than the tree-enclosed front and stretched over several acres down to the stables and the creek that defined the southern boundary. Libby could imagine sitting on the porch of a summer evening, watching as deep shadows took over the patchwork of green lawns, working gardens, and thickets of berry bushes. She thought the tangle of now winter-browned vegetation that stood man-high at the edge of the terrace might be honeysuckle, a treat for the taste buds come spring.

Inside the kitchen, two women were sitting at the big table drinking coffee, one of them dressed in plain servant gray. Libby moved quickly around the table's end and descended on the other woman, putting her arms around the narrow, bony shoulders and giving her aunt a big kiss, square on the mouth.

"Dear Aunt Lydia, that's a kiss from Mama!" She kissed her again. "And that one's from me."

3. LYDIA

ROBERT'S FIRST SIGHT of Elizabeth Brackett, standing on the station platform in Roulette, was of a tiny porcelain doll. She wore a fitted jacket of black silk taffeta and a flaring skirt of some duller fabric, perhaps black lamb's wool. Her hair, under a jaunty tam-o'-shanter of red, yellow, and blue plaid, was the color of old gold. It was drawn up from around her natural hairline and gathered on top of her head in the once-popular Gibson Girl style, now slightly old fashioned. The skin of her face and her wrists above the short leather gloves was as pale, and almost as translucent, as fine china with thin blue veins. When she smiled, her lips were bright red petals over teeth like smooth white pebbles. When she looked at him, her eyes were as bright and green as stones from the river.

She completely discombobulated him. In her presence, he mumbled and forgot his manners. He even drove the horse badly.

When they went into the kitchen and she kissed her aunt, Robert secretly glanced from one to the other, looking for a family resemblance. It was there, he thought, in the set of the head, the shape of the face, and in the eyes. But where Elizabeth's cheeks were full and round from smiling, Lydia's were gaunt from her perpetual frowns. Where Elizabeth's hair swept up like a golden cloud, Lydia's was tightly curled like ringlets of brass wire and dull with streaks of gray. Where Elizabeth's eyes were like freshly wetted moss, Lydia's had hardened into pieces of jade.

In all of Lydia's years in the house, Robert had never before thought of her as a woman—and certainly not as the shadow of a desirable woman. So now he was fascinated by his own reaction to Elizabeth.

When she had recovered from the kisses of her niece, Lydia looked up at him. "What are you gawking at?" she snapped. "You left the horse standing out in the cold, didn't you? I'll bet you drove him hard, too, and he's all in a sweat. You can kill a horse that way."

32

Robert's face went red but he kept his temper. "Yes, ma'am," he said.

"Aunt?" Elizabeth said. "I asked Cousin Robert to leave Jack— just for a minute."

"Well, you shouldn't have," Lydia said, but she smiled at the girl.

Elizabeth pressed her lips together and nodded.

Robert let himself out onto the porch. Behind him, as the kitchen door was closing, he heard a chair scrape on the floor tiles and Elizabeth start to say, "Oh, Aunt, as soon as we got the news …" But he was out of earshot before she could say what the news was. It was about Robert's father, of course. And the news was that his father was dead. That was all.

He walked around to the porte-cochère, where Jack waited patiently. He did not seem to be suffering from his brief time in the cold air. The horse had nuzzled out and was chewing at a patch of brown grass in the snow beyond the edge of the drive-way. Robert took the bridle in hand and walked him down to the barn. In the sudden, velvety darkness inside, he unhitched Jack from the sleigh's shafts, led him into the stall, and went back to turn the sleigh around. He took out Libby's suitcase and set it beside the door.

Robert then stripped off the horse collar and harness and wiped Jack down with a piece of burlap, one side and then the other: neck and shoulder, chest and foreleg, back and flank, buttock and thigh. As his hands pushed against the hard flesh, Robert thought about the structural similarity of all animals—all mammals, anyway. The smooth, tapering muscles and knobby bone-ends in Jack's leg were very like those of a dog, or a man. And if the leg of a horse was like a man's, then the leg of a wom-an could hardly be very different, belonging to the same species as they did. Robert found himself wondering what the leg looked like under the flare of that black lamb's-wool skirt.

His hands stopped in mid-stroke.

It was shameful to have such thoughts on the day of his fa-ther's funeral. Doubly shameful to have them about an innocent young girl like Elizabeth. And triply so because she was a relative of his, by marriage if not by blood.

The horse was dry now, and the barn was warm. Robert hung up the cloth, covered the horse with a blanket, and backed out of the stall. He started to give Jack his customary slap on the rump but held his hand.

Back in the kitchen, the women were still sitting around the table, talking. When Robert came in with her suitcase, Elizabeth looked up at him and smiled.

"Leave the door open a minute, please," she said. "The cold air feels good."

"Why, Elizabeth, you're flushed!" Lydia said, reaching a hand up to her forehead.

"No, it's just ..." The girl ducked her head. "That old wood stove throws off such a blast of heat. In Binghamton we have town gas, you know."

By this Robert understood her to mean a factory, such as he had seen in the slums around Boston, where coal was roasted in great, closed kettles. The burning coals gave off a lethal mixture of fumes—methane, carbon monoxide, and sulfurous gases—that had the one beneficial property of being instantly flammable. The gas companies piped it under the streets for heating and lighting.

"That's a business my father never got into," he said.

Elizabeth grinned, as if he had made a joke.

"Take Miss Elizabeth's things up to the east bedroom," Lydia told him.

Robert nodded and went out into the hall, up the stairs to the second floor, and across to the door of the bedroom Lydia had set aside for her niece. He stopped in front of it. Should he take the bag inside, as a matter of practical convenience? Or leave it outside the door, to show that he was a gentleman who respected a lady's privacy? Robert paused over the question, then opened the door. Technically, until her things were installed, the room was his—or part of the house that he would shortly inherit from his father—and thus no invasion was intended nor implied.

He set the suitcase at the foot of her bed, looked around to make sure everything was in order, and withdrew.

At the head of the stairs, he could hear light footsteps and hushed voices in the main hallway below: Lydia and her niece would be going into the parlor, for the obligatory viewing of the body. Robert moved silently down the stairs, so as not to disturb them, and slipped back into the kitchen.

Rosie was washing cups in the sink. "Didn't I tell you she was pretty?" she said without looking up.

"Well ... You were right." Robert went to the stove, picked up the coffee pot, felt how light it was, put it down. "I think ..." He stopped, waited, tried to work out his thoughts. But some thoughts cannot be controlled.

"Yes?" Rosie turned to stare at him. He could feel her eyes on his back.

"That's the woman I'm going to marry!" he blurted. Then he corrected himself: "I mean, *would* marry—if I were going to marry anyone."

She chuckled. "You'll be needing Lydia's permission then. And I can tell you now, she won't give it."

"But Elizabeth has a mother and father, doesn't she? Certainly they ..."

"Lydia is the elder sister. You'll have to go through her."

Robert did not have an answer for that. He just nodded. It was a passing fancy anyway. Nothing would come of it.

She pointed a sudsy finger at the big wall clock. "Townsfolk will be arriving in another hour. You'd better get ready."

He shrugged. "I've shaved, washed, dressed in my best ... picked up Miss Elizabeth ..."

"Did you shovel off the front porch and the walk?"

"They were clear when Elizabeth and I came in."

"Is that a fact now?" she said, not believing him.

"Maybe a little bit of ice," he admitted. "In patches."

"Well, they can't take your father out through the kitchen— though the good Lord knows everyone else tramps through here. It wouldn't be dignified, not to mention taking too many turns through the house. And yet wouldn't it be a terrible thing if they slipped on the ice while carrying his casket?"

"I'll shovel the front then," he agreed.

"Go out the back way and around," Rosie said. "Give Lydia these last minutes with your father."

4. ZACKY'S CAFÉ

As SOON AS Albert Waterman, conductor on the E&RR mixed train up to Roulette, had seen the last passenger off onto the platform, he collected the engine crew and headed for the only place in town where a person could buy a cooked meal. Or, in this case, some breakfast.

Zacky's was a converted store front on Main Street. Its two display windows on either side of the entrance door had nothing to display but the red-checked cloths of the tables inside. Down one side wall that was paneled in knotty pine stretched a zinc-covered counter with a row of nickel-plated swivel stools. Behind the counter was a coal-fired range, with an industrial-strength coffee pot and a vat of hot lard where Zacky dipped his homemade doughnuts. The rest of the kitchen—in full sight of the customers, as God had intended food to be made—was the carving board for cutting meat and sandwiches and a sink for washing up the crockery. Beyond the double-doors in the back wall were the storeroom and a one-holer that served both sexes, please knock before entering.

When Waterman and his crew—Nils the fireman and Johansson the engine driver—arrived after eight o'clock, the counter was full and the tables half-populated. Clarence, owner of the feed store, was digging into his usual eggs over easy and a short stack of pancakes, but Waterman knew he would have opened his shop at dawn, checked his orders, and topped up his bins. Reverend Stevens, on the other hand, would be dropping in for coffee and chat before making his first official call of the day. Mike and Little Tom, trappers from a ways down the Allegheny, were in town to sell their pelts. The only person who didn't have business to get back to was Malcolm Hurlbert, the county clerk. No one was going to open the courthouse today, not for business.

Hurlbert turned on his stool and eyed the three trainmen with disgust.

"I can understand your friends there, Waterman, not bothering to clean up for their employer's funeral. After all, they have to

37

work for a living. A show of coal dust and grease is fitting tribute, coming from them. But what's your excuse?"

"Hell, Malcolm! I *run* the railroad," Waterman said, pulling out his big silver fob watch. "I'm the only one of this bunch who can tell time."

That got a chuckle from the room, except for Hurlbert.

"You could be a mite more respectful of William Henry," the county clerk said. "*He* runs the railroad, always has and always will—at least in spirit."

"Hear, hear!" came softly from those present.

"Not to mention," Hurlbert went on, "being the best judge this county has ever seen. Twenty-three years on the bench, and not once has the Appellate Court down in Harrisburg reversed him."

"Not once," came the echo, and everyone looked thoughtful.

"Amen," Waterman whispered, and shooed his crew to an empty table.

"Seriously though …" said Nathan Birdsall, one of the farmers who had acreage close enough to town to make the trip in for coffee. "Who is going to run the railroad and the rest of the business, now that William Henry's gone?"

"Not that son of his," said another farmer.

"And why not?" Waterman asked pleasantly.

"Well …"

"Because," Hurlbert put in with authority, "his daddy didn't send him up to Harvard so he could stay around here and look after fifty miles of track, two broke-down engines, and you three hooligans. That boy is destined for better things."

"Such as …?" Waterman prompted.

"Corporate counsel. I happen to know that William Henry was in correspondence with three or four New York firms, lining up something choice for Master Robert."

"Such as …?" Waterman said again.

"I'm not at liberty to say."

"Oh, yeah."

"What I don't understand," said the second farmer, "is why Bobby hasn't joined the army, like everyone else? With all that education of his, he'd of started out an officer and been made general by now."

"Or dead on the high side of a trench," Little Tom said with a nod.

"William Henry wouldn't allow it," Hurlbert replied. "Said it was a fool's war in a foreign country. He wrote to Harrisburg and got Robert exempted from the draft, so he could finish law school. The old man said if this war lasted another three years, then his son would be more use in the adjutant general's office than over in France, carrying a rifle."

"The boy could enlist. You don't need your father's permission—not at his age."

"Master Robert would need permission, at any age."

"So who is going to run the railroad?"

Waterman raised his hand. "I am."

That got another laugh around the room.

And then, as if by consensus, the plates on the tables and at the counter were empty. Zacky had stopped pouring refills and was putting stray dishes in the sink.

"Is it time?" Clarence asked.

"Yes, it's time," said Reverend Stevens.

Among the men there were nods and a general scraping of chairs.

Waterman left his engine crew and sidled up to the counter. "Hey, Zack?"

"What is it?" The owner didn't look up from his soapsuds.

"Lend me a suit, will you?"

Now Zacky did look up, from his own five-foot-six to Waterman's more than six feet. "You've got to be kidding."

"No, I should dress for this. I'm a pall bearer."

"You should have thought of that this morning."

"Well ... yeah." Waterman was embarrassed.

"You *do* own a suit, don't you?"

"It ... never came up before."

"What do you wear to church?"

"Who told you I go to church?"

"Agh!" Zacky threw up his hands, spattering drops which sizzled on the hot stove. "All right! My brother-in-law's a big guy like you. Maybe he has a jacket or something. Come on up to the house."

"Thanks, Zacky."

"Nothing to it."

5. The Funeral

In picking out her wardrobe that morning, at the railroad hotel in Emporium, Libby had prepared for the day's solemnities with skirt and jacket, gloves and boots—all in black, even if the materials did not exactly match. Her one spot of color was the hat, a bright Scottish bonnet which kept her spirits up but would hardly do for a funeral. Once upstairs at the Wheelock house, with her face washed and hair pinned up again, Libby took from her suitcase the scarf her mother had packed, a yard of black silk lace with scalloped edging. She draped it over her head and adjusted the hang of it across her shoulders.

Someone rapped on her bedroom door, bare knuckles on thick wood.

"Yes?" Libby said.

"The men are about ready," Aunt Lydia called through the door.

"Coming!"

Down in the parlor, the pall bearers had already closed the coffin lid. William Henry's stern face, framed in side whiskers like stiff wire, and with a brush of fine gray hair down over his domed forehead, was shut away from sight forever. A large man—whom Libby recognized as the conductor from the train, but now wearing a shapeless black jacket with his overalls—was tightening the brass screws with a huge screwdriver that looked as if it came from his locomotive.

She saw Robert beyond the coffin, supporting himself with one hand on the carved mahogany mantelpiece. He was by far the best-dressed man in the room, although he still wore the thick boots from this morning. Libby tried to catch his eye, to offer him some kind reassurance, but he was looking steadfastly into the ashes of the fire.

"That's it," the conductor said, shoving the screwdriver into his back pocket.

41

Another man—a clerk, from the pallor of his face and the ink stains on his fingers—approached Lydia. "With your permission, ma'am?"

Aunt Lydia nodded, and the clerk arranged the bearers around the coffin. He put Robert at the head, on the right, and himself on the left. Each took hold of a curved, brass handle. "Up," the clerk said quietly.

They lifted the coffin to waist height, and there several of the men had to shift grips to raise it to their shoulders. One of them slipped, and the box lurched sideways. From inside, Libby heard a hollow *thunk* and imagined the body sliding on its bed of watered silk.

The clerk frowned and shook his head. "Forward," he said.

Rosie Cobb was waiting by the inner vestibule door. She opened it and passed ahead of the cortege to open the outer door. A swirl of dry snow came off the porch and glided over the dark wood of the coffin. Libby linked her arm firmly in Aunt Lydia's, and the two women followed it into the cold morning air.

Outside, the men took a turn and moved in cadence along the walkway to the porte-cochere. By coincidence, that high last step was now just level with the bed of a Ford motor truck which someone had parked in the space. They had already removed its slat railings so the bearers could carry the coffin straight across and lower it onto the truck's bed. A streamer of black crepe hung from the windshield.

Rosie Cobb had explained earlier, in the kitchen, that the town's only hearse—a horse-drawn conveyance of ebony and silver majesty with spindly wheels and no springs—had bogged down in the snow. The truck from Jaspers's feed store would get William Henry through and at the same time do honor to the owner, who was also one of the pall bearers.

When they had aligned the coffin on the bed and pegged it in place with wedges between the floorboards, the men stood looking at each other for a moment. Then Robert jumped off the back, onto the driveway. The others followed him and turned to lift the women down from the porte-cochere's last, awkward step.

Robert went around to the back of the house and returned with a large, green motorcar, a Pierce-Arrow, which he pulled up behind the truck. He helped the three women into the rear seat. The clerk and conductor joined him in front, and the rest got into the truck's cab with the owner.

They moved slowly down the long curve of the drive, past the withered cornfield, the hedges, and the screen of trees. At the street they paused before turning. The road to the center of town was lined on both sides with waiting vehicles—tall black sedans, several dull-colored farm trucks, more farm wagons, and even a sleigh or two. Thin steam from the engines' exhausts and horses' breaths mixed in the cold air while half the town, it looked like, waited for the truck that bore William Henry.

The procession went six blocks to the First Methodist Church, which as far as Libby could tell was the only church in town. It was a clapboard building with clear glass in windows with simple gothic arches; the open steeple displayed a black iron bell. The vehicles arranged themselves in order of precedence along the sidewalk, and the men got out. They handed the coffin down from the truck bed, carefully distributed the wedges to various pockets, carried William Henry into the church, and laid him across two sawhorses before the altar. As a member of the family, Libby sat in the front row beside Aunt Lydia. Robert sat on her aunt's other side, near the end of the pew. Rosie Cobb was in the row immediately behind them.

While the pastor, Reverend Stevens, read the service Libby's mind wandered. The inside of the church was as plain as white paint and bleached linen could make it. The lights overhead were frosted globes hanging from stamped metal arms. The pews were white oak and the floorboards matched spruce, both waxed to a high gloss. In one corner, the black iron stove puffed out wisps of gray smoke when the wind reversed the draft in the flue. From the smell of it, Libby guessed that the stove, like everything else in Pennsylvania, burned coal.

The only color in the church was a bank of flowers, bright yellow mums and red cabbage roses, to the left and right of the altar. Now, where did they get fresh flowers in the dead of winter? Libby didn't remember seeing any brought in on the train, and she doubted anyone in town could afford to keep a greenhouse. She squinted at the flowers, trying to focus her eyes. Something about the color of the roses … too bright … too uniform. They were made of velvet and tissue paper!

The pastor had finished and now was inviting individuals to come forward and speak. Rosie Cobb reached forward and nudged Robert, who frowned and shook his head. The cook practically had to push him off the pew.

Robert went up to the pulpit and put his big hands on either side of the Bible there. As he spoke, his fingertips riffled the corners of the pages. He was talking about William Henry's place in the community, but Libby couldn't follow: the names of people and places she did not know, and was unlikely ever to meet or visit, or even hear of again, became a buzz in her head. As he talked, Robert looked down at her once. He looked away, and then his gaze wandered back to her. Finally, he seemed to give up and hold her in his eye. He was smiling as he looked at her, but she could see the tears glazing his eyes.

Libby was feeling hot and lightheaded. Perhaps that was just the crowded church, or the fumes from the coal stove. However, what Robert was saying clearly moved the people around her. Libby heard small coughs turn into sobs and snuffs develop into sniffles. Rosie Cobb took out a surprisingly dainty hankie and wiped her nose. Even Aunt Lydia was nodding her head in time to the cadence of Robert's voice.

When Robert came to an end, the pastor stood and with a gesture invited others to come forward and speak. Libby looked around. Apparently, no one felt he could add to what the Judge's own son had said. So, after a pause, the pastor signed to the pall bearers. They assembled around the coffin, lifted it smoothly, and carried it back down the aisle.

The people in the pews waited a moment in awkward silence, expecting the family to make the first move. Rosie Cobb finally stood up, came around to the front pew, lifted Libby by her elbow, and set her gently in the aisle. Rosie went back and brought Aunt Lydia forward in a kind of daze. A little shove sent Libby ahead to lead the recessional.

As she passed the Judge's friends and neighbors, most had a sheen of tears below their eyes and sympathetic pouts stretching their faces. Libby felt she had to offer them something. She chose the first woman of her mother's age that she came to, moved closer, and spread her arms. The woman gave her such a powerful hug that Libby's ribcage creaked. A bit farther up the aisle, Libby embraced a younger woman, who kissed her cheek. At the same time, Libby extended a free hand to another woman farther down in the pew. And so the congregation went out of the church, with Libby in the lead, embracing, touching, occasionally kissing, and generally sharing the family's grief among the women of the county and even several of the suitably older men.

The cemetery was a mile outside of town proper along the river road. Because the ground was frozen, the men carried the coffin into a crypt near the entry gates. Libby understood that William Henry would be reburied in the spring, when the ground had thawed, under the Wheelock marker up on the hillside. She did not expect to be part of that second ceremony.

The crypt was a low cement building, itself half-buried, with a black-tile roof over the exposed part. The doors were black iron with a Greek key worked into the metal at top and bottom. They were normally secured with a chain, which now hung loose. The interior was so small that only the pallbearers and immediate family could fit inside. The only light came from the south-facing door and from a row of tiny square windows, high in the wall, that were so smeared with dust and cobwebs as to be barely translucent. After the bearers slid the coffin head-first into an open cavity in the wall, the railroad conductor and another big man lifted a dark bronze plate onto bolt-ends protruding from the wall's surface. While the other pall bearers withdrew, tipping their hats to Aunt Lydia, the conductor placed four knurled knobs over the bolts and tightened them one by one.

As the conductor performed this final service, Robert stood before the blank plate. With the last knob was in place, he took the glove off his right hand, reached forward, and brushed the metal with his bare fingertips. The bronze, Libby realized, would be as cold as the ground it had been resting on. Robert brought the hand up to his face, just below the eyes, as if convincing himself of the plate's reality. A sparkle of tears rolled over the back of his hand.

Libby wanted to put her arms around him then, but Rosie Cobb got there first. She folded the young man in a wide embrace and let him weep on her shoulder.

Libby thought she would cry herself now, but her eyes were strangely hot and dry, almost itchy, instead of moist. She thought it had to do with the cold air inside the crypt, some mold long dormant in this shut-up space. She turned to her aunt, who stood watching Robert's anguish with a look of disdain. Libby wanted to say something consoling, but when she tried her throat had closed up as if swollen.

Instead, she coughed into her glove, once politely. And then a wracking spasm came on so quickly that she did not have time to retrieve her handkerchief from her sleeve. The effort was like a fire in her chest. She was suddenly aware of being bent over with Lydia pounding on her back. Each blow sent a bolt of pain down Libby's arms.

"I'm—I'm—all—right," she finally managed to croak.

"Well I should hope so," Lydia said, backing off.

Libby straightened and turned away from the others, desperately trying to cope with what all that coughing had brought up. She took out her handkerchief and wiped her chin. Then she saw the palm of her black leather glove was covered with a substance that had the color and consistency of pea soup. Libby had never seen anything like it. She wiped it furiously with her hankie.

While she was cleaning the glove, another coughing fit came upon her. Libby's throat closed up and her lungs burned like white fire. She needed air. Stumbling out of the crypt, she tripped on the iron threshold and fell forward onto the muddy, trampled snow. At least it was cool.

6. Sickness in the House

At first, when her niece flopped face-down outside the crypt, Lydia Wheelock thought the girl was playing childish games, making a grotesque snow angel in the slush. Then Lydia saw the random flutter of Elizabeth's arms, the kick of her legs, and decided it was some kind of seizure. She grabbed Robert's elbow and pushed him forward. "Quickly," she said.

But the ninny held back, his eyes as round in his face as two millstones.

Lydia herself knelt by the girl, one hand gripping a quaking shoulder, the other lifting her head out of the muck. Even with melted snow stuck to her brow, Elizabeth was burning up. Lydia could feel the fever heat through her black gloves. She looked around for the big trainman, the conductor, Waterman. "You, Albert! Come here!"

Without hesitation he came forward, rolled the girl into his arms, and carried her on the run to Lydia's car. By that time Robert had bestirred himself enough to get behind the wheel and start the engine. They drove back to the house as fast as the roads would allow. Waterman cradled the girl on his lap in the back seat with Lydia crowded in beside him, wiping the flushed face with handfuls of clean snow. Rosie Cobb sat in front, half-turned in the passenger seat, reaching back with her hand and patting Elizabeth gently on the cheek, on the neck, anywhere a human touch might soothe her.

At the house, Lydia led the small procession up to the second floor guestroom. Waterman laid the girl on the bed, straightened up, and looked on with a frown as she rolled her head, kicked at her heavy skirt, and muttered incoherently. "I'm sorry, Missus," was all he could find to say.

"Thank you, Albert," Lydia acknowledged. Then she remembered what day it was. "People will be coming this afternoon to offer their condolences. Would you please stand by at the front door and thank them, but let them know we have sickness in the house?"

"Certainly, ma'am." He nodded once and quickly left the room.

Rosie was already at work, pushing Elizabeth's jacket back off her shoulders, pulling it down her arms, and starting to unfasten the buttons at the waist of her skirt. Lydia noticed Robert hanging in the doorway, looking on, and stopped Rosie with a loud "Ahem!" She turned to her stepson. "Fetch towels," she said. "And bowls of cold water with ice. Then put a pan on the stove and heat it, for she'll turn to ague in no time."

Robert chose to be obstinate. "Where am I going to find ice?"

"Go chop some from the river, of course," Lydia snapped.

He muttered something and left with his head down.

Rosie continued the undressing, pulling off the layered petticoats and leaving Elizabeth in just her shift. The girl clung to the cook's big arm and fought as Rosie tried to stuff her under the covers. "Let her lie on top for now," Lydia advised.

Then she went down the hall, to the bathroom, and considered the resources of her medicine chest. There was a bottle of Pinkham's elixir, which William Henry always swore by and was supposedly good for female complaints—although it never did anything for Lydia but make her light-headed. She also had sulfate of quinine, which was the specific for malarial fevers—but somehow Lydia doubted that Elizabeth had been bitten by a mosquito, or not recently. And then there was the new German drug, aspirin. It was known to be good for pain and was advertised for fever as well. Lydia put aside her nationalistic feelings and took the bottle down from the shelf. She drew water into a tooth glass.

When she got back to Elizabeth's room, Robert was just setting a bowl of water, with slabs of dark ice floating in it, on the table outside the door. He had already taken a pile of white towels from the linen closet. "Anything else?" he asked.

"Boil water," she reminded him. "And some prayers might be in order."

"Yes, ma'am." But he still didn't leave.

"What are you waiting for?" she asked.

"Perhaps I should call for Dr. Guillaume," he asked quietly.

Lydia snorted at the suggestion. If this had been a laceration or broken bone, she would not have hesitated. But people took to cramps and fever all the time without needing more than bed rest, an occasional tonic, and time. No call for spending money on a doctor. Still, her niece was as sick as anyone she had ever seen. "After you boil the water," she said grudgingly.

When he had gone, Lydia dipped two of the towels in the bowl, went back into the room, and shut the door. While Rosie cradled Elizabeth, she shook out two of the bitter pills and worked them between the girl's lips. Elizabeth's face screwed up and she tried to spit them out, but Lydia clamped her jaw with a hand and offered her the water. Elizabeth drank, and the pills disappeared.

Rosie laid her gently back on the pillows. Elizabeth opened her eyes wide—staring past the two women—then closed them in a slow blink. "You'll be all right, Lamb," the cook said.

Lydia wasn't so sure now. "We must watch her," she whispered.

The sweat was coming off Elizabeth so fast it soaked her shift and blotted the sheets around her shoulders and hips. Lydia took the first of the damp towels and wiped down the girl's neck and throat. When that towel was warm to the touch, she picked up another and began wiping her arms and legs. "Bring in the rest of it," she told Rosie.

Deep, wracking coughs punctuated the thrashings of Elizabeth's fever. The spasms bounced her on the bedsprings and brought up amazing amounts of mucus. Within half an hour, all of the towels Robert had gathered were either soaked or stained, and Lydia had to send Rosie through the house for more cloths.

When the vomiting started, Lydia held the girl's head over a chamber pot and wiped her mouth when she lay back. Then Lydia studied the curds in the mess, to see whether the pills had come up with the contents of Elizabeth's stomach. She could not be certain, but she did not want to force more vomiting by giving her more medicine. At least there was no blood in the bile.

"Oh, Aunt!" Elizabeth said during a lucid period. "Am I going to die now?"

"It's just a chill," Lydia replied. "You'll be feeling better soon enough."

"Please don't let anyone see me like this. Especially Cousin Robert."

"Don't worry. He's not one to notice."

She made Elizabeth drink more water then, against the sweating, and covered her when she finally dozed.

And so Lydia Wheelock spent the afternoon and evening of her husband's funeral tending her niece. The doctor came, examined the girl, and approved of what Lydia was doing. At night she had Rosie bring a pillow and a blanket, and made up a cocoon for herself in an armchair beside the bed. She watched while Elizabeth slept and smoothed her hair when she was wakeful. Finally, as that long night faded into dawn, Lydia arose and ventured downstairs.

The lights were on in the dining room, which opened off the front hall. Lydia was surprised to find the remains of what appeared to be a party: all of her rose-patterned Haviland china and Towle sterling were spread upon the white damask. But among them was a collection of iron pots, brown-glazed crockery, and rude baskets that were hardly fit for Lydia's kitchen, let alone her table. She looked into one and sniffed a casserole made mostly of beans. The people of the county had brought the family enough food for a week. Lydia was touched. She was also hungry.

She found a spoon and a plate, and served herself beans and cornbread for breakfast. There was also half a pot of coffee, cold now but still stimulating. When she lifted the silver pot to pour, a jolt of pain shot up her arm and through her shoulder. Lydia set down the pot and rubbed her elbow. She must have developed a crick, sitting up in a chair like that all night. She also felt a bit of a flush, but this Lydia attributed to sleeping in her clothes with a blanket wrapped around her.

While she ate, the sun came over the mountains.

7. Mineral Rights

By the end of the first day after his father's funeral, Robert found himself alone in a house with two sick women. Lydia had begun coughing and complaining of joint pains that morning, and in the late afternoon Rosie Cobb put her to bed with a high fever.

"Stay out of the way," the cook told him, as she rushed from one sickroom to the other with cups of broth, brown glass bottles that rattled with pills, and piles of towels that she herself washed out in the basement, drying them in front of the furnace. "If you get sick, I won't be responsible."

"And what if *you* get sick, Mrs. Cobb?" Robert returned.

"Don't be asking foolish questions," she said. "Forty-odd years I've been doing for this family and never missed a day to illness." And she crossed herself.

"Well, is there anything I can do for you?" he asked.

"Go chop more ice."

That evening the front doorbell rang at just one minute after eight o'clock. Robert went to answer it and through the heavy glass saw Nathan Birdsall, a potato farmer with property north of Roulette, standing outside. There was a man with him, clearly another farmer, because he was dressed in flannel shirt and bib overalls under a corduroy coat. Robert opened the door to them.

"Come in," he said as warmly as he could.

"We are not disturbing you, are we?" Birdsall asked.

"Not at all. However, I was not expecting a social ..."

"This is a matter of business, Mr. Wheelock," said the second man. "Unfinished business."

"We didn't quite know how to go about it," Birdsall explained. "This here is Ezra Stills, who farms the land next to mine ...?" He made it a question, as if reminding Robert of something he already knew.

"Pleased to meet you, Mr. Stills," Robert said, offering his hand.

"Likewise," the man replied, looking at the hand and finally taking it.

"You see," Birdsall went on, "your father helped me sell some of my land—two hundred acres of cleared timber east of Ulysses—you know of it?"

Robert blinked. "Not personally."

"Well, William Henry had worked up a proper bill of sale, all ready for us to sign, and then … the apoplexy."

"Tragic," Stills said automatically.

"And we know this may not be the best time and all," Birdsall continued, "but we did want to finish the deal before the spring planting."

"Lot of work to do on that land," Stills added.

"Why don't you come into my father's study," Robert said, leading them left off the main hall through the arch into the library. With everyone upstairs, he did not feel the need to pull the sliding doors for privacy, but Robert did close the brocaded portieres. The room was lined with glass-front cases that held William Henry's law books. In the corner next to the tower alcove were two metal filing cabinets—one painted dark green for the Judge's legal work, and one crinkled black for the railroad, electric company, and his other ventures. Beside them was a square, black safe. Robert seated the two men in front of the big, claw-footed table that had served his father for a desk and went to the first filing cabinet.

He guessed that the contract would be under "B," for "Birdsall," and it was. He opened the file and found three pages of typed onionskin. In back of them were the familiar blue-ruled yellow sheets filled with his father's close writing—his notes on the substance and nature of the sales agreement. Robert read through both quickly while he stood in front of the filing cabinet. The contract appeared to be in order, with space at the end for the signatures of the principals and two witnesses. There was no reason they could not conclude this business right now, tonight, with Robert as one witness and Rosie Cobb called down to serve as the other. He brought the file back to the desk and sat down behind it, in his father's chair.

There was just one thing.

"I don't see a reference to mineral rights," Robert said.

"There aren't any minerals," Stills said quickly.

"What kind of rights?" Birdsall asked.

"Well," Robert said, "the value of any minerals under the land's surface, like gold or iron ore, is usually treated separately from any productive use of the land, like farming or rents. That's because unlike, say, water rights, which can be directly observed and measured, the nature—indeed, the very presence—of any mineral values is entirely speculative until proven by investigation and assay."

Birdsall took a minute to digest that. "Is coal a mineral?" he asked.

"There's no coal for a hundred miles around here," Stills said.

"Yes," Robert said, answering the former question. "Coal is considered a mineral."

"How about oil?"

"Oil?" Stills nearly exploded. "Maybe a hundred miles west, at Titusville. But there is nothing like that under your land, Birdsall. We have a deal, and I'm ready to sign."

"Well, I don't know ..." Birdsall said slowly.

Robert saw that he had inadvertently upset the arrangement. Worse, he did not know, as a lawyer, which party he was supposed to represent. His father's notes, so precise in the survey references and other technical details, had left that part vague. As far as William Henry had been concerned, this was a friendly agreement between two neighbors. And now Robert had made it adversarial.

"These rights need have only nominal value," he said quickly.

"What does that mean?" Birdsall said, suspicious.

"That, since we don't really know what's down there, if anything," Robert said, "Mr. Stills would agree to pay a token amount, a few dollars, say, as a gesture of good will ..."

"Sounds fair," Birdsall said.

"Fair for you," Stills said. "Dollars may not mean much to you rich farmers, but I got to scrape for every one of mine and then squeeze 'em 'til the eagle screams. Anything that's down there—

if there's anything down there—I don't want it. I'll pay to farm that land, not to speculate it."

"But that is not the way the law reads," Robert said, realizing he was only getting in deeper. "Without a specific clause disposing of the mineral rights, they would automatically accrue to you as owner of the property."

"Don't want 'em," Stills said.

"I won't let them go for naught," Birdsall said.

It was a stalemate, Robert saw. This was his first attempt at practicing law—the real law, governing the affairs of real people—and he had botched it. He had turned an all-but-signed agreement into a feud between neighbors.

"If it's only a matter of a few dollars," he said slowly, "and as neither of you gentlemen wants these mineral rights, which are probably nonexistent anyway, what do you say to *my* acquiring them, in the interests of preserving this agreement? It might not be regular—"

"Done," said Birdsall.

"Fine by me," from Stills.

Robert sighed with relief at how easily the matter was resolved. "Then just let me draft a clause to that effect. We can append it to the contract and you can still sign tonight."

He opened the center drawer on his side of the table, looking for a pad to write on. Right there, in the middle of the drawer among the pencils and loose stationery, was a folded vellum packet. On the front was printed in Old English type, "Last Will and Testament of," followed by "William Henry Wheelock" in inked script nearly as grand. Robert took the document out of the drawer and held it under the lamp. He was surprised that his father would have kept it so carelessly. It belonged in the safe, if not in the bank's vault.

"What's that?" Stills asked.

"Oh, family business," Robert said, laying the packet aside. He would have to arrange a formal reading when Lydia was feeling better.

From the drawer he withdrew one of the familiar yellow pads. He quickly drafted language stating that he, Robert Wheelock, for a consideration of five dollars, was to acquire the mineral rights passed with this contract of sale. When the two farmers had read over the statement and nodded their agreement, Robert took the contract's onionskin pages to the skeletal typewriting machine on a table in the corner. He added the language as a final clause, going letter by letter with his two forefingers, squeezing the sentence into the space above the previously typed lines for signatures.

Leaving the farmers for a moment, he went upstairs and brought down Rosie Cobb, who was on watch in Lydia's room. Rosie was known to both men, of course, and so could witness their signing. Robert, who was now a party to the arrangement, however obliquely, felt a twinge of propriety about serving as the other witness. Technically, it might not be legal. But, rather than risk further upsetting the deal, he kept his qualms to himself.

With the document executed, the two men shook hands. Robert poured them each a small shot of bourbon from the decanter behind the desk, with one for himself and another for Rosie. They drank—Stills tossing his back, Birdsall sipping solemnly—and the ceremony was concluded.

Rosie Cobb bid the men good night and went upstairs again. Robert let the farmers out the front door, holding the contract between them, to be filed at the courthouse the next day.

After nearly losing it, Robert had negotiated his first transaction under the law.

8. ZACKY'S CAFÉ

It was a much reduced group that met at Zacky's for breakfast in the week following the funeral of William Henry Wheelock. Malcolm Hurlbert came in at eight-thirty and found the place less than half full. Nils and Johansson from the railroad were there but not Waterman, which was very strange. Hurlbert wondered if they'd had to run the train up from Emporium by themselves, without the conductor. For once, Nathan Birdsall had come in from his farm—but then he had a bit of money to spend after selling that parcel up north. Reverend Stevens was missing, as was Clarence from the feed store.

"Morning all," Hurlbert said.

Zacky flipped his towel behind the bar, by way of greeting.

"Where is everybody?" Hurlbert asked.

"Haven't you heard?" Zacky replied. "Half the town's taken sick."

Hurlbert considered for a moment: business was off at the courthouse, too. "What have they got?" he asked.

"Some call it the croup," said Zacky. "Some say *la grippe*. Doc Guillaume says it's the influenza, but I don't know. If that's influenza, it's almighty fierce. Takes hold like a regular bear."

"And it don't let go," from Nils.

"We've had three die so far," Zacky continued. "Mrs. Ames, her daughter Christy, and the Reverend Stevens's little Alice. You'll be getting the death certificates in a day or two, Hurlbert, after the Doc works through his live customers."

"Only among the women?" Hurlbert said, surprised.

"It started with the womenfolk. Some of the men are sick now."

"Then it's a good thing I'm not married. I won't get it."

"That's not all you're not getting, Hurlbert," Johansson said.

There was a general laugh at his expense—but not as bad as normal, when Zacky's was full up. Hurlbert decided to change the subject.

"You heard young Robert's started to do law work?"

"That a fact?" Zacky said.

"Yeah," from Birdsall. "He sold some of my land."

"And kept a piece of it for himself," Hurlbert said with a grin.

"Not a real piece. More like a legal fiction." Birdsall started laughing. "He paid five dollars to buy the mining rights—of which there aren't any."

"William Henry's gold mine," someone said.

"Big rock candy mountain."

Now the laughter was general, and not to Hurlbert's disadvantage.

"Do you suppose he'd want to buy the gold under my land?" said a farmer who was unknown to Hurlbert.

That made a pause, every one of them suddenly thinking.

"I got a little piece of land by the river," Johansson said.

"Five dollar' is a five dollar'," said Nils.

"The boy wouldn't be that much of a fool," Zacky said.

"Of course, he's a rich man now," Hurlbert said, "when you think that he'll inherit the railroad, along with William Henry's other holdings. Five dollars would not be the same thing to him as it is to you or me."

"But what would he buy it for? There's no gold, and you know it."

"For a chance to do something nice for the people around here," Hurlbert suggested. "A lot of the farmers are scrabbling, this time of year. Five dollars will feed a family, and buying these fictitious rights is a way of helping while letting them save face. It's what his father would have done."

"Are you saying he offered me charity?" Birdsall said heavily.

"No, no—you just took him for five dollars," Zacky replied.

More laughter greeted that, and the sickness in town was almost forgotten.

By the end of the morning, everyone present was convinced that young Robert Wheelock would pay five dollars for an invisible and largely nonexistent component of their land. More, if the land was really poor, or if they happened to mention the possibility of gold.

9. CONVALESCENCE

IT WASN'T REALLY decent. Her mother would not have approved. And if Aunt Lydia had known, she would have been furious. A proper young woman did not sit in the parlor in her aunt's borrowed dressing robe—in her *negligée*, her mother would have called it—and let a young man make love to her while the nearest chaperone, the cook, was upstairs, well out of earshot, and thoroughly distracted with a family crisis.

And yet what was Libby to do? She was weak as a cat in the aftermath of her illness, barely able to lift a hand, let alone fend off the attentions of an earnest young man like Robert. Besides, having seen herself in the bathroom mirror, Libby knew she looked ghastly: her hair down and tangled, suffering from only the most feeble of brushings; her face thinner if not absolutely haggard; and her skin roughened and red from the effects of fever and the drying heat indoors. The most she could do was sit blankly in a rocking chair beside the hearth and watch the low-angled sunbeams creep across the Turkish carpet.

And in truth Robert had been very attentive, although he was often called away on business. She gathered he was just starting his practice in town as an attorney. During the first two days of her convalescence the front doorbell had rung no less than a dozen times, and each time Robert had been drawn into some transaction—she did not know what. But in between times he stoked the fire, brought her soup out of Mrs. Cobb's endless stock pot, played cribbage with Libby and let her win by miscounting his own hand, and read to her.

He had started with the new Somerset Maugham novel, *Of Human Bondage*, but when it became clear to Libby that the story concerned a young man caught in a hopeless infatuation, she declared herself bored with it and suggested they try something else. Robert asked if she liked sea stories, and she said she had never read one. He came back from the library with a collection of Joseph Conrad, and Libby tried to show as much enthusiasm for the stories as possible, despite their gray-edged realism. And yet, oddly, they matched her inner mood of sober watchfulness.

"How do you feel?" Robert asked at one point, closing the book.

Libby made a meaningless gesture. She did not *feel* anything, and that was the new thing. The world no longer rushed along for her, buzzing with energy and emotions and opinions over a flower, a view, a new friend, or an afternoon's adventure. Now she hung between one word and the next, between the lift of Robert's eyes and their drop to the page, between the crack of a burning log and the fall of an ember. She watched the world to see what it might become. She waited for events to develop. She reserved judgment.

Partly, Libby knew, this was a temporary reaction to her illness, which had drained her of physical energy. But nonetheless she felt light, clean, and unattached to the events and images around her. She imagined this was how women felt after recovering from the pains of labor and childbirth—or the soldiers in Europe, from their wounds. Libby sensed that she had nearly died, and now she was reborn. How could she explain all this to Robert?

"Tired," she said, after a bit.

"Lydia is very sick," he told her. "Mrs. Cobb is afraid she may die, and Dr. Guillaume looks very concerned. If she succumbs to the fever and vomiting ..."

Libby reached out a hand and touched his arm. "Hush."

"Oh, I am sorry. This talk must be disturbing you."

She sat back, nodded. In a moment she was asleep.

10. FIVE DOLLARS IN GOLD

ROBERT HAD JUST set down his book when the doorbell rang again, a long double-ring that he was afraid would wake Miss Elizabeth. He rose quickly and went to answer, closing the sliding doors of the parlor so as not to disturb her.

It was becoming clear that since the night he had finalized the sale of acreage between Birdsall and Stills, they had told everyone in the county about his willingness to acquire mineral rights. Farmers from as far away as Port Allegany—and even one from Olean, over in New York State—would stop by when they happened to be in town and offer to sell Robert something they did not value, had never considered an asset, in return for crisp greenbacks. Whatever the size of the parcel involved, the sum they mentioned was invariably five dollars—another clue that this theory of newfound riches, or at least a dividend on their butter and egg money, had originated with either Birdsall or Stills. Probably both.

Each time Robert smiled and bought from them. First, because the sum was so small. He had money of his own, the family had resources, and the men who came to him, though they tried to look their best, were dressed shabbily enough that he could see a few dollars was a lot of money to them. And second, because these people were his future clients. If he expected to practice law in this town ... When had he decided that? he suddenly wondered. When his father had died and severed his access to all other possibilities, Robert realized. At any rate, it was required that these people think well of him. He would rather they thought him a fool in the matter of five dollars than a cold, unapproachable miser who would not open his door to them. So he bought the rights to their imaginary mineral wealth and paid in cash.

This time it is Valdemar Johansson, the engineer on the railroad. When Robert answered the door, Johansson took off his trainman's cap of blue ticking and held it in both hands. He tried to make conversation with his future employer, but after observations about the coldness of the weather and the shame about Robert's father, the well ran dry.

"What I want to ask," Johansson said at last, after Robert had automatically shown him into the study and offered him a chair, "was if you was interested in my fishing lodge, down on the river? It's got twenty-six acres under it."

"I don't think I need a fishing lodge," Robert said slowly.

"Oh, not to buy! But for, you know, the minerals."

A twitch of playfulness—in this case perhaps meanness—led Robert to pretend ignorance. "Do you think there *are* any minerals?" he asked. "Under your land?"

Johansson's face screwed up for a moment. "Well, maybe there's gold. I seen a gravel bar down there, right along the bank, on my side. Sometimes, when the light's just right, you can see something glinting in there among the stones. Something yellow-like."

"Do you really think it's gold?" Robert asked, smiling. That old story about his father's Canadian mine would never die.

"Well, I wouldn't swear to it," Johansson said, twisting his cap.

"Maybe not. Still, it's the best offer I've had this morning," Robert said, relenting. "I'll draw up the papers. You can sign them in a couple of days."

"Umm …" The man appeared to be in some distress. "Could I have the money now? You see, I owe Nils ten dollars."

"And you want that much for your gold?"

"Oh, no. Just the five, like everybody else. I'm not greedy."

Robert took out his wallet and found a five-dollar bill. "You'll still have to sign the papers," he warned.

"Sure, Mr. Wheelock," Johansson said. "Otherwise, you can dock my pay."

"That's right," Robert agreed, wondering if the engineer realized how impossible it would be to recoup a private debt from the Emporium & Roulette's corporate accounts.

"Everybody well at home?" Johansson asked at the door.

"As well as can be expected, I guess," Robert said quietly.

Johansson nodded gravely. "Good day to you, sir."

11. Mutual Discovery

Libby sat in the conservatory, writing a letter to her mother. She had gotten as far as the salutation and a general report on Aunt Lydia's health, which still verged on disastrous, when she put her pen down and looked around. This place had become a favorite of hers, despite the heavy air and a sense of creeping neglect.

It was a large, square room separated from the south end of the formal dining room by a wall of windows and a half-glassed door. The outer walls of the conservatory were double-paned glass, and the room was kept heated by exposed steam pipes that ran along the baseboards. The floor was gently sloping concrete, painted dark green, with a drain grate in the center to collect spills and drippings off the plants.

In the middle of the room, amid sprays of fan-sized leaves and exotic, bulbous flowers that Libby suspected might be orchids, were grouped a table and two chairs, all made of wicker. It was summer furniture and summerlike heat—with a view of sparkling snow and bare tree limbs just beyond the windows. When she closed her eyes, however, she could imagine she was in the fabled tropics.

Except for a tapping on the glass.

She opened her eyes and turned her head. Robert stood in the dining room, waving for her attention. She nodded to bid him enter.

"I didn't want to disturb you," he said.

"But you did," she countered. When his face fell, she added, "I was stuck with this anyway."

"Oh. With what?"

"A letter to Mama."

He sat down in the chair opposite her.

"What do you call that plant?" she asked, pointing past his shoulder.

He looked around. "I have no idea," he said. "Is it some kind of fern?"

"Then I suppose this is Aunt Lydia's private reserve—not yours?"

"Actually, it was my father's. He was interested in all sorts of flowers and shrubs. He built this room so he could explore the tropics."

"And you don't share his interest?"

"I've been too busy with schoolwork."

"Ah." Libby picked up her pen and tapped her lower lip.

"You must miss Binghamton," he said after a moment's pause.

She shrugged. "Roulette is not so bad. I've enjoyed my stay here—not the funeral, of course! Or being sick out of my head with fever."

"But there are people at home you must miss."

"My parents. My sister, although she's living down in New York City, with her husband."

"And school friends?" he suggested.

"A few of the girls, although we've grown apart since graduation."

Robert was silent again, as if waiting for something. She felt him willing her to say something more. He held the smooth edge of a broad, waxy leaf between his fingertips. Libby saw he was crimping it into a saw-tooth pattern, getting green sap under his immaculate nails.

"What will you do when you leave here?" he finally asked.

"I shall go home to Mama," she said simply.

"I mean, beyond that. Do you plan on going to college?"

"Now, what would I study in college? Latin and Greek?"

"Then ... do you want a career? Some kind of work ..."

"A position in trade, perhaps? Become a shop girl?" She laughed.

"No, I mean ... your future. Your whole life ..."

"I will probably get married, like my sister. And have children."

"Oh ... And do you have someone in mind?"

"Yes," she said.

That stopped him cold. Libby purposely didn't offer anything more. She knew he wanted to ask who it was, even if he would not know any of Binghamton's young men.

After letting him dangle a minute longer she said, "What about you, Robert? What are your plans for the future? Will you enlist for the war?"

Robert shook his head. "Father forbade it, and I cannot go against his wishes. I mean, a man should do his duty. I know that. Maybe, with the Judge's help, I might have become an officer and contributed something meaningful. But now … one more man with a rifle will probably not be missed. And I have other responsibilities, here in Roulette."

"Would you be happy in a town this small?"

"My father was. And they still need a good lawyer."

"And someone has to run the railroad?" she suggested.

"Yes, the Wheelocks have a place here. I am my family now." He seemed to brood on that.

"You loved your father very much, didn't you," she said quietly.

Robert hesitated, and she could see the thoughts working across his face. But she had not meant her observation to be a difficult question.

"I respected my father," Robert said carefully. "When I was a boy, he was the most intelligent man I ever knew. He was also the most educated man in town and, in affairs of business and politics, the most penetrating. It was like having God for a father. I think 'love' is too small a word."

"And your mother?" Libby asked.

"She was the wisest person. Wise and gentle. I loved her completely," Robert said. "And now I've lost them both. You are lucky to have your parents still living." He hesitated again. "You'll be returning to your family soon."

"You keep hinting at that—as if you wanted me to leave."

"No, of course not. It's just …"

"Whatever happens will depend on Aunt Lydia, don't you think? She may need me to stay and take care of her for quite a while."

"Yes, she might ... I'm sure she would want that."

"And would *you* want that?" Libby asked, looking directly at him.

Robert was studying one of the big, white flowers. "I would like that very much."

12. Epidemic

Holding his pocket watch in one hand and Lydia Wheelock's wrist in the other, Dr. Eric Guillaume silently counted the thready beats of her pulse. Although his family name was properly pronounced "Gee-ahm" in the original French, and his father always used the English form "Gwillem," the doctor knew that behind his back patients jocularly called him "Dr. Kill'em." Too often, in the past week, that macabre epithet had seemed to prove itself as he struggled for their lives against this voracious influenza, only to watch them one by one weaken and slip away. They went like old trees along the riverbank when the water is rising.

Not this woman, however. Although her heartbeat was weak and shallow, it was regular enough. Her chest, when he listened to it, was clear of that hideous rattle. And her sputum was laudably clear. She had lost almost twenty pounds, of course, which a woman as tiny and thin as Lydia Wheelock could hardly afford. But she would survive where many another in town, with more meat on their bones and fewer years to carry, had not.

"Well?" she croaked, looking up at him from one slitted eye.

Guillaume had thought she was asleep. "You are doing very well, madam."

"And you call yourself a doctor! I happen to be at death's door, you fool."

"Well, perhaps you were," he said. "But you're not going through it today."

Lydia Wheelock chuckled, opening both eyes. "I thought you were the Grim Reaper himself, taking my hand that way."

Guillaume laid her arm on the bedcovers and patted her wrist.

"Don't get familiar," she growled.

"I wouldn't think of it," he replied.

Guillaume turned and looked around the room.

For all the opulence of this house set on five acres of park-like grounds at the center of town, he had been surprised by the simplicity of Lydia Wheelock's bedroom. Aside from a bedstead of turned maple that had been waxed to a glowing yellow, the only furniture was a flat pine wardrobe and a dressing table with a comb and brush, a box of face powder, and one dusty perfume bottle. The chair in front of it was straight backed. Significantly, there was no mirror behind the dressing table. The window drapes were old green velvet over a sheer curtain of white gauze.

Under the edge of the bed, he found a covered porcelain chamber pot. Of course, the house had full indoor plumbing but, for a woman too weak to rise and walk, the pot would be most useful. He took it out and, rather than risk her embarrassment by examining it in Lydia Wheelock's presence, he carried it into the hall.

"Something amiss, sir?" asked the cook, Mrs. Cobb.

"Not at all," he replied.

He lifted the lid and examined the contents. They were laudable, too, if a bit sparse and dry.

"Mrs. Wheelock must drink more water," he said. "Fruit juice would be good as well, but at this time of year ..."

"We have lemons, sir."

"Excellent! Squeeze them, squeeze them dry. Then boil the rinds and give her the liquor mixed with a dollop of honey. You may also cut up fresh apples, if you can find them, and squeeze the pulp. But no cider—no alcohol of any kind."

"Mrs. Wheelock? Never, sir!"

"And no stimulants either, no coffee, no tea. Not for a few days anyway."

"Yes, sir." She bobbed. "No stimulants."

"You have been a good nurse to her, Mrs. Cobb. I wish I had a hundred like you."

"Thank you, sir." She dipped her chin and blushed.

"And now I'd better go see Miss Elizabeth."

"In the parlor, Doctor. With Master Robert."

"Oh?" Guillaume paused. When she moved as if to lead him, he said, "No, no. I can find my way. You stay with Mrs. Wheelock."

"Yes, sir."

He found the two young people at the parlor door, waiting for him. Elizabeth Brackett was fully dressed now, thinner and paler than she had been the day of William Henry's funeral, but standing straight. Robert was formal, as always, and slightly detached. Guillaume noted, however, that the two of them stood together, leaning towards each other slightly, almost touching. He wondered if they were aware of the posture.

"How is my aunt, Doctor?" Elizabeth asked.

"She will survive," he said. "She is still very weak, but out of danger."

"That's good to hear," Robert responded.

"Thank God," Elizabeth exclaimed. "And thank *you*, Dr. Guillaume."

"Nothing I did." He shook his head. "And I doubt God had much to do with it, either. Mrs. Wheelock is as tough a woman as I've ever known. I certainly wouldn't like to face her in a fight, sick or well."

"No, of course not," Elizabeth smiled.

"Nor would anyone, I think," Robert said.

"Mrs. Cobb has my directions for her care," Guillaume went on. "She should stay in bed for several days more—not up and around, like you, young lady."

"I'm sure Aunt Lydia will mind you better than I did," Elizabeth said.

"Don't tax her with the running of the house," he warned.

"We'll take care of her," Robert assured him.

"I'm sure you will." And with that, Guillaume allowed them to show him out. Others in town needed him more than these people did at present.

13. The Question

A FEW DAYS after the doctor's visit, when Lydia was sitting up and giving orders to the household, Robert again found Miss Elizabeth—"Libby," as he had begun to think of her—in the conservatory. She was bent over the tub that held what he thought was a rubber plant. Somewhere she had found his father's gardening gloves, which fit her tiny hands like a pair of baseball mitts, and a pair of well-honed pruning shears. She was methodically cutting away the leaves that showed edges of sickly yellow and dropping them on a piece of newspaper in the middle of the floor.

"Libby?" he asked.

She straightened suddenly. "Robert!"

"I thought I might find you in here. The place looks ... cared for."

"Plants need attention, just like people," she said. "Only they can't ask for it."

"Yes, that would be difficult for them." He paused. "Your aunt seems to have no trouble that way—asking for attention."

Libby smiled at this. "Hardly. From what Dr. Guillaume said, she will be returned to health soon enough. And Mrs. Cobb is taking very good care of her."

"I suppose that means you are free to go home."

"It's probably time," she agreed.

After nearly a week, Robert was still haunted by that "yes" Libby had given to his question about her marrying someone. It would be improper for Robert to press his suit if Libby was already committed to another, in her heart if not by her word. He expected her to mention the man now, but she very discreetly did not.

But then, he realized, she had never referred to any young man in their many conversations. The only letters she seemed to write were to her mother and sister. And, as far as he knew, they were the only people who wrote to her. Rosemary Cobb, who knew the gossip of three counties, had never hinted at a beau in

Miss Elizabeth's life. There was only that "yes" hanging between them.

"I should like it very much if you stayed here," he said slowly.

"But Aunt Lydia has no further need of me. So it would hardly seem proper."

"It would if …" Robert faltered. It was the simplest thing to ask—and the hardest.

"If what, sir?" She searched his face with her eyes, and her look was hopeful.

"If you agreed to become my wife."

"Oh, Robert! Is that a proposal?"

"Yes—yes, I suppose that it is."

"Then I accept," she said with a smile, taking off the gardening gloves and holding out her hands to him. "On the condition that my family approves, of course."

"Will they, do you think?" Robert asked, suddenly anxious as he remembered Rosie Cobb's warning. He gripped her slender fingers in his big, awkward hands.

"Oh, Mama will take to you right away." She moved closer to him and brought her face near to his hands, turning them over and planting a gentle kiss on the back of each one. "You are the sort of fiancé every mother dreams of. Handsome, too. Father will be standoffish, at first. He will ask what your prospects are, as if you hadn't any. But with your law school, and the railroad and electric businesses, he won't have any excuse."

"Then should we set a date?"

"Will you kiss me first?"

Robert stepped closer, conscious of how slender and fragile she was. She pulled his hands apart, guiding them back past her shoulders and releasing them, so that his arms could encircle her. Then she brought her own hands up and her fingertips touched his neck, the back of his head. He held her gently, lightly, like a rare bird's egg cuddled in a frail nest. He bent his head as she lifted her face, and suddenly their bodies brushed, touched, sliding together like cam to tappet, convex to concave, his hardness, her softness. Their lips brushed, touched, and joined, tentatively at first, and then with increasing pressure.

As their lips parted from that first kiss, she whispered, "I won't break, you know."

Robert took that as an invitation. His arms tightened around her. His lips pressed down on hers. He wanted to open his mouth and taste her lips, her skin—

She drew back, slightly but definitely.

He released her at once and stepped back.

But she was not angry. Her eyes were shining.

"I want to be married on the first day of spring," Libby said. "Here, in the garden. As soon as the snow is gone and the ground firms up. Just as all the buds are coming out."

"That won't be March twenty-first. More like mid-April."

"Whatever the date, I want to celebrate in our new home."

"We must tell Lydia," he said.

"Yes, of course."

14. Proposing to Lydia

Lydia Wheelock was sitting in the parlor with a cup of tea at her elbow, a book of American verse on her lap, and a blanket tucked around her knees when her niece and her stepson came in to see her.

"Aunt?" Elizabeth said. "Robert and I have some wonderful news."

Lydia raised her chin. After all the whispering and awkward glances that, according to Rosemary Cobb, had infested this house during the past week, "wonderful news" could only mean one thing. Lydia steeled herself. "Yes?"

"Robert has asked me to marry him!" Elizabeth said.

"Did he?" Lydia replied coldly. "And did you accept?"

"Yes, of course. We are in love. How could I not?"

Lydia turned to glare at Robert. "So! While I was lying on my deathbed, you took advantage of this young woman's trusting nature—worse, you preyed on the vulnerability created by her illness—to compromise her. Do I understand this correctly?"

"Aunt!" the girl exclaimed.

"Lydia, I hardly think that's fair," Robert said tightly. From the furrow in his brow and the color in his cheeks, he clearly could think of more to say but did not trust himself to speak. So her barb had hit home. Good!

"I am Miss Elizabeth's guardian," Lydia went on, "her chaperone while she is under my roof. Considering her age, your attentions are inappropriate, sir. Considering the existing relationship between you, they are incestuous."

Robert straightened. "Not legally so," he said. "The relation is connubial—through your marriage to my father—not consanguine. The law does not—"

"Don't go quoting the law to me, young man!" she flared. "Even if the attachment were legal, it would be a social disgrace. And even if it were publicly acceptable, I will not have it!"

"Aunt!" from Elizabeth.

"Do you object to me, madam?" Robert said.

"You are a callow boy, unprepared for life, and without prospects."

"I have prepared for the legal profession," he replied. "I shall take the bar in this state and practice in this very town. My father's clients—"

"They consider you a laughingstock! These foolish land deals you've been making, sending good money into the ground—for a mere whim!"

"What do you know about that?" he demanded.

"Don't think just because I've been sick abed that I don't hear things." Lydia had the story of the mineral rights from Rosemary Cobb, of course. "I shall write to my brother and tell him what a spendthrift wastrel you have become. He cannot approve of a man who throws his money around like that."

"The amount is negligible, given the good will it buys," Robert said quietly. "And I have resources—or soon will have."

"Yes, let's see how you're sitting after the will is read."

"What do you mean?" he demanded.

Lydia did not dare tell him what she knew, of course, or how she knew it. Instead she said, "Oh, I know a thing or two about your father's business affairs. You'll find a few surprises there."

"What surprises?"

"Wait and see."

Lydia took satisfaction in the frustration that distorted his smooth young face. Would Elizabeth now see what a weakling he was? If he could not win an argument with an old woman just a few days risen from her sickbed, how would he fare in a law court, even one as provincial as Roulette's?

Instead of the surprise and loathing she expected to find on Elizabeth's face, there was a serene confidence. The girl put a hand on Robert's arm and stood on tiptoe to whisper in his ear. Lydia saw his face clear.

"What's all this?" Lydia demanded. "Why are you whispering?"

Elizabeth turned to her. "I said, Aunt, that Robert should leave you to me."

"And what are *you* going to do, Miss Pert?"
"Wait and see," the girl said—and smiled.

15. Convincing Lydia

Libby waited until after breakfast the following day, which gave her aunt time to consider the proposed marriage and perhaps come to a more generous conclusion. Then, having sent Robert on an errand in town, Libby went to confront the old woman in her own parlor. Lydia, however, did not give her the chance to open her mouth.

"Well, Miss, what do you have to say for yourself?" she demanded.

"The summer of seventy-eight," Libby replied after a pause.

"What's that?" the other woman asked suspiciously.

"That was the summer Grandmama and Grandpapa took you and your little brother to Saratoga Springs, wasn't it? You were twenty then, and quite beautiful. I've seen the portrait, of course. It's still hanging in the parlor of Grandmama's house, above the mantelpiece. It was painted that year, I believe."

After a hesitation, Lydia said, "What of it?"

But Libby could see she had struck a nerve.

She knew that people were already calling the seventies of the last century the Gilded Age. It was the period when the Astors and the Vanderbilts ruled American society, and New York was the center of the world—New York City, of course. Not the rest of the state, nor any part of a dreary, industrial, hide-and-tallow town like Binghamton. For all their wealth, the Bracketts of Binghamton were not even on the fringes of real society. And so, with a daughter who needed to make a good marriage, and a son who needed to make those casual friendships that meant a lifetime of profitable contact, the family had gone to Saratoga Springs to mingle.

The portrait of Lydia Brackett—in a white silk *décolleté* gown, seated among red velvet pillows, her face nearly as flushed as the seat cushions, eyes bright, and mouth partly open—was all that remained of the venture. The painting, heavy with oils and still smelling faintly of turpentine forty years later, was framed with great slabs of beveled wood that were decorated with plaster rosettes and slathered in gold leaf. Exactly to the taste of an Upstate striver who had made his money in shoe leather, or so Libby's mother once said.

"Who commissioned that portrait?" Libby asked now. "A young cousin of the Stuyvesants, wasn't it? And it was painted, or so Mama told me, at the Adelphi Hotel, in one of the third-floor bedrooms. Sitting every afternoon … from two to four."

Libby's mother had whispered that sometimes Jimmy Stuyvesant kept the appointment in place of his artist friend, who was supposed to be a scion of Gilbert Stuart from the wrong side of the blanket. Apparently, Lydia did not mind with whom she spent her afternoons. But when Grandmother Brackett finally found out about those trysts, the family had returned to Binghamton, practically on the next train, with its pride in tatters.

"The artist must have been working from memory, I suppose," Libby went on, "because there certainly wasn't time to *paint* during those sittings, was there?" By now her aunt was glaring white-hot needles at her. "Did Jimmy Stuyvesant send the portrait after you as a token? I'm surprised Grandmama would keep such a thing in her house."

"You are an impudent girl!"

"That may be," Libby said coolly. "But I know what I want."

"And you will blackmail me to get it? Is that your idea?"

"You have built a good life here, Aunt. It may not have suited you, originally, being married off to a back-country lawyer who was already a widower. But your husband was a pillar in this town, and you have become something of a fixture here yourself. Although you may secretly despise these people, I believe you would feel badly if they did not think well of you."

"And what do you want?" Lydia asked sullenly.

"To marry Robert. I want you to write to Father recommending the match."

"Robert will be nothing but a small-town squire, as William Henry was," Lydia said. "You may think Roulette is charming. You may think this house and the life surrounding it are very grand. But you are young and naive. Wait until you have spent almost twenty years here, with the same dull people making the same dull jokes. With the same blizzard closing the roads for weeks on end every winter. And the same flood drowning the downtown every spring. It will drive you mad, Elizabeth."

"It may not be the life you wanted, but it's what I want. Robert is a good man."

"Then be married to him with my blessing, dear," Lydia said with a frosty smile. "And may you live to regret it."

"Thank you, Aunt."

16. Last Will and Testament

THE DAY ARRANGED for the reading of his father's will came late in the winter, when the sky appeared changeable, sunny one moment and clouded the next, and the dark earth seemed to be thinking about warming up and shedding its mantle of snow. Robert met Malcolm Hurlbert at the front door. The man nodded and said, "Morning, Robert," in keeping with the dignity of the occasion. Robert took Hurlbert's black overcoat and gray scarf, hung them carefully on the rack in the hall, and led the county clerk into the library.

Lydia was already waiting in there, on one of the hardwood chairs arrayed in a semicircle before the desk. Libby sat beside her but with her chair pushed a few inches back, out of alignment with the circle. This innate sensitivity showed her awareness that, although a member of the family, she was not a principal in the proceedings.

As Robert and Hurlbert entered, the sun came out from behind a cloud and was caught in the webwork of beveled glass around the high windows in the east wall, above the bookcases. The room lit up with finger-length rainbows. Then the sun went under again, and the wintry gray light returned.

Hurlbert seated himself behind the desk. Robert touched the will that he had discovered in the drawer and which now lay at the center of the blotter, then took the chair at the extreme right of the semicircle.

The county clerk picked up the vellum packet, read aloud the ornate script on the front side, and turned it over to examine the red-wax seal on the back. "Everything seems to be in order," he pronounced.

"Then why don't you open it?" Lydia suggested.

"Yes, ma'am." Hurlbert picked up William Henry's letter opener—a tiny crusader's sword with Constantine's motto on a medallion at the hilt—and tried to pry the wax off the paper without damaging the seal. He worked the blade against first one edge of the blob, then the other.

Lydia stood up, leaned across the desk, and held out her palm. "Give me that."

Hurlbert put the sword into her hand. She turned it so the pommel was in her fist and smashed down on the seal. Red shards skittered across the paper and flew to the four corners of the desk. The flaps of the packet opened of themselves. Lydia dropped the letter opener on the blotter. "Proceed, sir."

Hurlbert picked up the document, smoothed it, covertly brushing away bits of wax, and began to read.

" 'On this date, the seventh of April, Nineteen Hundred and Four, I, William Henry Wheelock, being of sound mind, do declare this document to be my last will and testament ...' "

As the clerk spoke the words, Robert focused on the date: 1904. Robert himself would have been twelve years old. His mother had been dead in the ground for half of his young life. That was the year his father brought home a stern-faced woman from Upstate New York, Lydia Brackett, intending her to be Robert's new mother. And Robert would have none of it. He despised Lydia on sight, although he probably would have hated any woman who presumed to replace his real mother.

William Henry and this woman were married in Harrisburg, while his father was attending to a brief appointment on the governor's staff in the hope of entering politics. The marriage had taken place in the spring—early April would be about right—so this will must have been made either just before or just after, to seal the union. Robert wondered what a spinster and an established widower would have to give each other.

He also wondered, briefly, why William Henry never made a new will once Robert had turned twenty-one. No longer a child then, he could be expected to share in the burdens of managing the estate, and so it would be natural to change the terms of the will. But, of course, lawyers were notoriously bad at handling their own affairs. The shoemaker's children ...

" 'One,' " Hurlbert read, " 'at my death, the Emporium & Roulette Railroad Company, of which I am sole owner and proprietor, and the Roulette Electric Company, of which I am the principal shareholder, are to be held in trust for their employees. Operations shall be conducted in a manner to provide liveli-hoods for the good people who have made these enterprises the lucrative concerns they are today, and to provide a service to Sylvan County and its various communities. Profit from the op-erations shall provide support for my wife, Lydia Wheelock née Brackett' "—Hurlbert stumbled and actually pronounced the strange word as *knee*—" 'for as long as she shall live. Thereafter, the proceeds shall support any future children, with whom may she and I be blessed, until they have attained their majority.' "

Hurlburt glanced up. *"Are* there children?"

"No," Lydia said shortly.

Robert nodded to himself. He had always supposed his father would make such an arrangement on Lydia's behalf. The railroad and the electric system were William Henry's toys, and he often said that Robert's future lay with a corporate practice in New York, if not a position as counsel to one of the many national companies his father had advised.

Of course, profits from the E&RR had shrunk in the last few years, compared to what they had been in 1904. The war was hard on the local economy. And now the gasoline engine had shown it could pull a load farther and longer than a pair of hors-es or a team of mules. Someone would find a way to fix the roads for winter hauling, and then the monopolistic railroad business would be a relic of the past.

The electric business was in a better position to grow. In fact, bringing in the weekly trainload of coal to feed the generating plant was about the biggest contract the E&RR had. But growth was a two-edged sword: more customers meant more poles to buy and wire to string. Sooner or later, too, the plant's boilers would need to be rebuilt, the generator rewound, or something equally costly. That meant capital investment, and Roulette's po-tential as an urban center in rural Sylvan County would make it hard to sell shares in the financial market.

Still, these were interesting problems, and Robert secretly would have liked to try his hand at dealing with them. However, for a modest fee, to be paid from operations, he supposed he could do the legal work of setting up the trust that would manage these businesses … for the benefit of the employees and Lydia.

"The trust papers are all drawn up here," Hurlbert said as an aside, displaying a set of loose sheets that had been folded with the will. "They name a Harrisburg law firm, Hughes and Thayer, as administrator. So William Henry seems to have thought of everything."

"Thank you, Malcolm," Lydia said. "Please go on."

" 'Two, the balance of my assets shall pass to my son, Robert Wren Wheelock, to be held in trust by Hughes and Thayer until such time as he attains his majority.' … Then there's a list of these assets," Hurlbert explained.

"Read them," Lydia instructed.

Hurlbert read them off. They included large amounts of stock in Tidewater Oil Company, in the Yellow Knife Gold Mining Company, and various parcels of property around the county.

As the clerk went down the list, Robert slowly came to realize that the assets named were mostly worthless. The Tidewater stock was sold off years ago to pay for expanding the railroad and electric businesses and maintaining them during a time of financial reverses. The Yellow Knife mine played out not long after the will was made. So, aside from rents off a few pieces of land, it appeared that Robert was to be left penniless.

" 'Three,' " Hurlbert began anew, " 'the great house that I have built I leave to my son, Robert. The five acres of land under and surrounding it I leave to my wife Lydia, in the hope that they may share this property and occupy it jointly in a spirit of family and friendship.' … And that's it. The rest is just William Henry's signature, witnessed by two lawyers from the Harrisburg firm."

It looked as if Robert's only major asset was going to be a house in town.

Lydia turned to him with a grim smile. "I'll give you thirty days to move your house off my land."

"But—" Words escaped him. Robert looked around the room, at the dark carved woodwork, the solid lath-and-plaster walls, fine-grained maple floorboards, leaded windows with sand-stone sills. The house was three stories, thirteen large rooms not counting hallways and bathrooms, red-brick outer walls, and a black-slate roof. The weight of all that! He was no engineer, but common sense told him what was possible. "Moving this house would be impossible!"

"Do be reasonable, Aunt!" Libby said.

"I am being reasonable," Lydia replied. "The house is his. The land is mine. I want his house off my land."

"It cannot be done!" Robert insisted.

"Then you can vacate the premises," Lydia said. "You have thirty days."

"But, Aunt!" Libby said. "We're going to be married. This will be our home."

"Marry if you want to, my dear. But you and he will not be living here."

Robert glanced at Hurlbert, saw him looking beyond the circle of quarreling relatives, to the snow sliding off the trees along the driveway. Robert could imagine the stories he would have to tell in town.

"All right, Lydia," Robert said. "I give you leave to use this house, up until your death—but on the condition that Libby and I can be married here in the spring."

"Young man, you are in no position to bargain!" Lydia flared.

"Oh, yes," Robert said. "The coin I offer is my acquiescence. I'll make no challenge to this will. There will be no scandal. You get to keep the house, the railroad—everything my father built." He made his smile just as grim as hers. "And may it comfort you."

17. ZACKY'S CAFÉ

THE MORNING AFTER the reading of Judge Wheelock's will, Malcolm Hurlbert found a full house waiting for him at Zacky's. He took his time ordering eggs and sausage, hash browns and coffee. He took his time pouring cream in his coffee and stirring in the sugar.

"So are you going to tell us?" Albert Waterman asked. "Or should we go off to work?"

"You?" Hurlbert smiled. "Work?" He kept on stirring.

"I've been known to, from time to time. What happens to the railroad?"

"Held in trust," the county clerk said. "So you and the boys still have someone to watch over you in your sinecure."

Waterman's brow wrinkled. "I'll take that as an insult, I guess."

"Profits from the railroad and electric company will go to support the widow," Hurlbert said.

"Not much money there," said Nils, the fireman. "Not for ten year and more."

"Barely enough revenue to support ourselves," the engine driver, Johansson, agreed. "Let alone a great lady, too."

"But—with Lydia Wheelock in charge?" Waterman said. "She could squeeze sap from a peach stone."

"So good times are here again," Johansson said sourly.

"That's not all the news," Hurlbert said. "Young Robert and the Brackett girl are getting married."

"I knew it!" said Waterman.

"She's awful pretty," from Nils.

"What does Lydia say?" Zacky asked.

"Nothing good," Hurlbert replied. "But evidently she's allowing it."

"Big of her," from Johansson.

"They'll bring new life to this town, a young couple in high places," Zacky predicted. "Open up that big house for entertaining and all."

"Yeah, the upper crust of Sylvan County," said Waterman, lifting his pinkie.

"And you can cater for 'em, Zacky," Johansson said.

"Now that's the thing," Hurlbert interjected. "According to the terms of the Judge's will, Robert gets the house, but Lydia gets the land. She's kicking him out."

"Can she do that?" from Waterman.

"Move the house or move himself," Hurlbert replied.

"Sure, under writ of eminent domain," from Nils.

Hurlbert sniffed at this misuse of the legal term.

"Can't move that house," Johansson said. "Can't!"

"Of course not," Hurlbert said. "Stupid idea in the first place. But it's her way of getting back at the boy."

"For what?" Waterman asked.

"How should I know what for? For being the Judge's only son. For wanting to marry her only niece. For the simple fact that she's Lydia Wheelock and always expects to have her way."

"Where do you think Robert will go?" asked Clarence, the feed store owner.

"Too early to say," Hurlbert judged. "Maybe he'll head for the big city, finally."

"You don't think he'll do that, do you?" Johansson said. "He won't leave town."

"What do you care?" Hurlbert asked.

"He might want his money back."

That quieted them all.

"Naw," Waterman said after a minute. "He wouldn't welch on your deal."

"Not for five dollars," Hurlbert agreed.

18. THE HOUSE AT THE END OF THE LANE

ROBERT'S LAW PRACTICE doubled in early spring when he acquired a land case—a legitimate dispute of trespass and nothing to do with mineral rights. It promised to go to court unless his client accepted a thousand-dollar settlement on the misadventures of a bull involving ten yards of broken fencing and the claimed souring of a well heretofore producing eighteen hundred gallons of potable water a day. Robert knew he could win at trial; so his fees were assured in any event. They would establish him in a store-front office in town and enable him to plan for his and Libby's future.

With the question of how they would live all but decided, that only left the matter of *where*.

One morning during the first good thaw he was walking down the driveway on his way to court and happened to glance at the abandoned house at the end of the lane. This was the original homestead on the acreage when his father bought it, thirty years ago. Rather than tear it down in preparation for building the three-story Queen Anne–style manse he envisioned, William Henry had moved it out to the edge of the road, for it was a small frame structure of only three or four rooms. The Judge's first groundsman, an Italian immigrant named Vincenzo, had lived here and raised a family of five children. That was when Robert was a boy and had a nodding acquaintance with the eldest son, Eddie, who could punch with the force of a mallet driving a croquet ball.

In time, William Henry had sold the man this house and a hundred-foot strip of land along the road out of the total five acres of property. Now, as Robert approached the house, he could see the iron stakes which had marked the rows in Vincenzo's long-defunct garden, poking up through the melting snow. Robert remembered broad, bulging peapods growing there and some kind of beans—maybe kidney beans, because they always started off dull green and finished up dark red.

The house appeared to be in bad shape. The clapboards were gray and furred with splinters. The porch sagged at one end. But sandpaper and paint would take care of the one—white paint, he thought, with blue trim—and a proper cement footing and some shoring would put the other right. New shutters would help the windows … and new sashes with fresh glass.

Robert went up to the back door, stepping carefully on the uneven boards, and tried the lock. It snapped under pressure, and the knob came off in his hand—one more thing to fix.

The kitchen was small, square, and dingy. Reflected light from the snow outside made the interior seem brighter than it actually was. There were no appliances, except for a rusted iron stove that was missing its doors and all the lids on the range top. There was a bare line in the darkened paint along one wall where a counter and, judging by the drain hole underneath it, a sink had once stood. The oilcloth flooring was stained and wrinkled and littered with bits of moldy paper, evidence of rats. Mrs. Vincenzo would have shrieked and then run for her broom.

There were two other rooms on the ground floor: a dining room—or alcove, actually—that opened off the kitchen. An archway separated the dining room from the parlor that ran across the front of the house. Up the single staircase were two bedrooms with no plumbing in sight. Robert recalled now that the family had used a privy over a pit at the end of the garden. But something could probably be arranged in one of the closets—they were narrow but serviceable—or constructed in a corner between the two bedrooms. And, of course, the whole building would have to be wired for electricity.

Robert stamped his heel on the floorboards and felt for how the house reacted. He sensed no subtle shifts, heard no ominous creaks. Other than the porch, the structure seemed sound enough.

He imagined this room with fresh plaster, the floor sanded and waxed, curtains on the windows instead of cobwebs. Would Libby agree to live in such a house? She had told him she did not mind losing the big house to Lydia. It was Robert she loved, not the setting. But still, would she accept the gardener's house in return?

The one person who would have no say in the matter was Lydia. The deed to the house and strip of land was clear. Although Vincenzo had died and the family moved away to Ohio, Robert knew for certain that William Henry had never reacquired title. Robert could locate the wife or the children and make them an offer on the house. He would sell some of the property he had inherited around the county to come up with the purchase price.

He looked though the cracked pane in the bedroom window. In the middle distance, beyond the spruce trees, he could see the roof line of his father's house and one of the turrets. Could he wake up to that view every morning? Yes, he could—every morning until Lydia Wheelock was in her grave.

19. Dearly Beloved

THE HONEYSUCKLE WAS in bloom along the back terrace on the day Libby and Robert were to be married. Libby took that as an auspicious sign. Their tiny white flowers perfumed the air with a musky, wood-flavored scent.

The edge of the terrace was decorated with the tubs of orchids, ferns, and other green plants she had watered and pruned in the conservatory, brought out to the sunlight by the trainmen under the direction of Albert Waterman. Between the tubs, Libby's mother had arranged vases of early cabbage roses from the formal garden, and these Libby had also tended since the ground outside had awakened.

When they were planning the wedding, her mother had at first wanted to hold it in Binghamton, where most of her school friends still lived. But Libby insisted the wedding should be where her life would be, here in Roulette. Aunt Lydia tried to back out of her agreement with Robert about holding the ceremony at the great house, first by claiming not to remember, and then by insisting there had been no legal contract. It was only when Libby's father made a personal plea, brother to sister—with Robert looking on in a cold rage—and finally offered to pay, that her aunt at last relented.

Libby regretted that she and Robert would not be able to live in his father's house with its three grand stories, its white columns, and its fairytale turrets. But Robert had done a wonderful job of fixing up the house at the end of the lane. She was halfway in love with the fresh white paint and blue shutters. Though the rooms were small, she thought the house would be adequate for the two of them. What they would do when a family came was another matter.

As soon as Robert had completed the most basic repairs to the house, Lydia made him move out of the suite on the third floor. He took his law books and his suits and camped among the bare boards and open laths of the new house. But now the place was nice and clean. Libby had even turned over the good black earth of the garden out in back and started planting rows of squash and beans.

This morning, as Libby was putting on her mother's wedding dress of silver-colored silk that was heavy with white lace, Lydia had told her to pack her things.

"Of course she's packing," her mother had replied. "Tonight she will be sleeping in her own home."

"Just so you understand," Lydia had said primly.

When the final pins were in place and her mother pronounced her ready for the world, Libby gathered the four-foot-long train of the dress under her right arm and started carefully down the carpeted stairs. She went out through the front hall and around the driveway to the back of the house, rather than pass through the kitchen with its steams and its potential for stains. Her mother and aunt followed closely to make sure her leather pumps did not take a turn on the gravel and that none of the pins was slipping. At the corner by the conservatory she came into sight of the wedding party on the terrace. Her father was waiting with Mrs. Cobb, who laid a bouquet of white chrysanthemums—brought in on the railroad, everyone said, all the way from New York City—in the crook of Libby's left arm, lifted the trailing hem of the dress, and bent to straighten it across the verge of grass and flagstones that defined the terrace edge. When that was done, Libby's father took her free arm.

"I love you," he whispered, and she almost started to cry.

Up on the porch, where the trainmen had wrestled a spinet piano last night, the organist from the First Methodist Church struck the first chords of the wedding march. Libby's sister, Eunice, who was matron of honor, held a bouquet of violets and baby's breath up in front of her chin and turned to step off in front of them. Libby and her father walked slowly behind her, toward the far end of the terrace under the honeysuckle, using the step-halt-step that they had been practicing for the past three days.

From folding chairs on either side of the aisle, her family and friends from Binghamton, and Robert's smaller circle of acquaintances from Roulette, all rose to their feet. Happy faces turned towards her. But Libby could only see the man standing in front of the bank of fragile white blossoms.

According to the tradition, on this her wedding day she had not laid eyes on her groom until this moment. He was his same grave self: the brown hair brushed straight back, the cleft chin lifted in Libby's direction, the gray eyes shining as they always did whenever he looked at her. Today he wore a starched white collar and wide, gray-silk tie, a black coat with swallowtails, and gray pants with pinstripes. He looked like a banker, although he stood with his hands clasped behind his back, like a schoolboy. From the broad smile that creased his face, Robert looked as if he had just won a great prize. And Libby was shyly pleased to think that prize was herself.

Reverend Stevens stood somewhat off center, almost among the honeysuckle, his dull black robes making a shadow hole in the array of bright blossoms. Drawing closer, Libby could see that his face bore new, deep lines and his eyes were dark with sadness. He had put aside, for the moment, the death of his daughter to officiate at Libby's wedding, and for that she was grateful.

As Libby came up next to Robert, her father squeezed her arm once, then went to sit in the first row of chairs. She and Robert turned to face the minister, and he stepped out to meet them. "Dearly beloved," he began.

Libby heard almost none of what the minister said. She was conscious only of the man beside her: immensely tall, standing solid as a post, radiating a warm presence, like a second sun come down from the sky. And when he spoke, repeating the minister's droned words, it was almost a shock to her how they stood out on the air as if etched in light: "I, Robert, take thee, Elizabeth, to be my lawfully wedded wife, to have and to hold, for richer and for poorer, in sickness and in health, from this day forward, until death us do part."

Then it was Libby's turn. She followed the words that were said to her, quite in a daze. Although the formula was as familiar to a girl her age as any child's prayer, she could not remember from one second to the next what she was saying.

Finally, at the minister's bidding, Robert produced from his pocket a ring of yellow gold, round and heavy, looking far too large for her. She put out her left hand with the fingers spread stiffly. He slipped the ring over her third finger, giving it a little twist across the knuckle bones, and settled the weight of it against the web of her hand. "With this ring I thee wed."

The ceremony was completed with a dry brush of a kiss that Libby's lips hardly felt—his mouth was there and gone so fast in front of all these near-strangers. She opened her eyes. His arms were still around her shoulders, his face six inches from hers. He was grinning, his eyes dancing, as if the two of them shared a secret. That was when the reality of the situation became clear to her. With just those few words, Libby Brackett had gone away—replaced by Mrs. Robert Wheelock, Esquire, of Roulette, Pennsylvania. Now and forever.

20. First Night

THE LIGHT WAS a small reading lamp that had been at his father's bedside. It had a round base of patinaed bronze and a glass shade with a finish of fired gold, so that it gave an orange-yellow glow to the whole room.

"Turn it off," Libby said.

Her hair was down now, trailing across her bare shoulders, and to Robert it seemed to change color from golden blonde to deep russet as she turned from the direct light into shadow. She had removed the wedding dress in the bathroom. She would not let him help her because of the pins, she said. Now she wore a long white sheath with a low neckline that fastened with a ribbon bow and a row of tiny buttons. It might have been part of her underwear and might be her nightdress—Robert did not know enough about such things to make a judgment. But her eyes shone with complicity, a shared secret, a new understanding of what they were about to undertake. It was a look both shameful and wonderful at the same time.

He turned off the light.

While Libby was undressing in the other room, Robert had stripped off the patent-leather shoes, his black wool socks, and the boiled shirt. Now he shucked the suspenders off his shoulders and stepped out of his pants. Not knowing what might be customary, he left on his long cotton underwear. Besides, there was a chill in the room. He stood on his side of the bed, and she on hers, waiting.

"Robert," she whispered.

He came around the end and found her in the dark.

"Dear husband," she said, lifting her arms around his neck and kissing him.

He could feel her lips smiling under his, and then her mouth opened. Her tongue was suddenly inside his lips, pushing between his teeth, searching for him. Her obvious excitement aroused him, freeing him to imagine every form of sensuality. Robert's hands left their firm grip under her shoulderblades and traveled downward, meeting no resistance from corset or stays. His palms settled beneath the round softness of her bottom, and he lifted her. She spread her legs, hooking her knees around his hips, and thrust herself forward.

The two of them unbalanced and he crashed backward onto the bed.

Libby was on top of him then, laughing uncontrollably.

"Hush!" he whispered, feeling scandalized.

"There's no one to hear," she whispered back.

"It's just that—it doesn't seem—"

"Proper?" Libby suggested, giving him a squeeze.

She snuggled her head down beside his jawbone and pressed her elbows into the mattress on either side of his shoulders. Still spread-eagled on top of him, she arched her back, then relaxed. She repeated the movement, rubbing herself against him from collarbone to thigh. Robert's hands were still clasped around her bottom, and they slipped lower with this motion, chafing the backs of her hams and pulling up the hem of her nightdress.

He was growing beneath her.

Feeling it, she chuckled.

Libby kept up the rocking movements until Robert thought he could no longer stand it. "I'm afraid ... I have to ..."

She rolled off him like a cat. Her nightdress was now up around her ribs. Her fingers scrabbled at the buttons below his waist. When she had freed him, she measured his member against the length of her thumb and guided it. Her free hand pulled at his hip to urge him over on top of her. He entered her just at the moment of release.

One brief spasm, and it was finished.

She made a quick intake of breath.

"I'm sorry," he said, embarrassed.

"It's all right," she said. "There will be other times."

But that was the night William Henry II was conceived.

SPRING 1928

1. Spring Cleaning

"Mother, may I keep this?" William Henry asked, holding out his closed hand to her. Behind him stood his sister, Eugenia, watching with big eyes. Libby knew he was the leader of their tiny band, and whatever nine-year-old Willie got away with, seven-year-old Genie was sure to try. In fact, from the way the girl had her hands clenched at her sides, Libby guessed she was hiding another of whatever her big brother was holding.

"Open your hand," Libby told him.

It was a shard of ceramic, smooth edged and slightly concave—part of a cup or bowl, the dull green clay suggesting Wedgwood. Libby's heart sank, because Aunt Lydia collected Wedgwood. He turned the piece over, and the other side had the white figure of a lady in Greek drapery. A broken-off olive branch entered the piece above her head.

"It's pretty," he said innocently.

"How did it break?" she asked.

"It was already broken. Really."

"Where did you find it?"

"Upstairs, on the third floor."

"At the front or back?" Libby asked, but the boy only looked confused. "Was there a long window?" she clarified. "And little round rooms on either side?"

"No, small windows," William Henry said. "And I could see the barn from up there."

That would have been the cook's old rooms. The jasperware was likely a piece that Rosie Cobb might once have broken, then hidden so as to avoid Lydia's wrath. No matter now, because Rosie had been dead for more than a year.

The children had been exploring while Libby commanded a crew of town girls in a general spring cleaning of the big house, because the woman who came in once a day to cook for Lydia and do her laundry was not up to the task. Over the winter the carpets had absorbed stains and grains of caked mud. The turnings of the woodwork were deep in dust. The windowpanes were smeared, and the basins all had edgings of dark green mildew.

Willie and Genie were probably aware they had a family connection with the great house across the park behind their home and with the mysterious old woman who lived there. Robert never spoke of her and, while Libby acknowledged her aunt, she generally avoided their questions. Clearly, a place so large and empty fascinated them. There were bedrooms on the second floor that had not been occupied in ten years. The children could visit them only after creeping, with much whispering, past the room where Lydia stayed in her bed.

At home they did not have such amounts of space. When Genie was born, Robert had moved Libby and himself into the small bedroom in the house at the end of the lane and divided the larger room for the children. Libby did not know what they would do when—or rather, if—there was a third child. She was only glad there was no third sex that would require a separate accommodation.

As she swept and scrubbed, Libby was saddened by much of what she saw in the great house. The shelves in the library were empty and smelled of mice, while Robert kept his law books and his growing collection of first editions—mostly American mystery writers like Edgar Allan Poe and Melville Davisson Post—on shelves made of bricks and boards in the front room of their home. The conservatory was empty, too. Not just the plants were gone, but the tubs and worktable and the summer furniture as well. All that richness squandered, while Libby consoled herself with a pot of herbs in her kitchen window. She also wouldn't mind having the big kitchen, with its huge range that had eight lids and a built-in griddle—even if it did burn wood—to cook for her growing family.

"So, may I keep it?" Willie repeated, gesturing with his hand.

Genie wanted to help, so she showed Libby her piece. It was not as big as her brother's, nor as complete: she only had the rest of the olive tree.

"Those pieces don't belong to you," Libby said.

"No … But they're not good for anything."

"That's not the point. Someone left those in the house, rather than throw them away. Maybe that person planned to glue the broken pieces together someday. If you steal this much, then the design can never be whole again."

"We didn't *steal* them!" he protested.

"You wanted to take them for yourself," she said.

Libby knew her argument was unreasonable. No one would want the shards. Lydia, who did not leave her room for more than a few hours a day now, hardly looked at her Wedgwood collection displayed around the parlor and along the plate rack in the dining room. She had no time to hunt up an old broken piece and mend it. Still, Libby was reluctant to let the children take anything from this house, no matter how useless. If Robert should find the pieces—and she could not warn the children against showing them off, because that would lead to embarrassing questions—he would guess where they had come from. It would hurt Robert, his sense of honor, his pride, to have his children gleaning toys and trinkets from the house he had not entered in ten years. It would disappoint him to think that Libby did not understand this.

"No," she said finally. "You must put the pieces back."

"Mother!" Genie wailed.

"None of that. Go along now."

Willie looked rebellious, but he went and Genie followed. Libby knew they would not sneak the pieces into their pockets as soon as they were out of sight. She knew that, if she went up to the third floor and searched Rosie's old room, she would find all the shards of green Wedgwood, including the Greek lady and the broken tree. Libby was raising honest children. She could trust them.

2. THE CREEK

ROBERT STOOD BEHIND the barn on Lydia's property and watched brown water slide over the rocks. Only the biggest rocks stood above the surface now. And soon—perhaps by the end of the morning—they would be mere lumps under the rolling water. For most of the year, Miller's Creek was as clear as well water and flashed with bubbles as it danced over the sandy riffles in its shallow bed. Now it was the color of coffee with cream and gave an impression of sluggishness, as if it had been mixed with corn starch.

Mrs. Sharp, who was Lydia's new housekeeper, had called him that morning with a voice of concern. Lydia had seen the creek from her bedroom window and was worried. Of course, Lydia never told her to call Robert. She simply wanted something done about the barn, and Robert was the only person Mrs. Sharp could think of.

He had been careful, in coming here, not to let himself be seen from the house. Lydia would leave her bed to call the sheriff to report a trespasser or swear out a warrant or something. So he approached the barn the long way around: from Main Street coming down Miller's Lane along the eastern edge of the property, which had the heaviest screen of trees, then following the path along the creek bank and keeping his head down.

He looked downstream, to where the creek joined the Allegheny River in a curve that defined the western side of the property. From a half-hour spent standing on the Main Street bridge, he knew the river was already high. Not flood stage yet, but not far from it. Miller's Creek would get no relief there. In fact, as the river swelled, it would back up into this channel for a mile or more. Robert knew what that meant. Once the creek topped its banks, the water would spread sideways like a rising brown army, through the barn, over the lawns and back gardens, and come right up to besiege the terrace. Then the river would follow in a day or two, and the property would become a still brown lake, undermining the tree roots and damaging the outbuildings.

100

The great house itself, on its slight rise in the middle of the property, would not be harmed. In all his years in the house, Robert could not remember ever seeing water in the basement.

He did not care about the rest, which belonged to Lydia.

Still, the barn could be a concern. Although Lydia had sold the horse Jack Wax years ago, there were still sheep to be kept from hoof rot, or from drowning in a panic … or worse. Robert was shocked at the deterioration of the bank behind the barn. From years of neglect, the ground had been allowed to undercut the fieldstone foundation wall. It was already sagging and soon to collapse—perhaps even this spring. The wooden beam that provided a footing for the frame above the stonework was in bad shape, too.

Robert opened the large blade of his clasp knife and probed the exposed wood under the crumbling layers of oxidized red paint. The tip went in more than an inch. So dry rot had taken hold. About five years ago he had written a letter to Lydia suggesting some basic improvements to the property, including renewing the gravel fill along this very bank, but Lydia had not answered him. Clearly, she had never done anything about the bank, either.

There was nothing he could do now. When the water rose, as it always did, Robert would pull on waders and try to get the poor animals to the higher ground of his strip along the road. Then Lydia could charge him with sheep stealing, if she wanted.

And when the barn finally did collapse, he would hire a contractor to come and haul the rubble away. Or he would pay the damages when the hulk floated into one of the local bridges and knocked it down, because Lydia would never think to pay.

Shaking his head, Robert crouched down and duck-walked back upstream, until he was behind the screen of trees again.

3. FLOOD WATER

WHEN HER MOTHER said there was not going to be any school, Genie worried that she wouldn't be seeing her second-grade classmates for a long time. Then Mother tried to keep her and Willie indoors for the day, and Genie was sure something very bad had happened. They started playing Indian chiefs by pulling the cloth down on one side of the dining room table, to make a tent, but Willie soon grew bored. He called it a baby's game and started to roughhouse. So Mother sent them outside. "Don't leave the yard," was the last thing she said. "And don't go into Great Aunt Lydia's yard."

The grass was spongy beyond the doorstep, and the dirt path through the garden had big puddles. But when Genie raised her eyes to the other side of the fence, she saw a magical land. The trees stood upon their own reflections, as if the surface of the world had become a black mirror. The gray fog moved between them, making some of the trees stand out and others quietly disappear. The gravel driveway up to Great Aunt Lydia's house curved across this glassy surface like a long white ribbon. Genie's feet itched to walk upon it. Her fingers wanted to touch those ghost trees that grew upside down. In a trance, she started to climb the fence.

"We're supposed to stay here," Willie called.

"It's all right," she said over her shoulder.

Then Genie stopped and turned back. "You should get your sailboat," she said.

It was a model that Father had made for Willie. "A real Barbary pirate corsair," Father called it. The boat had a long, low hull with a high stern that was fitted with bits of mirror, for the windows. Genie could imagine the pirates in there, cutting hair. Father had stuck the ends of clothes pins in the sides and painted them gold, for the guns. There were two masts with two triangular sails, made of old table napkins dyed red with ink. The boat itself was painted dead black—"the pirate color," Father had said.

"It's just for show," Willie said. "I don't think it will float."

"How do you know if you won't try!" she replied.

"It's just meant to be pretty," he insisted.

"It would be prettier on the water."

"I don't know. Mother said …"

"Father made you a pirate ship," Genie told him. "And *that*—" She pointed out over the dark water. "—is a pirate sea."

"All right," Willie replied, defeated by her logic. "But just for a little bit. Just to see how it looks." He started for the back door.

"Go in the front," Genie said, "so Mother won't see you."

He came back a few minutes later with the boat held stiffly before him, to keep the rigging, made from lengths of fishing line, from snagging on the front of his jacket. Genie climbed over the fence and carefully took the boat from him, cradling the long hull in her open hands. Willie climbed over after her. She carried the ship up the driveway until she found a likely cove against the banked gravel. "You launch it," she said, offering him the ship.

Willie knelt down and took it into his hands. She saw him fingering the overlapped planks of the side, wondering if they would keep out the water. "Father must have built it right," she told him. "He knows about these things."

"Of course he does!" Willie said.

He leaned far out and gently dipped the bow into the still water. Ripples spread outward from that first touch, like a stone hitting the surface. He quickly dropped the stern, so that the bow wouldn't slide under the water and fill. He gave the hull a little push. The pirate ship leaned over on one side, wetting the lower corner of the triangular sails, then righted itself. It rode majestically off, catching up with its own widening band of ripples and riding over them as if crossing the waves.

"It's beautiful," she whispered.

"Yes," he replied.

But no sooner had he spoken than Genie could see that something was wrong. The farther the ship went, the more it leaned, until the sail was dragging in the water all the time now. The boat turned toward that side and slowly stopped. It was a good ten feet out from the bank. She sensed it getting lower in the water by the minute.

"It's sinking!" Willie cried. "My boat'll be ruined!"

The red ink was already fading from the sail's wetted corner.

"Maybe it will drift back this way," she suggested hopefully.

"No, it won't," he said.

"Well ..." Genie hesitated.

"This was your idea. You should go and get it."

"But I'll get wet!"

"Go on!"

Genie held her breath and stepped off the firm white gravel of the driveway. Cold water filled her shoes and soaked her stockings. The grass was slippery beneath her feet. The flood had turned the soil under the sod into soft mud. She reached back and took Willie's hand for support, but their arms would only stretch so far. Eventually, she had to let go and walk into deeper water.

The ship's carved railing was only an inch above the surface now.

She leaned out and just touched the end of the boom. One foot slid out from under her, and she flopped face-down in the pool. She came up drenched from head to foot. Her braids were soaked and slapped heavily against her chest. Liquid mud was actually dribbling out of her ears. She spat and blew brown foam out of her nose.

"I'm all wet!" she shouted.

"Get my boat!" Willie cried.

Genie looked around. Her great splash had sent the sluggish vessel only a foot further along. She couldn't get any wetter now. She slogged forward and reached under the boat. The hull was heavy with the water it held. When she lifted it clear, streams of brown water drizzled out along the keel. She turned and carried it back to shore.

Willie took the pirate ship from her gently. He fussed with the discolored edges of the sails and tried to wipe the little flecks of mud on the deck and rigging, while rivers of water spread across the gravel.

"Well, what about me?" Genie said.

"Serves you right," he replied crossly. "It was a stupid idea, trying to sail my boat in this stuff. You'll catch hell when Mother sees you."

"Well, maybe I can …" But Genie didn't know what she could do. Even if she managed to sneak inside, she was sure to leave footprints. And then Mother would find her muddy clothes in the laundry. And Genie couldn't wash the stink out of her hair and redo the braids without Mother's help. There was only one thing to do. "I'll tell her you were swearing," Genie threatened.

"You'll still catch hell," he said, repeating the word.

"Yes," she acknowledged glumly. "I guess I will."

4. ZACKY'S CAFÉ

MALCOLM HURLBERT FOUND a much reduced attendance at Zacky's when he entered on a midweek morning. Reverend Stevens and Clarence from the feed store were at their usual tables. Stovall, who managed the lumber operation over Denton Hill, was in town to pick up supplies. But none of the local farmers had made an appearance, which was hardly surprising given the amount of work they had to accomplish in order to plow and plant as soon as the water went down. What did surprise him was the absence of the train crew, who had not missed a working day's breakfast since the blizzard three years ago.

"You tie your boat up good and tight?" Clarence asked as Hurlbert hung his oilskin on the coat rack.

For answer, Hurlbert lifted one leg to show off the wet, black rubber of his fishing waders. "Water's not that deep this year," he said.

"At least it's not over your head," Stovall said.

"What's it like up at your camp?" Hurlbert asked.

"Dry as bone, except for the rain. We work the hillsides, not the streambeds."

"Lucky you," Hurlbert said. Then to the rest of the room, "Where are the boys?"

"Bridge's out at Austin, according to the telegraph," Zacky said and snapped a towel.

Hurlbert whistled. "We won't see them for a month then. Lydia's not going to pay to replace that bridge. Put a dent in her profit structure."

"It's only a tree snag," Clarence volunteered. "The flood crest is pushing water over the tracks. And that McKee is a cautious man." McKee was the new conductor, who had replaced the late Albert Waterman five—no, six years ago now. "He wouldn't take responsibility for going ahead."

"Three foot of water," Zacky supplied. "That'll just about reach the firebox."

"And who knows what the sidewise pressure is doing to the track alignment," Stovall added.

"You got all that from a telegram?" Hurlbert asked.

"No," from Clarence, "McKee telephoned me from Austin, on account of a shipment I'm expecting."

"Right considerate," Hurlbert said, "considering the time of year."

"Yeah, except there's not going to be any customers today."

"Something should be done about these spring floods," Zacky said.

"Like what?" Hurlbert asked contemptuously. "Ask God to stop the rain? How about making the snow pack disappear?"

"Well … something."

5. Life in a Small Town

Although Robert lived in a small house in a small town in central Pennsylvania with a small legal practice among farmers and shopkeepers, he still liked to get the news from what he thought of as the big world outside. So, at some expense and with a delay of two to three days, he had *The New York Times* brought in on the train. He would read it every morning with his coffee before going downtown to his office. In the week after the spring floods receded, an article with a dateline somewhere in California caught his eye.

"Now here's an interesting thing," he said to Libby.

"What's that, dear?" she asked from in front of the stove.

"What's that, Daddy?" his daughter echoed from across the table.

"A company out in California has found gas in the ground and is building a pipeline to take it to market," he said.

Robert had read the story through because, after another long winter, he had been thinking about fuel—even nursing a grudge against it. When he lived in the big house across the park, it had been Robert's job to shovel coal into the furnace every morning. And even now Lydia hired a man to come in and do it for her. He and Libby did not have such a monster in the basement, because the house at the end of the lane did not have a basement. But there was a monster in their living room: a pot-bellied stove that glowed red hot in the evening, threatened to spit sparks and drop clinkers onto the rug, and wanted to be fed every hour. In an age when they could turn a switch to get light, and even plug in a tabletop device to make toast, messing about with chunks of coal and sifting coal dust in the living room—and feeding the kitchen range with splits of wood—just seemed barbaric. Getting clean, silent gas through a pipe would be so much more civilized.

"Oh," Libby said. "I see. ... And where do they usually find gas?"

"They don't find it. They make it in a factory, by heating anthracite," Robert explained. "Or rather, they do that in cities large enough to make the operation profitable. This article says there are also some fractional amounts of gas in the California oil wells, around Los Angeles, but not enough to build a pipeline."

"Don't they have oil wells out in the western part of Pennsylvania?" Libby asked.

"Yes, but that's not the point. They're talking about a different kind of gas. These gas wells are at a place called Kettleman Hills, and the gas is mostly methane. They call it 'natural gas' because—"

Robert stopped short.

Of course, Libby was right.

There *was* oil in Pennsylvania, at Franklin and Oil City. And that was about eighty miles to the west of Sylvan County—about as far as this place called Kettleman was supposed to be from the oil wells around Bakersfield, in California. And pockets of methane were also to be found in coal deposits—everyone knew that. There were coal fields at Scranton, and that place, too, was about eighty miles from Sylvan County. So … if Robert were a betting man, he would bet that the right kind of well, put into the ground right under this kitchen, might bring up some of that natural gas. The question was, how deep a well? And would it be the right kind of gas?

If it were, then they could pipe it around town. The gas would be a boon to the community. No one would have to burn coal and wood for heat. Libby could have a clean-burning stove in her kitchen, as they had when she was a girl in Binghamton. And Robert would no longer have to chop kindling in the morning and split balks of timber on Saturday afternoons. Perhaps, if there were enough of this gas, they could even run a pipeline across the hills to nearby towns, and then—

"Penny for your thoughts," Libby said. She was standing at his shoulder, smiling down at him.

"I'm afraid they're not worth even that much," he said folding the paper. "Just daydreaming."

"You'd better get down to the office."

"Yes, I had better."

As it was a bright, sunny day, Robert decided to walk to work. The trip along Main Street showed him the extent of the flood damage. The front yards of the houses around his, but on lower ground, had the look of drained swamps with the trees showing high-water marks, and the flowers and shrubs looking drowned. The town's main bridge over the Allegheny River had mud in its gutters and a thin layer of silt over the paving of the sidewalk.

Robert's law office was on the second floor of a building in back of the courthouse square, and so it never felt the effects of the flood. When he put his key in the front door lock, however, he found it was already open. He walked in and hallooed up the stairs. "Hello?"

"Is that you, Mr. Wheelock?" his secretary Helen called out.

"Yes, of course," Robert replied, coming up. "You're here early, aren't you?"

"Well ... I'm here to clean out my desk, sir. You see, I have decided to retire."

Robert was taken aback. "Oh? Why? After—what is it—ten years?"

"Eight and a half, sir. But my daughter in Harrisburg has taken ill, and I need to move down there to take care of her."

"That's sad news. What is it that ails her?" Robert asked.

"The crab," Helen answered laconically, by which he understood her to mean a cancer of some kind. It would be indelicate of him to inquire of its nature and extent. The fact that Helen was leaving Roulette, apparently for good, suggested the illness was grave and likely to be mortal.

"I am so sorry," he said, putting a hand on her arm.

"It comes to us all," she said. "But I hate leaving you with this mess."

Robert looked around at the desks, his and hers, piled with books and papers, the row of green metal cabinets, the wall of shelves with the regular spines of legal bindings in tan and gold, banded in maroon and blue. He would have to find some way to maintain it all. Robert could type—a bit—and that would take care of his correspondence and legal briefs, given the current flux of business. But he was unfamiliar with the filing system she had created for the office. And accounting and billing were utter mysteries to him. The pool of trained secretaries in a town like Roulette was not large. In fact, he had been lucky, all those years ago, to hire Helen Grant from the railroad dispatch office in Emporium, and singlehandedly she had set up and systematized his practice.

"I suppose I could keep my eyes and ears open," she said.

"Excuse me?"

"To find someone for you," she explained. "To run the office for you."

She had been reading his mind again. It was a talent he was going to miss.

"Why, thank you, Mrs. Grant," he said. "However, I expect you will be impossible to replace."

That made her smile. He suspected it would be her last smile for a long time.

6. MARGOT

THE SONG GOING through Margot Dobray's head as she walked down Main Street was accompanied by a slick jazz trumpet. And that trumpet wasn't staying in the background.

If your woes have just begun,
Find your place—in the sun—
And there that trumpet went: *Bree-dup! Bree-dup!*
Up on top of the RAIN-bow,
Sweepin' the clouds away!

Margot gave a little dance kick and—Damn! Her last pair of silk stockings let go with a runner halfway up her calf. And it felt like an inch wide.

She turned and lifted her leg to survey the damage. She noticed two men on the street stop to do likewise. She made a face at them, and they hurried on. Alone in her own bubble again, Margot raised her skirt above the knee to adjust her garter. It was a pretty garter, with black lace ruffles around a band of red silk. It was a pretty knee, too, with dimples. And, until a moment ago, it had been a pretty pair of stockings, with the kind of smooth white shine that she loved so well.

What was she going to do now?

Margot had come to Roulette to collect money—not a hustle or anything, just a debt owed to a friend of a friend, back in Chicago. All perfectly legal. She had put up her last two hundred dollars, minus fifty for travel expenses, to collect two thousand that was due on the sale of some property. That money was going to set Margot up in her singing career in New York.

But when she tried to find the address, no one could help her. They couldn't even tell her where Pennsylvania Street was. And when she asked at the post office, they said there was no such street in this town. Yes, the postmark on the letter she had was genuine, but the return address did not exist.

They suggested she try at the courthouse—at least it wasn't the police station—to consult the county tax rolls. The old man who was the clerk there could tell her without even turning to

112

look in his wall of books. "You won't find her," he said. "I know a family of Ryans up near Ulysses, but none of the daughters is named Fay."

Margot realized she had fallen for the oldest play in the book, chapter one, page one. And all they had needed was a long-distance telephone call, one sheet of fancy legal letterhead, and the price of a stamp. God damn it!

Still ... the play had gotten her out of Chicago, at least. And Chicago was, for various reasons, all having to do with men and money, not a place she could be anymore.

But the question remained. With three dollars in her purse, and just fifteen more tucked into her shoe, what was Margot going to do now?

Glancing down a side street, she saw a sign in front of a large, two-story house on a narrow lot. The paint on the clapboards was more gray than white, and some of the shingles were missing from the edge of the roof. The sign out front said "Rooms for Rent." With no hotel in town—as Margot had learned by asking the county clerk—a boarding house seemed like the next best thing, so long as the landlady wasn't too snoopy. But then, Margot had lots of experience with snoopy landladies. The plaque by the front doorbell said, "Clara Endicott, Prop." Well, Mrs. Endicott had just met her match.

"Yes?" the woman said from behind a crack in the door.

"I'd like a room," Margot said.

"We have one available." The door opened an inch wider, revealing a suspicious gray eye. "Are you new in town, then?"

"Yes, ma'am," Margot agreed. "Just arrived."

The door opened another inch, showing a long nose to go with the eye. "Are you here with your husband?"

Margot didn't hesitate. "I'm not married." In her experience, a woman's marital status could always be checked: a wire to the husband's employer, a demand to produce the marriage certificate, or any other evidence the landlord required. A single woman, on the other hand, needed no proofs.

"We generally don't take unattached females." The door closed an inch.

"That is," Margot lowered her voice and blinked her eyes. "My husband died. I'm ... a widow."

"You poor dear!" The door opened to shoulder width and Mrs. Endicott's head came out. "My own husband died ten years ago. In the Great War."

Margot nodded soberly, hunched her shoulders submissively, and waited for the game to continue.

"What brings you to Roulette?" Mrs. Endicott asked.

Margot knew the only possible answer to that one. "A job."

"I see ... And what do you do?"

Margot said the first thing that popped into her head. "I'm a secretary." And then, out of the blue, the second thing. "A legal secretary."

"Oh!" A light came into Mrs. Endicott's face. "You must be Robert Wheelock's new girl."

Margot knew an opportunity when it presented itself. "Oh, yes! That's me."

"I'm glad he found someone so quickly. Isn't it a shame about Mrs. Grant's daughter?"

"Yes, it is," Margot said.

"I understand it's supposed to be a cancer."

"Why, I believe so. But I really don't know the details." Margot would have to look up this Wheelock person right away, in case there were going to be more conversations like this. "Could you show me the room now?"

"Of course. It's second floor, at the back." The door opened wide and Mrs. Endicott beckoned her in. "Silly of me to keep you standing on the porch in this wind. The room is five dollars a week—in advance."

Margot stood on one foot and slipped off her shoe to take out the money. "Here you go."

"I run a clean house," the landlady said, accepting the bills and leading her across the hallway to the stairs. "No drinking, of course, no men friends, and curfew is at ten o'clock sharp," she said over her shoulder. "Those are the rules."

"Yes, ma'am," Margot replied dutifully.

Mrs. Endicott stopped and turned around suddenly, looking suspicious. "Don't you have any luggage?"

"I left it at the train station, until things got arranged."

"Oh … Well, that's sensible."

"Could we see the room?"

"Certainly. Right this way."

7. TYPING LESSON

ROBERT HAD HIS letters all drawn up. Or the first drafts, at least, written out in longhand on yellow legal pads. Now came the laborious process of typing them on the office Underwood without making too many errors that would mess up the paper with corrections or, to satisfy his penchant for neatness, force him to start over again.

To the chairman of the Geology Department at the Pennsylvania State University, after the appropriate salutations: "… Can you recommend a consulting geologist, one with extensive knowledge of the countryside centering on Sylvan County?"

To one of his father's old contacts in the Legal Department of Tidewater Oil: "I was hoping you could direct me to a commercial drilling firm with experience in deep wells …" Robert did not say what kind of wells. It seemed best to let his correspondent assume *oil* wells. Nor did he specify how deep because, at this point, Robert could only hazard a guess that hundreds of feet would only tap the water table, and thousands of feet might be out of the realm of possibility. Better to let the recipient fill in the gaps.

To the manager of the Purchasing Department at …

"Hello?" A voice came from inside the front door on the ground floor. "Anybody home?" A female voice.

"Yes, up here." he called out. "One moment, please." Robert arranged and covered his papers, in case it might be a client, then stood up and went to the top of the stairs.

A young woman was standing at the bottom. She wore a red-felt hat that fitted her head like a conquistador's helmet, a thin silk dress that barely covered her limbs and anyway looked like underwear, and too much makeup. "Are you Mr. Robert Wheelock?" she asked.

"I am Wheelock, yes," Robert replied. "Won't you come up?"

"Oh, thanks! It's freezing down here."

She ran up the stairs, pumping her legs so that Robert could see the dark bands at the tops of her stockings with a width of pale flesh above. As she came nearer, into the electric light of the office, he decided that it wasn't just the makeup. She really did have huge eyes, black eyes, and lids lightly veined with blue. Her lips really were full and red and just slightly wet. Her cheeks and throat were both pale and flushed at the same time. And, at the back of her neck, from beneath the lower edge of her stiff hat, fell a long skein of straight hair that glistened blackly in the hard light and begged to be smoothed by a man's hand.

"Can I help you?" Robert asked politely.

"Probably it's me that can help *you*." She paused to glance around the office, exposed behind him in its current state of clutter. "My name's Margot Dobray and I'm a secretary." She looked directly into Robert's eyes. "A legal secretary. Somebody said you could use one."

"Oh!" Robert took her meaning immediately. "Helen Grant sent you."

"Yes … Shame about her daughter."

"We're all very sad for her."

"I'm sure you are."

"Well … um …" Robert could not break away from those eyes. "Do you have any experience?"

"Yes, with a legal firm in Chicago."

"Oh, that's excellent. Really excellent!"

"Can you tell me what the job pays here?"

"Oh …" Robert paused until she took her eyes off him, which left him free to think. He had paid Helen Grant twenty dollars a week, but that was only after eight years of service. Eight and a half, actually. She had started at twelve dollars, but that was in the hard economic times right after the war. And this Margot Dobray, with experience at a big law firm in Chicago, would be better trained than Helen had been, in the beginning. "Shall we say eighteen dollars a week?" he suggested.

The woman's head drew back. "Gee, that's—"

"It's a small town," Robert explained quickly. "With not a lot of business, I'm afraid. But I suppose we could stretch to, well … twenty?"

"A week?" she asked in confirmation.

"Of course. And, as my caseload develops, we could expect to improve on that."

"Why, that's handsome!" she said, offering him her eyes again. "I'll take it."

"Good. And when can you begin working?"

"How about right now? What comes first?"

"I have some business correspondence." Robert led her back to his desk and uncovered the yellow pads. "Just some letters."

"Oh, good!" She seemed genuinely eager. "I like letters."

"And you will be sitting over here." He took her to Helen's desk and pulled the cover off the Underwood. "It has a fresh ribbon. And the paper's in the top left drawer."

"Thanks." She sat down in the swivel chair, crossed her legs, and swung the seat side to side experimentally. "Comfy!"

Robert could not take his eyes off the hem of her dress as it rode gently back and forth across the top of her knee. "Yes ... um ..."

"Why don't I get started on these?" Margot suggested, twisting her body around on the seat to reach the drawer. Her dress moved even higher, and Robert gulped.

She took out a thick stack of onionskin and slapped it down beside the typewriter. Wetting her finger with the pink tip of her tongue, she plucked off the top sheet, grasped it in both hands, and approached the machine. She hesitated, then pushed the paper down in front of the roller, seesawing it past the guides. When she had worked the sheet deep enough not to fall out, she reached for the platen knobs and cranked them backwards. The paper sank into the machine and accordioned on itself below the carriage mechanism.

"I think," Robert said slowly, "the paper goes *behind* the roller." He pointed to the place. "In that slot there."

"Oh, sure!" She yanked out the sheet, balled it up, and tossed it into the wastebasket. "I've just never worked with this model before."

"Apparently not."

Margot took another sheet, fed it in correctly this time—figuring out the restraining bails after only a second—and cranked the platen in the right direction to raise the top edge of the paper into typing position. She gave the return lever three expert slaps to bring the carriage back and establish a top margin. Then she settled the yellow pad with the first letter draft in front of her and studied it.

"You have very nice handwriting," she said.

"Thank you."

"We could practically send this right off without even typing it."

"I think it would look more professional coming from the machine," he said.

"Oh, sure," Margot agreed.

She pushed the shift key with her left index finger, raising the carriage. *Clunk!* Her right index finger circled over the keyboard, looking for the first letter. She found it. *Clack!* She looked up at him and smiled.

"Very good," Robert said, with some misgivings. "I'll just leave you to it."

"Sure. Be done in a jiffy." And her head bent to find another key.

Robert went back to his desk. Margot Dobray would probably work out, he told himself. She might just be having the first-day jitters. He realized he should have asked for references, of course, written to that law firm in Chicago, and checked her story with Helen, before extending so very generous a salary offer—which Margot was so quick to accept. Given that her skills were clearly less than she claimed, Robert knew he could cite volumes of contract law to abrogate their arrangement.

But, on the other hand, it had taken spunk and determination for her to approach him out of the blue like that, and spunk was a quality mostly lacking in the women of Roulette. On top of which, Margot was not hard to look at—also unusual among any of the local women he might hope to employ. It would do Robert's practice good to have an eye-catching female greeting his mostly male clients. And, truth to tell, Robert himself felt a thrill having the forbidden fruit so close at hand.

It looked like he was going to be stuck with her.

8. ZACKY'S CAFÉ

WITHIN A WEEK of Margot Dobray's arrival in town, she had become a topic of general conversation—not to say rampant speculation—among the breakfast regulars at Zacky's. Because he was, arguably, the first person to have seen and talked to her, Malcolm Hurlbert considered himself an authority on the new woman. It turned out that Bud Lloyd, over at the post office, could legitimately claim to have seen her first, had examined the mysterious letter she was carrying, and then sent her on to Hurlbert at the courthouse to locate the fictitious sender, the woman known as "Fay Ryan." But Lloyd wasn't a regular, and so Hurlbert's position on the matter remained secure.

"Did I hear correctly," said McKee, the train conductor, as soon as he came through the door and hung up his jacket, "that she's working for Bob Wheelock now?"

"You did," Hurlbert affirmed.

McKee paused. "As what?"

"Secretary, replacing Helen Grant."

"Hell, I'd have guessed something else."

"What other work would Mr. Wheelock have for her?" Hurlbert asked, perhaps too quietly. Malcolm naturally had to defend the family honor, because of his former professional relationship with Robert's father, the Judge. "Mr. Wheelock is a gentleman."

"I've never seen a hootchy-kootchy girl before," Clarence said dreamily.

"You know Mrs. Endicott wouldn't tolerate any of that," Hurlbert said primly.

"And you ain't seen one yet," Stovall said to Clarence. "That gal's a flapper."

"And just what is a flapper?" asked Reverend Stevens.

"It's a kind of a dancer, padre," Stovall explained.

"Endicott won't allow dancing, either," Clarence said glumly.

"And can a woman make *money* from dancing?" the reverend asked, wide-eyed.

121

"Well … not exactly—not from the dancing part." Stovall got all red in the face.

"He's pulling your leg," Hurlbert assured Stovall, for he had seen the twinkle in the reverend's eye. "Miss Dobray came here from Chicago to collect some money from a mutual acquaintance, and that's a fact. Only it turns out she was misdirected."

"Why doesn't she go back to Chicago?" Reverend Stevens asked seriously.

"How should I know?" Hurlbert said. Then, because this admission robbed him of his position of authority, he added, "It's my theory she was unlucky in love, out there."

"So she used the letter as a ruse, sort of, to come to our town?" Clarence asked.

"Yes, on account of Roulette being so very popular this year," Stovall sneered.

"She stays on because she needs time," Hurlbert opined. "Time to heal love's wounds," he explained.

"Oh, my!" from Clarence, who squirmed in his chair at the thought.

"Horse apples!" Stovall said. "You mark my words. That gal is just mischief on the make. Plain and simple."

9. Geology Lesson

The job with the lawyer was really a bore. Each day Margot came to the upstairs office as long after his stated opening time as she dared. He was always there ahead of her, having made a pot of coffee on the tiny electric plate. She always started by arranging the pads and pencils on her desk, taking the cover off the typewriter, and cranking in a sheet of the crinkly, translucent paper he called "onionskin." Then she settled down to spend the hours until lunch trying to look busy. Some days he actually gave her something to type, and that would fill the time nicely, picking over the round black keys, looking for the little white letters. At least she didn't make too many mistakes that way.

But during the second week this quiet routine broke: Robert Wheelock, Esquire, actually had a visitor.

At first, Margot thought he was one of the farmers who seemed to be Wheelock's only clients, except he always went out to the countryside to do business with them, because of the spring planting. This new man wore fitted, khaki-colored riding breeches, baggy at the outside of the thigh and bloused into his boots at the knee; a long-sleeved, red-plaid shirt, open at the neck; and a gray felt hat with a sweat-stained band, which is what she supposed a farmer would wear out in the sun. But his high-laced boots, which had thick soles of brown gutta-percha and expensive waxed stitching, seemed wrong for walking through mud and manure. And anyway, they were too clean. Besides, he was a young man—and Margot hadn't noticed too many of those among the farmers around here.

Yes, the skin of his round, snub-nosed face was tanned brown, but it wasn't cracked and dried by the dusty wind. Under that shirt he had muscles that had been made by heavy lifting and hauling, maybe working with big machinery, not by following a plow. And his eyes were wide-set and gray, with the far-seeing look she associated with men who came from the great mountains beyond the plains.

123

"My name is John Loring," he said, as she met him coming up the stairs. "I'm here to see Mr. Wheelock." Suddenly, this new young man was looking down at her from a height of more than six feet.

"Oh, yes," Margot said breathlessly. "And is he expecting you?"

"I am," Wheelock said from across the room. "Would you make us a fresh pot of coffee, please, Miss Dobray?"

"I'm Margot Dobray," she said to Loring.

"I gathered that," he said with a little smile.

"Then ... I guess I'll go make the coffee."

She drew water at the sink in the bathroom while Wheelock took over their guest, shook his hand, and seated him beside the big desk on the far side of the office. While she rattled around with the pot and spoon, Margot stole glances at the back of Loring's close-cropped blond head and the set of his shoulders. She noticed that he didn't cross his legs, like a city man, but sat straight up with his legs bent at the knee and his feet tucked under, like a hawk perched and ready to swoop.

"I understand you have some questions about the geology of this area," Loring said to Wheelock. He had an outdoor voice that easily carried. "Is this going to be testimony for a law case you're trying?"

"No, not at all," Wheelock said, so softly that she could hardly make out his words. "It's more in the nature of a personal inquiry."

"Well, after I got your letter, I did some background reading on the county." The man then launched into what sounded to Margot like a lecture. He used a lot of funny words, like Ordovician, Silurian, and—not surprisingly—Pennsylvanian. After a while, she figured out he was talking about rocks. Really old rocks.

"That's all very interesting," Wheelock interrupted him. "But what I mainly want to know is the underlying ..." and there his voice went so low that Margot lost the thread entirely.

She decided that the coffee was ready. She hurriedly poured two cups, put them on the little Bakelite tray, and took them over to the lawyer's desk. She placed one at Wheelock's elbow and handed the other to Loring directly. "Cream and sugar?" she asked brightly.

"No, thank you," from Loring.

"Please," Wheelock said.

Getting the cream from the window ledge outside—where Wheelock insisted on keeping it in a wire cage against the squirrels—and pouring it into the delftware pitcher was the work of a minute. When she returned to the men, she caught Wheelock saying, "… mineral resources."

"What kind of minerals?" Loring asked.

Margot moved off to her desk, about ten feet away, and settled her hands on the typewriter keyboard. There she made herself invisible, listening.

"Well, this natural gas," Wheelock said. "Out in California—"

"I was out there!" Loring said excitedly. "I've drilled for it."

"That's why I asked for you," Wheelock said. "You see, it's my theory that, with gas being found in both coal mines and oil wells, and we have both in Pennsylvania, then there must surely be commercial quantities of gas somewhere around here."

"Well, yes," Loring said slowly. "That would seem to make sense, I guess, to the man in the street. But you've got to understand these mountains have many synclinal formations—complex folds. The gas, if it was ever there, might have been relieved eons ago. Or it may have plunged to such depths that no well could find it."

"But do you think it's worth a look?"

"So long as you've got the money."

"I'm prepared to back an exploratory well."

"One well isn't going to tell you much of anything," Loring said. "No more than a potshot in the brush will bring down your buck. You must have a drilling plan, a pattern of likely sites—"

"How many wells, do you think?"

"About five should tell us something. We'll stop after eight or ten, if there's no encouragement."

"And what would each well cost?" the lawyer asked.

"Oh, figure a hundred dollars per thousand feet of depth."

Margot started to let out a whistle and held herself. That was some big money the men were talking.

"How do you know when to stop?" Wheelock sounded curious.

"When the drill no longer turns, then you stop. Usually after about five or ten thousand feet, depending on the ground."

"So eight wells—" Margot could hear Wheelock's pencil scratching. "—at an average, say, of seventy-five hundred feet, or seven hundred fifty dollars each—"

"Plus the cost of equipment," Loring put in quickly.

"How much?"

"Four thousand for the rig itself. Plus a heavy-duty truck. Donkey engine. Pumps. Pipe. Rack. Bits ... Say, eight thousand all told."

"On top of six thousand dollars, average cost basis, for all eight wells. We're treading perilously close to fifteen thousand dollars."

"Don't forget the cost of leases, the mineral rights—"

"Those are accounted for," Wheelock said.

"Really?" Loring sounded surprised.

"Don't you worry about it."

"So ... um ... do you have that kind of money?"

Margot listened to the silence, not daring to breathe.

"I can raise it," Wheelock said at last. "I may have to sell some property."

"Oh." Loring sounded disappointed. "Well, you know where to reach me."

"But it's a good market, right now," the lawyer said quickly. "I can write you a check, to get started. Why don't you begin hiring men and ordering what you'll need?"

Out of the corner of her eye, Margot saw Wheelock stand up behind the desk. Loring's chair scraped as he got to his feet, and the two men shook hands.

Margot didn't move, more than to work her typewriter carriage in dumb show. But she did turn her head to watch Loring's rear end stir against his tight khaki pants as he headed for the stairs. Then she thought back over all that she had heard.

Robert Wheelock was definitely pursuing something, a play of some kind, maybe a confidence game. She was sure of it. So the country-mouse lawyer was not as dumb, nor as chivalrous, as he looked.

She knew there was a reason she had taken this stupid job.

10. First Well

Five and a half miles out along the county road, according to the pencil lines Robert Wheelock had marked on the U.S. Geological Survey quadrangle map, John Loring found the field they had discussed. Someone had turned the dark earth in neat furrows that ran straight across the curve of the land, like comb marks in a dandy's pomaded hair.

That curve was going to be a problem. The derrick had to be footed solidly, and on level ground, to support the weight of the casing as it went into the hole. Loring didn't relish having to cut and grade a platform, not for an exploratory well that most likely would come up dry.

He stopped the truck at the side of the road and got out. "Wait here," he told the two roughnecks riding in the cab with him.

"Where we goin'ta go?" Chalker asked.

"Around here?" Suggs put in.

Loring nodded and walked out into the field, kicking over the moist, black clods with the side of his right foot. The land sloped down to the west, from the sharply defined edge of the forest that cut across the top of the hill, into a tangle of brushwood on the low side. More forest showed beyond the brush, and those trees were on rising ground. So Loring would bet that brushwood was the bottom of this little valley. He started downhill.

The brush was some kind of flowering shrub with broad, waxy leaves. It only came up chest-high on Loring. The ends of the branches were just starting to sprout what looked to be big bunches of purple and white flowers. Really pretty. He pushed them aside and stepped onto harder soil that had never been plowed. It was damp, though, and not far away was the murmur of running water. In another ten paces that took him twisting through the interlaced branches, he found the stream. It was so narrow he could just about step across it. By midsummer it would be long gone—but then, so would he.

The ground at this spot was nearly level, or could be made so with a couple of blocks to shore the rig. And the water was not a problem. Half a day with shovels and a bag of cement, and the boys could make a diversion dam and sluice that would take it around their drilling site. And the stream had already cleared the topsoil here, bringing the drill bit that much closer to solid rock.

He marked the spot with his neckerchief and went back to the truck.

"You see where I went into that line of brush?" he said to Chalker.

"Yeah, we were watchin'," the big man replied.

"Take a couple of spades and clear a patch ten feet either side."

"How far back?" Chalker asked.

"Till you come to the stream."

"Then what?" from Suggs.

"Drive down and unload the truck."

"*Then* what?" from Chalker.

"Start digging," Loring said.

By the second morning the three men had diverted the stream a dozen feet to the west. With the sharp end of his rock hammer, Loring had ceremoniously made a gouge in the gray, drying streambed where he wanted the drill to bite, and they had placed the rotary table and kelly bushing over the spot. Then Loring and Chalker set the footings for the rig. Out on the edge of the field, they had pieced together the box frame of the small derrick, a four-sided tower twenty-five feet tall.

Now they carried the derrick into the brush and positioned the legs of the lower side onto the footings. Loring threaded a long rope through the crown block and tailed the ends back to two pulleys secured by loops to two sturdy trees at the edge of the woods. Then he walked the ends out into the field and handed one to Chalker, the other to Suggs.

"A nice even pull, please," he said. "On three." He went back to the rig and blocked the tower legs on their marks with balks of timber. "One … Two … Pull!"

The roughnecks took up the slack and started giving it some muscle. Loring put his shoulder against the framework, halfway toward the top, and felt it shimmy as the derrick started from the ground. Without standing directly under it—in case the rope should part or one of the pulleys slipped—he steadied its rise.

The derrick was just below a forty-five degree angle, at its most vulnerable point of equilibrium, when Loring heard the tail end of a shout from across the field, "... *hell* are you doing?"

He looked up in time to see Chalker and Suggs turn toward the sound, letting the line slacken momentarily. Loring roared at them: "Hang onto that rope!"

The men tried to take a grip, but it was already too late. The tower had started on its way back down, and all they could do was slow its fall. Loring got out of the way. The uprights slapped the uneven ground, and the framework rocked awkwardly. The bolts on two of the diagonal pieces sheared, and the square cross section assumed a more rhomboid shape. Damn! That was going to be another morning's work to true it up and start the erection all over again.

"What *is* that thing?" A man in dungaree overalls was stomping across the furrows. "And why is it on my land?"

Loring squinted at him. "Who are you?" he asked tiredly.

"I'm Ezra Stills. I own this field. And you're trespassing."

"I think you'll find we have a right to be here," Loring said.

"No, you don't. This is my land. What are you building there?"

Loring contained his impatience. "It's the derrick for a drilling rig," he explained. "We're going to drill a well over there." He pointed toward the bushes.

"What for? I've got all the water I need. And who sent you?"

"We're not drilling for water, but for natural gas," Loring said.

"Gas?" the man said, disbelieving. "Out of the ground? Horse shit!"

"Well, speaking as a geologist, I'd say the ground was very favorable."

"For gas," the man said. "Not oil?"

"No, for gas," Loring assured him.

"And that'll be worth something?"

"Well, the price depends on the market and the pipeline distance, of course, but out in California they're getting thirty cents a thousand cubic feet."

"How many cubic feet do you reckon are down there?" Stills asked, pointing towards his own feet.

"No telling—until we drill and find some."

"But I'd get thirty cents a thousand for it."

"I don't know about that," Loring said. "We were hired by Mr. Robert Wheelock, the lawyer. He holds the mineral rights to this land."

"Mineral rights?" Stills repeated, and Loring could see the light fade in his eyes.

"Wheelock's office is in Roulette. If you want to discuss the matter, go see him."

"Damn right, I will."

11. Mineral Rights

At ten o'clock in the morning Robert was dictating letters that answered interrogatories in the matter of a shipper's claim against the railroad, and taking care to spell out the words for Margot's benefit, when the outer door of the office slammed and heavy boots stamped upon the stairs. In short order the gray head of Ezra Stills topped the end of the banister. Robert had more or less been expecting him.

"We'll continue this later," he told his secretary. And then to Stills, "Good morning, Ezra."

"Morning yourself, Wheelock." And then, without pausing to pass the time of day: "You've put a geologist fellow on my land, moving the stream around and building things. Nice of you to tell me."

"I sent notification," Robert said. "Didn't you read my letter?"

"I didn't get any letter."

Out of the corner of his eye, Robert saw Margot's head sink down. His gaze went to the office out-basket, which was unnaturally full. Later, they would also have to discuss prompt posting of the mail.

"Well, I'm sorry, Ezra. You should have received notification," Robert said. "The drilling will take no more than a few days and shouldn't interfere with your planting. And, when they're done, they'll put everything back as it was. You will not suffer in any material way."

"The fellow says he's looking for gas."

"Yes, just like the new discoveries—"

"Out in California, yes. He mentioned that ..." Stills seemed to be choosing his words. "If he finds anything, he says, I'm due to get thirty cents for a thousand feet of it."

Robert went cold. "I don't think that's quite right, Ezra. I can't imagine Loring saying anything like that."

"But he said the gas would get a price somewhere in that neighborhood."

"The price is still to be determined. However, you'll remember we had an agreement, when you sold the land ten years ago. I bought the mineral rights from you, remember? Because you would not pay Nathan Birdsall for them."

"That might be the way it was," Stills said, temporizing. "You paid me five dollars. The gas will be worth a lot more than that."

"We had a written agreement," Robert said.

"We did," Stills said. "And I'll hold to it …"

"Besides, this presumes there's any gas at all."

"If there is, it's on my land. I still own the land, don't I? And it's my land that your man is digging up."

"I suppose we could work out an easement," Robert said. "A payment for use of your property," he explained.

"How much? And it better be more than five dollars."

"Ten dollars," Robert suggested. "Per diem, for as long as the drilling goes on."

"You said that would only be a couple of days."

"And if they find something, you can charge a right of way for us to run a pipeline across the field."

"How big a pipe?" Stills asked dubiously.

"Oh, two or three inches in diameter," Robert ventured. "No more. And it would be buried, too, of course."

"And what will you pay for this right of way?"

"That would depend on the direction and distance, of course. What would you say to one dollar per hundred feet, payable monthly?"

"This isn't nineteen-eighteen, you know. No way in hell you get my gas for a dollar. Prices have gone up."

"All right … what would be fair?"

"Ten dollars a hundred feet."

Robert laughed. "Three."

"Seven."

"Four and a half."

"Done." Stills put out his hand, and Robert shook it.

The amount was really more than Robert wanted to pay, but it would satisfy Ezra Stills. And if Stills was satisfied, others would be, when it came their turn to negotiate. And perhaps, after all, this first well would not find anything. Then Robert would be in a better position to bargain. Or, after eight such wells, he would not have to bargain at all.

12. Seduction

After Wheelock's meeting with the farmer, Margot was surer than ever that the lawyer had some kind of game going. So, when he went home for lunch she determined to find out what it was.

She knew from watching him around the office that he kept the papers related to his practice in the green filing cabinet at the back of the room, and his private business in the black one. She also knew where he kept the keys to each, although he always pretended to be fiddling with the potted geranium on the table in the corner, picking at its leaves or testing the soil moisture, as he reached behind for the hook concealed below the wainscoting. Margot got the keys now and unlocked the black cabinet.

What she found inside was a gold mine. There were files for the railroad business, of which it appeared that Wheelock—or at least his mother, his stepmother, whatever—was the owner, or chief shareholder, or something. More files on the power company, of which ditto. Plus real estate interests, stocks, bonds, and yes, a whole folder by itself, three inches thick, labeled "Mineral Rights." She pulled that one out and laid it crosswise on top of the others in the open drawer. Then she started reading.

After half an hour of back-and-forth comparisons among the documents, she had the picture. Robert Wheelock held the rights to whatever was under the ground in more than half of this godforsaken county. And he had acquired them cheap, too, for five dollars here, ten dollars there, regardless of the size or actual value of the parcel involved. If John Loring, that geologist fellow, found gas—or oil, or iron ore, or diamonds, for that matter—Wheelock was going to be very rich. Or very much richer, depending on your point of view. And all of that on a bet made with a few dollars here and there. Why, he—

"What are you doing?" Wheelock's voice came from behind her. Margot had never heard the door, down below, or his step upon the stairs.

Margot lifted her head fractionally. Her hair was hanging forward, and she did not move it aside as she turned her head, so that she was looking at him as through a veil. She stood erect slowly, straightened her shoulders, and threw out her chest, to give him the profile that she knew he would like.

"I ... wanted to find out what that farmer had on you, Robert," she said, pushing her hair aside and looking at him directly. "The things he said scared me."

"Scared you?" Wheelock's face was still as dark as thunder, but now there was doubt. "Why?"

During her days in the law office Margot had sensed how Wheelock watched her as she moved around. She always knew where his eyes were going. She felt his interest, his hidden lust—had known about it from the first day, even if he did not. So she knew he was vulnerable. And now, when she was caught in the act like this, was the time to use every advantage.

"Because I care about you, Robert. I don't want you to get into any trouble."

"Why would you think I'm in trouble?"

"Well ..." Margot stepped close to him. When dealing with an angry man, close was better than far—unless he was too angry, and then you got hit. "From the way he talked, the two of you have had dealings before. And he wasn't happy about them."

"You shouldn't listen to conversations that take place in this office."

"How can I not?" she said, laying her palms on the lapels of his jacket. "With you so near?"

Wheelock put his hands over hers, to move them away. Instead, Margot slipped her hands up to his collarbones—then around his neck. After a pause, he still didn't remove them. She moved closer and laid her body against his. He stiffened and raised his hands again to take hers away. She mewed and reached up with her mouth, pulling down on his head at the same time. She met resistance in his neck, but it yielded to firm pressure. When his lips were on hers, Margot knew she had won.

The rest was a simple matter of logistics. The cracked leather couch under the windowsill, where Wheelock occasionally liked to nap in the afternoon—that was the obvious place. And be damned to the stains.

13. REMORSE

ROBERT HAD BROKEN his word, trampled his pledge, violated his sacred vow of marriage. He had betrayed Libby's trust. He had betrayed himself. And for what? A few moments of carnal congress. A spasm of white-hot pleasure. And a welter of emotions—with animal stupefaction and confusion dominant. Robert sat on the couch, slowly buttoning his shirt, smoothing his fly, and examining both for telltale signs. Margot was in the office's tiny bathroom, doing whatever it was women did ... afterward.

Libby would do that, too. But she did not go in so quickly, nor with her face twisted in such a frown. As if she hadn't enjoyed the act. Libby always enjoyed their conjugal encounters, although recently the opportunities had become less frequent. The house was small, with thin walls and two pairs of sharp young ears on the other side. And the problem, truth to tell, was the children more than the house.

Willie and Genie had always been a handful, but this spring they seemed to be attached to each other with magnets. Teasing. Fighting. Telling lies, both for and about each other. And Libby was caught in the middle. She was constant mother, occasional referee to their fights, sometime victim of their pranks—and slowly losing her mind, or so she said. By bedtime she would climb in beside him, pull the covers up over her head, and start snoring before Robert could even put down his book.

But none of that excused, let alone justified, what Robert had just done. He could hardly explain it to himself. One moment, he had been confronting Margot over her prying into his personal files, and the next he was on the couch, burrowing in her clothing like a pig going after truffles.

Aside from Margot's obvious physical attractions, the sudden personal interest she had shown in him—or was it feigned?—as well as his own weakness as a man, there was no reason. Worse, Robert understood Margot was a self-centered woman given to opportunistic designs. He guessed she would be a bitter opponent in any confrontation. In fact, the person she most resembled, of all his acquaintance, was his stepmother Lydia, and this thought horrified him. That he might be attracted to such a woman, when he had a pure and gentle soul like Libby waiting for him at home, both shamed and troubled him.

Robert stood up and approached the door to the bathroom. "Look," he said.

No response from the other side.

"What just happened," he went on, raising his voice, "it was not—"

"Nothing happened," she yelled through the door.

"What? But you, I mean, we just—"

"Forget it," through the door again.

"But I can't forget it. That was so …" He meant to say "unlike me," but thought better of it. What would such a declaration mean to a woman who had just shared her most intimate favors? Nothing good.

Before he could come up with something better, she opened the door six inches. From the thunk it made, he knew she had her foot blocking the door from the inside, to keep him from pushing it open any further. Through the crack, he could see one dark eye, half of her pale face, and one shoulder, bare except for a pair of pink satin straps. By now, he knew just where those straps attached and what they held. In her hand was a towel, soaked through, as if she had been using it as a washcloth.

"What do you think happened, Robert? We had sex. It was no big thing."

"Then why are you so angry about it?" he blurted, feeling … hurt.

"If you actually loved me, then it would be a big thing."

He knew what she expected him to say. It would be mere reflex for a man to say "I love you" at such a moment, whether he meant it or not. But Robert could not say it. Not to her.

"Yeah, but you don't love me," she said with a sigh. "So go home to your wife." And she slammed the bathroom door on him.

Robert gathered up his jacket and, at the unheard-of hour of two in the afternoon, left the office for home.

14. ZACKY'S CAFÉ

When Nathan Birdsall dropped into the café for a late breakfast, the room was humming with talk of the doings north of town. It seemed a geologist was out in the hills, punching holes in the ground. Looking for water, said McKee from the railroad—which didn't make a lot of sense, seeing as the man started his drilling in a streambed. Looking for oil, said Hurlbert from the courthouse, although everybody knew the oil stopped somewhere to the west of them, in McKean County.

"Does anyone *know* why he's here?" Clarence asked.

"Ezra Stills says it's for the gas," Reverend Stevens said.

"Gas? From the ground?" Birdsall couldn't believe it.

"That's Ezra's story. He says he's going to make three thousand dollars on it."

"Stills hired himself a geologist?" Birdsall asked, curious now.

"No, Wheelock hired him. But he's drilling on Ezra's land, so Stills stands to profit from it."

"Except Wheelock bought the mineral rights," Hurlbert said. "If anyone's going to profit, it's Wheelock."

"By poking holes in the dirt," Birdsall said scornfully.

"His father had the touch," Hurlbert observed. "The Judge started the railroad and the electric company. They made him the man he was."

"Yes, but those were real businesses, investments, right out in the open," Birdsall objected. "You build 'em, you run 'em, and you make money. Not like drilling for oil—"

"Gas," the reverend said.

"—which is more like gambling," Birdsall finished.

"Wheelock's got the money to gamble with," Clarence observed.

"Not that much," said Hurlbert. "And he's a young man with a family yet. He should be thinking about them. Their future."

"One imagines that is what he's doing," the reverend said.

"Well, he's going to break their hearts then," Hurlbert said.

"Not the man his father was," Birdsall said.

"No, not the man," Hurlbert agreed.

15. Fever Dreams

ON THE FIRST morning that the spring air was moist and muggy, like it was already summer, Genie woke up with a dull headache and a creaky feeling in her wrists and ankles. She got out of bed more slowly than usual and washed her face with just dabs and wipes, because her hands hurt and her face stung when the cold water touched it. She dressed slowly, because the clothes scraped her skin like it was peeling back layers.

She stepped off at the top of the stairs and, by the time she reached the bottom, she was floating several feet above the floor. When she went into the kitchen, she was surprised at how dark it was, even with the sun shining outside the windows. Genie took her place at the table, beside her brother. Willie nudged her with his elbow, and she nudged back listlessly.

Father sat reading his newspaper. He turned and folded the pages, making a noise like Mother did when she folded a huge, white bed sheet. The flapping set up a little breeze that fanned Genie's face.

Mother was at the stove, stirring the oatmeal in the pot. She brought it over to the table, and began spooning out globs … of … sheep's brains.

Genie turned her face aside and vomited on the floor.

"Eugenia!" her mother cried.

Genie straightened up. "I'm sorry."

"Are you sick?" Mother felt her forehead.

Genie heard the rustle of the newspaper again and felt her father's stare. She looked up at her mother. "Do I have to go to school today?"

"No, you have to go back to bed."

"Is it a fever?" Father asked.

"Pretty high." Mother bit her lip.

"Should we call Dr. Guillaume?"

"Well … Children have fevers all the time," Mother said. "Remember how often she got sick as a baby?"

"She's not a baby anymore," Father said.

143

"And they usually recover without a trace," Mother went on.

"Why don't you take her upstairs?" he said. "I'll mop the floor."

"What about your breakfast, Robert?"

"It can wait. You take care of the little one."

Genie got up from the chair, being careful to step around the puddle of lumpy yellow stuff on the floor. She took hold her mother's hand, and then her legs went out from under her. She pulled on her mother's fingers as she went down.

She heard Mother call out, "Robert!"

Strong hands moved under her armpits and then under her knees. Genie put her arms up around Father's neck, but they wouldn't stay there, falling of themselves onto her lap.

Suddenly, she was floating again, but this time nearly six feet off the floor. Father carried her back through the living room and up the stairs. Her head almost touched the ceiling as they went up to the second floor.

He laid her on the bed. Her sheets were cold, like deep snow. As Mother pulled off Genie's clothes, her limbs grew cold one by one. She shut her eyes and went out to play in the snow.

16. The Fishing Lodge

Judge Larry LeConte waited in his book-lined chambers at the back of the Sylvan County Courthouse. The furniture was dark and heavy, crammed into the narrow room, with the big roll-top desk and his swivel chair crowding out the two round-backed captain's chairs he kept for guests. Anyone who wanted to use the spittoon—and some members of the bar were still countrified enough to take a chaw—had to stand up, lean to one side, and aim well into the shadows at the foot of the hat rack.

LeConte was waiting for the sheriff to find and bring before him the young attorney, Robert Wheelock. Well, not so young anymore, as Wheelock had been advising and representing clients in the county for ten years now—a few of them holdovers from his father's old practice. As an attorney himself, before taking the bench two years back, LeConte had frequently crossed swords with Wheelock. He found the younger man possessed of a keen mind, an expensive Harvard education, an exaggerated sense of personal honor, and small practical experience. But all in all Wheelock had made a good career for himself in the years since the old judge's death. It would be a shame if the matter at hand were to ruin him now.

He picked up the piece of paper on the desk in front of him. White paper lined in faint blue, it had obviously been torn from a school copybook. Yellowed with age, the edges furred, it might have been stuck at the back of a drawer for years, waiting to be used. But the writing on it was in pencil and fresh, without the fuzziness that time and abrasion give to pencil marks. The hand that wrote it was unconnected and uncertain, the letters wavering between capitals and lower case, like a child's writing. And then it had been folded into a neat square with sharp creases.

"To Those Who Find me: A man's got to know when his own Good Time has come. The gunshot you find me Dead of here was no foul play and no accident either. So be it, and I am Glad to go. I do not have much to leave the world but this Fishing Camp, which is already bespoke to the Lawyer Wheelock, who bought it off me years ago for the sum of Five Dollars. Also, this deer rifle that I got down in Harrisburg and the man said it is worth One Hundred dollars. It might as well belong to the Lawyer too, as there is no one else Kin to me anyway. Good bye. God bless."

LeConte contemplated the dismal effect of these words. He tried to imagine the scale of a life so small, so constrained that, at its end, this was all the man could find to say to the world—the disposal of a piece of land and a prized rifle. And even one of these bequests was dictated by circumstance and not by his own choice. What a pitiful cross between a suicide note and a last will and testament!

There came a soft knock at his door. "Judge? Your Honor?"

"Yeah?" LeConte found a thickness in his throat.

"I brought the lawyer," said the sheriff.

"The door's open," he called.

Robert Wheelock felt his way into the room, moving cautiously in the gloom. The sheriff hung back in the doorway. Wheelock removed his hat and ran a hand through his hair. "Good morning, Your Honor."

"Sit down, Counselor," LeConte said quietly. "You and I have something very interesting to discuss."

Wheelock looked puzzled. "I don't have a case before you right now."

"No, it's not an active case. It may be nothing at all." LeConte considered his line of approach, like examining any witness, conscious that Wheelock's reactions at any point might be telling. "Have you had any dealings with Valdemar Johansson?"

"He worked on my father's railroad. As engineer, I think, until he retired a couple of years ago."

"Any transactions between you and him? Anything at all?"

"Not that I recall …" Wheelock paused in thought. "Well, there was that business with the mineral rights—more of a joke, really."

"Oh! I remember," LeConte said. "About ten years ago, wasn't it? People all over town were suddenly rushing to sell them."

Wheelock nodded and picked up the story. "You see, I had just completed a land deal between two farmers, and I made the mistake of mentioning the mineral rights—"

"You ended up absorbing them yourself," LeConte said, chuckling. "And the consideration was five dollars. When word of that got out, everyone wanted to sell you their mineral rights."

"I was a laughingstock," Wheelock conceded.

"Maybe. But it was also a shrewd move in a town like this. You showed yourself a good sport, and people tend to remember that. But you don't want to appear shrewd, Counselor. Not with your geologist out there finding gas—"

"He hasn't found anything yet, and maybe never will."

"If he does, you could become rich. People will get angry, you know, if they think you've swindled them. That would jeopardize your place in this community."

"I hear you," Wheelock said bleakly. "But you asked about Johansson. Does he want his money back?"

"Not at all. In fact …" Le Conte decided to show him the suicide note.

Wheelock took the paper, angled it to the light, and scanned the contents in a few seconds. He frowned, started to hand the note back, then pulled it away and lingered on certain words. He turned it over to check the reverse, then returned it to the judge's hand. "When?" was what he finally asked.

"Sheriff's deputy found Johansson at his cabin this morning. No one had seen him around town for a few days, so we sent people out looking for him. He was dead at his kitchen table from a gunshot wound. To all appearances, acquired while cleaning that big deer rifle of his. Possibly accidental. Probably self-inflicted … But perhaps something more sinister. Anyway, they found that note with him."

"Which says he died by his own hand," Wheelock observed.

"Yeah, the obvious conclusion," LeConte replied. "Except a man who takes his own life is usually expected to state a reason. Johansson had his pension and twenty-six good acres along the river bottom. He wasn't sick—Dr. Guillaume confirms that. He didn't get flooded out and lose everything—that cabin is high up the bank and stayed dry. And everyone agrees he wasn't morbid nor inclined to mope. So why, on a fine spring day, would a man so blessed take a rifle and blow his brains out? Why, with deer season a full six months away, would he even be cleaning that rifle? Those are questions the law has to ask."

"Who can know the darkness in a man's heart?" Wheelock murmured. Then he seemed to shake himself awake. "And do you think I have the answers, Your Honor?"

"No, I called you in because he put your name on that paper."

"Five dollars is what he got for his mineral rights—same as everyone else."

"Then what did Johansson mean, 'bought it off me,' Counselor?"

"He was confused, I guess. A man would be a fool to sell his land for such a sum. Johansson was no fool."

LeConte sighed. "For the record then, there was no understanding that you were paying for the land?"

"If he was under that impression, it was his mistake. And anyway, what would I do with a fishing camp? I'm not a fisherman."

"Which leaves us with that piece of paper. ..."

The judge had pretty much made up his mind about Johansson's situation and Wheelock's lack of involvement in the death. But he still couldn't resist having some fun with the serious young lawyer.

"Given all these uncertainties," he went on, "what I have to decide is whether that note is genuine. Is that really Johansson's handwriting? Or a forgery to cover up a murder? Counselor, do you think the railroad office might have a sample of his writing? Any kind of correspondence? Maybe a work order on his locomotive?"

"You could check. But it was the conductor, Albert Waterman, who handled all the paperwork."

"Would anyone recognize this handwriting? How about the fireman?"

"That man shoveled coal for a living. I doubt he could read."

"Then, Counselor, we have a problem," LeConte said.

"Why so?"

"Because if that note's genuine, then I have to rule it the last will and testament of Valdemar Johansson. In which case you become the owner of twenty-six acres of prime bottom land and a fine deer rifle. But if it's not genuine, then Johansson died by foul play. And you become the prime suspect, because of those aforementioned acres, and the rifle could be your murder weapon."

"Your Honor! If you think it's in me to kill a man—"

"Calm down, Bob!" LeConte tried to hide a smile. "You'll remember I've seen samples of your handwriting, plenty of times. Not to mention your fine legal style and perfect syntax. It would kill you to write a note like that. And, as to motive, why, I have your own words—you don't even fish."

"So, what are you going to do?"

LeConte thought about that a moment. "See what other clues the sheriff might turn up when his deputies take that cabin apart. If nothing else suggests a murder, and no other heirs become apparent, then I'm going to honor the bequest. Maybe you can take up fishing after all."

17. GUSHER

AT THE DRILLING site nestled in among the mountain laurel, John Loring sat in a canvas camp chair and was starting to doze in the afternoon sun, lulled by the rhythmic thump and wheeze of the donkey engine. As it drove the rotary table, the drill pipe rattled against the casing with a hollow clank that echoed over its length of nearly five thousand feet. Only when the sound changed did Loring lift his head.

The pipe paused in its turning, just for a fraction of a second, and then it did a little spin before settling into a slightly faster rotation. Loring knew from experience that the drill bit had broken through one layer of rock into the next, and the pipe behind it—which was not perfectly rigid nor inflexible—had twisted and untwisted as it took up and released the torque. From the subsequent speedup, he knew that the bit was now in softer material, perhaps even sand. But that was not what made him sit upright in his chair.

The clanking was rising in pitch, like notes going up a scale. For the past week he had listened to it grow deeper and deeper as the pipe lengthened, like letting out the slide on a trombone. Now the process was reversing itself, and right quickly too. Something was coming up the well casing, quenching the vibrations.

Loring stopped the donkey engine and leaned over the rotary to put his ear against the kelly that drove the drill string. There was a low rumble, almost a gurgle, and it was rapidly growing louder. The gap under the rotary started to whistle with the escape of residual air in the casing.

He stepped back from the platform. He looked around to locate Chalker and Suggs, but they were nowhere in sight—probably in the tent, sleeping off the effects of last night in town. Good, that meant they were out of danger.

The whistle rose to a scream, and he could hear the underlying rumble clearly from where he was standing, now about a dozen feet away from the rig. The ground started to vibrate.

A puff of fog blew out from beneath the rotary, followed by a solid jet that broke against its underside. The rotary rose up on one side and toppled over. The stream of water blew away the kelly and batted around the chain fall that hung inside the derrick. Inside a minute, Loring himself was soaked.

Above the roar of the water, Loring heard a human scream. He turned and worked his way through the bushes to the edge of the open field. The farmer, Ezra Stills, was standing there, doubled over. The high-pitched sound he made was actually peals of shrill laughter.

"Water," he said at last, as Loring came up to him. "I could have told you," Stills went on as he caught his breath. "Drill around here, and you get water."

Loring grinned and ran a hand over his face. Then he grabbed Stills by the elbow and dragged him within range of the shower that was coming down around the derrick. In a moment the farmer was soaked and sputtering. "Taste it," Loring commanded.

Stills ran his tongue over his lips. "Salt water!"

"Brine," Loring affirmed. "We've got a dome down there."

"What does that mean?" The farmer squinted at him.

"It's a good sign. A salt dome is a likely formation."

"Ayuh," Stills said. "And when does the gas come out?"

"From this well? Probably never."

"So, it's a bust," Stills concluded. "And what about my field? Sow it with salt, and it'll never produce again. Fill that streambed with brine, and you'll poison all the fields downstream."

"Oh, we'll cap this well—just as soon as the pressure relieves. At this depth, it only takes an hour or two."

"And then what? You drill another well? Nearby?"

Loring thought for a moment. "Somewhere close."

"On my land?"

"Can't say yet."

"Damnation!" the farmer swore and stamped his foot. "I thought you didn't want me drilling on your land."

"I changed my mind."

18. The Smell of Salt

LIBBY WAS IN the kitchen at the back of their tiny house, peeling potatoes for dinner, when she heard a rapid knock—one-two-three-four-five—on the front door. She dried her hands and went out through the dining room. Before she had gone halfway across the parlor, the imperious knocking started again.

"I'm coming!" she called, stopping just long enough to take off her apron and throw it over the back of a chair.

When she opened the door there was a man on the stoop. He was young looking—or rather, younger in the tan smoothness of his face and the lithe narrowness of his body than the time-hardened squint in his eyes might suggest. Libby guessed he was about her own age, if not a couple of years older. His reddish blonde hair, which glowed in the late afternoon sunlight, was cut so close that it stood up in pixie points. He was dressed roughly, like most of the working men in Roulette, although she could see that his clothes had quality, like good western wear. But what set this man apart was that he was drenched to the skin, and there wasn't a cloud in the sky.

"May I help you?" she asked.

"I'm looking for Robert Wheelock."

"He should be downtown now, at his office."

"Oh, right! I just—in my hurry—this was nearer."

"Do you want to come in?" she asked. "You need a towel."

The man looked down at himself. "I guess I do. Much obliged, ma'am."

Libby stepped back to let him into the entryway. As he passed, she got the distinct smell of salt water, like a summer by the seashore. "How did you get so—?"

"Wet?" He grinned. "We had a gusher. Couple of thousand gallons per minute."

"Oh!" Libby said, suddenly understanding. "You're the geologist."

"John Loring, ma'am." He put out his hand. "Pleased to meet you."

Libby shook the hand and felt its strength. His grip was warm despite the calluses across his palm and the lingering dampness.

"But I'm making a mess of your floors."

"Never mind that. Let me get your towel."

Libby ran up the stairs and found two of the terrycloth bath sheets that Robert so liked. She bunched them in her arms and brought them back down.

Loring took them and patted across the front of his plaid shirt and the inner thighs of his fawn-colored trousers. Then he squeezed the excess moisture out of his shirt cuffs and toweled off his head. The fuzz of blonde hair lay flat against his skull for an instant before springing up again. The salt smell of the sea increased in the room.

"I really should offer you a shower."

"Thank you, but I've just had one."

"I mean with soap and sweet water."

"Another time, perhaps. I really do want to find your husband."

"As I said, he's at his office. There until five, generally. Do you know where—?"

"Of course. Downtown, back of the courthouse." He handed her the towels. "Thank you for your trouble."

"It was nothing."

In a moment John Loring climbed back in his truck and was gone. Libby stood leaning against the door, hugging the towels until the wet terrycloth dampened the front of her dress. She knew she was acting like a schoolgirl. Still, she could not help putting her face into them and inhaling deeply. She was looking for the scent of the man but found only the smell of the sea.

19. PAYOUT

FOR THE FIRST couple of days, Robert had walked around his own law office on eggshells, expecting Margot to make some allusion to their illicit experience. Worse, he feared she might remark upon it to one of her women friends, if she had any, or talk about it around town. But Margot appeared to be the soul of discretion and conducted herself like a lady in his presence. She even took to wearing dark, ankle-length skirts and white shirtwaists with collars up to her chin when she came to work. All in all, it was a relief.

Toward the end of that week, late in the afternoon, John Loring came running into the office—the first time he had reported in since going to the field. "Have I got good news for you, Mr. Wheelock!"

Robert couldn't help smiling as he looked up at the handsome young man. "And what is that?"

"We got brine in our first well."

"Brine?" Robert felt his face change. "As in salt water? How is that good news?"

"Look here," Loring said, going over to the claw-footed mahogany table with the carved lion heads that stood in front of the shelves full of law books, in the part of his office that Robert called his library. The geologist unrolled a topological map and ran his finger in a circle around the X marking their first well. "I chose this area because it's an anticline—kind of like a hill with its roots underground."

"Well, of course ..." Robert said. He sniffed and found that the man actually smelled of brine.

"It's an upward fold, bringing whatever may be deeper in the ground toward the surface. If there's an easy place to find your gas, an anticline would be it."

"But you found water instead."

"Yes, but not groundwater, not surface runoff. This is a dome, filled with sediment and an aquifer so ancient that it's leached out the salts."

"And why is this good for us?"

"Because it means the ground is porous. Porous rock traps gas. And an aquifer will provide the pressure to drive it out. If there's any gas down there, this is the kind of ground you want it to be in."

"Another *if* …" Robert said, not trying to hide his disappointment.

"This venture was always a gamble," Loring said slowly. "I thought we were agreed on that."

"Well, yes, but I always assumed … we would find … something."

"And we're on track. This well is very promising, but … I hate to bring the matter up, but there's not going to be a better time. We're just about out of money. If we're going to start another well, I'm going to need another check from you."

"Oh," Robert said. "So … this is the decision point."

"Yes," Loring said shortly.

"Oh, well. Hung for a lamb, hung for a ram. I'll have the check ready tomorrow."

"I'll select a site for our second well." Loring said, rolling his map.

Robert nodded. "Please keep me informed."

"Of course, sir."

On his way to the stairs, Loring stopped by Margot's desk. She looked up and smiled at him. They obviously exchanged words. Robert could not hear what they said, and he busied himself with the papers at his desk. Clearly, the geologist was paying court to a good-looking woman. That was nothing unusual—it had just never happened in Robert's office before. Loring laughed at something Margot said, and she beamed at him in response.

Robert cleared his throat.

The two of them glanced over at him.

"Nothing," Robert said. "Just a cough."

Loring nodded. "I must get back to the field."

" 'Bye now," Margot said in reply.

20. YELLOW EYES

FOR A WEEK Libby nursed her daughter through fretful days and feverish nights. Genie weakly insisted she was feeling better even as she looked worse. School was out of the question. Libby let her sit out in the backyard, wrapped in a blanket against sudden bouts of chills, to see what fresh air and sunshine would do. Libby's mother would not have approved, saying that utter quiet in a darkened room was what the sick required, but Libby followed the modern regimen.

On the sixth morning, however, when she went into her daughter's bedroom to see if she was wake, the girl was lying on her back, mouth open, and breathing so shallowly that Libby at first thought she had stopped breathing altogether.

"Genie?" She rushed to the bed, grabbed both of the girl's shoulders, and shook her. "Wake up, Genie!"

Her eyes opened slowly, looked up at Libby. The whites had turned the color of blooming daffodils. The blue-gray of the irises reflected a sickly green, as did her skin under the natural childhood tan.

Libby let out a shriek.

"Mother? What is it?"

"You've got jaundice!"

"Oh? Is that what's making me sick?"

Libby did not know. She had heard that jaundice was a bad thing, the sign of serious illness and glands gone wrong. But with fever and lassitude her daughter's illness was already serious enough. This was no simple childhood infection, quickly shaken off. Libby went downstairs to the telephone and asked for Doctor Guillaume's number.

After hearing Libby describe the symptoms, the doctor was there inside an hour. He probed the unresisting girl's stomach and, when his fingers touched her right side, elicited a flinch and a deep groan. He took her temperature and pulse, peeled back an eyelid and looked deep within. All the time he kept his lips tightly compressed. Finally, he laid Genie back on the pillows, which Libby had plumped and arranged. The doctor gave her daughter an absent pat on the head and motioned Libby out into the hall.

"Hepatitis," he said quietly.

Libby, listening for any sign of hope or despair in his voice and, hearing neither, did not quite understand. "What's that?" she asked distractedly.

"It's liver disease," Doctor Guillaume explained.

Libby knew what the liver was, more or less. It was an organ that every animal had, although her experience of it was more as a meat sautéed with onions. The fact that the organ's name was associated with the words "to live" and "life" had not penetrated her awareness until now. "That sounds serious," she said with renewed fear.

"Well … it *can* be. If the liver is deeply scarred—or goes into failure—"

"*Is* her liver failing?" Libby asked quickly.

"There's no way to tell," Doctor Guillaume said. "The jaundice is not a good sign, of course, especially in a child so young. Most of them pass off the infection without any visible symptoms. Most of them survive this illness without lasting effect."

Libby had a sudden vision of the grubby, probably verminous, farm children at Genie's school who had imperiled her daughter with a sneeze or a touch. "So you're telling me there are other sick children! Did one of them give it to her?"

"No, it's not transmitted that way," he said. "Not like a head cold. The causes are not completely understood."

"Then why my daughter?" she asked. "Why is Genie sick?"

"Well, there is the theory of the—ahem—fecal-oral route."

Libby was aghast. "What do you mean? She ate … *dirt?*"

"No," he said with embarrassment, "specifically feces. Um … shit."

"But Genie is a clean child. Where would she …?"

"Did she go out during the spring floods? The rising water generally dredges out the cesspits on the surrounding farms and backs up the sewers in town."

"Oh my God! But that was weeks ago."

"The disease often takes weeks to develop," Dr. Guillaume said. "It's called the incubation period."

Libby was still trying to absorb all this. "What can you do for her? Are there medicines? My husband and I will gladly pay—"

"Nothing that would help." He was shaking his head. "We can keep her quiet. Give her plenty of fluids to wash out her system. She's a strong little girl. Her body will surely fight off this thing."

"So all we can do is wait," Libby concluded.

"And we watch," he agreed.

21. PAVANE FOR A DEAD PRINCESS

STANDING BESIDE HIS seven-year-old daughter's open grave, Robert realized what a stately dance the death rite had become. Four pall bearers—with Willie among them, reaching up above his head to grasp the bronze handle—carried the tiny coffin up the hillside. The box was made of some pale wood, oak or maple, waxed and polished until it resembled the pale amber of the little girl's braids. The bearers set it on the grass, over two canvas straps laid crosswise and coiled at the ends like four brown snakes.

Reverend Stevens stepped forward to stand at the coffin's head. He spoke soothing words that included "innocence," "understanding," and "love," but Robert could not connect them. He could only remember the past week in which his wife had alternated between sitting patiently at her daughter's bedside, murmuring lullabies and bathing the yellow-green skin of limbs and forehead, and then kneeling in her own bedroom, hands clasped before her face like a child, promising God a hundred good works, a thousand pieties, if He would let the little one survive and grow strong again.

But He did not.

Libby had not joined the rite this day. She was at home in bed, pale and gaunt, her face turned to the wall, waiting for the pain to pass. At least God would, in time, grant her that.

Lydia had come to her great niece's funeral. She stood beside Robert now, a wraith in black bombazine, her face shrouded in dark lace, so that he could not tell if she was weeping or bearing the loss more stoically. But her carriage was erect, her head unbowed even when the reverend invited them to prayer.

Willie took his place next to Robert. The boy was wearing his first dark suit, his first long pants. His fair hair was freshly clipped and combed sideways with pomade. Not all of that finery could touch the blank, uncomprehending misery of his face. He had not just lost a sister, Robert realized, but a compatriot in their small country of two, a sometime comrade in arms, and a friend.

He was really too young to be facing such a loss, but there was nothing a father could do about that.

On the far side of the hole and the coffin, opposite the three of them, stood friends of the family and those of the townspeople who wished to show respect. At the back of this small gathering, almost in hiding, Robert had glimpsed Margot Dobray, soberly dressed with a net veil over her face. He had looked for John Loring as well, but the geologist had not come in from the field.

Reverend Stevens offered a final prayer and signaled to the pallbearers. The three men—McKee and one of the enginemen from the railroad, and Bemis, who managed the electric plant—took their places at the canvas straps. Willie started blindly forward to fulfill the last of his duty to his sister, but Robert put a hand on his arm. "Let me, son," he murmured.

Robert stepped around the boy, and Willie backed up. Out of the corner of his eye, Robert saw Lydia take him by the shoulders and draw him close to her. There must be some feeling in the old woman, after all.

With the straps drawn tight under the coffin, the four men walked it around the end of the grave, over the hole, and lined it up with the edges of green turf.

"Lower away," McKee said quietly, and they began paying out in measured amounts, hand over hand. The blond-colored wood sank into the dark earth until shadows covered it.

When it thumped on the solid earth at the bottom, McKee looked at Robert and Bemis opposite him. "You let go." Then McKee and the engineer drew up the straps and folded them.

Mallory, who kept the cemetery, came up with a pair of shovels. He offered one to Robert, but Robert turned his head. He went to the wreath of white roses standing behind the reverend and pulled one loose. With his thumbnail, he peeled away the thorns along the stem as he carried it to the grave. When it was free of its stings, he dropped the rose into the darkness. Then he turned away to his family.

Behind him, McKee and Bemis had accepted the shovels and dug into the pile of freshly turned earth. Robert tried to close his ears to the thud it made against his daughter's coffin. The pressure of the effort squeezed his eyes, and his tears finally came.

22. A Fountain of Fire

ON LORING'S THIRD exploratory well, the telltale clatter started much earlier—at less than three thousand feet—and the sound increased both in volume and pitch much more rapidly than with the two previous wells. He barely had time to step off the platform before the pressure blew the rotary table clear away, sending it flying like a huge black disk through the struts of the derrick and off into the brush. The impact crippled the tower: it creaked and metal screeched as the structure started to topple sideways.

He turned on one foot to see how bad the damage was going to be. The scream of air rushing up the pipe turned to a rumble and then a gurgle. More brine, Loring thought sourly. This drilling campaign in Pennsylvania was not turning out at all as he had hoped. The open pipe coughed up its usual puff of steam, followed by a white column that mushroomed over at the top and rained salt water over the boards of the platform.

Loring started forward, to see if he could shore up the derrick before it twisted itself irreparably. The wellhead sputtered and shot a blank of clear air into the column of froth, followed by a bomb of water, then with a shriek, more air. Except it couldn't be air—not from thousands of feet underground.

The chain fall hanging high up at the crown block was still swinging from the impact of the flying rotary. Against all probability, because of the dousing the structure had already taken, it was striking sparks against the in-bent leg of the tower. Loring perceived all of this with one-quarter of his mind, while another quarter engaged his muscles to turn his hips and put his legs in motion. But fully half of his brain was congratulating itself upon his deductions, his superb sense of the ground, and his success in proving the existence of natural gas in the twisted geology of the ancient Allegheny Mountains.

John Loring did not see the spark that set off the pressurized column of gas. He barely heard the boom of ignition. But he did feel the giant hand that lifted him by the seat of his pants and threw him squarely against the broad bole of the tree he was intending to dodge around. Fortunately, the impact stunned him so that he never felt the fire that consumed him.

23. REQUIESCAT

Reverend Stevens always found something strangely familiar about the public parlor of Adolphus Shute's funeral home. It was not just that he had been a frequent visitor over the years, arranging with the rotund mortician for the rites of viewing, transporting, and burying his congregants. No, he thought, it was something in the room itself. Perhaps the modestly styled, cream-painted woodwork that bore the scuffs of daily traffic, very like the interior of First Methodist. Still, what nagged at him was something more primal and insistent, something in the nose.

Then it struck Stevens that the faint odor of decay, which he had always assumed to rise from the workrooms in the basement, or to linger in the drapes and carpet from the presence of corpses airing in open caskets for a night and a day, actually had nothing to do with the bodies or the work of the house. What he was smelling was the jungle rot of dead flowers and the murky water in their vases. Stevens could smell it in his church on Sunday evenings, when he was clearing out the bouquets from morning service and, for a while, the odor of dead vegetation overpowered the smells of beeswax and floor polish that otherwise dominated.

Having solved that little mystery, the reverend turned his mind to the business at hand. He admired the coffin on display at the end of the room. Under the faux stained glass, a nondenominational harlequin pattern in blue and violet with embedded lozenges of yellow, the coffin's fine-grained mahogany and layers of varnish seemed even deeper and redder. The handles were heavily scrolled in fluted brass. The lid was closed.

"That's a nice piece of work," he observed quietly.

"Yes, Wheelock insisted on paying for the best quality."

"If he was willing to spend all that, why not send Loring home to his people?"

"Ah, and who would they be?" Adolphus Shute asked. "Talk is, he came from somewhere in Colorado, and while it's not

164

nearly as populated as Pennsylvania, it's still a big place to go knocking on doors."

"But he must have left something with an address—a driver's license, an electric bill, letters from home—some clue about whom to contact."

"I've got his effects in my office, along with a suitcase full of work clothes, a set of collar studs, and some books. No papers, nothing personal. Well, in one of the books we did find a photograph, Loring with a woman."

"There you go. He had a family, a wife or sister—"

"Possibly, Reverend. But the back of the photo was stamped from a shop in New Orleans. And, judging by the way the woman was dressed and made up, it would seem they had a more, um, professional relationship."

"Loring must have carried a wallet," Stevens observed.

"If so, he was wearing it at the time of the accident."

"Ah, yes? And so the contents would show—"

"You don't understand," Shute said. "Why do you think that coffin's closed? By the time Loring's men put out the fire and got a cap on the well, the man was hardly bigger than a singed monkey, all curled around himself. His pocket watch and chain were just a little trickle of gold melted into his ribcage. If he was carrying any papers, they're ash and cinders now. Wheelock paid me handsomely to prepare the body, but there was just nothing to be done. You never hope to see such a blackened mess."

"What an awful way to die," Stevens murmured.

"When I explained all this to Wheelock, he still insisted on doing the most for Loring. He's even having the man's likeness carved into the headstone, full-on of the face in bas-relief, taken from that photograph—but without his companion, of course. That's work for a sculptor, not a stone mason, and Wheelock paid for it freely. He said it was so people around here wouldn't forget the geologist entirely."

"Robert's a very thoughtful person."

"Yes, he bought space for him in the cemetery, too, just a little down the hill and a row back from the family plot. ... You know,

I'm glad to have the business. But if you asked me candidly, I'd say all this is a waste of money, really, for someone who was, all things said and done, a stranger."

"Even if the death was an accident, I believe Robert felt there was a debt to pay."

"Does it bother you," Shute asked, "taking Loring into your church and burying him on sanctified ground, when you don't know if he was baptized, or even Christian?"

"Robert and I discussed that. We both agreed that God would make room for the unfortunate stranger."

As the men talked, Stevens saw over the mortician's shoulder that someone had come into the room. It was Wheelock's secretary, dressed in a dark coat and with her red cloche hat pulled down over her face. For a moment, he thought she had further instructions from the lawyer, but she never looked at the two men.

She walked slowly up to the coffin and stood beside it for a long moment. At her side, hanging from her hand, was a spray of bright color. When she laid it on the coffin, the reverend recognized a ragged bouquet of flowers she had obviously picked from the beds around the courthouse square. The woman rested her hand on the lid for another moment, still holding the stems. Then she spread her fingers and let stems and blossoms fan out across the dark wood.

She turned and walked away.

Stevens shook his head.

"What?" Shute asked.

"Nothing," he said.

24. A Plan for the Future

THE FIRST RED rays of early dawn were just coming through the windows of Robert's office when he put the last line to the letter he had drafted on a yellow legal tablet. Beside his inkwell was a shot glass with a brown stain in the bottom and smudges around the lip. As he turned out the desk light, he picked up the glass, sniffed the sharp medicinal smell for comfort, and set it back down.

It was contraband, of course, under the terms of the Volstead Act. One of Robert's clients provided an occasional bottle "for medical emergencies," straight off the boat from Canada. As an officer of the court, Robert could be disbarred for accepting, possessing, and using the liquor, and up until the death of his daughter he had scrupulously complied with the law. After that, it became harder. And so he kept the bottle in a locked drawer of his desk—one to which Margot Dobray did *not* have the key.

Still, he had to ask himself, had the drink affected his judgment? Probably. But Robert would stand behind what he had written. It was a good proposal, a sound plan, suffering not a bit because its composition had been motivated by his personal loss and lubricated with Canadian whiskey. He read it over again, following in his mind's eye the flow of water.

It sheeted from the steep mountain slopes and seeped from springs, swelling the river and filling the creekbed. The floods collected in the first catch basin and dropped a certain amount of silt that later, in the dry months, would have to be reclaimed and trucked into the forest or spread on the fields. From the basin, the overflow went into a concrete ditch, twenty feet deep and forty feet wide, with sides slanted like the faces of Cheops's pyramid. That ditch replaced the shallow course of the creek as it went past Aunt Lydia's property and through the town, widening bridges and shortening backyards. Some would call it an eyesore, but it would channel the spring floods away from their basements and, in too many cases, from their front parlors. On the other side of town, the river would enter a deeper canyon of

167

gray concrete, with vertical walls and twice the carrying capacity of the remade creek.

Robert had racked his brains for an alternative: a diversion channel, a dam, something that would take the excess water away from the town and let them have their shaded green banks and languid flow for most of the year, with fishing and swimming holes in the summer, skating parties and easy crossings in the winter. But Roulette was situated in a deep valley. Aside from the path through town, there was no place for the water to go except back up the hills, and that the water would not do. Of course, a major dam upstream of the town might hold the spring runoff and meter it out a little at a time through the rest of the year. But dams required space behind them, whole valleys to retain the lakes they built up, and there was no such configuration in the land upstream—not until you got to the continental divide and started going back downstream on the Susquehanna or the Genesee.

No, Robert had described the best plan, the most reasonable plan, for dealing with the floods that passed through Roulette at least once, and sometimes twice, each year. And, after all, he did not have to design the perfect plan, merely propose something solid, something feasible, to show that it could be done, to demonstrate for any reasonable, fair-minded person how it ought to be done. There was a way to free the town from its muddy shackles and the waves of sickness—dysentery, hepatitis, and some years even cholera and typhoid fever—that plagued the people and regularly took their toll.

Including, not to mention, Robert's own daughter.

He put the papers down and stared out the window, across the square, to the stone abutments and iron trusses of the Main Street bridge where it crossed the Allegheny River. In the right hands, these sheets of yellow paper had the power to remake the landscape, to remove that bridge and replace it with another one.

He would give them to Margot to type when she came in. After weeks of patience, Robert had turned her into an acceptable secretary. She was reasonably fast, fairly accurate, and immensely intuitive. He had come to trust her judgment where evaluation of people was concerned, once he learned to discount her innate cynicism. She had an unerring instinct, however, for a deadbeat. And she could tell within a minute if someone was telling the truth or a lie—not a bad talent in a legal secretary.

The door to the street opened and closed. Robert heard steps on the stairs. It was too early for Margot, although no one else had a key to the office. But then, the steps he heard were slow and even, where she usually ran up pell-mell. He watched the end of the banister and was surprised to see her red felt hat appear.

"Is that you, Margot?" he called.

She turned a pale face with blank eyes.

"Bit early for you, isn't it?" he said, trying to smile.

She shrugged and put her handbag on the desk by her typewriter.

"That's good, though," he went on, "because I have letters for you."

"I'm not typing any more of your damn letters," she said quietly.

"What?" Robert was not sure he had heard correctly. "Why not?"

"I'm leaving. I'm going to New York. Like I planned all along."

"But I need you here. You have a job. You have a future here."

As he said this, Margot shook her head, a baleful look in her eyes.

His protests trailed away. He returned her stare. "What is it?"

"I'm pregnant. I'm going to have your child."

Robert swallowed. "Are you sure?"

"A woman always knows."

"Well … Maybe you could see Dr. Guillaume. He might be able to—"

"That old gossip?" Margot sneered. "Do you want the whole town to know?"

"Then someone else, perhaps in Austin or Emporium, where you're—"

"Or perhaps in New York, where I was going anyway, when I came here."

"All right," Robert said, accepting the situation. "For that, you'll need money."

"I've got my wages coming," she said.

Twenty dollars, Robert realized, for the past week. Twelve more, to bring this week up to date. He opened the ledger that kept the office accounts and made note of her wages. "It would probably be more convenient, seeing as you'll be traveling, if I paid you in cash," he said, reaching for the box in the side drawer of his desk.

"Don't bother," she said quickly. "I'll take a check."

"Of course." Robert took out his checkbook, made out the amount, tore the check loose, and fanned it to dry the ink. As he handed it over, he said, "You'll need more than that to—to get started."

"Yes," she agreed.

"I suppose I could manage another hundred," he said.

"I'd appreciate it."

He wrote out another check. "You probably don't want to cash this one at the bank in town. There might be questions."

"Will any other bank take it?" she asked suspiciously. "One in New York, for instance?"

"You have to provide proof of identity, of course," he said. "And it will take a day or two to clear."

Margot nodded at this. "I can wait."

She folded the two checks together and put them in her handbag.

"It's not much," she said. "Not for raising a child."

"Raise it? I thought you were going to … take care of it."

"That's still my decision, isn't it?" she said sharply.

"I suppose it is," he agreed.

"I'll let you know when I get settled."

"Please do that," he said. "But write to the office."

"Of course."

She turned to go. She had brought nothing with her when she came. There was nothing to take out of her desk. She walked to the stairs, put her hand on the newel post, and started down. At the third step, she stopped and turned to look at him with her head just above the banister.

Robert thought she was going to say good-bye after all their time together.

"Oh yeah," she said. "I cleaned out the petty cash box yesterday. You'll want to refill it before you try to buy stamps or something."

When the outside door had slammed and she had certainly gone, Robert sat for a moment, thinking and remembering.

Then he went over to Margot's desk—her former desk—and took the cover off the Underwood typewriter. He pulled up her wheeled typing chair, with the tiny swivel seat and the back that flopped over, and perched himself on it. He cranked the first piece of paper into the platen and began typing the first of his letters: "The Honorable—" he left a space to fill in the name after he looked it up "—Secretary of State of the Commonwealth of Pennsylvania …"

Half an hour later, Robert started on the next letter: "Bureau of Reclamation, U.S. Department of the Interior …"

And the third: "Department of the Army, Corps of Engineers, Eastern District …"

By noon he had finished the cover letters for his first salvo in the fight for the Sylvan County Flood Control Project.

SUMMER 1938

1. Breaking Ground

THE HIGH SCHOOL band finished *America the Beautiful* and started thumping and tooting into the opening bars of *My Country 'Tis of Thee*. The sweat trickled down the back of Robert's neck and into his collar, while the slats of the wooden folding chair dug into the bones of his nether regions. Beside him, in a trim white linen suit and flowered hat, Libby shaded her eyes with one gloved hand against the sun that reflected off the ripples of the Allegheny River. The coordinators of this ceremony had set up the speakers' platform along the north bank, just two blocks from the center of town, and facing the water across fifty feet of cleared earth that was once a bramble patch. The gathering of townspeople stood on that spot now, with the river and its glare behind them, listening to the music and waiting patiently for the politicians.

The band stumbled to a stop, all within a beat of the ending, either way. Robert tended to notice such things after Willie had been promoted to first-chair trumpet—"It's called a *cornet*, Dad. There's a difference"—during his senior year in high school.

In the pause after the music, the mayor of Roulette, Walter Dufour, stood up to speak. When Dufour wasn't performing his official duties, he ran the town's electric plant, which had sold out six years ago to Duquesne Light and Power Company. That was progress, of a sort, because the local business could not compete with the regional utility on coal contracts. Selling out had kept the electric lights burning in Roulette during the darkest days after the Crash. Progress was what Dufour was talking about now, too: the power of men to change the course of mighty rivers and protect their property against the encroachments of nature.

Hearing these words, Robert felt a slight dislocation. The river before them was at the low point of the season—just a collection of silvery streams and jade-colored holes threaded among bare, mud-colored rocks. No one, looking at it today, would think the Allegheny required the work they were about to propose. But

Robert remembered, and so would everyone else, the floods of springtime and what they took from the town each year.

After Dufour finished, there came a project manager from the district office of the Works Progress Administration, who spoke about the promises of the current government in Washington, D.C. He was followed by the Secretary of State for the Commonwealth of Pennsylvania, who said the same things about Harrisburg. And after him came a colonel in the U.S. Army Corps of Engineers, which had worked up a construction plan from Robert's earliest sketches and sent out a surveying team in the spring to walk the ground and measure the river.

As each man spoke in turn, Robert relived the past ten years of writing letters and attending meetings and reading the reports of various commissions and their hearings. He had met personally with his congressman in Emporium, with the bureaucrats who variously oversaw farmland and forestry, streams and rivers, and soil conservation at their offices in Harrisburg, and with this same colonel at the Department of the Army headquarters in Washington.

At first, their story had been that rivers simply flooded—always had, always would—and nothing could be done about it. Then, as the economy slid into Depression and the national mood darkened, the answer was that there was no money—never had been money, never would be money—to serve a secondary priority like flood control, not when farmers were going under with the drought out west. But finally the man with the smile had taken up residence in the White House. He preached that spending money on public programs was a good thing, because it put people to work. While Robert disagreed with that man on many issues in principle, he could see an opportunity when one was offered. And so Robert had applied for a WPA grant to build the flood control. After two years of waiting, with nothing else for him to try, the authorization had finally come through. And here they were today, gathered by the river, about to see the first dirt moved.

Robert himself had not been asked to speak. His contribution to the proceedings had been recognized by the fact that he and Libby were seated on the platform at all. But after the speeches there had to be positive action. It was part of the rite.

Dufour asked the three other speakers—and Robert—to stand up. As they had rehearsed, they filed to the left, off the boards and onto the cleared ground. The crowd made way for them as they walked toward the river bank. A workman in coveralls and canvas gloves came forward with five shovels bought new from the feed store and painted with the same gold paint the county used on the courthouse trim. The workman passed out the shovels among the five of them, and they lined up two yards from the water. Dufour waved for the photographers from newspapers as far away as Emporium and Harrisburg to come forward with their Speed Graphics. To get the best shots, they splashed through the shallows and squatted with their pants legs dipped in the floating duckweed.

"On three, gentlemen," Dufour said quietly.

"One …" He planted the blade of his shovel in the brown, hard-packed alluvial soil, and the others did likewise. He placed one foot on the back of the blade, and they followed suit. Three of them used their right foot, as did the mayor, but the bureaucrat from the WPA started off with his left foot and then quickly changed.

"Two …" Dufour pushed and wedged his blade into the dirt. The rest of them struggled to match him for angle and depth.

"And three!" He pulled up a good half-bucketful of brown Pennsylvania earth.

The others lifted their own loads and then looked up for the cameras.

The flashbulbs exploded, memorializing the moment.

One thing they had not rehearsed was what to do with the collective first shovel of dirt. Dufour threw his forward, into the water—which ran counter, symbolically, to the intent of the floor control plan. Robert and two of the others turned quietly and emptied their shovels behind them on the shore. The bureaucrat dropped his back into the hole he had just made.

And so the work was under way.

2. An Unearthly Noise

THE NOISE THAT the earth-movers made, working down in the creek-bed, was indeed a terrible thing. The big chrome-yellow and soot-black machines grunted like a herd of pigs, then bellowed like bulls. The belted plates that they had instead of wheels clanked and rattled. And when the shiny steel blades scraped across rock, the high-pitched squeal went right up Libby's nerves. She could not recollect hearing a bird, not even the incessant blue jays, since the morning the flood control work had started.

"Can't you make it stop?" Lydia asked from the depths of her pillows. She had broken her left hip in a fall on the back steps late in the spring, and now she was bedridden for real. Libby, as the woman's only local relative, had taken it upon herself to look in on her aunt and nurse her back to health.

"Do you want me to close the window?" she asked.

"No, this is the only breeze I'll get all day," her aunt replied.

"We could move you to the other side of the house."

"There's no breeze over there. Besides, this is my bedroom."

"Well then …"

"You could get them to go away."

"The men have a job to do, Aunt."

"This is all because of Robert."

"Of course. I'm proud of him."

"Terrible machines. What do you call them? 'Clatter-pillars'?"

"No, caterpillars … like the inchworm."

"Maybe. But I like my word better."

Upon reflection, Libby did too.

"This is just a plot for Robert to get his hands on my property."

Libby sighed. "And how do you figure that?"

"With all that money he's made, he still cannot buy my land. So he asks the government to steal it for him, three feet at a time. He may think he's smart, but I know his game."

"That's absurd, Aunt. The flood control will do good things for Roulette. And it will keep your yard from being inundated every year. I would think a little strip of land under eminent domain is

179

a small price to pay for that. Besides, the land will belong to the county, not to Robert."

"Think what you will. But Robert's behind all this."

Libby sighed again and kept her mouth shut. Arguing didn't do any good. Not with Lydia. Not in this mood.

"Still," her aunt went on, "I do wonder what will become of the property, when my time comes."

"Surely you've made your will."

"Why would you assume that?"

"Well, as a lawyer's wife …"

"I was planning to live forever."

There was nothing to say to that.

"But now I believe I'll have to do something," Lydia said after a pause. She was looking down at her left leg, which no longer moved.

Libby knew that Robert could draw up his stepmother's will in twenty minutes. Aside from the small incomes allotted from her late husband's businesses—which would end with her death—there were only her personal possessions in this house and the large tract of property under it. Robert would do the legal work for free because she was, still and all, family. And Lydia would have nothing to do with it. So it would be pointless for Libby even to mention the possibility.

"Do you happen to know a good lawyer?" Lydia asked.

Libby clamped her tongue firmly between her front teeth.

"Perhaps Jim Harris could draw up a will," Lydia went on.

Harris was Robert's biggest competitor. They often faced each other from opposite sides of Judge Lawrence LeConte's courtroom. The choice of Harris to arrange Lydia's affairs would be a bitter blow to Robert. And, of course, Libby would not stoop to explain this to her aunt, because it might sound too much like pleading.

"Would you talk to him for me?" Lydia asked, meaning Harris.

"If that's what you want."

"I think it's time," she said, laying her head back into the pillows.

3. Ruby's Café

The front was the same, with narrow shop windows on either side of the door where a store owner would have set up displays of his merchandise. The tables in the windows still had red-checked tablecloths; the difference was that now they also had flowers in little ceramic vases. They were paper flowers, true, but the thought was there.

Zacky had cashed out when business died off after the Crash, and the store front had stayed empty for a year. Then Ruby Pearson had come to town, rented the space, and painted over the sign with her name instead of his. But she kept the same blocky, green letters with the white edging.

Another thing that was the same but different was the kitchen. It was still out in plain sight behind the zinc-covered counter, but Ruby had brought in a number of new appliances, including a Hamilton Beach mixer for making milkshakes and a freezer to keep a generous supply of ice cream. Ruby liked ice cream and wanted to share with her customers. And, of course, a big gas range and griddle replaced the old coal-fired stove. The greatest change of all was in the back, however, where she sacrificed part of the storeroom to make a second bathroom, separate for the ladies.

The clientele had changed in the past ten years, too. Walter Dufour was a regular now, and people said he understood his constituency so well because he drank coffee with them every morning. Another new face was Sheriff Rafe Cobb, who was a grand-nephew of Judge Wheelock's old housekeeper and had come down from Binghamton during the Depression to try his hand at law enforcement. More recently, Malcolm Hurlbert had retired to Florida, for the sun, but the new county clerk, Harold Burke, took his breakfast in the same chair at the same table every day before opening the courthouse. Inside of two weeks, no one could tell the difference. McKee was still coming in from the railroad, but the line had switched from steam locomotives to the new diesel and was moving mostly freight now. The new

181

engineer and fireman ate their breakfast in Emporium, before the run. Clarence was still coming in after opening his feed store. Stovall had disappeared when the lumber camp on the other side of Denton Hill closed down.

"All I'm saying," said McKee, picking at the thread of a very old discussion, "is that this town has seen *nothing* of the Depression. Not compared to Austin and Wharton and places along the line that are hardly *there* anymore. Sure, we deserve the flood control. Sure, we pay our taxes—and even that's a luxury some do not have. But we've enjoyed an easy ride, is all. Compared to some."

"I suppose it's just our natural talent and good looks," said Reverend Stevens.

"It's the gas, of course," said Burke. "That's what's kept this town from want."

"So do we owe *everything* to the Wheelocks?" Clarence said with a moan.

"Well, Robert's the one who brought in that geologist fellow," McKee said reasonably. "What was his name?"

"Loring," Reverend Stevens supplied. "Christian name John."

McKee turned to one of the farmers sitting at a table along the wall. "Nathan, how much did you take out of the ground last quarter?"

"Fifteen hundred," Birdsall said.

"And is that in dollars or cubic feet?"

"I didn't bother to ask." Birdsall grinned.

"You just cashed the check, right?"

"Ayuh!"

"Not many farmers down around Costello could say the same."

"Still, Wheelock has made a pretty penny for himself," said Clarence.

"Yeah," said another farmer with wellheads on his land. "Wheelock makes the big money, owning the ground rights and all. That was a bit of sharp practice, buying them up before anyone knew the gas was there."

"How much money, do you reckon?" Birdsall asked. "I mean, all told?"

"Has to be a million dollars," said Walt Dufour. "Two, maybe."

"Nathan?" McKee interposed. "How much you get selling that dog of yours?"

"Heh?" said the farmer.

"Not that it's any of my business," McKee added quickly.

"My dog? What the hell's *that* got to do with anything?"

"Just making a point," said the conductor equably.

"All that money," said Clarence, "and Wheelock still lives in that pokey little house at the end of the lane. Couldn't he buy—or build himself—a better one?"

"He makes do with what he has and doesn't strive for show," said Reverend Stevens. "That, my friends, is character."

"Or he's waiting to get his hands on the big house across the park," said Dufour. "The one his daddy built."

"Won't be long now," said Harold Burke. "Not according to Dr. Guillaume."

"Nonsense," said McKee. "It won't be *ever*. Lydia will burn that house down before she lets Wheelock have it."

"But wasn't it his house to begin with?" asked Dufour. "According to the will?"

"That's in the public record," said Burke.

"It's her house now, by common law," said Birdsall.

"That only works for marriages," said Clarence. "Not for property."

"Robert Wheelock still owns the house," Burke concluded, "just not the land underneath it."

"Well, all I can say," said McKee, "is he'd better join the fire brigade."

4. A Fine Mind

THE METAL FILINGS on the floor of the living room around Robert's chair would not come out of the rug. Libby had tried sweeping and brushing, but the sharp edges caught in the cross fibers. She had tried using that newfangled device, the vacuum cleaner, but found it could not blow, or suck, or whatever it did hard enough to remove them. In the end Libby was forced to get on her knees and pick them out one by one with her fingernails.

She had asked Robert nicely to put down a newspaper before he started repairing an old flintlock musket he'd bought from one of the farm families, and he had done so. But the metal filings tended to fly when he was working, and then they dropped from his lap when he stood up, so the paper was mostly wasted effort. It was the same with the copper work he did on her kitchen table: she had asked him to use a block of wood to soften the blows when he started hammering, and so she got big square dents in the table's surface instead of small round ones.

Libby wasn't angry, not really, not with Robert.

He was a brilliant man, classically educated with many practical and artistic interests, but he was caught in a political and cultural backwater. Robert loved the town and its people. He had tried to fill his father's shoes, both as their lawyer and as an agent of change, and by any measure he had been a success at it. He had become quite a public figure both in Roulette and in Sylvan County as a whole, and Libby was proud of him. But her husband was clearly restless, seeking outlets for his energy and creativity, and sometimes she thought he felt stifled. So his hobbies were a way for him to pass the long evenings after his legal work, such as it was, was done for the day.

In addition to his budding collection of firearms, there were the bracelets, ashtrays, vases, and lamps that Robert fashioned from sheets of copper and bits of brass. He also had a closet full of cameras in the front hall, both for still and moving pictures; for the past several years he had photographed and filmed the life of the county. And William Henry's interest in botany had

184

finally come out in the six different varieties of gladiolus bulbs that were now sprouting in Libby's garden in back of the house, after spending all winter in her kitchen behind the gas stove, in what used to be the wood box.

It was almost as if Robert was frantically trying to find some meaning in the encapsulated existence he had chosen for himself and Libby. And yet, there seemed to be a dark element to all this activity as well. Libby could not put a hard name to any single deed, or word, or facial expression of his. But, looking back over the past ten years of their marriage, she thought she could detect a cooling in his attitude. Robert acted as if he was unhappy, or quietly angry, or perhaps even feeling guilty about something. But about what, she did not know.

Ow! The pieces of metal were sharp and stabbed the ends of her fingers. ...

Libby thought the veil had dropped between the two of them at about the time Genie died. At first, she supposed that Robert blamed her for the death—for not supervising their daughter more closely during the flood, for not being more attentive at her bedside, for not willing Genie to live through the disease that killed her. But when Libby and Robert had talked about it, some months later, he expressed only sorrow and no recrimination against her.

What else he might be feeling, Libby did not know. In other circumstances, she might suspect another woman. But if he was straying now, after all these years, she expected there would be some evidence. Roulette was a small town, where everyone knew everyone else's business, and Robert did not travel regularly enough to be carrying on an affair somewhere else. Libby could not abide a philanderer. Handsome and sweet-natured as Robert was, if he had ever shown the least sign of infidelity, she knew she would have left him and taken the children straight back to Binghamton. But, thank God, there was never anything of that sort to worry about.

All in all, Libby imagined that every couple married for twenty years or more harbored such silent places, marked their own territories that could not be entered, and erected barriers around similar lonely feelings. She just regretted that these dark thoughts were making Robert so unhappy.

Ouch! One of the metal filings had been driven under her fingernail far enough to raise a blood spot. Libby thought there had to be an easier way to pick them up. Well … coming from an old gun, it stood to reason the slivers were either steel or iron. That meant they would be magnetic. And Robert probably had a magnet in his toolbox. She got up and went to the kitchen. Predictably, he had every kind of tool, including a small horseshoe magnet, painted red, stuck to the inside of the lid.

At least that was one problem solved.

5. Letter from London

Dear Dad—

Today I went to the British Museum and spent eight hours there, right up until closing time. The first impression you get, when you walk into this great hall on the ground floor, is of many lurking figures. The walls and pillars each have their resident deity, waiting with impassive faces and hooded eyes. And then, when you start looking at these sculptures of gods and pharaohs and mystical creatures, you see how many kinds of stone are represented. The Mesopotamian figures are sandstone, I think. At least, they are the color of sand. Some of the Egyptian statues are a hard, reddish rock that they pound and polish until it gleams like chocolate. Others are a granite that turns as dark as cast iron.

The giant wall carvings from Mesopotamia are lions with wings and the faces of bearded kings. Did you know that each one has five legs? When you face them, the two front legs go straight down. And when you look from the side, the body has four legs in profile, with one of the front legs angled slightly backward, behind the other. So, altogether, five legs. I wonder that no one ever stood at the corner and looked at them from an angle. The error is quite obvious from that point of view.

The best thing in the hall, however, was one flat stone—made of black basalt, I think. It was surprisingly small, so that you could cover it with an old blanket. There are just these lines of white letters cut into its face. I recognized the lines across the bottom as Greek, of course, although I couldn't read them. Just above them are letters that look something similar but are really different when you look closely. And at the top are Egyptian hieroglyphics, made up of bird signs and body parts mixed with lumps and squares that might almost be letters. This is the Rosetta Stone, which the placard says helped the scholars interpret the Egyptian writing and read it for the first time.

I wanted to touch it, to run my fingers over those incised letters, but of course they don't let you do that. Still, I looked at it for about half an hour. Other people would come up, glance at it, and go on. I just got lost in the tiny white lines. The Greek is almost familiar. I could recognize *M* and *H*, *P* and *W*, among other letters that are almost but not quite like the Latin we studied in high school. But none of the words made sense. How that led them to Egyptian, another language in another alphabet, is not exactly clear to me. Still, I know now that I want to study Greek and the classics. And I'm really looking forward to Rome, walking in the Forum and seeing the Senate building and the Coliseum.

Those hieroglyphics make me think there must be other languages out there, still undiscovered and undeciphered. Celtic runes and Mexican feather-serpents. If I studied really hard, starting with the Greek and maybe going on to Sanskrit or Hebrew, do you think I might be the first person to read them aloud? That would be exciting!

The London newspapers are all talking about the international situation, of course. Especially after the Austrians voted to a man (well, ninety-eight percent of them) to join up with the Germans. If Hitler is such a bad fellow, why would so many people want to go his way? The English are not fooled, of course. They see Hitler as another Napoleon, risen again after a hundred and fifty years. That's just like the unstable Europeans, they say—give them a few years of hard times and they turn to the Tyrant to solve their problems. All very un-English, don't you know?

The papers talk of another war—a continuation of 1918. Although, some people think it will be worse because the Germans were never really beaten in the first place. I don't know. I don't suppose anyone wants to go through *that* again.

I am glad to be just a visitor here, and able to go back across the Atlantic—or "the pond," as the English call it—when this summer is over and I go on to college. We are so lucky to live in a great and democratic country without enemies. These national grudges seem to me so, well, antique. Like people don't have anything better to do.

Thank you again for sending me on this trip, and for trusting me to do it on my own. I am having the best time!

Your loving son,

William.

6. KEEPER OF THE HILLS

ONCE MORE ROBERT found himself seated with Libby on a ceremonial stage at the river's edge. But this time, instead of a patch of cleared brush in the hot sun along the river bank in town, they were under trees on the grounds of Valdemar Johansson's old fishing lodge. The other difference was the wardrobe of the dignitaries seated with them. Rather than the starched shirts and worsted suits of state and county officials, Chief Gregory Darnell and the tribal elders of the Seneca Nation were decked out in buckskins and war paint. Darnell even wore a feather bonnet and carried a tomahawk, although he insisted that no Indian ever wore feathers, except in Hollywood's imagination, and the last time he used a hatchet was to chop kindling.

Robert's gaze went to the flags set up at the front corners of the platform. On the left stood the American flag on an eagle-headed standard. On the right, the dark-blue flag with gold fleur-de-lis of the Boy Scouts of America stood next to the flag of the Seneca Nation, which held between its folds a roundel with silhouettes of birds and animals.

Each Tuesday afternoon during the preceding weeks, Robert had sat in a small room that smelled like a cedar closet inside the tribe's community hall. And there Chief Darnell taught him the names of those animals: bear and fox, heron and owl, elk, turtle, and beaver. The names worked into long poems of rising and falling monosyllables in the Iroquois language, although just two or three hours after learning them Robert could remember only fragmentary rhythms. These were animals sacred to the Seneca Indians. They were now—and, he realized suddenly, had always had been—the animals of his world, too, of the Allegheny Valley, Sylvan County, and the mountains surrounding his home in Roulette.

On those long afternoons Darnell had worn the regular clothes of any farming community, khaki pants and plaid flannels. In addition to tribal chief, he also happened to be mayor of

Salamanca, New York—across the state border from Roulette—
and his tribal council was also the town's board of supervisors.

Now under the trees, Robert and Libby and their hosts waited
while the local scout troop went through its dedication ceremo-
nies, which were supposed to be based on a native American
powwow.

After acquiring the fishing lodge under tragic circumstances,
Robert and his family had visited it only three or four times in the
succeeding years. He paid for the property's upkeep, improved
the rustic lodge house with a new roof and plumbing, added a
well, and graded the track down from the main road. But Robert never really considered the place to be his. And then, late
last year, the Boy Scouts had approached him about leasing the
lodge for a summer camp. Rather than lease it, Robert decided to
make an outright gift of the property and had set up a small trust
to maintain it and hire a member of the Seneca tribe to teach the
boys Indian lore and survival skills. And so Valdemar Johansson's
twenty-six run-down acres along the Allegheny River had become "Camp Moxie" and sported an archery range and a dozen
bentwood canoes.

"But it's not just for the gift of the camp and the teaching stipend that we're honoring you," Darnell had explained when
they met for Robert's instruction. "Over the years you've been a
good friend of the tribe."

When the Senecas had needed cash to meet their commit-
ments in the early days of the Depression, Wheelock helped the
tribe find a logging company that would harvest some of its vast
acreage. He negotiated a fair price for the lumber and even arranged for the company to hire the young men of the reservation.

When those same young men occasionally crossed the border into Sylvan County and sometimes ran afoul of Pennsylvania
laws—fished or shot a deer out of season, perhaps having taken
too much of the white man's alcohol—Wheelock represented
them in court and got them fair treatment. Within the provisions
of white law, he tried to have them returned to the tribal elders
for judgment and proper punishment.

When the State of New York wanted to charge the tribe for plowing snow on the public highways within its territory, Robert found precedents in both white and Indian law for providing access to all under the existing rights of way.

Now at the edge of the river, when the scouts had finished their own parades and speeches, Chief Darnell stood up on the platform and invited Robert to stand and face him. "For your many acts of kindness to the Seneca Nation," Darnell intoned, "and for your gift of this land, you have shown yourself to be a man of the people and mindful of the tribe's welfare.

"And so I name you 'Hah-Nuh-Dise-Suh,' which translates into your language as 'Keeper of the Hills.' You shall be a member of our tribe and a chief at the council table for all of your days."

During the training sessions, Darnell had explained to Robert that he would be the first Pennsylvanian accepted into the tribe since William Penn—and Robert pretended to believe that.

One of the tribal elders now handed Darnell a small, flat package. The chief stripped off the paper, revealing a plain box of polished, dark-brown wood. He opened the cover and offered it to Robert.

Inside, curled across a bed of blue velvet, was a black snake. Its mouth was open, with sharp white teeth winking in the sunlight, poised to bite. The snake unfolded itself and writhed out of the box as Darnell thrust it forward.

Instinctively, Robert grabbed it in back of the head, to control the strike.

Libby, still seated with her face at striking level, let out a little scream.

The snake's long body swung languidly from behind his grip and wrapped itself once around his forearm.

Robert expected the reptile to be cold to the touch, but he was surprised at how hard it was. After a moment of dislocation, he realized that the snake was a doll or a puppet: a long train of bell-shaped shells carved of dense, black wood and fitted together like beads on a string. The head was made of the same dark wood with the teeth whitened and set into the open jaws. A forked red tongue showed behind those teeth. The tail was ribbed and hollowed to simulate rattles. This was meant to represent a rattlesnake.

"Chief Robert, this is your totem animal," Darnell said. "The snake is wise in the ways of the wild. He feeds but once a month and husbands his strength. He draws his life from the warmth of the sun. He is cunning and moves swiftly at need. He avoids the eyes and attentions of man. Be like the snake and enjoy a long life."

Robert met Darnell's eye throughout this explanation. He wondered if they were making a joke at the white man's expense. Robert hoped his face did not show what he was thinking in parallel with the chief's words—that in the Christian religion the snake was the devil, the tempter of old, the deceiver, the enemy of man; that rattlesnakes were supposed to be low and vicious creatures. But these were ideas from another culture and would have no bearing on the virtues the Seneca elder was describing. So Robert patted the slender wooden head and said, "I will try to do that."

"Then go forth with the blessings of the nation," Darnell concluded.

Everyone around them broke into applause. Libby squeezed his arm as he sat down. Robert held his snake, still behind the pits of the head, and tried to look pleased.

7. The Bequest

The temperature had gone down during night, and there was even a thin fog off the river that covered the town by morning. When she had departed the evening before, Libby offered to leave the windows wide open in Lydia's bedroom, to take advantage of the cool air. She promised to leave a quilt within reach of the bed, in case the old woman got too cold. But Lydia, although she had complained of the stifling heat at regular intervals all day long, like the chiming of the brass eight-day clock on the mantelpiece, refused the offer. The windows stayed closed and the room's walls turned as warm as the plaster covering a chimney flue. And now the morning fog was burning off and the still air outside was becoming glary bright in preparation for another July day with no relief in sight.

"The lawyer is coming at ten o'clock," Libby reminded her aunt when Lydia had finished her tea and sugar cookies, which constituted her only breakfast.

"Which lawyer is that?" Lydia replied cautiously.

"James Harris, who's to prepare your will, of course."

"Oh! So you think my time is drawing near, do you?"

"You asked me to talk to him. He agreed to come here."

"My will …" Lydia said thoughtfully. "For when I'm dead."

"You wanted to see about the property. Don't you remember?"

"Oh, yes. I want to give it to the town," Lydia said. "To make a park."

"That's … an interesting thought," Libby replied.

"They can build a bandstand out on that spit of land where the river and the creek converge. Then on Sunday afternoons and the Fourth of July they can play for the people. And everyone can promenade up and down among the trees, and through the gardens—they'll replant the gardens, just like William Henry had them—and listen to the music."

"*Who* can play?" Libby wondered aloud.

"The band—the one Willie plays in."

"You mean the *high school* band?"

"That's the one," Lydia agreed.

"But that was last year—"

"Well, whenever."

"And what about this house?" Libby prompted.

"Oh, they can tear it down. Or use it for civic events. They can give recitals of chamber music—"

"Chamber music?" Libby repeated. Her aunt had become very musical this morning—for a woman who discouraged whistling or humming indoors and who dismissed Robert's vast collection of symphonies and opera on phonograph disks as so much noise. Lydia seemed to have forgotten that the house was not hers to donate for anything, and that Robert as owner would certainly have the final say in what became of it. But this line of talk had put her aunt in a cheerful mood, and it did not seem necessary to raise the question just then.

"Yes, recitals in the front parlor," her aunt babbled on. "And the Ladies Garden Society can have the conservatory to grow hothouse flowers during the cold months."

Libby brought to mind the conservatory as it now stood. To heat the glassed-in room during the winter, iron pipes around the outside walls were fed steam from a boiler in the basement through a big brass valve. These pipes had never been properly drained, once the old Judge had died, and now their joints showed veils of weeping rust. Hothouse flowers indeed!

"And the daughters of the town can have their weddings on the back terrace—just as you had yours," Lydia finished up with enthusiasm.

"You seem to have it all worked out," Libby said evenly.

"They'll find a use for the house. Or, as I said, tear it down."

"*Après moi le deluge?*"

"What did you say?"

"Nothing, Aunt."

―――――

James Harris had never been inside the big house built by the legendary Judge William Henry Wheelock. Neither had Harris ever practiced before the Judge, having come to Sylvan County in the last sunny days before the stock market crashed. He had stayed on in Roulette because, sparse as the pickings were, many another town had suffered worse during the past ten years. He and the Judge's son, Robert, were the only two lawyers in the county who amounted to anything, so they met often in the courtroom. And now, as he understood it, Wheelock's stepmother was asking Harris to arrange her will instead of her stepson.

Harris wondered what kind of surprise she might be arranging. From everything he had heard about Lydia Wheelock, it would not be a pleasant one.

As befitted the formality of the occasion, Harris had parked in the loop of the driveway and gone to the front door of the imposing Queen Anne–style house. He pushed the door bell, a round button set in a bronze rosette, but heard nothing from the inside. After several minutes and a second push of the bell, he decided that the button was no longer connected. He went along the walkway by the side of the house, down the stone steps of the porte-cochere, and around to the back. Up on the porch was the half-glassed door to the kitchen with another bell push, this one considerably less ornate. When he pushed it, however, he could hear a bell ringing from somewhere in the house.

After a minute or two, Robert Wheelock's wife Elizabeth, who had arranged the appointment, appeared at the door. She was a trim woman, not yet in her forties, but already there was a touch of silver-gray in her piled-up hair, and a deep seriousness shaped her mouth. Harris supposed she had experienced some sadness in her life, although he knew nothing about the family except what was common talk around the town. But then, making a will was naturally a sad occasion.

"Won't you come in Mr. Harris?" she said, holding the door open.

"Thank you, ma'am."

"My aunt is upstairs," she said, turning away to lead him through the high-ceilinged kitchen and into the back hall. "She's bedridden, of course—"

"So I understood."

"—and cannot meet you in the parlor, as befits a lady."

"Of course not."

Elizabeth Wheelock took him up the grand staircase, with its deeply carved banister and rich, red wool carpet. The carpet was held in place with mahogany battens screwed to the risers with brass caps in the shape of pine cones, or maybe it was lotus flowers. The house was beautiful but old … and dark. The silvered wallpaper in the front hall had tarnished to a gloomy brown, and there was dust in the niches of the woodwork. If Lydia Wheelock was going to die, this was the house to do it in.

From the bedroom door, Harris finally saw the woman. His first impression was that he had come not a moment too soon: she was a pale wraith against the pillows, thin and fragile like an effigy made of tissue paper. Only her voice was strong.

"This is the lawyer?" the woman said without moving her head.

"Yes, Aunt."

"Well, bring him over here where I can see the two of you."

Harris approached the bed, and Elizabeth brought up a straight chair for him to sit on. He opened his brief case and took out a legal pad and his fountain pen.

"How are you, Mrs. Wheelock?" he asked conversationally.

"Well, how do I look?"

"In the peak of health," he lied politely.

"Libby, you've brought me a fool," the old woman said.

"Now, Aunt …"

"I suppose you can draw up a legal document," Lydia said to Harris.

"Yes, ma'am." He decided to keep his answers short.

"I want to dispose of my property before I shuffle off."

"Your daughter-in-law has provided a list of assets."

"She's not my daughter-in-law. She's my niece."

"I see," Harris said. For years he had heard the town's stories about the enmity between the stepmother and stepson. He knew that, technically, Elizabeth Wheelock was related to the old woman both by blood and by marriage. But from Lydia's choice of terms he understood that she was denying the latter, and so denying any relationship with Robert Wheelock. Her hatred went that deep.

"According to the terms of your husband's will, which your—niece—also supplied to me," he went on, "the only major asset available for disposal is the acreage under this house. The rest of the assets are ... encumbered."

"He has a nice way with words," Lydia told Elizabeth.

"It's the truth, Aunt."

"I want to leave the property to the town, to make a park out of it," the old woman said. "You write that up so it's legally binding, so that a lawyer like yourself can't break it, and then I'll sign it."

"Well," Harris temporized. "I can make it legal, but I'm not sure I can make it ... stick."

"What's that? Why not?"

"While I'm sure the people of Roulette would be grateful for the bequest, it would entail some expense. You would be asking them to take on the care and maintenance of a large property while simultaneously removing it from the tax rolls. This would place a fiscal burden on the town, one which the city fathers might not be in a position to accept. And then there's the matter of the house."

"What about the house? It would make a grand centerpiece—"

"But it is not yours to give. To complete the acquisition, the town would have to buy it from your stepson."

"He would have to sell," the old woman said with a glint. "That's the law. Move it, or lose it."

"Yes, but Mr. Wheelock would be in a position to ask whatever price he wanted."

"Then the town could take it by eminent domain—same as they took my land."

Harris had heard about the fight over the strip of property for flood control, too.

Now he considered his position in all this. He had no reason to love Robert Wheelock but no reason to hate him, either. He understood the man to be honorable, fair minded, and public spirited. So far as Harris knew, Wheelock had lived up to his father's reputation and Roulette's expectations of the family. And Harris had no wish to support the stepmother in her vendetta. Moreover, as her attorney, he had a responsibility to raise and address the reasonable, legal objections that her scheme might meet with.

"Yes, eminent domain is a possibility," he said slowly. "But that is a tool to be used only when great public benefit is at stake. Your stepson is liked and respected in this town—"

"Bah!" Lydia Wheelock said. "He's nothing compared to his father."

"—and the people around here might not agree to taking his property without due recompense."

"You mean, he'll finagle it for himself, just like everything else."

"I'm only trying to advise you …"

"You're only trying to help him get this land," Lydia flared, "and that's the one thing I won't—"

"Aunt?" Elizabeth interposed suddenly. "I have a suggestion! If you really don't want to leave the property to Robert, why not bequeath it to Eunice?"

"This is whom?" Harris asked, confused.

"My elder sister," Elizabeth answered. "Her other niece."

"She would just give it to you," Lydia said petulantly.

"No," Elizabeth replied. "Eunice and her husband Teddy have long admired the property. They would use it for a summer place, up here in the mountains."

"Teddy would still have to buy the house from Robert," Lydia said.

"I'm sure he could afford it," Elizabeth said. In an aside to Harris, she explained: "He's a banker in New York City. He put all his money into government bonds."

Harris nodded. It was the only way to have survived the Crash.

"Ah, but would Robert sell to him?" Lydia asked.

"Well ... we could use the money," Elizabeth said in a low voice.

"Humph! I knew your husband would turn out a spendthrift."

"Mr. Harris, do you have any legal objections to this disposition?" Elizabeth asked.

"If the house has a willing buyer and a willing seller, then of course not," he said. "I was only concerned that the town—"

"Then there's the solution to your problem, Aunt," Elizabeth concluded.

"Give the land to Eunice," Lydia mused. "And let Teddy haggle with Robert ..."

"You know how they are. You can be sure Teddy will drive a hard bargain."

"I suppose ..." Lydia paused, considering. "It's the best solution, after all."

"I'm sure you won't regret it," Elizabeth said soothingly.

"I won't be here to see it," the old woman said tartly.

8. A Piece of Walnut

To complete the old gun that Robert was working on, he needed a piece of walnut. He'd done everything else for the restoration: cleaned and blued the pitted steel of the barrel, touched up the incised scrollwork on the lock plate, dug the rust out of the trigger mechanism and cleaned it with solvent, straightened the bent parts of the flint holder and pan cover, and polished up the brass furniture. But the stock was a total loss to rainwater and dry rot.

Because of that destroyed stock, Lance Maires had sold Robert the gun for ten dollars and thought he got the best of the bargain, even when Robert had insisted it was old, definitely an antique, and probably valuable.

"Just look at the octagonal cross section of the barrel," Robert had said. "No one has made a gun barrel like that in a hundred years. Well—not in the last seventy-five, certainly. And it's smooth bore, like a musket."

"My daddy said it was for birds," Maires said. "Some kind of shotgun."

"A fowling piece. Probably English. Perhaps even eighteenth century."

"But so busted up you can't fire it," Maires concluded. "And if you did, the stock would put splinters right through your shoulder. No, sir. You take that gun with my blessing."

Robert had accepted with thanks and gone to work. He knew that, as far as restoration was concerned, his repairs were more practical and decorative than strictly authentic. A museum would have left the rust and verdigris intact and tried to stop the dry rot with a fixative. But Robert wanted a working gun, a serviceable mechanism, a restored weapon, and something with a shine on it as well. For that he would need a piece of walnut about thirty-inches long, eight inches wide, and not less than four inches thick through the narrowest part.

He had tried Harold Binion at the lumber yard. "Well, Robert, you've got some nice black walnut in that grove of your father's," Binion had said. "Why don't you take an ax to one of them?"

Robert was horrified by the idea. "I only want about two feet of wood, Harold—not the whole tree!"

"I can't help you there. Walnut's a furniture wood. I sell construction materials."

And that had given Robert the idea of writing to Lowe's, down in Wharton. They were the nearest thing to a fine furniture store in three counties, although they did—and this was what interested him—buy up households and estates as well as sell new-made goods. Robert didn't have the heart to take a new piece of furniture and cut it apart to repair a gun. But if something old came in trade, maybe with one leg broken already, or a lot of surface scratches, then Robert would take it for the wood. Old was even better than new, because then he would know the wood was properly dried and had done all the warping and splitting it was going to do.

He wrote the letter after his regular office hours—not wishing to use his secretary, Dorothy Greer, for his personal correspondence. As usual, he made a first draft in longhand on a yellow pad before tackling the office Underwood.

"… Let me repeat that I am not concerned with the nature of the piece," he wrote, "whether a table, a large chair, or even a well-built armoire, so long as at least one part is made of solid wood, no veneer, and fits the dimensions specified above. Nor am I concerned with surface appearance. The finish does not matter, and deep scratches are acceptable. However, the area that matches my dimensions should have no deep cracks or splits. The price is negotiable, based on the quality of the section I have described. …"

When Robert had gotten the phrasing to his liking—anxious not to be mistaken for an antique collector hunting out a bargain—he signed his name, addressed the envelope, and put the letter on the pile for Dorothy to stamp and mail.

Then came the other piece of personal business—one that he also would not share with his secretary. Robert took out his personal checkbook and made a check to Margaret Dobray for two hundred dollars. He signed his name, addressed an envelope to the post office box number in New York City, put in the check without a note or other cover, and sealed it. But, rather than leave it for Dorothy to handle, he found a stamp in the secretary's desk, put the postage on it himself, and slid the letter into his pocket. He would mail it from the box in the street.

Once a month he did this, as regularly as paying any other bill, even though the unknowns of the situation were starting to crowd his mind. Robert had not had a word from Margot in more than nine years, not since she sent him a card with the box number soon after arriving in New York. He had assumed that she preferred a post office box to a street address because she did not want him to put the detectives on her, but perhaps she had to move around a lot in a city as large and fast-paced as New York.

Robert always assumed, also, that Margot had kept the child—their child, the object of their lust—and brought it to term. He tacitly intended this monthly stipend to pay for its care and up-keep. But, in reality, he did not know if the child was even alive or had ever existed, except as a story in Margot's mouth.

He did know that the checks were cashed every month. Once, years ago, he had worried that someone at his bank would no-tice the checks, remember Margot's name, and mention it about town. But nothing like that had ever happened. Bankers—and their tellers, clerks, and other minions—apparently had their own code of ethics governing privileged dealings between bank and customer. But again, he did not know for certain, and he dared not ask.

Robert paid his money, and Margot kept her silence. And so the matter stood. As far as Robert knew, he had a second family living just a few hundred miles to the east of Roulette. He should be happy enough that, after all these years, no one had discov-ered his secret. But not being able to discuss it with anyone—es-pecially not with Libby, who was supposed to be his helpmate and his best friend—was beginning to wear at him.

Since nothing had ever been said, nothing took place ... or that was the popular view of the society in which Robert lived. And yet there was the fact—the putative fact—of the child, about which nothing had ever been said, either. Robert had been paying for the child all these years. He did not object, of course, because to pay was his duty. But he was also conscious that he had never seen the child, did not know its name, did not even know whether the child or its mother were still alive—other than the definitive fact that his checks were being cashed. And the incomprehensible scribble endorsing them across the back *might*, when viewed from certain angles, be read as "Margot Dobray."

9. LETTER FROM PARIS

DEAR DAD—

I have been in this city a week, and it's taken me this long to figure out what is wrong around here: the French are scared. You can feel it in the cafés and on the Metro, like a harmonic hanging in the air after a heavy chord has died away. You sense it sometimes when a waiter drops a tray of dishes, and everyone laughs. Or when two men are arguing in the street, come to the point of blows, then stop and clap each other on the shoulder. The little differences melt away before something bigger but still unspoken.

The unspoken thing, of course, is the Germans. There are reports of violence in Berlin, of marches and protests that get out of hand and end up as riots. The English thought it was the doing of "that man Hitler," but the French just see it as the "German disease" ready to break out again. Maybe they're not wrong, either. Sixty years ago the Germans marched down the Champs Elysées, and twenty years ago you could hear the guns of the front just by stepping out of any door in Paris. If there's a war, the French know they are in its path.

This is not just my own opinion, you understand. I have made a friend of a man who calls himself "a traveler from the East." Actually, in spite of his using that phrase, Niklaus Riesenberg and his wife Alma are Jews from Poland. Niklaus is a professor of economics from the University of Cracow, and Alma is a tutor in languages and teaches the violin. Their status is apparently that of displaced persons. Niklaus says Poland stands in the way of the Germans, too, when they eventually go after the Soviet Union. And I don't think *les Boches* will be gentlemanly in passing through, because of Poland's tolerance for the Jews.

I met the Riesenbergs after an unfortunate incident as soon as I arrived here. I had eaten supper at a bistro in the Montmartre District and, I blush to say, may have had one too many of the licorice-flavored liqueurs that are served as a *digestif*. As I was going down a long flight of steps, on the way back to my hotel room, two young Frenchmen stopped me to ask the time. Before I could respond, one took my arm and the other struck me on the side of the head. They knocked me down several of the steps, where I fetched up against the handrail. They took my wallet with all my ready money and fled into a side alley.

First let me say that I am all right—just a few scrapes and bruises. And the robbers did me no actual harm as, at your suggestion, I keep my passport, train tickets, and the largest portion of my capital pinned inside my underwear. The men did not think to take the watch you gave me upon graduation. So I was more chagrined than injured.

Anyway, as I lay there deciding whether it was time to move yet, Niklaus came down the steps. There was no use in a hue and cry, but he helped me up, felt over my head, offered me his handkerchief for the raw patch on my chin, and led me to inventory my possessions. Then, as I was about to go on my way, he insisted on taking me home to his apartment, which was nearby. There Alma tut-tutted over me and fed me black tea with milk and shortbread cookies that were folded into a triangle shape and filled with apricot jam. She called these pastries "Hammond's ears"—but never explained who Hammond was or why anybody wanted to cut his ears off.

Niklaus then showed me his library of history books and yearly economic summaries for most of Europe over the past twenty years. He is compiling a manuscript on the German economic reforms as they relate to increasing military production. Professor Riesenberg's point seems to be that National Socialism isn't really socialism at all but a form of state-supported capitalism. He also maintains that it's a conspiracy to hide Germany's preparations for the next war under innocuous-seeming domestic expenditures. I don't understand all the details, but what he says makes sense to me.

Since that night, I've spent a lot more time with the Riesenbergs. We toured the Louvre together, or at least a couple of rooms one afternoon, with Alma explaining the paintings and Niklaus providing historical footnotes on the people portrayed and their times. A city like this is so much more enjoyable when you have someone who knows what to look for.

The Riesenbergs are worried about the coming war. They left Poland because Niklaus predicted an eventual Nazi onslaught, but now France seems no more secure. Maybe England will be safe, but he says the Pas de Calais will give the Germans a good jumping off place for an amphibious invasion of Britain. Only America is safe, he says, but it is not always possible to pass immigration, especially when you're a native Pole starting the journey from a foreign country like France.

Maybe you know somebody in the State Department, Dad. If you would put in a good word for the Riesenbergs, I'm sure the government would let them in.

Your loving son,
William.

10. Between Sisters

On a Sunday afternoon Libby placed her monthly long-distance call to her sister in New York. This time—rather than make it a family affair, with Robert and the children waiting by her chair, ready to take the receiver and give their greetings—she chose a time when they were outside in the yard. And she kept her voice down.

"Eunice?" she said, as soon as the other end was picked up.

"No, it's Teddy," came the familiar, deep male voice. "Is this Libby?"

"Yes, Teddy. I need to talk to Eunice right away. Is she there?"

"Is there trouble?" he asked, concerned.

"No, just … I need to talk to her."

"I'll get her." There was a *clunk!* as he put the phone down. And a rattle as someone picked it up again. "Hello?"

"Eunice, it's Libby. Can you talk privately?"

"What's all the mystery, Sis?"

"I have something for your ears alone."

Libby heard a rustle as Eunice put her hand over the mouthpiece, although she could still hear: "Teddy Bear, this is private." Then the hand came off.

"What's going on?" Eunice said brightly. "Has Robert been cheating on you?"

"Oh, Lord no!" Libby laughed, then sobered. "It's about Aunt Lydia."

There was an intake of breath on the other end. "Is she any better?"

"Not really. Doctor Guillaume tries to sound encouraging but … she probably won't make it through the summer."

"That's too bad," Eunice said sadly, "though I guess it's to be expected."

Libby waited a moment, then went on. "I made her agree to give you and Teddy the property in town. It took some doing, but she finally allowed the lawyer to put it in her will, and she's signed it."

"Oh?" A pause. "Oh!" Another pause. "But what would we do with five acres out in the middle of Pennsylvania?"

"Exactly," Libby said. "So, when you receive title, you know what to do?"

"Certainly."

"But don't tell anyone."

"Especially Aunt Lydia?" Eunice suggested.

"You understand perfectly."

11. Setting the Bear Loose

DURING THE SECOND week in July, two of the local rangers with the Pennsylvania Game Commission, Jim Gresham and Harry Dillard, invited Robert on an expedition to release a large black bear they had trapped up near Ulysses. They were taking it down into the Black Forest region, where it would be less of a nuisance. So, on a Saturday morning before sunrise, Robert packed up his movie camera, put on high-top boots and an old field jacket, and met the two men at the driveway entrance to Gresham's acreage, half a mile outside Roulette. They already had the trap loaded on the back of the official PGC truck and were waiting with the engine idling.

The trap was a great box, built of heavy balks of four-by-four timber painted dark green, with a vertical sliding door at one end. There was a rope-and-pulley mechanism folded down over the top, and that obviously connected to a trigger plate somewhere inside. In the half-light, Robert peered in through the gaps in the side. He told himself he was trying to see the trigger, but actually he was looking for the bear.

Dillard got out of the truck cab and came back to help him.

"You can ride up front, you know," Dillard said.

"Is he in there?" Robert asked. "Or she?"

"Was last night. Still got a bellyful of mutton to sleep off."

"You fed the bear, did you?"

"That was the bait. Didn't have any reason to take it out."

Robert nodded at that. You'd need a very good reason to go in and take anything so juicy as a sheep carcass out of that box with the bear still inside.

They squeezed into the cab with Robert's equipment and started east on Route 6. About twenty miles out of town, they turned off on a secondary road that, as it climbed into the mountains, went from tar macadam to gravel. The truck's tires kicked up a cloud of dust in the rear-view mirror. In another dozen miles they were well beyond the limits of private property and rural delivery mailboxes. And then there was nothing but trees: dense, brooding forest with a visibility of less than 50 feet on either side of the road. Soon the branches seemed to join overhead and block out the glow in the sky from the rising sun.

"You have a place in mind?" Dillard asked Gresham.

"Meadow up here a couple of miles," Gresham said.

And that, Robert reflected, was the sum of conversation in the cab since the expedition had started. The two rangers might have asked him about his camera and what he planned to do with the movies he was making. In that case, he would have explained his latest project, which was to film the everyday events in Sylvan County. He wanted to make a record of life in this place and time in all its simple richness. He didn't know what he was going to do with the films—perhaps send them to the historical society. But he sensed they would have value one day.

However, since the men did not ask, Robert did not offer an explanation.

About when Gresham had predicted, he turned the truck off onto a track between the trees. After a hundred yards of bumping and bouncing over tree roots, it opened out into a grassy saddleback meadow with a stream running across its middle. Gresham pulled the truck through a turn of one hundred and eighty degrees, so that it was facing back toward the entry point. He parked at the meadow's highest elevation and set the brake.

The two rangers got out on the driver's side, and Robert got out on the other.

"You need a hand?" he asked.

"Naw, we got it," Dillard said.

They fed a pair of ash poles into loops on either end of the trap and, working from the sides of the truck, slipped the box off the back and lowered it to the ground. The sliding door faced the deep part of the meadow, the stream, and the distant tree line.

"You probably want to set up on the bed," Gresham told Robert.

"Good idea. Better view up there," he replied.

"And out of the bear's way."

Robert laughed at that. He unfolded his tripod and set its points into the scarred planks of the truckbed. He took the camera out of its case, made sure the spring mechanism was fully wound, and screwed the case onto the tripod head. He had already loaded it with film. He took off the lens cap, made a reading with his light meter, and adjusted the settings on the camera. While he fiddled, the rangers waited patiently beside the trap.

"Do you have to prepare anything?" Robert asked.

"Yeah, wake up the bear," said Gresham, whacking the side of the box with the end of his pole. In response he got a low, throaty growl.

Dillard went around to the truck cab, got in, and closed the door.

Gresham handed Robert a rope attached to the pulley on the trap.

"When you're ready, just pull on that."

"Aren't you going to release the bear?"

"You'll do fine," Gresham said, retreating to the cab as well.

Robert found that the wooden box was shaking from side to side: the bear was fully awake and aroused. He made one final check of his equipment, sighted the camera along the bear's probable path from the trap to the tree line, and started it rolling. Then he stood aside and pulled on the rope.

The door in the end swung up and flapped back on top of the trap. Before it could bounce, a black streak with a blur of legs launched itself across the lush grass and headed downhill toward the stream.

Robert stepped back to his camera, crouched slightly, and looked through the view finder. The bear was well within frame. Normally, Robert avoided panning his shots, preferring instead to set up a view and let the action happen within it. But now he had his hand on the camera, ready to shift the view in case the bear swerved.

The humping black rump was moving rapidly, heading straight away from the truck. Robert wondered what kind of action he would get when the bear came to the stream: would it make a spectacular leap across, or splash through, or maybe stop to take a drink?

The bear did none of these things. As it came up to the bank, it turned, moving sideways along the stream for a half-dozen steps, then it turned again, back toward the truck. Robert had the impression the bear was remembering it had forgotten something—maybe the rest of that sheep, still in the trap.

He shifted the camera's alignment to keep the bear centered in the frame. Instead of growing smaller and less defined, now the black shape was growing rapidly in the view finder. Robert could make out the tawny hair around the muzzle, then the glint of teeth in its open mouth, the sparkle of its beady eyes. The bear dodged around the trap and headed for the rear of the truck.

Robert was a brave man but not a foolish one. He abandoned the camera, scooted backwards the length of the truckbed, and hitched his posterior up on the roof of the cab. The bear crashed into the edge of the bed, making the camera wobble violently on its tripod. With no one handy to eat, the bear turned and headed off downhill again.

From his perch on the cab, Robert eyeballed the alignment of camera and bear: it was close enough for his purposes. He watched from up there as the animal took the bank of the stream in stride, splashed through, and made a straight line for the far trees. In five seconds, it was gone.

Robert got down and went to stop the camera.

Muffled laughter came to him from the truck's cab. Then the doors opened on either side.

"We thought you were dinner," Gresham said.

"Or breakfast, as might be," Dillard added.

"Never thought I'd see a town man move so fast."

"Why didn't you warn me he would turn?" Robert asked evenly.

"They don't, generally, unless they get good and riled," Gresham said.

"Maybe he was camera-shy," Dillard said, still giggling.

Robert had to laugh along with them. And anyway, he'd taken some superb footage. Even if the camera was making its own pictures, there at the end, the sight of that bear charging up at the camera would excite—no, terrify—his audiences for years to come.

12. QUIET PASSING

LIBBY WATCHED BY her aunt's bedside in the middle of a still August night. The reading lamp on the nightstand glowed faintly, its normal sixty-watt bulb replaced by one of twenty-five watts, and then the metal lampshade was pushed down almost to the tabletop, so that only a crack of light escaped into the room. Libby and the duty nurse had arranged this feeble glow so that they could take readings from the gauge on the oxygen cylinder and know when to change it.

As Dr. Guillaume had predicted, the prolonged inactivity, lying flat on her back for going on two months now, had caused Lydia's lungs to fill with fluid, and pneumonia set in. He had rigged a tent of faintly yellowed plastic—now shining redly in the light from the night lamp—over her head and tucked it beneath the pillows and covers. The oxygen flowing into this protected space enriched her breathing and, so far as Libby could see, was the only thing keeping her alive.

For three days Libby and the nurse had fed Lydia through a zippered opening in the tent, and had to rearrange it every time they tended to her bodily functions. Through it all, Lydia complained of strangling on the air inside the tent, of the "smell" of the oxygen—which she compared to raw gin—and of the hissing noise made by the hose near her left ear.

And then, two days ago, the complaints had stopped when Lydia fell asleep in the middle of the afternoon, snoring with a great and terrible snuffling sound—almost like a pig going after its favorite food, Libby thought—and did not wake up for dinner.

For the past thirty-six hours, last night and this, Libby had sat in an armchair beside the tent, checked the valves, felt her aunt's wrist for a pulse as the doctor had showed her, and listened. She listened for the snores as they diminished steadily, first to occasional snags in the back of her throat, then to childlike whimpers, and finally to a deep, gurgling rumble inside her chest. Libby listened for the hiss of the oxygen as it gradually came to

215

dominate every other sound in the room, including the tick-tock of the clock on the mantelpiece.

She listened, and then she dozed. But even as she dozed, one ear stayed alert to monitor the balance between the breathing and the hissing.

Finally, just after the clock chimed twice, the oxygen was the only sound left.

Libby opened her eyes and raised her head. She listened once more. Nothing but the drawn-out hiss from the hose. She reached in under the bedclothes and found Lydia's wrist. It was warm but still. Libby's fingertips probed among the old bones and brittle tendons under the paper-dry skin, but she could detect no sign of life.

She unzipped the window in the tent and put her head through. (It did smell faintly of gin!) She laid her cheek next to Lydia's half-opened mouth, alert for any hint of wind or moisture or movement, but there was nothing.

Libby pulled her head back and left the window unzipped. She straightened, turned to the oxygen tank, and closed the valve. She decided not to wake the nurse, who had borne the bulk of the chores during the day and needed her sleep. It never occurred to Libby to call Dr. Guillaume. And there would be time, in the morning, to call Adolphus Shute, the undertaker.

None of this was unexpected.

Except perhaps by Lydia herself.

13. Letter from Rome

Dear Dad—

This is the most beautiful city in the world.

There's nothing I could add to that statement.

Or a thousand things, bit by bit, over a lifetime.

It's not a complete city, a jewel, like Paris or London. In fact, the sense you get just from walking around Rome is of an incredible ruin, and shabbiness, with the dust of ages kicking up under your feet. If the Emperor Augustus claimed to have found this city made of brick and clothed it in marble, then by now it's back to the brick, and fairly well-worn bricks at that. The only gleaming white structure I have seen so far is the memorial to Victor Immanuel, and that was started in the last century but only completed three years ago. Artistically, it is not the best thing in Rome.

The Forum, the real Rome, the original from the time of the Caesars, is all these broken columns and halves of buildings, located about ten feet below the current street level. They mostly show the brick foundation walls from which centuries of later builders (and vandals) have stripped off the emperor's marble facing. The place is a jumble of temples, crowded façade to buttress, with paths between them that are practically haunted at night. But the Forum is so real you can almost hear the legions marching through in triumph. The original Senate house is still intact—a small, square building with a steep gabled roof and a tall front door of latticed iron—but I didn't manage to get the inside.

The best thing I've seen in Rome is the Pantheon, built by the emperor's friend Marcus Agrippa, over on the western side of the city near the Piazza Navono. It has been in continuous use as a church or temple since the second century A.D. Imagine that! You can walk over the same stone threshold and across the same marble floor that senators and generals, slaves and courtesans, Goths and Visigoths have walked on. The building is one huge dome, shaped like the inside of an egg, with the square indents from the egg carton imprinted against the inner surface. That's because the dome is all concrete (a Roman invention) and needs the indents to give it strength (I think). At the very top is just an open hole that lets in sunlight, rain, and snow—if they have snow here. It's the most impressive space I've ever stood in.

Well, after Saint Peter's, I guess. That church does not feel ancient, like the Pantheon, but is very well kept: polished marble, gilded brass, mosaic inlays, stained glass windows, and fresh flowers every day. Each pope has his tomb in a patch of wall space somewhere on the ground floor, with life-sized angels and lions draping themselves beside his catafalque. And there's a frieze that goes all the way around the inside of the building, up near the ceiling, that has practically the whole Bible, in Latin, engraved in golden letters three feet tall. Amazing!

I will need another whole letter to describe the things in the Vatican museum.

The Roman people seem very nice and friendly, greeting me and everyone else with *Buongiorno!* and *Ciao!* But I am not so sure of the government here—or the military-style groups that run around in the government's name. At first I thought they were some kind of older Boy Scouts, except with black shirts and side arms and their own marching songs. But not now.

First, let me say that Gypsies are indeed a problem in Rome. You don't see the men so much, during the day, but the women stand outside the restaurants and the churches, thrust their babies at you, and beg in a language that is not Italian. Underneath the bundle of her little *bambino*—which, like as not, is just a doll fixed to a wooden arm strapped against the woman's side—her hand is grasping for your watch and wallet. The children don't bother with such gimmicks but just gather around you, singing and dancing, and try to strip you. The guards warned me about them at the train station.

Between the Fascists and the Gypsies there is open war. I was walking on the Via Imperiale when a group of the Black Shirts came upon a man selling trinkets on the sidewalk. They must have known he was a Gypsy by his clothing—the dark jacket that is never quite the right cut, the brightly striped shirt, the floppy hat, the neckerchief—and began harassing him. First they fingered his goods, as if they wanted to buy. Then they started playing catch with the better pieces, waiting for him to protest. And when he did, in a flash, they overturned his tray, stamped on his things, and threw him into the street.

In Paris, even in Berlin, it might have stopped there. But these Black Shirts had their blood up. They kicked the man into the gutter while the traffic went by and nobody stopped to lift a hand. They took turns stomping the Gypsy until he went entirely limp. One of them, the leader, looked around at the others, as if asking what to do next. They shrugged in return. He drew his gun and shot the man in the head. The Black Shirts laughed as if this were the punch line to a joke, then linked their arms and went off singing.

I could only watch, horrified, but no one else even seemed to notice.

They left the man lying there, like a piece of garbage, as if nothing had happened. It was pure murder, and no one did anything about it. I thought of reporting the matter to the Carabiniere, the police, as an eye witness. But I was too far away, the other side of the wide street—a boulevard really, busy with traffic—and I wouldn't be able to identify any of the killers. So I was powerless, too.

This is a beautiful city, but I fear it hides some ugly things.

I do not like it so well today as I did yesterday.

Your loving son,

William.

14. RUBY'S CAFÉ

RIGHT AFTER LYDIA Wheelock's funeral, the regulars all came into the café at once. Ruby Pearson had announced the day before that she would serve a special pork chop and fried apple dinner starting at two o'clock, free to all the town's mourners. So McKee the conductor, Mayor Dufour, Sheriff Cobb, Burke the county clerk, Clarence from the feed store, and all the others filed in wearing their best black suits—or at least something nice in a sober dark color—and hung their jackets on the coat rack. It was a sweltering day, and one of the women had actually fainted from the heat during the service.

"Where's the reverend?" asked McKee, looking around as they sat down.

"He obviously felt it inappropriate to feast with his parishioners after such a solemn occasion," said Walter Dufour.

No one commented on the fact that Robert and Libby Wheelock were also absent. They had stood for Lydia at her graveside and now, as family, were presumed to be in polite seclusion, no matter that everyone in town knew the real nature of their relations with the deceased.

"Nice of Ruby to do this," said Cobb. "Assuring Lydia of a crowd to give her a good sendoff."

"Not that Lydia needed it," Dufour put in hastily.

"Not at all," McKee agreed, a bit too solemnly.

"That's not what I meant, of course," said the sheriff.

"Mrs. Wheelock has been a benefactress to this town," Walt Dufour said handsomely. "The way she's run the railroad and the power company, all without a thought for her own profit, has kept this town a going concern."

"Hear, hear," from around the room.

"Of course," said Burke, "not that she had much choice, according to the terms of the old Judge's will." Burke was in a position to know such things.

"Choice or not," Dufour said, "she always thought of the town first."

"Yes, indeed," from around the room.

Ruby brought out platters with layered stacks of brown chops and heaps of red-and-yellow apple pieces smelling of cinnamon and butter. Then there were bowls of mashed potatoes and a tureen of pan gravy. Plates were already on the tables, as were brown bottles of beer and pots of steaming coffee.

"I wonder what will happen to the property now," said McKee.

"You mean the land under the house?" asked Burke.

"She won't leave it to Robert," said McKee.

"Not in a million years," said Cobb.

"I suppose James Harris knows," said Burke. "He drew up her will."

"Did he file a copy at the courthouse?" McKee asked.

"Even if he did," said Burke, "it's certainly not my business to know the contents—or talk about them."

"Just asking," the conductor said.

"Perhaps she left the property to the town," Dufour mused. "It would make a wonderful city park, being so central …"

"And do what with house?" Burke asked. "You know it's not hers to give."

"She has to leave it all to Robert, doesn't she?" asked Clarence. "That's the law."

"No law to say how you dispose of your own goods," Burke declared.

"Then she could leave it to Libby, her niece," said Clarence.

"Which would be the same as leaving it to Robert."

"Oh … that's true, too," Clarence admitted.

"Lydia will find some way to get the last laugh," Cobb said.

"We won't know until the will is read," Dufour said.

"If it's our business, even then," from Burke.

A silence descended while knives and forks worried the chop bones down to the last scraps of meat.

"Who will succeed Judge LeConte?" Dufour asked the room at large.

"Are you sure he's even going to retire?" the sheriff asked.

"He said as how he's had enough of the job," said Burke. "Time to go fishing."

"Then it's going to be Wheelock," Clarence predicted.

"Or Jim Harris," said Nathan Birdsall. "He's a good man, too."

"Wheelock's been here longer. And his daddy was judge long before LeConte."

"Well, don't we all get to vote?" Birdsall asked.

"Sure," said Clarence, "for whoever they decide will run. Or, you can vote for the stooge they run that they know you won't want anyway."

"And who is 'they,' exactly?" Dufour asked.

"The party, the powers that be, *they*," said Clarence.

"I don't remember any *they* when I ran for mayor. I put my name before the County Commission—which as I remember included Harold here, and Judge LeConte, Reverend Stevens, and a few other familiar faces. You all put me on the ballot, along with that fellow from Ulysses. Nothing underhanded there, as he had a business in town and was well liked. Election came, and I won."

"Yeah, we always wondered about that, Walt," the sheriff observed.

"We couldn't find *anyone* to admit they voted for you," Birdsall said.

"Must have been a fluke of nature, don't you think?" laughed Cobb.

"Or those other things—sunspots!"

"Yeah, sunspots!"

"They'll do that, every time."

15. LYDIA'S WILL

TWO WEEKS AFTER the funeral, the family gathered in the law offices of James Harris, Esq., for the reading of Lydia's will.

As he held the chair for Libby in front of the attorney's scrolled walnut desk, Robert looked around the room. This was where Harris, his chief adversary in a town as small as Roulette, had plotted most of Robert's professional setbacks over the past few years, although Harris sometimes also managed to maneuver himself onto tricky legal ground that eventually offered Robert a victory. From outward appearances, Harris had the more prosperous practice. Instead of the piles of law books and papers on every flat surface, as in Robert's own office, here there was order. The bookshelves inside their glass-front cabinets had not a volume out of place. The side tables held only items of convenience to visitors and clients: a Tiffany-shaded lamp, a crystal ash tray, an expensive cigarette lighter, all arranged with artistic casualness. And Harris maintained two secretaries and a clerk to take orders and bring coffee. It was all very handsome.

But Robert had long felt that, when it came to the law, Harris just wasn't as smart as he appeared. He wasn't a bad attorney, no. In fact, he could be fairly clever. But sometimes his arguments were too clever, too educated, too involved. He could leave a jury of the local farmers and tradesman staring with open-mouthed wonder. However, admiration for a learned argument and confidence that it would lead them to the truth were two different things. A likable enough man to chat with or have a drink with, Harris lacked the insight, the feel for humanity, that made the law a working proposition.

As she sat in the chair Robert held for her, Libby turned her head to thank him with a nod but did not look directly at him. She had been more distant this morning than usual. Indeed, now that Robert thought of it, she had been acting strangely ever since Lydia's death … and for some weeks before that. She would respond to his overtures with monosyllables, and she would not meet his eyes. Of course, the current situation—a serious illness

223

in the family, death, and the reading of a will—all called for gravity and subdued reflection. But Robert and Libby had been through this in the past and not lost contact with each other. Now, it appeared, Libby had closed her heart to him.

The other thing that was strange, though less so than his wife's recent coolness, was the sudden appearance of her sister Eunice and husband Teddy. They had come hundreds of miles from New York City, not for Lydia's funeral, but for the reading of her will. Robert supposed they had no more love for Aunt Lydia than anyone else in the immediate family, and no more reason to be remembered in her will than he and Libby had themselves. So why were they there?

This morning, when Robert had asked his wife that question, though not in such bald terms, she had replied: "I asked her to come."

"But why, particularly?" Robert pressed.

"Oh, for emotional support."

"That's really …" He was about to say "a long way to come for the sake of sentiment." But Robert realized it would make him sound hard and unfeeling. Besides, Eunice could have come alone, without dragging Teddy away from his banking business in the middle of the week.

"Oh!" he said when another interpretation occurred to him: Eunice and Teddy must have come to supply the support that Libby did not feel Robert was giving. With her aunt—his own stepmother, whom Libby had served and cared for so long—now gone, she was turning to her sister and brother-in-law for the comfort that she might have found in her husband.

That thought made him deeply sad, and so he had not pursued the topic.

Now Eunice and Teddy sat on Libby's other side. Their greetings to Robert had been strained, their faces stiff, their postures awkward in the soft chairs that James Harris made available to his guests. Clearly, they felt disapproving of the whole situation, too.

Robert's gloom deepened.

"Shall we begin?" Harris asked with a patent smile.

Libby and her family nodded. Robert waited passively.

Harris opened the document from his files and read out: " 'I, Lydia Brackett Wheelock, being of sound mind, do hereby declare this to be my true intent. …' "

The attorney droned through the preamble, a version of the same language Robert had written a hundred times over the years for various members of the community. In fact, Lydia's will was one of the few that Robert had not handled, as Harris was a newcomer to the town and really more interested in criminal law—what there was of it in the county—than in estates, contracts, and other mundane concerns. But Robert understood why Lydia had gone to someone else: the enmity against her stepson was deep and unrelenting.

It did not matter. Robert knew that the businesses his father had established and left to her twenty years ago were still being run under the trusts incorporated by the old will, providing a only modest living for Lydia. She owned nothing of value there, and so could not convey her interest. The profits from the railroad and the electric company reverted to each business upon her death.

As he read from her will, Harris was communicating this much, although in far grander language.

The only property she possessed was the land under her house—his house, actually—and Robert knew in his heart that she had found some way to deny it to him. If she could have sunk the acres in the ocean, or burned them up in a fire, she would have done so to spite him. But since the ground itself cannot disintegrate, there only remained the interesting issue of what means Lydia had found to give it away or destroy its inherent value. Not that Robert cared, except as an academic question in law.

" '… this property, all five and one-fifth acres,' " Harris continued reading, " 'with all improvements and appurtenances, I leave to my niece, Eunice Taylor née Brackett, who is my blood relative.' "

Of course! That explained Eunice and Teddy's presence to-day. They must have known Lydia was going to do this. Libby must have known and told them so. Robert did wonder what Harris had meant when he wrote "appurtenances" into the will. The water and electrical connections, perhaps? The septic tank? Certainly he would have known that the house itself was encumbered by Robert's prior claim under the old will. What exactly was Harris thinking? What was Lydia planning?

Did they believe—had Lydia believed—that she could pass on her malice to the next generation? Was she leaving Eunice the property in order to make Robert fight for the house? And was that word, "appurtenances," thrown in to cloud the legal title and so encourage Eunice to continue the game?

Well, it would not work. Robert did not want the great house his father had built. Not now. He and Libby had their own home, small but comfortable, at the end of the lane. It was twenty years since Robert had set foot in the house across the park, and he did not miss the place. Eunice and Teddy could keep it and live there, or sell it for a dovecote, for all he cared.

And yet, when Lydia's illness took its final turn for the worse, Robert discovered that he had been hoping, subconsciously, that she might have relented. That making him suffer in exile all these years might have been enough, and she could finally leave the property to him. It was just a flicker of a thought, barely brighter than a candle at the edge of his mind, and he had put no trust in it—with good reason, it turned out.

"I have the deed to the property here," Harris was saying. He held up a sheaf of yellowed legal onionskin with the imprint and seal of the Clerk of Records of Sylvan County, signed by Malcolm Hurlbert's predecessor when William Henry Wheelock had acquired the land in town. Harris reached across the desk and offered it to Eunice, who was sitting next to Libby.

"You will want to have the transfer notarized," he said. "My secretary can take care of that for you."

"That won't be necessary," Eunice said. She turned and gave the deed to Libby. Robert noticed that his wife's hands were already reaching out for it. "This is yours, Sis," Eunice said with a smile. "I relinquish all claims."

Robert expected Teddy to object, but his brother-in-law was smiling as well. Teddy even winked at him.

Libby turned and passed the papers to Robert. Her face was radiant.

"What … what does this mean?" he asked, amazed.

"The house is yours, dear. It has always been yours."

Then she leaned forward and kissed him on the lips.

16. THE JUDGE

AFTER TWO WEEKS of negotiations, and with just three days to the start of trial in the civil case of *Jensen v. Roulette Feed & Grain*—over a matter of thirteen bags of millet seed found to be in rust at some indeterminate time after delivery, the facts being unclear as to the exact onset, progression, and eventual discovery of the blight itself—the plaintiff, represented by James Harris, Esq., and the defendant, represented by Robert Wheelock, Esq., came to terms in the chambers of Judge Lawrence LeConte. With a bit of prompting from the judge, the plaintiff reluctantly agreed to accept return of one-half the seed's purchase cost, which the defendant reluctantly agreed to remit.

With that settled, and because everyone was in such an agreeable mood, LeConte decided it was time to broach a matter of his own with the county's two most prominent attorneys.

"Gentlemen, if you wouldn't mind staying behind a moment? Please?" he said, putting a hand on either man's arm as their clients, Hobart Jensen and Clarence Jaspers, preceded them through the door.

"Of course, Your Honor," said Wheelock.

"Certainly, Larry," said Harris.

"Please do sit down."

The two men naturally took the seats they had just vacated, at opposite ends of the judge's huge desk. LeConte sat between them and rested his hands on the sheet of tempered glass that covered the inlaid marquetry of the desktop. This gaudy thing was not his own furniture, of course, but a piece installed when the new sandstone and slate-tiled courthouse was built, back in '34. The county bought the desk to match the paneling in the judge's chambers, in the courtroom, and throughout the whole building: dark oak trimmed with red mahogany fillets and finished to a glaze with thick coats of lacquer. This decoration was a souvenir of the natural-gas money that had kept the town whole and growing during the darkest days of the Depression while the rest of the country fell apart.

228

LeConte rubbed at a smear on the glass surface, trying to decide how to begin.

"I've been on the bench here in Roulette twelve years," he said at last.

"Good years, too, I should hope, Larry," Harris said.

Wheelock nodded also but said nothing.

"Good years," LeConte agreed. "Well, most of them."

A judge saw human nature at its most fragile. LeConte remembered one hard winter when the game wardens brought in a—well, "cartel" was too grand a word—of poachers to be tried for selling wholesale venison out of season. And he had carried on a perennial battle with private distillers of moonshine, both before and after the repeal of Prohibition. Then there was that string of robberies, out at the west end of town, that had ended in a manslaughter trial. Ole Granger—driven by desperation, no doubt, with a family of ten to feed on a handyman's wages after the tannery closed down—had turned to breaking and entering, picked an occupied house, and got himself shot in the process. Just plain folly. There were no criminal masterminds, LeConte reflected, just people pushed to the edge.

"Was there something you wanted to tell us?" Wheelock prompted gently.

"Do I go away like that in the courtroom?" LeConte asked wonderingly.

"No more than anyone else, I suppose," Wheelock answered with a smile.

"Just as well, then, that I've decided to retire. Twelve years is long enough."

"It's been a pleasure appearing before you," Wheelock said.

"Yes, we'll miss you, Larry," Harris said.

LeConte nodded at the sentiment. "That only leaves the question of who will succeed me," he said. "As the two most capable attorneys in the county, one or the other of you should put yourself forward for the bench."

Wheelock and Harris exchanged wary glances.

"Surely you've thought of it," LeConte prompted.

"Well, of course," Harris responded quickly.

"Become the judge ..." Wheelock said slowly.

"You'd be following in your father's footsteps."

"I know," Wheelock replied. "It's a daunting thought."

"You've done a lot of good for the community, Robert," the other lawyer said generously. "You arranged to have this courthouse built when it meant jobs to people in the trades. And you worked all those years to bring in the flood control. Everyone in the county knows and respects you."

"You've quite a reputation yourself," Wheelock said chivalrously.

LeConte laughed out loud. "So we can count on you, Robert?"

"If it's the right thing, then yes. I'll run for election, come the fall."

"And if you don't mind," said Harris, "I'll give you a run for your money."

"Ah, a brawl!" LeConte said. "The people of Roulette will love it!"

"Well," Wheelock said, "let's try not to make this thing *too* exciting."

"Perhaps we should establish some guidelines," the judge said. "Just among gentlemen?"

"Fine by me," Harris replied. "Wheelock's the one with the deep pockets."

"We could agree on a spending limit for our campaigns," Wheelock agreed. "How about two thousand dollars for signs, printed literature, and entertainments at any event?"

"How about one thousand?" the other countered.

"Done," Wheelock replied. "But no limit on volunteer canvassing."

"Done," Harris agreed, although with somewhat less enthusiasm.

"No rallies or parades until two weeks before the election."

"May we even announce ourselves?" Harris asked.

"Just the usual notice of filing in the newspaper."

"And how will the cost of that be borne?"

"We'll file jointly and split the fee."

"So we're agreed," said Harris.

"Then come out swinging," LeConte said. "And may the best man win."

17. Moving Day

During the first week of September, on her first day as mistress of the house across the park, Libby made a tour of inspection before the men brought in the furniture—what little there was of it—from the house at the end of the lane. The men were from the railroad, whose general manager had offered their assistance in the middle of the day, between the morning run up from Emporium and the afternoon run back down. Robert, of course, was busy in his law office, seeing clients or preparing for a case or arranging some business of his own. So instead of her husband, she had the conductor, McKee, to accompany her through the rooms of the great house and take notes on where to put her things.

"And what is this room supposed to be, ma'am?" he asked, from the doorway into the conservatory.

Libby, standing in the dining room, turned to look through the thickly smudged glass of the interior windows. "It's a hot house of sorts, for flowers and tropical plants."

"Flowers. I see," McKee said doubtfully.

The room was still full of summer furniture. The green wicker chairs and tables had never made it out this year, because of Lydia's illness. The black wooden frames that would normally enclose the back porch with wire screens now leaned, dust- and fly-spotted, against the brickwork of the conservatory's west wall. And a striped canvas bundle along the outer wall under the exterior windows held the rolled awnings. When Libby put her head into the room she smelled mildew for certain and mice for a maybe.

"We'll air it all out later," she said.

"Yes, ma'am."

Libby returned her attention to the dining room itself. The long, sectioned table and chairs to seat sixteen were in good condition. If Robert were to become the judge, she would be expected to do more entertaining. And even if he failed to be elected, a dinner party now and then for the town notables would certainly help his law practice.

The one piece that did not fit in this room, literally, was the sideboard. While the rest of the dining furniture was light maple with a close-grained pattern, this piece was made from slabs of dark walnut. Where the table and chairs were a curved and tapering French provincial, this was blocky Italianate, its panels edged with rosettes and scallops.

Worse, the wall space where the sideboard was positioned, between the narrow door into the pantry and the archway into the front hall, was barely long enough for it. But when workmen installed the new gas furnace six years ago, they had cut the hole for a forced-air duct in the floor right against the wainscoting of this wall. To accommodate the awkward placement, they had simply shoved the sideboard to the left until it overlapped the pantry door by six inches. Libby would never have permitted such sloppiness herself, but then, her aunt had not asked her to supervise the furnace work. And Lydia, who never entertained anymore, apparently did not care that the dining room was rendered inconvenient—not to say unsightly—by the alteration.

Libby turned and surveyed the rest of the room. Just by eye, she could tell the sideboard would not fit across the north wall, because the fireplace was set aslant in that corner. The east wall had three deep windows that looked out into the porte-cochere: the sideboard was too tall and would block them if she put it there. And the middle of the south wall had the conservatory door in its center and the interior windows on either side.

"Do you want us to move that to another room?" McKee asked, pointing at the sideboard while she was still considering.

"You could," she said, temporizing. "But it really belongs in a dining room. Just not *this* dining room."

"Perhaps in the attic?" he suggested.

"Or I might sell it."

"It's a good piece," McKee said, running his hand along the flower garlands cut into the front panels. "Does Mr. Wheelock have any attachment to it, do you think?"

"Oh, Robert never notices such things. And, anyway he hasn't been in this house in twenty years. He'll never miss it." Libby had all but decided to sell the sideboard, preferably before Robert could see it and have an opinion of his own.

Then she and McKee went out into the hall and down to examine the front of the house with the parlor and library.

"I don't think we need any changes in here," Libby said, after they had taken a turn through the parlor. "Nothing Robert and I have is as good as this. You can put our furniture on the third floor, for the time being."

In the room opposite, McKee said, "This was the Judge's study."

"Yes, leave the furniture in here, too. It will give Robert someplace to meet people privately," Libby said, "away from his law office or the courthouse."

"Very appropriate."

Upstairs, she and McKee looked into the master bedroom, with its circular tower alcove. Lydia had occupied this room, at the end.

"You'll want us to put your bed here, I suppose," McKee said.

"Robert thought we would use his old apartment, up on the third floor."

"It's a long way to climb—up at night and back down in the morning."

"Well, yes. And this room has its own bath, too."

It occurred to her that Robert might feel awkward, sleeping in the room his father and stepmother had shared while he lived in the house. But Libby did not think he was that sentimental, or that superstitious. And the windows did have a nice view over the Judge's small orchard to the river.

"I think this will be very satisfactory."

"It's a lot of room," McKee said.

"We could have used it when the children were growing up."

"And now Master William is going off to college, isn't he?"

"Yes." She sighed. "So it's all this for just two people."

"For twenty years it was just the one," he observed.

"That couldn't be helped," Libby said sharply.

"No, ma'am," McKee said. "Not at all."

18. The Barn Raising

Ernst Bauer had emigrated from Germany as a boy with his father and mother in 1920, during the privations resulting from the Great War. The family prospered in the stony soil of the Pennsylvania mountains, raising potatoes on a cleared hillside that the father had picked up cheap because of the trees and stones. Young Ernst grew strong of back and thick of arm clearing the land with his father.

When he came of age, his father had arranged a loan through Robert Wheelock to buy the old Moody place, nine hundred acres north of town. Young Bauer was a sober and industrious farmer who made his expenses year after year, Depression or no. In this year of 1938 he had even expected to make a small profit on his potato crop, of which he was justly proud. And then, in early August, a lightning strike reduced his barn to charred planks and a roof beam plunging into the stone foundation like a handful of blackened jackstraws. The town folks said perhaps they didn't have lightning rods in Germany, or that Bauer had never thought to maintain his. When a neighbor asked him about it, the young farmer was said to look blankly back at the man. Likely the rod's insulating ball had cracked or its conductor had parted with the ground sometime over the years, the neighbor said, and that the device had failed in practice.

When Bauer came to Robert and asked his help in securing a loan to rebuild the barn, while quietly bemoaning the cost of building, Robert had suggested a barn raising to reduce the expense. Given the community's generally high regard for Bauer, he said, people were sure to come.

"What is this, please?" Bauer asked "The barn rises? How?"

"People raise it," Robert said. "Working together. Generally in just one day."

"I have not heard of such a thing." And he added with a smile, "Something else we do not have in Germany."

Robert arranged to put an ad in the paper. And, during the week that preceded the announced date in September, a few of Bauer's closest neighbors helped him pull out the blackened debris, patch the grout between the stonework, and clear the ground. The lumber yard in town delivered beams and planks precut to specifications that one of the neighbors drew up, working from a sketch he and Bauer had made and measured to scale, plus two barrels of nails and ten bales of red cedar shingles.

And so, on a foggy Saturday morning in mid-September, with the chill of autumn just beginning to set in, Robert put on a pair of dungaree overalls and gathered his woodworking tools. Libby was going with him, as was the custom, having baked two apple pies for the picnic supper. Almost as an afterthought, Robert packed his movie camera, several cans of film, and a tripod.

"Do you really want to take all that?" Libby asked.

"This will be an event for the town," he said. "Worth capturing."

"But won't you be busy, sawing and hammering along with everyone else?"

"Others will stop to rest. I'll stop to take a few pictures."

At the entrance to the farm Ernst Bauer, big of stature, with a flat face and sober eyes, his skin colored like old oak from the sun in his fields, directed parking of the cars and farm trucks around the perimeter of the yard and along the lane leading in from the road. "Willkommen, wilkommen," he greeted the men and directed them to the stone-lined hole that the foundation made, where the supplies were stacked. The women with their baskets he waved in the direction of trestle tables under the trees at the side of the house, where his wife Emily waited with hands folded in front of her starched white apron.

When everyone was gathered and waiting patiently, Bauer's grin faltered. "And … now … how do we begin?" he asked.

Reverend Stevens stepped forward. "With a blessing, of course."

While the men gathered removed their hats, and the women bowed their heads, the reverend spoke briefly, asked God to bless the barn, the farm, and the family and that everyone come through the day safely. The murmured "ah-men" from the crowd echoed off the back of the house.

The men who had earlier helped Bauer take measurements and prepare the stonework now directed laying out the footers along the ends and sides of the foundation. They sent teams to find, among the stacks of wood, framing pieces of the right size and length and carry them into position on the grass and in the dooryard, all according to their diagram. Rather than join in this scramble, Robert went to set up his camera, picking the best angle on the scene with the sun against his back. He was loaded and rolling as the first of the long yellow beams, flexing slightly between the shoulders of the men carrying them, were moved from stack to ground.

Once the main beams were laid out, checked, and squared up, other teams began fitting the corners and hammering the diagonally driven nails that would hold the wood at right angles. The work went on for an hour until, by about ten o'clock, they had the four walls of the barn, minus the plank exterior, lying flat on the ground, as if the new barn had simply fallen apart. So far it was all pickup work, where hands found things to do without any great need of coordination. And Robert caught it all in close detail.

But then came time to raise the back wall and an adjoining side. This took men to hold the footers in place, men to raise the frames to shoulder height, more men with poles to raise the frames to vertical, and still more to climb the uprights and nail the corners together. As all the neighbors—including Reverend Stevens and several of the stronger women—moved into position, Bauer looked to Robert behind his camera. "Will you come?" he called.

"Of course," Robert said. He had a fresh reel of film in the camera and decided to set it rolling and let it run out on the scene. Then he ran to take a pole.

By noon the four walls were up, and men were pulling the joists across to secure a footing for framing the roof. Then Bauer called for a break and lunch.

While everyone was eating, Jim Harris, who had quietly joined the work about midway through the morning, stood up and moved to the end of a trestle table.

"Friends," he began in a commanding voice. "Friends, I just want to say how much I admire what you're all doing here today. In hard times like these, we know that poor farmers such as Mr. Bauer here can't always afford the insurance to protect his barn and rebuild it when tragedy strikes. Some people might expect the government to step in and build the barn for him. But I'm gratified to see the local community step forward ..."

As he went on for some minutes in this vein, Bauer turned to Robert at his table. "Is this true? The government would rebuild my barn?"

"That's what some people want from Washington," Robert replied cautiously.

Bauer showed surprised at this. "Even through I'm not a citizen?"

"You're not?" Now Robert was surprised. "I thought you were naturalized."

"My father asked once, but the expense and paperwork were too much."

"Still, you'd like to be a citizen? No thoughts of returning to Germany?"

Bauer rolled his eyes. "These days? Of course not. My life is here."

"Then I'll see what we can do."

Bauer held his gaze and then nodded. "Is good."

Robert returned his attention to Jim Harris. The man had managed to bring the subject of community spirit around to listing the issues that were facing the county and why he was the best choice to take the bench after Larry LeConte. Robert tried to gauge how people were receiving this stump speech: most seemed to be concentrating on their fried chicken; some listened and seemed to agree.

Harris finally wound up his pitch and turned to Robert. "Wheelock? Would you like to say a few words?"

Robert stood up and wiped his lips with a napkin. "I'm glad everyone could come today. But I think we'd all better get back to work, don't you?"

19. The Sponsor

"I HEREBY DECLARE, on oath, that I absolutely and entirely renounce and abjure all allegiance and fidelity to any foreign prince, potentate, state, or sovereignty of whom or which I have heretofore been a subject or citizen; …"

For once Robert Wheelock was standing behind the railing in a courtroom. He watched with some pride as Ernst Bauer stood before a judge in the Federal court in Philadelphia, with right hand raised, and took the oath of citizenship.

"… that I will support and defend the Constitution and laws of the United States of America against all enemies, foreign and domestic; that I will bear true faith and allegiance to the same; …"

Robert had done the paperwork on Bauer's application and coached him through the studies that enabled him to pass the naturalization examination. Because he was a German national, Ernst had feared there might, in the current political climate, be some difficulty about his seeking citizenship. And so he glad of Robert's help.

"… that I will bear arms on behalf of the United States when required by law; that I will perform noncombatant service in the Armed Forces of the United States when required by the law; that I will perform work of national importance under civilian direction when required by the law; …"

Ernst was a good man and an asset to the community. He was also a simple man and plain spoken. Today, instead of his customary bib overalls, he was wearing a suit of rough gray tweed—the best he had—with a white shirt and a patterned tie. He took the proceedings very seriously.

Beside him stood his pretty young wife, Emily. Emily Herzteufel she had been, Robert recalled, before marrying Ernst. She might have been taking the oath this day alongside her husband, except that she lacked the residence requirements, having come over just two years ago. But one day, Ernst hoped, she would become a citizen in her own right.

"... and that I take this obligation freely without any mental reservation or purpose of evasion; so help me God."

When Bauer finished the oath, the judge leaned forward and said, "Welcome to America, sir." Then he banged his gavel and turned to other business.

Ernst and Emily came through the gate in the railing, arm in arm, beaming as if they had just been married all over again. Robert moved sideways into the aisle to meet them.

"Thank you, Mr. Wheelock," Ernst said. "I am so happy this day."

"No need to thank me," Robert said. "You did it all yourself."

Together they went out into the corridor and down to the street. When they stepped out of the cool shadows inside the courthouse, with its active ceiling fans, the late summer air was suddenly thick with heat and humidity. Robert's shirt quickly stuck to his collarbones and around his ribs under the weight of his woolen suit and vest.

"Will you join us in a celebratory lunch, sir?" Bauer asked.

Robert looked at his watch. "I would certainly like that," he said, "but I have another errand to attend to. However, may I suggest you seek out Wanamaker's department store? Their cafeteria sets an excellent table." In making the recommendation, Robert was conscious of the young couple's budget, their tastes, and the opportunity for Ernst to buy his pretty wife a gift on this momentous day.

Bauer nodded. "We will do so. Thank you again." He took his wife's hand. "Come, Emily."

They headed off up Market Street, and Robert went in the other direction, down toward Second and Chestnut streets, where the regional offices of the U.S. Department of Justice were located. It had been some months since he had received William Henry's letter from Paris. As Robert happened to be in Philadelphia on similar business, it seemed as good a time as any to follow up on his son's request. When he found the large, limestone-clad building he saw listed on the engraved plaque beside the street door: "Immigration and Naturalization Service." He hoped it would be cooler inside.

The lobby directory sent him up to the third floor. The gorgeously paneled elevator had bronze doors that bore the seal of the Office of the U.S. Attorney General. The corridor beyond on the upper floor were lined with marble and punctuated with imposing doorways framed in dark wood. The doors all had frosted glass windows with their department names in gold-edged letters. From beyond, he could hear the languid pecking of typewriters and the occasional ringing of a telephone. The hot weather sealed the corridor like the inside of an Egyptian tomb. When he found the right office Robert knocked, but there was no response. So he quietly opened the door and put his head through.

Five feet inside the room there was a long wooden counter. On the other side was a woman wearing a bulky telephone headset and seated at a massive switchboard festooned with black wires. She was talking in a low but commanding voice into a microphone that was anchored around her neck.

Robert entered the chamber and waited for her to look up, but she never did. Finally, he leaned over the counter and waved gently at the side of her face. She turned and glared at him, pulled the plug on her conversation, and lifted one of the headphone cups away from her ear. A drop of sweat crept out of her upswept hair and crawled down her neck.

"Yes?" she said in no very friendly tone.

"I want to speak to someone about immigration."

"Are you a foreign national?"

"No, I'm a U.S. citizen."

"Oh, then you want to *sponsor* a foreign national."

"No … well …" Robert realized he had not thought this business through. Did he really want to sponsor the Riesenbergs in America? It was a step he had not been required to undertake even for a client like Ernest Bauer. But then, his son already had a personal connection with the couple, which was something to consider. "I suppose that might be an option," he said finally. "What does sponsorship involve?"

"I can't explain it all," the woman said. "And I'm busy with the phones here." She reached into a box behind the counter's edge and handed him a sheaf of papers. "You fill out these forms, then come back and talk to a case manager."

Robert counted the pages, eight in all. As he glanced through them, he saw extensive questions about his own background, his financial condition, his personal associations and affiliations, his criminal history, and other details from what Robert would normally consider his private life. There was very little space to introduce the person being sponsored. He put the forms down on the countertop.

"Couldn't I just talk to someone?" he asked.

The woman, who had gone back to her plugs and wires, lifted the earphone again. "Do you have an appointment?" she asked.

"No, but ..."

An inner door opened behind her, and a man in his late fifties wearing gray flannel came out. "Louise? Is there some problem?"

"This person wants to talk to someone about immigration."

The man looked Robert up and down and came to a decision.

"My name is Jones, sir. My time is limited, but maybe I can help you."

"I am Robert Wheelock, an attorney in town from Sylvan County. I am *investigating*"—he thought it would be best to put a semi-official face on these proceedings—"the situation of a displaced person, a Pole now living in France, who wishes to come to this country."

"Visas are handled through the State Department," Jones said.

"I am aware of that, but I understand Mr. Riesenberg and his wife are seeking permanent residence. In fact"—as long as Robert was making this up, why not make it good?—"they wish to become citizens."

"That would necessitate a suitable sponsor, who is also a U.S. citizen."

"So your receptionist implied," Robert said, indicating Louise, who was deep in her telephones again. "Can you tell me what exactly is required?"

"Well, we handle these requests on a case by case basis," Jones said. "But essentially it amounts to your providing a job for this person, arranging housing, taking responsibility for all his debts, and so on. You pledge your good name and character and vouch for his future conduct—and his wife's, too, of course. You would need to have considerable resources to undertake this."

"I understand."

"That's why we require an in-depth review of the sponsor's financial and social standing, you see." Jones put a finger on the forms that lay on the counter and pushed them an inch in Robert's direction. "You fill those out, submit them to this office, and then we will talk again."

Robert opened his briefcase and scooped up the papers. "Thank you for your time, Mr. Jones."

The man smiled. "That's what we're here for." But then, as Robert turned to leave the office, Jones called out behind him, "Did you say the name was *Riesenberg?*"

Robert turned. "Yes, that's the name."

"Jews?"

"I believe so."

"You understand that can have no bearing on the case. The Department has no official position in matters of foreign policy."

"Of course," Robert agreed. "This would be entirely a personal arrangement."

"Exactly."

20. The Lowenback

During the first crisp days of autumn, Libby was sitting out on the back porch in the afternoon while the sun was still high enough to warm her. In her lap were three small ears of late corn that she meant to husk for Robert's dinner. It was a task of just a few minutes, but the mess that corn silk might make gave her an excuse to sit out and enjoy the weather before frost closed in on the Allegheny Valley. She was halfway through the first ear when she heard a heavy vehicle crunching gravel as it came down the driveway.

"Now who could that be?" she asked herself. Libby was expecting no deliveries, and Robert was at his office in town; so it wouldn't be one of his farming clients. The hood of a large green truck appeared around the corner of the conservatory, followed by its long, boxed-in back. The sign on the side read "Lowe's Emporium" in great brown-and-gold swash lettering, with "Wharton, Pa." in smaller, square letters down in the corner. It looked very like the truck that had come by a month ago to haul away Lydia's sideboard.

The truck went a little ways beyond the parking space beside the terrace, then backed in so that its rear gate was facing her. Libby put aside her corn and came down the steps.

"Can I help you?" she said.

The driver opened his door and swung down out of the cab. It was the same man who had taken the sideboard.

"Why, Mrs. Wheelock!" he said, sounding surprised. He looked at the clipboard in his hand. "Yes, this is the address."

"Address for what?" she asked.

"My delivery—of a walnut sideboard."

He opened the double-doors at the back of the truck, and Libby could see the square end of the piece, with its incised panels and garlanded top. Italianate *rococo*, come home to roost.

"What's the matter? Did no one want it?" she asked. "It wasn't in your store for very long."

246

"Not at all," the driver said, and Libby seemed to remember his name was Isaac. "It just fit the bill of a standing order we have from Mr. Wheelock."

"And what does Mr. Wheelock want with my sideboard?"

"I don't know that he particularly wanted a sideboard. Or that he intended to buy back his own furniture, for that matter. He wrote to us some months ago looking for a piece of walnut, being careful about the kind and quality of the wood, but not what it was attached to—if you get my meaning."

"I'm beginning to," Libby said.

"It's my guess he wants it for some bit of wood-working or other."

The man's helper came around the other side of the truck, yawning and scratching himself.

"So where do you want us to put it?" the driver asked.

"Not up here." She pointed down the drive toward the garage that Lydia had built after the barn collapsed, when she thought she might finally want to buy herself an automobile. It was a modest clapboard building, painted creamy yellow, having a cement floor and two wide doors with their corners angled at the top, in the Dutch style. Robert had already appropriated half of the garage for his projects, knocking out part of one wall and installing a glassed-in lean-to for his potting and seedlings. He also had a heavy wooden bench for his gun-smithing and other metal work.

"Take it down there," she said.

"Would you sign for it, ma'am?"

"I might as well. That will keep it in the family. May I ask what my husband is paying for that thing?"

"He agreed to abide by the seller's—that is, your—asking price."

Libby sniffed. "He's paying too much for it then."

"His business, I guess."

"My gain." She smiled.

The thought crossed her mind that, since Robert had not seen the sideboard in twenty years, he might not even remember that it came from this house. He certainly had not seen the Lowe's truck take the piece away, so he need never know that he was buying back his own property. And then, too ... it was undoubtedly some of the furniture that Lydia had brought to her marriage with the Judge, because Libby could remember seeing pieces like it in her grandmother's house in Binghamton. So Libby could, with some justification, put the money in her own pocket, maybe use it to do a bit of shopping for herself. She was already considering when she might next be going down to Harrisburg when the driver interrupted her thoughts.

"Nice piece like this," he said, closing the truck's doors for the further drive down to the garage. "It'd be a shame to break it up."

"Let's just say it has a history," Libby said.

"I'm sure it does, ma'am."

21. THE HIDING PLACE

ROBERT RAN HIS hands over the walnut sideboard. Under the hard electric lights in his workshop, the darkly grained surface shone with a warmth and luster that reminded him of candlelight. The people at Lowe's had put a coat of oil on the piece, even though his letter had made clear that he was unconcerned about the wood's surface condition. Robert could admire such thorough-going craftsmen, who adhered to their own standards rather than the prerequisites of others.

Libby had explained the sideboard's origin when they discussed it earlier in the evening. With a tight smile she had started calling it "the Lowe-and-back." She had only thought to sell it, she said, because she had seen a similar piece in the Binghamton house and believed it had once belonged to Lydia and would therefore be unpalatable to him. Robert knew he could smash such flimsy feminine logic on cross-examination but thought better of that in his own kitchen. Besides, Libby said, the sideboard didn't fit in the dining room anymore—whatever that meant.

While she might not have wanted it, the sideboard carried some happy memories for Robert. Among them were the important dinners his father had given that Robert was old enough to attend. The Judge would stand at this very spot—Robert unconsciously assumed his father's position in front of the sideboard—with carving knife and serving fork raised over a joint of venison or a brace of pheasants and interrogate each diner as to preference. On state occasions, the Judge always served, and he wished to keep the clutter of platters and bowls from destroying the elegant symmetry of his dinner table.

Robert was less enthusiastic, now, about breaking up this piece for gunstocks and other knickknacks. If Libby was adamant about having it out of the house, then he might keep it down here in the garage and use it for a tool chest or storage cabinet. However, on the off-chance that Libby's set against the sideboard was to remove it from the premises entirely, Robert decided to see if it had salvageable wood. He knew they could never return it to Lowe's, not after the folly of sending it the first time and getting it back.

He opened the doors in the front and pulled out the drawers one by one. They were lined with white paper—the kind that had a white glazed surface, such as butchers used to hold in the meat juices. Robert tore the edge of one piece to see what the wood underneath looked like.

It was good enough, so he ripped out the paper in all the drawers. He hated stopgaps like antimacassars, doilies, and shelf paper. They were all designed to halt, or at least delay, the wear-and-tear of time. The real world had scratches on it. Well-used furniture and utensils showed them proudly.

When the drawers were stacked neatly crosswise in his work area, Robert squatted down to examine the interior of the cabinet. He knew instinctively that the panels, doors, and drawer fronts were too thin to shape a stock for his fowling piece. It was only among the uprights and cross braces of the internal carpentry, if anywhere, that he was likely to find a piece of wood thick enough in at least two dimensions for a gun stock.

There was more paper stuck up inside the space left by one of the upper drawers. Probably some of the butcher paper from an earlier application had torn off and lodged between the drawer rails.

He reached in, scraping his bare arm on the unbeveled edges of the opening. What he felt was more than a single sheet of paper—more like a wad of the stuff. He pulled slowly, so as not to tear it and make more work for himself.

When Robert brought his hand out into the harsh glare of electric light, the papers had the appearance of a legal document. He unfolded them. On the front was printed in Old English type, "Last Will and Testament of," followed by "William Henry Wheelock" in inked script that had not changed a jot from a similar version that Robert had seen more than twenty years ago. The only difference was the date inside: 1916. The will that was read after his father's funeral had been made in 1904.

Robert scanned it quickly, decoding the fine legal language and assembling the provisions in his mind against the division of property that had been made under the earlier will. This one left both the house and land to Robert, as well as control of the railroad and electric companies that his father had established. It made only a small bequest of stocks and cash to Lydia for her continued support.

So she never had a claim to the property in town at all!

Trembling with some feeling he could not describe—exasperation, indignation, mystification, anticipation, or a mixture of them all—Robert took the document up to the kitchen, where Libby was just finishing with the dishes. He showed it to her silently.

Wrinkling her brow, but sensing that something important was at stake, Libby took the will in her still-damp hands and read it through. At last she asked, "Where did you find this?"

He described how it had been wedged into the sideboard.

"Would your father have kept it there?" she asked. "Maybe it got stacked on top of something else and jammed—"

"The Judge never kept business papers anywhere but in his files or the safe."

"Then someone must have moved it." His wife paused. "No, wait. Lydia moved it, of course, because she knew what it contained."

"You mean she hid it," Robert said neutrally.

"Yes, that's exactly what I mean. ... What are you going to do?"

Her question clarified the storm that was brewing in Robert's mind. It passed like clouds parting to reveal the afternoon sun. "About what?" he said with a grin. "Lydia's gone now, and we have the house."

"Well, what about the companies?"

"They're in good hands. I think Father would approve the way that his business has been conducted over the years—better than I could have done."

"You don't know that. I think you would have made a wonderful businessman," she added loyally.

"Still, I can't complain about the current set of managers. Walter Dufour is a fixture in this town."

"And Billy McKee," Libby said, "who actually runs that railroad, could be the mayor after him. That is, if Billy didn't have to live in Emporium so he could catch the morning run up to Roulette. ... But that's not the point, is it."

"Then what is the point?" Robert asked patiently.

"You've been cheated. Deprived of what was rightfully yours."

"And still, we haven't done so badly," he said. "We've had some good years, while others have suffered with hard times."

"Ooooh!" She swung an open-handed blow at his shoulder. "Why don't you get *mad!* Why don't you *shout!* You have a right to, you know. I give you permission."

"Because Lydia was your aunt?" he asked curiously.

"Because you're a man. You're supposed to get angry when a stingy old woman gets the better of you."

"I did get mad," he said thoughtfully, "or at least confused, as I was coming up the drive with that piece of paper. But now I ask myself, would I give up what we've got together in order to have had the things promised in that will? No, I would not. Would I have become as good a lawyer—assuming that I am—"

"You are!"

"—or thought to bring in that geologist to find the natural gas, or done a dozen other things, if I'd been distracted by the possessions and responsibilities my father had?"

"You'd have done better!"

"Or lost it all in the Crash and never recovered," he said. "No, that paper was hidden for a reason, I think. Not Lydia's reason, which was mean and small, but a reason I can agree with."

"So what are you going to do?" she asked.

"This," Robert said, taking the document from her hands and thrusting it into the waste bin. It landed on top of the greasy scraps from dinner, and the fine clear paper was quickly spotted.

"And what about the sideboard?" Libby asked. "Will you still tear it apart?"

"It's a good piece," he said slowly. "We could put it in the second floor hallway, for linens. Or I could take it in the bedroom, to hold my shirts and collar studs and such."

"You want to keep it?"

"I think it deserves a reprieve" he said. "For services rendered."

22. INTO A NEW WORLD

ALL DURING THE long train ride that morning, as the rickety wooden coaches swaying on their absurd four-wheeled trucks followed the growling, fuming diesel engine into the mountains, the melodramatic strains of Antonín Dvorák's Symphony No. 9 in E minor, *Z Noveho Sveta*, or "From the New World," kept playing inside Niklaus Riesenberg's head. Perhaps the composer had found something energetic and resolute in this country of America. All that Riesenberg himself had seen so far was noisy and dirty cities filled with loud and vulgar people. Once they left Philadelphia, he had watched a patchwork of small, poverty-stricken farms pass by the window. And now they were traveling through a million hectares of dusty green forest that baked in the heat of what the conductor called "Indian Summer."

At that, Alma had perked up and asked if they would see real Indians.

The conductor just shook his head at her and walked off down the aisle.

"Seriously, Klaus," she said, turning to Riesenberg, "will we see them?"

"I think, my dear, we are—conservatively—a hundred years too late for that."

"Oh," his wife said. "I had hoped, once we arrived in the wilderness, we might discover those savages and get to observe their curious customs."

"No, we will only see more Americans."

Klaus remembered the young man to whom, as much as anyone, they owed their present circumstances. William Henry—"but, please, call me Willie"—had been eager, friendly, naïve, and far too confiding. He had goggled at everything and would believe anything Klaus told him. He absorbed bits of reason and fantasy, admiration and outrage, hatred and love, and packed them all into his personal world view as easily as a mason lays bricks. In fact, that was a good metaphor for the Americans: they took every kind of experience, chipped off the awkward bits until the sides were flat and the corners all matched, and then built straight, logical walls that had no flavor but would stand against all but hurricane winds. Europeans, on the other hand, selected from among odd-shaped stones and lumpy bricks, slathered them with mortar, and built topsy-turvy structures that leaned and swayed and sometimes fell down. But at least, while they stood, they were true to themselves and usually pleasing to the eye.

In fact, it was to escape the current European collapse—built on a world view made out of humbug and rotten cheese, and not pleasing at all—that Klaus and his wife were now in flight. He had been a *Herr-Doktor-Doktor* and lecturer in economic theory, first at Wien and then in Cracow, and now he was to become a groundsman, a kind of gardener, for a rich lawyer in the outlands of Pennsylvania. And Alma, who could carry on two conversations at once in any pair of six different languages and who played the violin with the passion of a *Zigeuner*, was to be a household domestic for this lawyer's wife. But such were the fortunes of war.

And make no mistake about it, Niklaus Riesenberg was at war. He had been fighting since before 1917.

As the train descended from the mountains into a sheltered valley, the conductor came up the aisle caroling, "Roulette! Roulette next stop. End of the line!" The name of the town was a pretty French word that sounded flat and ugly in the mouths of these Americans. It reminded Klaus that, as in most games of chance, the wheel of fortune was spun by a hand other than one's own. And it paid to keep your eye on the little white ball—the seed of truth among the dark pockets of chance—as it bounced erratically around its course.

He craned his neck to look ahead at the town that would soon be his own. The setting had the pocket closeness of a village in the Tyrolean Alps, although the surrounding mountains were nothing like so tall, not even extending above the tree line. The buildings were made of red brick instead of the shaped logs of a chalet. And while they all had pitched roofs, like in a good European village, the Americans hid the end gable behind a square front of brickwork or boards, designed to look from the street like a second or third story where none, in fact, existed. The center of town was trying to look like a great metropolis instead of the village it was.

As the train pulled into the station, Klaus scanned the platform for the sight of his benefactor. He was looking for an older version of William Henry: a fair-haired boy now grown to middle age. And there he was. Robert Wheelock was a tall man with light-brown hair, thin features, and long, elegant fingers. Klaus could see the son peeking out of the father's face. Beside him stood his wife—Elizabeth, although she was said to prefer some other name, something outlandish that sounded like "Liberté"—a petite woman whose blonde hair was still more gold than silver, just as the boy had described her.

"Come, Alma," he said, standing up and taking their hand luggage down from the overhead rack. "Time to humiliate ourselves."

"Tut, Klaus!" she scolded "They may be nice. After all, the boy was nice."

"A baron may be nice to you, but he is still a baron."

Alma simply nodded, unwilling to fight with him.

They made their way to the end of the car and down onto the platform.

"You must be Doctor Riesenberg," said the tall man, coming forward with his right hand outstretched.

"Why, yes, it is so," Klaus said, changing the bag to his other hand in order to take and shake Wheelock's hand. "And you are *Herr* Wheelock?"

"Please, call me Robert," said Wheelock.

"Mrs. Riesenberg?" said the Liberté woman.

"Yes, *madame*?" his wife answered politely.

"It's so good to finally meet you."

"Yes, *madame*."

"You two are exactly as Willie described you."

"Oh, is that true? And where is the boy?"

"He's at college now," the father said. "Went off last month."

"I had hoped we might see him again," Klaus said.

"You will, you will, when he comes home at Christmastime."

"Robert!" his wife exclaimed. "Call it 'Hanukkah.' Remember they are …"

"Don't mind us," Klaus said. "The Jews have learned to be tolerant. If the boy will be back in your home for Christmas, the celebration proper to your faith, then Alma and I are enriched as well."

"Of course," said Wheelock. "Now, do you have any other baggage?"

"Tons of it," Klaus rolled his eyes. "At the back end of the train, I think."

"Then Libby and the porter will get it while I bring the car around."

"That is good of you," Klaus said. "Really very kind."

"Nothing to it. Welcome to America."

23. Moving Pictures

Robert treated the campaign for the bench seriously, and that had meant going out of his way to meet people and learn about their lives, their wants, and their needs. He took a more active role in the local Masonic lodge and began to rise in the degrees. He took Libby to a square dance and was invited to call a set, which he did manfully, although later the fiddler passed him a tumbler full of sipping whisky and suggested Robert take a swig to loosen himself up, because in truth he seemed to have no natural sense of rhythm.

But the one thing he did well and felt good about was to take his collection of films out to the countryside. He would contact the principal of a school in one of the townships away from Roulette, the county seat, and arrange for a "moving picture night." The principal—and in some cases his contact was simply the local teacher, and the school was one room where all grades were taught together—would announce the event through the children. Children and parents both invited.

Most of the schools had electricity, and for those that didn't Robert purchased for himself a portable gasoline generator that could power his projector. He had a folding projection screen, but it was small. So for larger rooms and bigger audiences he borrowed one of Libby's bed sheets and stretched it with thumb tacks through the frame of the blackboard.

Robert knew the Liberty Theater in Roulette was the only moving picture palace in the county. Although he and Libby did not go to the shows much, he understood that for most country people the cinema was an unknown luxury: too distant, too expensive, too strange for them to bother with. And so the experience of moving pictures was relatively unknown outside of town.

Rather than introduce these folks to the strange worlds depicted in the Hollywood cinema—American cowboys, English detectives, big city gangsters, heroes and princes out of costumed histories—Robert showed them the world they knew in color and motion against a white sheet. And when, occasionally, the

258

children saw themselves or a family member up there, the shout of laughter was greater than if they had met Douglas Fairbanks or Mary Pickford in person.

He showed the reels he had shot and edited of farmers tapping maple trees for sap in the early spring and then sugaring off with snow still on the ground, of them shearing sheep and bailing the fleeces in late springtime, of the volunteer firemen practicing with their hoses at high pressure in the early summer, of the game wardens trapping beaver and bear, of the bathing beauties parading in their knee-length swimming costumes and children cannonballing into the local plunge, of the county agricultural agent trying out a new mechanical potato-extractor in the fall. The largest part of his collection, however, dealt with the railroad, showing freight trains highballing on the main line, yard engines making up trains in the switchyard, and operations in all weathers.

The one reel that drew the most excitement from the children was his outings with the train crews in heavy snow. The E&RR didn't have a large inventory of rolling stock, and a plow with ducted fans that could break up the snowdrifts and blow them far off the right-of-way—as they did on the mainline—was not among them. So when the snow gathered three and four feet deep across the tracks, the crews had only momentum and the weight of the engine to clear it. Robert would get down from the train with his camera, trudge one or two hundred yards up the line, and set up. Then the crew would back up the steam engine, get a running start, and crash through the drift, exploding snow in all directions.

If the snow was powdery enough and not too deep, this worked to clear the tracks. If it was too dense or too high, the engine would ride up over the packed snow and derail itself. Then the railroad had to call out a crane from the Emporium yards to put it back on track.

But that moment of exploding snow, with the blackened engine barreling through, was always a thrill for the children. For the parents, too. Robert had lost count of the times that people filing out of the school room at the end of a show had stopped by the projector. Some shared their memories of the subject in one of the films. Others praised his work as a photographer. And once a woman had simply taken his hand and mouthed the words, "Thank you."

24. RUBY'S CAFÉ

ON A FREEZING Tuesday in November the people of Roulette went quietly, by twos and threes, through the rain and sleet to mark their ballots for the office of County Judge as well as other offices. Given the weather, it was surprising so many people showed up at the polling place—held in Leonard Kingston's garage, since it was near the center of town—that a line formed out the door and nearly to the street. The past couple of weeks had climaxed what many people called the pokiest, most polite, least rancorous, and, on the whole, least satisfying campaign that the town had ever witnessed: no big promises, no great speeches from the courthouse steps, only a few quiet discussions after church or in the aisles of the A&P, and just one paid-for engagement at the Masonic Lodge. The regular clientele at Ruby's commented on the curiously subdued campaign at lunchtime that Tuesday.

"Yes, I was at the wing-ding, over at the hall," Clarence said in answer to a question from Harold Burke.

" 'Wing-ding,' you call it?" Sheriff Cobb interrupted. "Man, you have no sense of fun, do you? A bowl of pretzels and a barrel of near-beer—like it was still Prohibition!"

"I noticed you drank enough to get buzzed," Clarence replied.

"Well, the two candidates spoke for about ten minutes apiece," Cobb said. "And they still didn't say a thing."

"Oh, but they did," said Reverend Stevens. "They offered praise for the character, integrity, and legal skills of the other fellow. A very charitable way to campaign."

"Dang!" said Cobb. "What fun is *that?*"

"How are people supposed to know which way to vote?" McKee asked.

"You could consult your conscience," the reverend said quietly.

"Wheelock's done a lot for the people in this town," said Henry Barnes, who ran the grocery story. "Look at how he got the Bauer boy his citizenship. And he brought over that couple from France."

"Foreigners," said Clarence drily. "And Germans."

"Actually," said Burke, the county clerk, "the Riesenbergs originated in Poland. They're Polish Jews."

"Still foreigners."

"Who does LeConte like?" McKee asked Burke.

"He isn't saying," Burke answered.

"Well then, who do you *think* he likes?" Cobb asked.

"It's not my business to guess—or tell," Burke said primly.

"Personally, I couldn't vote for that man," said Ezra Stills.

"Which one?" several people in the room asked.

"The skinny one—Wheelock."

"Why in hell not?" asked McKee.

"Because he's gotten rich off the people of this county, is why."

"You'll have to defend a claim like that with facts," the conductor warned.

"Twenty years ago," Stills said, "Robert Wheelock went around buying up rights to the minerals under everyone's land. He paid a song for 'em, too. Then he turns around and drills for oil and gas and what-not. And when he finds it, he doesn't have to pay a cent to take all that wealth out of the ground you own. That's shady dealing in my book."

"I never heard that story," said Cobb.

"Happened to me. Happened to a lot of us."

"It might not have been *exactly* like that," Reverend Stevens said.

"Close enough for Wheelock to have a bucketful of cash and I'm still digging potatoes."

"Maybe he was willing to take a chance where you weren't," McKee said.

"And maybe he knew something ahead of time when we didn't," Stills replied.

"All I know," said another farmer, who like Stills was in town for the election, "is every year he takes a couple of thousand dollars out of my pasture."

"So you're going to vote for *Harris?*" McKee said. "That man's a fool."

"He's qualified," Stills said. "He knows his law books."

"Yeah, but he doesn't know this *town*."

McKee looked to Burke. "Tell us what you think of Harris."

"Seeing as I chair the Election Commission, it wouldn't be right for me to offer an opinion," Burke said. "But I do believe that Mr. Harris is competent. Even Mr. Wheelock acknowledges this."

"But will Harris make a good judge? Will he treat people fairly?"

"I'm sure he'll do what's right."

The conductor snorted. "I'll take Robert Wheelock, for all his money, over a smiling, glad-handing phony like Harris any day."

"Your opinion," said Stills evenly.

"And as good as the next man's."

"Be nice if you were eligible to vote," Burke observed.

"Then I'll move here, so I can give Wheelock a boost in the next election."

"That'll be too late," Stills said, "because Harris is winning this year."

25. Election Night

Robert and Libby Wheelock waited by the telephone in the library for a call from the courthouse, where Harold Burke presided over the election commissioners counting the ballots. As the hours drew on toward midnight, Robert paced in front of his desk. Libby sat in one of his office chairs, reading a magazine—although she hadn't turned a page in twenty minutes. It was clear to Robert, as he spun at the end of his groove in the carpet, that her eyes were no longer moving back and forth but instead were fixed in some middle distance beyond the page, lost in thought.

Although he had refused to make an ugly fight of the campaign against Jim Harris, Robert discovered that he did want to become judge, and he appreciated how much his life would change if he won. From being a private citizen, although well liked and respected around the county, he would become a public figure. His actions would be noted and discussed by people who had a right to examine his philosophies, his morals, and his person in general. Robert's decisions would change lives and perhaps, through the mechanism of precedent, even change the law itself. He would be the public conscience of the county, the arbiter of right and wrong, the final authority—with only the Supreme Court of the Commonwealth of Pennsylvania to gainsay him—on all matters having to do with the law.

For her part, Libby would automatically become one of the leaders of their small community. She would be sought out by her peers, not just for access to him, but as a respected voice in all things dear to women: fashion and floral arrangements, manners and moral advice. With one step, she would pass over the gray-haired ladies who ran the social scene. She would gain the kind of power that mere money and a big house could not command.

Tonight was the turning point in both Robert's and Libby's lives—momentous enough to set Robert to pacing and send Libby off to study the universe with her thousand-mile stare.

They both jumped when the doorbell rang.

"I'll get it," Robert said. "I'm already up."

"Maybe there's news," she said quietly.

He looked at his watch. "It's possible."

Outside, standing in the light over the front door, he found the Riesenbergs. After coming to Roulette, they had moved into the house at the end of the lane, and Robert's first thought was that they had experienced a broken pipe or some other trouble and come to him as their landlord. Robert opened the door to them.

"Niklaus," he said, putting his hand out. "Alma," with a smile. "What can I do for you at this time of night?"

"Is there word?" Riesenberg asked eagerly.

"Oh, you mean the election. No, nothing yet."

"We knew you'd be concerned, yes?" said *Frau* Riesenberg. "So we came to keep you company."

"That's very thoughtful," Robert said. He was willing to accept their best wishes and then retire.

He must have made a subtle movement with the door, because the professor put out a hand to stop it. "And we want to see this democracy of yours in action," he said.

"Then won't you come in?" Robert said, opening the door wide.

"Gladly," Riesenberg said, guiding his wife through the doorway.

"Libby?" Robert called into the library. "Look who's here to join us."

His wife came out into the hall, cordial and smiling as ever.

"How good of you both," she said, but Robert saw a wariness in her eyes.

Libby took them into the parlor and asked what they wanted to drink.

"Actually," Riesenberg said, "I wish to share with you a cordial."

"Oh, Klaus!" said his wife, sounding exasperated.

"What is it?" Robert asked.

"It is the water of life."

"Aquavit? Usquebaugh?"

"Something better."

Riesenberg opened his ever-present book bag and took out a stout, square bottle, unlabeled, made of clear glass. Like an expensive whiskey, it was stoppered with a round Bakelite or ceramic cap attached to the cork. Although Robert knew a thing or two about whiskeys, he did not recognize it. The liquid inside was clear, like vodka or schnapps.

"Glasses, please?" Riesenberg asked Libby.

She glanced at Alma, who shook her head. Libby went out to the kitchen and came back with two shot glasses, holding an ounce and a half each, on a tray. She set the tray on a side table.

Riesenberg poured the liquor with a careful hand, spilling not a drop, up to the one-ounce line etched on the side of each glass. He offered one to Robert and took the other for himself.

"To the fulfillment of your dreams," the professor said.

Robert nodded and held the glass under his nose. He thought there would be some scent from the liquor, some evanescence of the alcohol at least, but he smelled nothing.

They both drank.

The liquor was flat, bland, lying on the tongue like tap water.

Riesenberg was grinning at him. "Good, eh?"

"This doesn't have any ... taste," Robert said.

"Nor should it."

"But what is it?"

"Water from the River Jordan."

Robert held the half-empty glass up to the light. It was merely water, but he knew it to be something more. This was water that had flowed out of the Sea of Galilee, where Jesus had walked and called Peter and Andrew to follow Him and become fishers of men. This water had been the instrument of John the Baptist, who first recognized the Master and whose rite of cleansing the soul prefigured His new teachings. And, after flowing just one hundred miles through the center of the Holy Land, this water entered into the Dead Sea, the lowest point on earth. By its southern shore Sodom and Gomorrah had been blasted, and

Lot's wife turned to salt, as a sign to the ancients of God's wrath. For three thousand years this water had been …

"The soul of the oldest civilization on earth," Riesenberg murmured, as if sharing Robert's very thoughts.

"All contained in a single glass," Robert said. He was about to comment further when the phone rang in the library. "Would you excuse me?" he said.

When he picked up the phone, before he could even say hello, a voice said, "You did it, Wheelock. It's yours. Congratulations."

"Who—?" Then Robert recognized the voice. "Mr. Burke? Is the vote in?"

"In and counted," Harold Burke said. "And it's Wheelock by a margin of two hundred and sixteen votes."

"Is that good?" Robert asked.

"A landslide. You're the judge."

"Why, thank you, sir."

"Not at all, Your Honor." Burke laughed. "You stop by the courthouse in the morning, and LeConte and I will set up a transition, brief you on the docket, and show you where we keep the washroom key."

"Very good," Robert said. He wanted to say more but the man, interrupted him with " 'Night now," and rang off.

Robert replaced the receiver and stood for a moment in thought. The phone rang again while Robert's hand was still on it, sending a jolt through his body.

"Hello?" he said.

"I guess you deserve it," said the voice of Jim Harris. "Congratulations, Judge."

"From what I understand," Robert said, "it could have gone either way."

"Very chivalrous, but it didn't. The people of Roulette have spoken."

"Well, yes," Robert said, "but in a couple of years it'll be your turn."

"You better remember that when you're handing down decisions."

The men shared a laugh. Then Harris wished him luck and they hung up together.

Robert stood for a bit yet, letting Libby handle their guests in the parlor.

He had made the bench. For most attorneys, it was the culmination of a life's work. It certainly had been the making of his father. And now Robert was to follow in the old man's footsteps. The moment marked the high point of his life, and Robert savored it without a thought for what that might mean.

FALL 1948

1. THE LAST DIME

As HE DID every night, Robert counted out and examined the coins from his pants pocket on the surface of his dresser. It had become a game with him over the past couple of months to take change from his purchases in coins rather than bills and specifically ask for dimes when he could get them. He was looking for a specific coin, the silver Winged Liberty Head, showing the mythological goddess Liberty wearing an ancient freedom cap with feathered wings above her ears. On the reverse were the fasces, or bundled sticks, of the Roman Republic. But it was the head that he wanted.

His quest had started when he once noted that the face in profile resembled his wife Libby's. Not so much for the unfortunate jut of the figure's chin, but for her delicate skull, slender neck, and for the clear set of her eyes. Remarking upon these features, Robert had conceived a project that required three dimes, each one dated to their wedding year of 1918 and to the tenth anniversary since. Initially, he had wanted four dimes, so that the set would include the current decade, but soon discovered that the U.S. Treasury stopped minting the coin three years ago. He settled for the three years 1918, 1928, and 1938. He also thought, at the start, that all dimes should come from the Philadelphia mint, in their home state. But Robert quickly decided that imposing such a rule on himself would extend his search almost indefinitely.

He preferred to use the passive method of letting the dimes find him through his daily purchases, rather than contacting a collector or agency and placing an order. It just seemed … luckier, was the word, he guessed, to let the coins come to him. More like putting the project in the hands of the gods. More … fortuitous.

So far, he had found just two of the dimes he sought. Robert had a near-mint condition 1918 that he had quickly set aside. He had his choice of three 1938s, one in worn condition, one with a gouge across the face that he thought he could polish out, but only if he would accept an even more worn look, and one in fair condition that he would probably end up using. But no 1928 of any condition had yet crossed his path.

Robert wasn't exactly sure what he would do with the dimes when he found them all. They would be a gift for Libby, certainly, probably in the form of jewelry he would craft himself. The actual piece and its design was still up in the air, but he wanted it to be something she could wear in daily use and treasure always.

The fact that he could sort his pocket change, holding up individual coins to the light and evaluating them, and not arouse Libby's curiosity was due to their current—and now presumably permanent—sleeping arrangements. Sometime in the last ten years, after William Henry had left the house to go off to college and then to war, Libby had started making her bed in the room across the hall. At first she would leave in the middle of the night, claiming that his snoring kept her awake. Robert was not aware of any snoring, but he accepted her reasons all the same.

Then Libby had started making up the bed and keeping her clothes in that room. Robert was still free to visit her there from time to time, but she always pushed him out before he could fall asleep.

Now it was an accepted thing that they would keep separate bedrooms, with no formal declarations or discussions having taken place. From time to time Robert would ponder the matter, searching for signs of coldness or resentment, either on Libby's part or his own. He couldn't detect anything different about their marriage. She still greeted him cheerily in the morning and bid him happily goodnight in the evening, kissing him with smiling warmth.

But Robert knew their marriage had, all unannounced, crossed the border into a different country. There were no more mornings when he woke with her arm casually resting across his stomach or her leg warmly nestled against his thigh. There were no more evenings when they undressed together, cherishing each other's bodies and, in doing so, spoke the little intimacies that passed between wife and husband.

He had no illusions that a piece of jewelry celebrating their years together would change any of that. But it gave him pleasure to think of giving Libby one more gift.

Robert put the last coin from his pocket down on the dresser and glanced at it. It had the Roman fasces—the bundle of sticks with an ax head—just what he'd been looking for. He turned it over and saw the Winged Liberty. Then he picked it up and carried it to the reading lamp at the bedside to check the date.

It was the 1928. The mint mark was P for "Philadelphia." And the condition was very good. So his search was complete.

Now, what was he going to make with these three dimes?

2. Simmering Resentment

"Objection, Your Honor," snapped District Attorney Peter Twombley, even before James Harris could quite complete his sentence. "Counsel is leading the witness."

"Sustained. Mr. Harris, please rephrase your question."

"Yes, Your Honor."

Harris paused for a moment to gather himself. Certainly, he and everyone else in court knew where this line of testimony was bound to go. Martin Christensen was the only eye-witness outside the feed store. On direct testimony, he had already described the man who allegedly emerged after the robbery—a description matching Harris's client. And Harris was merely walking the witness through the early parts of his story, working toward the points of contention about hair color, jacket color, gait, and Christensen's own eyesight. But, clearly, Twombley and the judge wanted Harris to proceed more slowly. So he would break his line of attack down into bite-size questions.

As he fought to control his breathing, Harris reflected that he was appearing in Judge Robert Wheelock's court for perhaps the one-hundredth time over the past ten years. And this was about the five-hundredth time that Wheelock had ruled against him. Harris could not say it was sign of any judicial bias, no. And, in truth, Harris knew he had a legal style probably more attuned to the cases he argued in Harrisburg, Scranton, and Philadelphia than this rustic courtroom in Sylvan County. Still, it rankled.

He could not help but think that Wheelock's long, pale face, staring down at him from the height of the bench, with his reading glasses down on the tip of his nose, and those bony shoulders elegantly draped in his black-silk robes, were mocking Jim Harris personally. There—but for a few votes lost in a stupid "gentleman's campaign," with its arbitrarily limited funding and an utter lack of effective public speaking—might be sitting Judge James Harris. And then Bob Wheelock would be the one down at the counsel's table clawing for his cases and enduring objection after God-damned sustained objection.

274

Well … it was an election year. Wheelock was running again, and Harris had already put his hat in the ring against him.

The problem was, Wheelock was popular. People liked his measured style. They liked his integrity. And his cases usually resulted in verdicts that they could agree were fair and just. The people around here didn't begrudge Wheelock's money, because he kept doing the damnedest things, folksy things. Like donating sprays of red, yellow, and purple gladioluses—gladiolii?—from his personal garden to the hospital, the churches, and many of the local weddings. Or making the sconces for alongside the courthouse doors, his own design commemorating the oil lamps from the old tannery west of town, and executed by his own hand in copper and brass.

Jim Harris simply couldn't compete with that sort of down-home, carnival-act behavior. And he couldn't compete on money, because Wheelock could afford to paper the county from end to end with campaign bills, if he had a mind to. But the man had to have a weakness, somewhere, some hidden fault that would shock the people of Sylvan County and turn their votes against him. Jim Harris had pondered the issue often enough before.

If only he could find that weakness and exploit it properly.

There had to be something he could use.

Oh, well … back to work.

"Now, Mr. Christensen," he began again. "How long were you standing on the street across from the feed store?"

"About ten minutes."

"And what time of day was this … ?"

3. WHAT EVERY MOTHER BELIEVES

ON SUNDAYS THE family sat down to dinner at the big table in the formal dining room. Libby always positioned herself at the end near the door to the pantry, which led into the kitchen, in case anything was needed. Robert was seated at the far end, near the archway into the front hall, where he could lead their guests in retiring to the parlor afterwards. The middle part of the table on this Sunday was for Willie and the person who had become his most frequent guest at Libby's table, Barbara Eccles.

Barbara was a nice enough young woman, in her middle twenties, the daughter of a local potato farmer. The best thing that Libby could find to say about her was that she had good skin to go with her straight blonde hair and uncertain blue eyes.

"Ooh, Mrs. Wheelock!" she exclaimed, on cutting into her chicken breast. "What's this green stuff inside?"

"Spinach, dear," Libby replied, keeping her eyes on Robert, who was pretending not to hear. "The style is called Florentine." It was a recipe that Alma Riesenberg, who always officiated at Sunday dinner, prepared to perfection.

"Imagine that!" Barbara said. "Putting the vegetables inside the meat!"

"It's something our cook brought over from Europe," Willie explained.

"But then, how does she get the leaves inside?"

"I suppose she could slice the meat sideways."

Libby wanted to cry out that the dish was neither unusual nor exotic, that her own mother had served chicken Florentine at home in Binghamton, thirty years ago, and back then no one had thought it clever. But she bit her tongue instead.

It was not just that Barbara was plain, with a face that shared the contours of one of her father's fat potatoes. Nor was it just that she was unsophisticated and exclaimed over the simplest of dishes—Libby had once served avocados, which her green grocer brought in from California on Libby's order, and Barbara had talked about them for twenty minutes. In Roulette, after all,

Libby was surrounded by people with comparable faces and tastes. The real problem was that the girl was not right for Willie.

Her son had a college education—or most of one, anyway. He had toured Europe several years before he went over there to fight. He was a reserve officer in the United States Army. He was a gentleman, son of the county judge, and grandson of the county's greatest landholder and capitalist entrepreneur. Willie could become anything he wanted to be, and he deserved a mate of equal potential.

Barbara Eccles was not that person.

She had at most a high school education and, in the seven or eight years since, had apparently made no effort to advance herself—except by dating Willie. She lived on her father's farm, taking care of a cow, two pigs, and a flock of chickens. Libby supposed that Barbara milked the cow herself, and might even be handy at butchering one of the pigs in season. But beyond that her skills were not apparent. If she made her own clothes, she was an indifferent seamstress. And it was already obvious she had no talent for the kitchen.

In fact, Libby could not explain what might draw Willie to such a person—unless it was sex. Whether this girl had indeed shared her generous body with him was still unknown. Libby might guess, she might suppose, but her son was close-lipped on the subject. And if he confided in his father, neither of them was telling her.

And, really, was this relationship with Willie even fair to Barbara herself? One day Willie was bound to get restless and want to move on. Would Barbara then be happy in New York, or San Francisco, or wherever it was that life took him? If she was merely an infatuation for Willie—sharing her favors without receiving adequate promises from him in return—then Barbara was doomed to disappointment.

The most comfort Libby could take from the situation was that the fascination between the young people seemed to be fraying. At first, Willie had been solicitous of his young lady's opinions and patient with her gaffes. But today, for example, in explaining how the chicken breast might be prepared, he seemed terse and dry. Perhaps he was even making a joke at Barbara's expense. That was a good sign. It meant Willie might begin to see how unsuitable this girl actually was.

Next week, Libby decided, she would serve artichokes and not clip the tops of the leaves. Let him discover how his beloved dealt with those little thorns.

4. The Librarian

Of all the ways of ordering thoughts that Niklaus Riesenberg had to master in a long and complex life, the Dewey Decimal System was perhaps the easiest. After five years of working as gardener and occasional chauffeur for the Wheelock family, Klaus had seen a chance to advance himself when the position of Sylvan County librarian opened after the death of Gladys Euler at age eighty-seven. He discussed the position with the Judge and found that the one qualification he lacked was versatility with this system.

Klaus had used an offshoot of the system during his university days in Europe, of course, but as a patron and not as the person responsible for organizing all the books. So he went to the library, checked out a manual for the system, and learned it in one night. When he went before the board of trustees to defend his application, it took ten minutes to convince them he was the only person in town qualified for the job. The Judge had supported Klaus in this and arranged for someone else to mow his lawns and help with landscaping his flower beds.

Alma had stayed with the family as cook and housekeeper. However, she added to her income by tutoring the local schoolchildren in languages and giving violin and piano lessons. For these, Mrs. Wheelock had kindly allowed Alma to use her parlor, saying the music filled the great house with joy … at least when Alma took up the bow or sat at the keyboard herself to show the child how it was done.

The Dewey Decimal System came into play on the morning in mid-September that the lawyer, James Harris, came into the library and approached the main desk. "Say there, Professor."

"Yes, sir?" Klaus answered politely, although he was no longer accredited with any university and could not lay claim to the title "professor."

"Can you recommend a book on the Jewish religion?"

"Certainly, that would be Section 296." Klaus pointed. "Fourth aisle, middle shelf on the right, halfway down."

"Oh, well." Harris smiled in a way that Klaus did not like. "What I meant, do you have a book that you *personally* like and recommend."

"Such as the Old Testament?" he suggested.

"Don't you Jews call it something else?"

Klaus sighed. He would have thought all of that, the *Juden Hass*, had ended with the bonfire outside the bunker in Berlin. But perhaps not. "The Jews call the first five books the Torah," he explained. "But I'm not, personally, Jewish."

"Isn't Riesenberg a Jewish name?"

"Not at all. It's of German origin—although my wife and I were both born in Poland," he added quickly. Feelings about the war still ran fairly strong in town.

"And is your wife German, too?" Harris asked.

"No, she is Jewish and observant. I, however, am not."

"So what *are* you, Professor?" the man asked with a smooth smile.

"If you mean, what is my religion, I don't believe in an actual God, as such."

"No God? Then what do you believe in?"

"The historical process."

The man's lips moved, mouthing the words, as if he had heard them somewhere but could not place their meaning. After a moment Harris asked, "You're a Communist then?"

"Democratic Socialist."

"I didn't know there was a difference."

"When people say 'Communist,' they generally mean a Bolshevik, such as those who took control in Russia after the October Revolution," he explained. "However, they were only one faction of the Russian Social Democratic Labor Party, going back to the split that Vladimir Ilyich Ulyanov engineered at the party congress of 1912. The actual majority of the party—although 'menshevik' technically means 'minority member'—has remained far more egalitarian and populist. They, we, believe in achieving the aims of socialism by parliamentary and democratic means."

James Harris followed this explanation with a strange light in his eyes. His mouth hung slightly open. When Klaus finished, he swallowed. Then he said, "Is that a fact?"

"I would think it is common knowledge," Klaus said.

"Oh, yeah, sure. 'Social Democrat.' Forget I asked."

The lawyer turned away, still with that light in his eyes, and left the library.

5. Peccadillo

Alma Riesenberg guided the Judge's big black car very slowly through the white-painted gateposts and into the dooryard of the Ernst Bauer farm. Alma was still unaccustomed to driving, having received her license only two years ago, delayed by wartime gasoline rationing and a lack of any purpose to the undertaking. She was made doubly nervous by the car itself—what Klaus called an eight-cylinder Chrysler sedan—and feared putting a scrape on the fender or suffering some other misfortune with her employer's property. But now Alma needed some way to get around, having taken up tutoring in mathematics, languages, and history to supplement her modest income as cook to the Wheelocks and Klaus's as town librarian.

These teaching jobs usually paid in cash when she worked with the middle class families in Roulette proper, and then Alma could walk to their houses. The members of the agricultural class often paid in kind, and they lived on small farms scattered across Sylvan County, in which case she had to obtain some mode of transportation. The Judge had reasonably suggested that, since he himself was in court all day or doing business around town, Alma might borrow the car during the afternoons, so long as she had it back behind the courthouse before six o'clock.

The Bauer twins were the exception to the economic rule. Even though the family was bound to a farm, they always paid cash. Yet Mrs. Bauer—who liked to be called Emily—knew that Klaus had a sweet tooth and always added something for his palate: a small brown paper bag of fruit, a jar of pear preserves, or a wedge of honeycomb folded into a piece of waxed paper.

Even though Ernst Bauer had come to America thirty years ago, he adhered to the Old World values. The farm itself reminded Alma powerfully of the small holdings in Schwabia and the Tyrol: squared-off fields cut and patterned to the hilly landscape, but still with the furrows as regular as the marks on a ruler. The farmhouse was two stories tall and made of white clapboards, as were most of the buildings in America. But Bauer painted his

282

window trimmings, the flower boxes, and shutters afresh every year with bright green paint. In the same way, he whitewashed the small stones that bordered the patch of lawn in front of the house. And the grass was cut to within a millimeter, like a Prussian haircut. Everything was orderly. Prosperous. Strict.

The two Bauer daughters were like that, too: neat, clean, braided, and blonde. When Alma parked the car beside the barn, she found them sitting on the wooden bench next to the back door with their hands folded in their laps.

"*Was ist los?*" Alma called out.

"Mother wanted us outside," said Trude.

"But we're not to play," said Hannah.

"We are to wait for you," said Trude.

"And here I am," Alma agreed.

"I have new books for you," she added, taking a pair of geometry texts from the car's front seat. "And the tools"—a pad of drafting paper, pencils, two straight edges, and an ancient mechanical compass that had come from Klaus's desk at home—"to begin some very advanced study today. For my two best pupils."

The girls looked at her warily.

"We can't study with you today," said Trude.

"Mother wanted us to *stay* outside," said Hannah.

"This doesn't look like arithmetic," said Trude, opening one of the books.

"Of course not," Alma said. "But it's an important part of mathematics, which *includes* the basic functions of arithmetic. However, to study geometry, we will need the kitchen table."

Hannah frowned more deeply, but Trude's eyes lit up. Alma took that as a "yes" and let the girls into the kitchen. She didn't have to clear a place on the table for the girls because it was, as always, preternaturally neat. The wood had the scrubbed and worn look that Alma was accustomed to seeing in German kitchens. She sat the twins down, one on either side of her, and arranged a book in front of each. She peeled three sheets of paper off the pad for each girl, and gave each one a pencil. Alma reserved the straight edges and compass for later in the lesson.

"We start with the simplest of all geometric objects," she said, "the point. Please pick up your pencil. Be sure to test it for sharpness." The girls dutifully felt the needle points that Alma had put on the pencils at home before setting out. "And touch it at once to the center of the paper, making the smallest possible mark—not a circle, not a tick, but a tiny, tiny, round, dark point."

They did so, then set the pencils down to wait for an explanation.

Alma was launched into the concept of dimension—of length, width, and depth, and how the point had none of these—when they heard footsteps on the back stairs. Foot*falls* was more like it: a loud, rattling clamor with hardly any rhythm to it.

The three of them paused, looking toward the bottom of the stairwell where it entered the kitchen. Heavy work boots appeared, followed by faded denim trousers, a slack belt holding up an overflowing belly in a khaki shirt, and finally a lean, pale face, topped by a shock of red hair. The girls saw the man and relaxed.

"Hello, Mr. Maires," Trude and Hannah caroled together.

"Hello, girls," the man said smoothly enough, although Alma thought he seemed surprised. Perhaps even embarrassed.

Maires stared at her for a long minute. Alma sat patiently at the table, waiting to be introduced. Then the man nodded to himself, picked up a felt hat from the sideboard, and headed out the back door. He closed it hard, with a slam that rattled the windows and set the curtains swinging.

"Who is that man?" Alma asked.

"He works here," answered Trude.

"His name is Lance," Hannah explained.

"But we're supposed to call him 'Mr. Maires.' "

"What does he do?" Alma asked.

"Chores," Trude said with a shrug.

"He helps papa with the farm," said Hannah.

Alma had barely restarted the lesson, picking up from the interruption and being about to introduce a second point, the straight edge, and the concept of *line*, when they heard more footsteps on the stairs. These were light and fast, with a fluttering left-right-left-right syncopation. That was Emily Bauer's step—Alma had heard it around the house before—and immediately the woman appeared at the foot of the stairs.

Emily Bauer was the image of what the two girls would one day become: pretty and trim, with a cinched waist between generous breasts and full hips, and with graceful hands, long fingers, and bright red nails. She was patting strands of her blonde hair into place when she saw the trio sitting at the table.

"Hello!" she said—too loudly, Alma thought.

"Hello, Mama," the girls replied in chorus.

"*Guten Tag, gnädige Frau*," said Alma Riesenberg.

"I thought you were going to stay outside," Mrs. Bauer said. "This day is much too beautiful for you to be cooped up in here."

"We're learning geometry," said Hannah.

"It's a part of mathematics," said Trude.

"I see," the woman replied, "but you could still do it outside, couldn't you?"

"We need to make drawings," said Trude.

"If Frau Riesenberg will let us," Hannah added doubtfully.

"Well, I have to start dinner here in about a minute," their mother said. "Why don't you clean up those things and say good-bye to her?"

"But we've hardly begun," said Hannah.

"We only got to make one mark," said Trude.

"The lesson will keep for another day," Alma said.

Emily Bauer gave her a flashing smile—but with a hard edge.

Alma sensed that, under the woman's patently cheerful manner, there was a glint of anger. A good mother did not like being disobeyed in her own kitchen, of course, but this went deeper. Alma had some intuition as to what the trouble might be.

"I will let you keep the books," she told the girls. "Try to read and understand the first lesson—but no looking ahead!" Alma warned with mock-severity, expecting them to have reached at least Chapter 5 by the time she returned. "And practice making those points."

"We will," they said together.

Emily Bauer went to the cabinet and took out a familiar envelope. "We'll pay for the whole lesson," she said, "even though I cut it short."

"Thank you," she said gravely.

From a side drawer Frau Bauer took out an empty paper bag, unfolded it, and turned to the cookie jar by the stove. It was in the shape of a colorful clown's head with a conical hat. She removed the hat with her right hand and held it aloft while she reached in, took out two of her thick, white sugar cookies, and put them in the bag on the counter. She paused, then added a third. "I baked these yesterday," she said. There was more to her look than mere baker's pride. "I know how your husband likes them."

"Thank you again," she said.

"Now you must go," the woman said.

Alma waved to the girls and left by the kitchen door. All the way across the dooryard to the Judge's car, she could feel three pairs of eyes on her back. Two of them were slightly sad and bewildered, and one pair was burning neat, round holes.

6. Ruby's Café

Leonard Kingston had come to Roulette in the year after the war ended and bought three house lots at the corner of Main Street and Miller's Lane, across the road from Judge Wheelock's extensive property. Inside a month, he had torn down the houses, leveled the ground, and paved it over with tar macadam. He put up a small, cream-colored office building with wide windows on the outer corner of this empty lot, a shedlike garage with two grease pits at the back, and gone into business selling Chryslers and Buicks. To anyone who asked, he would point to the steady flow of out-of-town traffic on Main Street—which at the city limits again became State Route 6, running all the way across the northern tier of Pennsylvania—and say that the automobile was here to stay. Then, usually, he would sell the inquirer a car.

On a crisp September morning before opening his office, Kingston stopped at Ruby's Café for breakfast. As he entered and headed for his customary table, he gathered nods from the other regulars: Harold Burke from the courthouse, Clarence from the feed store, Walt Dufour from the electric company, Doc Ramsey from the new hospital, and Sheriff Cobb. He looked around for McKee, the conductor from the railroad, but then remembered that this wasn't his day. The railroad only made two runs a week now, and sometimes they switched the days around, depending on the freight loads available. Kingston could have told them to expect more of that, because the long-haul trucker was here to stay, too.

As his table was kitty-corner to Burke's, he felt the need to make conversation while waiting for his scrambled eggs. "The Judge's son doesn't talk about the war much," Kingston said. It was a fair observation, because William Henry Wheelock worked for him as a salesman. A bright young man, Willie was, and well liked around town. "He was in, wasn't he?"

"Came out a captain in the army," Burke said.

"So did he see any action? Where did he serve?"

"North Africa, Italy, then with the invasion in France."

287

"He must have been a war hero," Kingston said.

"No, he was in the quartermaster's corps."

"Then he was some kind of clerk."

"Some kind ... he ran a unit of the Red Ball Express. Ever hear of them?"

"Sure, supply trucks running bumper to tailgate, twenty-four hours a day."

"And not always behind the lines, because the lines kept moving, too."

"I heard the drivers were all Negroes. ... Kill you soon as look at you."

"Some of them. ... An officer would have to earn respect in that outfit."

"And Willie earned their respect?" Kingston asked.

"He came out alive, didn't he?" Burke said with a grin.

"I guess I'm lucky to have him working for me."

"If you can keep him," Walt Dufour said from the next table.

"Well, I pay him good wages," Kingston replied.

"A man like that doesn't work just for wages."

"Willie has a sense of purpose," said Burke. "Like his father."

"Didn't he go to college?" Cobb asked. "I thought he had a degree."

"Three years at Harvard, like his father, then cut short by Pearl Harbor."

"But he'll go back one day, won't he?" Cobb said.

"He never talks about it," the county clerk said. "But I have a hunch ..."

"He's doing real well selling cars, I can tell you," Kingston said quickly.

"William Henry would do well at anything he tried," Burke said. "He just hasn't figured out what his purpose is yet."

"Betcha it's not selling cars," observed the sheriff.

"Or not for long," Dufour added with a grin.

7. Ernst Bauer

While Sheriff Rafe Cobb was in town eating lunch at Ruby's Café, one of his deputies, Jim Stanton, pulled up to the curb outside the front door, parked all catawampus, and ran inside. He slid into the empty chair at Cobb's table and leaned in close. "We got trouble, Rafe," he whispered so that the other patrons couldn't hear.

"What's that?" the sheriff whispered back.

"Got a phone call from the Bauer farm. Mrs. Bauer says she heard a couple of shots. She asks for you to come quick. Juney on dispatch's been calling your radio for the last ten minutes."

"And I've been in here, away from the radio. So … shots." Cobb thought for a minute. "Too early for deer season, unless it's poachers. Could be going after varmints or the useless class of birds."

"Emily Bauer's not one to get skittish about someone popping off in the woods. And Juney said she sounded real scared."

"Okay." Cobb reached for his Smokey Bear hat and took out his wallet to pay for his meal, even though Ruby usually pushed his money back across the counter. "I'll go calm the womenfolk."

"Want me to come along?"

"What for?" Cobb asked.

"In case there's trouble."

"If shots have been fired, I'd say the trouble's come and gone. You get back on patrol."

"Okay, Rafe."

Cobb arrived at the Bauer place in twenty minutes or so—by his reckoning maybe half an hour after Emily Bauer's call. The dooryard was deserted, which was unusual for a family with young daughters on a busy farm. Cobb parked and went to the back door. By the dim light coming through the curtained windows he could see into the kitchen. It looked like nobody home, but he knocked anyway.

No response from inside.

After two minutes by his wristwatch, Cobb knocked again.

With still no answer, he called out, "Hello? It's the sheriff!"

He beat on the door with the flat of his hand until the house reverberated, as if hollowed out of all life. Otherwise nothing ... except that something white fluttered down. A piece of paper had been stuck quite deeply between the door and jamb and was dislodged by his pounding. Cobb picked it up and unfolded it.

"Dear Frau Riesenberg," the note said, "today we are playing over at Mary Jane Thorvald's house across the valley. Can we do our lessons with you next week instead?"

There was no signature, but Cobb figured one of the twins wrote it. Still, he was taken by the handwriting, which was done in black ink with the kind of flat-nib pen that ladies used for calligraphy and calling cards. The letters were graceful and evenly spaced. It didn't look like the message from any child.

He looked around the yard, wondering what to do next.

"Hello?" came a small voice from above him.

Cobb stood back and saw an open window on the second floor with a pale face withdrawn into the room beyond it. "Emily Bauer?" he called.

"Is that the sheriff?" she answered.

"Yes, of course. Do you want to come down and open the door?"

"Have they gone away?"

"What's that? Who's gone?"

"The men who fired the shots."

"There's no one around here, Emily."

"I heard shots—explosions—coming from the direction of the barn," she said, louder now. "I got scared and hid up here."

"Where's Ernst?" Cobb asked.

"I don't know. Out in the fields, I think."

"Don't you have a hired hand, too?"

"You mean Lance? I think Ernst sent him into town."

Cobb paused to think through his next move.

"Would you just please check the barn?" Emily said.

"All right," he agreed. "I'll go check the barn."

Before he crossed the dooryard, however, he took out his weapon, checked the loads, and put it back, leaving the retaining strap of the holster unhooked.

As he drew near the barn, a faint sound caught his attention—the crying of a cat.

The great double doors of the barn were closed. Cobb put his weight against one of them and slid it back enough to slip through. It was dark and stuffy inside, with only indirect light coming down from the hay loft. It took a minute for his eyes to adjust.

"Cat?" he called out. "Kitty-kit?"

Twenty feet away, in a patch of shadow to one side below the loft opening, Cobb saw a tiny bit of movement. Two masses of shadow in the darkness—one was a long, inverted triangle, the other upright and hunched—seemed to be attached to each other by a round, ball-shaped object that was moving rhythmically up and down. Timed to this movement he heard a mewling, whimpering sound. The sheriff approached this anomaly over the wide planks of the barn floor, placing his feet carefully and stepping around intermittent drifts of dry, light-colored straw to avoid disturbing any evidence.

The ball was the head of a cat, and the movement was its … licking at something in the shadows. Cobb was very near before the cat looked up, fixed him with pale yellow eyes, and cried again. Then it turned and disappeared in a blur.

That left the shadow on the floor. It was dark, approximately six feet long.

Drawing closer, Cobb didn't need even the dim light coming from the loft to recognize Ernst Bauer. The man was lying on his back in a cleared space below the open trap door. It wasn't the face Cobb recognized, because that had become a mangle of bone and bloody tissue. But Cobb had known Ernst personally and recognized, even in death, the width of his bull-like shoulders and span of his capable hands. He was lying with his head toward Cobb and his legs away, splayed out and steepled at the knees.

The sheriff walked around the body without touching anything, again keeping to the exposed parts of the floor. A large pool of blood surrounded the head and shoulders, overflowing the cracks between the planks. Even with that much physical trauma, Ernst Bauer's heart had kept on beating, draining his body. Strong heart!

So ... some person or persons had unloaded what had to be a shotgun, probably both barrels, directly into Bauer's neck and face. By studying the damage, Cobb could begin to read the shot patterns: one blast about eight inches below the other. The weapon was either an over-and-under in steady hands at a distance of about ... make it, nine or ten feet ... or the first and lower of the shots had raised the weapon slightly before the second was fired, and both would likely be from somewhat closer. However, the distance might not be guessable—without detailed forensic work—because there was no telling how far the force of the blast and his own spasmodic reaction had thrown Bauer back from the point of impact.

Cobb stood up straight and turned in a slow circle, gathering impressions of the crime scene. Predictably, the barn was tidy. The dedicated, compulsive, Germanic kind of tidy. The work bench over in the corner had outlines drawn on the tool board to show where every wrench and hammer should go. The floor was even swept, except for those drifts of straw. Now, where had they come from?

The sheriff walked beyond the body, into the shadows on the other side of the loft opening. There he found an oblong block of baled hay. The edges were slumped over and leaking straw, as if someone had rolled it across the floor. That might account for the drifts. Other than the fact that such untidiness was out of keeping with the barn's general appearance, Cobb couldn't see that it mattered.

He resisted the impulse to find a tarp and cover the dead man's face. Cobb didn't want to disturb the tissues, loose pellets, wad fragments, and possible hair and fiber evidence until the coroner had a chance to examine the body.

Cobb sighed. Well, first things first.

He made his way out of the barn, blinking in the bright September sunlight, and went over to his car. He opened the door and sat inside, using the radio to call his wife June, who worked dispatch in the office.

"Hi, hon," she responded to his call sign.

"Yeah, that phone call from the Bauer place? Afraid it's real bad news," he told her. "Ernst is dead. Shot in the face. Would you round up two of the deputies and send them out here with a van or something? Tell them to bring Doc Ramsey, if he'll come, along with the office forensics kit and the Speed Graflex."

"Got it. Anything else?"

"I guess not," he said. "Oh, wait! Call Cathy Thorvald and tell her to keep the Bauer twins with her for the afternoon. I don't want them walking in on this thing until we get the body out."

"Will do."

"And, just for good measure, ask any of the deputies if they've seen Lance Maires around town."

"Has he gone missing?" Juney asked.

"Don't know that yet. Just ask while it's fresh in everybody's mind."

"Okay. Team will be out there in forty minutes or so, depending."

"Thank you, darlin'," he finished.

Now it was time to go and tell Emily.

He crossed to the back door and knocked.

She was in the kitchen and came to the door.

"Emily. I am so sorry." The words failed him then.

She sagged against the jamb. "What is it? What is wrong?"

"I'm afraid the shots were Ernst. He's, um … dead, out in the barn."

Her face went white. "Dead? But how can that be?"

Cobb had been afraid she would break down, have hysterics, or otherwise react like a frail female. But although Emily Bauer was tiny and thin, barely taller than her half-grown daughters, just a sparrow of a woman compared to husband's hulking frame, Cobb reflected that she was German, too. She would do her sobbing in private.

"I don't know anything more than that right now," he said. "I've called for a team to come out and tend to things. We're also asking Mrs. Thorvald to take care of your daughters until the ... barn is cleared. And I want you to stay in the house for now. Is that all right?"

"Yes. I guess." The woman's eyes had gone glassy. "Would you like a cup of coffee, please?"

"Not right now, thank you. We have work to do."

"Yes. Certainly. I understand."

Since she was taking things so calmly, Cobb decided to venture a question. "One thing you can tell me. What kind of shotgun does Ernst have?"

Emily's brow furrowed. "Why, no kind. Ernst does not hunt the birds."

"Oh. Then does Lance Maires keep a gun around the place?"

"If he does, I have not seen it," she said. "I'm sorry."

"No trouble," Cobb replied. "Just checking."

He went back to the barn to wait for his deputies. It was going to be a long afternoon.

8. The Man on the Slab

Dr. Alexander Ramsey was chief of pathology at Roulette's War Memorial Hospital. In this capacity he also served as county coroner and ran the morgue in the basement of the east wing. Pathology was a routine science, a practice with regular hours, no house calls, and not a lot of need for bedside manner. You looked at slides, you wrote reports, and you let other people care whether the patient lived or died. You did your job and went home at five—unless the sheriff called up in a sweat and said he had a body, the victim of a probable homicide, and he wanted an autopsy done right away.

"Probable homicide," Ramsey muttered. "Too right."

Two of Cobb's deputies had requisitioned the hospital's one and only ambulance for the ride out to the farm, although a panel truck would have served just as well. At first everyone wanted Ramsey to drop what he was doing and go with them, to examine the body *in situ.* Given his case load at the hospital, he told them to just bundle up the body and bring it. So, after puttering around at the farm for a couple of hours, taking pictures of the crime scene and bagging the evidence, the deputies carried Ernst Bauer into the morgue at six-fifteen. They set the basket down beside the table and lifted out the body. Bauer was—had been— a big man, well over six feet, almost six and a half, and thick through the shoulders.

Ramsey directed the deputies in positioning the body on its dorsal surface, so he could study and photograph the major wounds. He made them stay while he examined the clothing, took snips and samples for blood tests, and correlated its physical damage with the injuries. Finally, he had the deputies strip the body, catalog the garments, and reposition Bauer with limbs straight.

Then he let the men go, because the rest of his work involved sights no healthy young buck should be paid to see. Hell, he himself had seen entirely too much of this sort of death when he was practicing in central Philadelphia. He came up to Sylvan

295

County just to find a place where people, on the whole, died of natural causes.

Ramsey did a general tactile examination of the head, neck, thorax, abdomen, and as much as he could reach along the spine. The skin of shoulders and back was pale with splotches of plum-colored bruising that corresponded to pressure points against the floor where Bauer had lain. Ramsay scraped the fingernails, turned the head and swabbed the exposed cavities—what was left of them—and peeled back the lid on the remaining eye to shine a light on the retina for signs of central nervous system bleeding, which was copious.

By now it was nearly eight o'clock, and Ramsey was just beginning the Y-cut to expose the abdominal cavity. Bauer had a good layer of fat down there, and it puffed out slick and yellow on either side of the scalpel. Upon reaching the pubis, the coroner put aside the blade and spread the major incision with his gloved hands. Ramsey was head down, practically inside the cavity, juggling the stomach and first yard or so of the small intestine in one hand to clear a path to the liver, reaching for a temperature probe with the other.

He heard the swinging doors of the morgue open, but he didn't pause to look up and see who it was. "Go away," he said.

"Doctor Ramsey?" a voice called out.

"All right, if you won't leave, make yourself useful."

"What can I do?" the voice said, sounding sincerely helpful.

"Hold this," the doctor said, pushing stomach and loops of gut across the table. A pair of tanned hands came forward to take the organs—and they were ungloved. Ramsey snatched the mass back. "No, no! Don't touch it."

"But you said—"

Ramsey looked up. It was Rafe Cobb, the sheriff. He wondered what the man was doing here. He would certainly have seen enough of Bauer and his condition, out at the farm, to last most people a lifetime.

"If you're going to hang around, you'd better put on a mask." He pointed with his chin at the box on the counter. "Don't touch anything, either, unless you put on gloves."

While Cobb went to get outfitted, Ramsey found his probe, made a space, and plunged it into the liver. Then he settled back on his heels. They'd get a reading real soon now.

"What can you tell me about him?" Cobb said, coming back to the table.

"Well, for one thing, he's dead," Ramsey said, never tiring of his little joke.

"Can you tell me exactly when Bauer died?" The sheriff peered into the cavity.

Ramsey noted that Cobb skipped the obvious questions about cause of death.

"If you mean, to the minute, then no," he replied. "But after the temperature probe I just placed equilibrates, I'll take a reading and do a bit of fancy math. But all that'll tell me is he died sometime before noon."

"How do you know that?"

"*Livor* and *rigor mortis*."

"Because of his *liver*?"

"No, from his skin and joints, and their state subsequent to death. After you meet enough dead people, you get an eye for it. I first saw the deceased at six o'clock tonight, or shortly thereafter. He'd been down a long time, many hours, six or seven at least."

"Are you absolutely certain about that?"

Ramsey shrugged. "This work is partly art and partly science. Which part do you want to believe?"

"But not after lunch," Cobb pressed.

"If he went down that recently, it would surprise me."

"What can you tell me about the wounds?"

"They were lethal," Ramsey said drily, enjoying his second-favorite joke.

"But that's all? Two shotgun blasts? No other marks?"

"Two is all I see. Why do you ask?"

"Oh," Cobb paused. "Just a feeling. I'm thinking it's kind of hard to surprise a man in his own barn. If I wanted to kill a big man like Ernst Bauer, I'd come at him from behind. Either slug him or shoot him in the back, just get him down so I could finish him off with the gun at close range."

"Well, that's not the case," Ramsey said. "There's no sign of dorsal trauma. I felt the back of his head. There's slight discoloration on the occipital, but not enough force even to knock him out. I'd say he bumped his head when he went over backwards and lived just long enough after those two blasts for the blow to leave a mark. The rest is gravitational bruising."

"You'd swear to that in court?"

"I'll put it in my report."

"What range would you say the shots came from?"

"Not close," Ramsey said. "Six to ten feet. Some bits of wadding in the wounds, but no powder burns on skin or clothing. Not closer than about five feet. Dispersal pattern is consistent with that, too."

"And what angle?" Cobb asked.

"Hard to tell with a shotgun. You don't have a bullet pathway you can put a probe through. And with these shots to the face and neck ... If you tell me what he was doing at the time— looking down, looking up, tying his shoe—then I'll tell you the angle."

"Assume he was just walking across the floor, staring ahead into the shadows."

"Then I'd say dead on."

"The assailant was—?"

"Six feet, six and a half, same as Bauer."

"Well, that rules out most of the county."

"I can't do your job for you." Ramsey grinned.

"Can you tell me what kind of shot it was?"

"If you wait while I finish here—" The doctor nodded at the abdominal incision. "—it'll take me a couple of hours to pick the pellets out of his face and neck. From that, we can approximate the cartridge from the pellet size and load. And from *that,* you can figure the gauge of the gun. Can't be more than five or six hundred shotguns in the county. Of course, nothing will tell you which gun fired the actual shots, but the gauge will eliminate a lot of them."

"And if I don't want to wait around?"

"I'll put it in my report."

"Okay, Doc. Thank you."

"As always, it's a pleasure."

9. BEHIND FRIENDLY LINES

WILLIAM HENRY WHEELOCK was putting a coat of paste wax on the trunk lid of a powder-blue Buick sedan when he saw the young man come onto Leonard Kingston's new car lot. The young man was boyishly slender, dressed in bib overalls and a blue denim work shirt. He had bright red hair and fair skin, very pale, but so covered with freckles that they joined up in islands and archipelagoes and made him seem to be wearing a piebald tan.

Willie shuddered to see him but stepped forward anyway. "May I help you, sir?" he asked neutrally.

The young man looked at him without at trace of recognition. Of course, there was no reason the man should recognize Willie, except ...

Willie had been in charge of hauling a mixed load of infantry supplies—rifle ammunition and C-rations—in an M-35 "deuce and a half." His driver was Pfc Albert Simms, a quiet-spoken black man from Atlanta, Georgia. Their route took them across the Ardennes region, a thinly patrolled part of the Allied front between the U.S. First and Ninth Armies in the north, which were heading for Cologne and Bonn, and the Third Army in the south, which was attacking into Germany across the Saar River. It was early in November 1944, with a chill in the air and the promise of snow.

On a narrow track through the forest, they suddenly came upon a large tree lying across the road. It might have been a windfall, with three soldiers already working to clear it, except that the men were not really working. When the truck braked to a stop, they casually picked up their weapons, turned to face Willie and Simms, and moved to position themselves around the cab.

Then Willie noticed that although they were all privates together, a glance at their insignia patches showed they were all out of different units. That was the first tip-off. The second was a warning from headquarters earlier in the week that American deserters were active in the area. According to reports, they had been attacking lone trucks to sell the war materiel on the black market. In a moment, Willie had gone from worrying about making his schedule to worrying about being killed for a load of 30.06 ammunition and tins of potted meat.

The soldier on the left approached the driver's window. Simms rolled it down politely to hear what he had to say.

"We'll take your load now," the man said. His voice was almost friendly, and the rifle was cradled loosely in his arms. But his finger, Willie saw, was inside the trigger guard.

Simms turned to look at Willie, as if asking what he should do next.

On the passenger side of the truck, right next to Willie, stood the boy with the red hair. His face was so flushed that his masses of freckles stood out in pale spots. He was visibly trembling—but whether from the cold, or nervous tension, or impatience with the driver's hesitation, Willie could not tell. The boy held his rifle at the ready, its muzzle pointed up into the cab. While Simms gaped at Willie, the boy yelled, "Get out of there!" A second later he fired a shot through the windshield between them, leaving a hole in it about a foot wide and dropping a double handful of glass shards into their laps.

The boy paused to see what effect this would have. In that moment, Willie pulled his service automatic from its holster, racked the slide as part of the same motion, and shot outward through the truck's thin metal door panel. The boy was thrown back onto the rutted ground. A pulsing, red blossom grew on the front of his battle fatigues.

Now the soldier standing directly in front of the truck turned and brought his weapon to bear. Willie opened the door, stepped out with the swing of it onto the running board, raised his pistol to aim through the window and across the truck's hood, and shot the man through the head. The .45 bullet neatly removed the back half of his skull.

The man standing on the driver's side, the one who had started it all, opened his hands and let his rifle drop into the mud. "Don't shoot!" he called. "Please, don't shoot."

While Willie covered their single prisoner with his sidearm, the three of them watched the boy with the chest wound die. They did not have to confirm that the man in the middle of the road was already dead. Willie had killed exactly two people in his life—both in the last three minutes. Together he and Simms bound the remaining man hand and foot with a long piece of wire and hoisted him into the back of the truck. Then they put the bodies of his companions in with him.

When he felt steady enough, Willie turned to Simms. "You're my witness."

"To what?" the driver asked.

"To these two deaths," Willie said patiently. "Did these men try to hold us up?"

"I guess so." Simms did not seem to understand the implications.

"Did the red-headed one shoot at us?" Willie persisted.

Simms's face brightened at that. "Oh, yes, suh!"

"So the killing was justifiable, wasn't it?"

The man looked at him. "Justifiable?"

"It was necessary. I had to kill them."

"Yes, suh," Simms said. "That's so."

"And you'll say that at headquarters?"

"Say whatever you want, suh."

A month or two later, Willie received by mail a commendation citing his quick thinking and positive action in the Ardennes forest. By the end of the war, the U.S. Army had court-martialed and hanged a total of 49 American soldiers for crimes committed on French soil after D-Day. More than 100 civilians had been murdered by deserters just like those men in the Ardennes. In that light, Willie was some kind of a hero.

But there were still two people dead because of him, one of them a red-haired boy with freckles.

"No, thank you," the young man on the car lot said politely. "I think I'll just look around."

"Well, let me know if something interests you," Willie replied.

Seeing this man—who might be a brother or a cousin of the boy he had killed—suddenly brought the affair in the forest into focus for Willie. Those killings had been in the line of duty, and the men involved had fairly earned their fate—not like this man the whole town was talking about, Ernst Bauer, who had been wantonly shot to death in his own barn.

Willie had come out of the war terribly tired, weighed down by the years of rude action, of lethal decisions, of heat and cold, mud and death. And so he had welcomed a quiet place like Roulette to recuperate, to avoid the crush of responsibility, to relax and drift downstream as it were. Under other circumstances, that boy in the forest might have come home, too, and gone to work on his father's farm or gone back to school on the G.I. Bill—except for the unwise choices he had made, and the automatic responses Willie had made in turn. But now, seeing that boy apparently alive again, grown to manhood, and doing something so trivial as looking at a new car laid him to rest in Willie's mind. The past had actually become the past.

Perhaps it was time for Willie himself to move on.

10. Ruby's Café

A DAY OR two after Ernst Bauer was killed, the sheriff's deputy who was just going off graveyard and the two about to go on day shift went over to Ruby's Café for breakfast. They joined their boss, Rafe Cobb, at one of the tables near the back. He was listening to Doc Ramsey enthrall the regulars with his autopsy findings. Although the coroner was polite in his language and used euphemisms for the technical parts of his job, the sheriff and his men noted that most of the customers put their forks down and now contemplated their breakfasts with sober and sometimes green faces. Ruby herself, who listened with a scowl from behind the counter, was silently counting up the damage done to normally healthy appetites.

"A man's not safe in his own barn anymore," observed Ezra Stills. "Makes you wonder, doesn't it?"

"It must have been somebody with a grudge against Bauer," said Harold Burke. Here he was only stating what, to most of the crowd, was the obvious.

"Could be drifters," said Clarence. "Been a lot of people cut loose since the war."

"Drifters don't have reason," said Walt Dufour. "Not to shoot a man to death."

"They would if he came upon them sudden-like," Clarence insisted. "Surprised them."

"But they don't have the hate and anger," said Burke. "Not to shoot twice."

"Well then … who?" Ezra Stills asked.

One of the deputies started to open his mouth.

Cobb kicked him, hard, under the table.

"It could have been Klaus Riesenberg," Harold Burke said quietly.

"Why would *Riesenberg* want to do it?" asked Leonard Kingston, who owned the car dealership.

"Well, he is a Jew," Burke offered.

"Now why is that significant?"

"Bauer was German, wasn't he?"

"You're saying this was a vengeance killing? Because of the Nazis?" Dufour said. "That doesn't sound like the professor."

"And anyway, Bauer was an American citizen," said Reverend Stevens, who still came in for breakfast although he had formally retired from the ministry some years earlier. "It was Ernst's father who came over, after the first war. Ernst's wife, Emily, was a German national but she emigrated back in thirty-six. That hardly fits your theory, Harold."

"And furthermore," said James Harris, who didn't usually eat breakfast at Ruby's but had started coming in the last couple of weeks, "Riesenberg isn't Jewish at all. I just found that out."

"So what is he?" Burke asked.

"He's a Red. A Communist. Judge Wheelock's been harboring a Communist here amongst us since before the war, first as his gardener and then as town librarian." From the way he smiled as he said this, Harris sounded … triumphant. "He's working on our minds from the inside."

"Well, Communists hate the Nazis, too, don't they?" said Burke.

"Riesenberg's from Poland." Ezra Stills shrugged. "Anyone from Poland is a Red by definition."

"Everyone knows Klaus's politics," said Reverend Stevens. "Sure, he's a socialist but no Bolshevik."

"He's done wonders for the library," added Dufour. "You can actually find a book in there now."

"His wife tutors my little Sarah," said one of the deputies. "The kid loves her."

"Well then … who?" Stills repeated, returning to the subject of murder.

People looked uncomfortable, and the center of attention shifted to Cobb's table.

"A killer like that can't stay hid," the sheriff said. "We'll find whoever did it."

"You'll have to," said Walter Dufour, who was also the mayor. "This is going to be the biggest case to hit this town in ten years."

11. SUSPICIONS

ON THE AFTERNOON that Ernst Bauer was killed, Alma Riesenberg had driven over to the farm for the usual lessons with the twins and been turned away by the sheriff's deputies. They had given her the note from the Bauer twins, left in the kitchen door and found by the sheriff, that proved her services were not needed that day.

Out of consideration for the feelings of Emily Bauer, Alma was slow to call her about further tutoring. And when Alma did call later in the week, Frau Bauer answered the phone, told her *"Einen Moment,"* and then quietly hung up. Alma Riesenberg tried to be understanding.

A week or more after the murder, a letter came to the house at the end of the lane for "Frau Riesenberg." Alma opened and read it. She sat on the sofa in the front parlor and read it again. She put it aside, made a cup of tea, and read it a third time. Then she put it on Klaus's desk and spent the afternoon thinking.

In the evening, when her husband returned home from the library, she greeted him at the door, took his coat, and handed him the letter.

"What is this?" he asked, taking it.

The envelope was small and square, as if for a greeting card. The address was written in pencil with a blocky, childish hand that he would not recognize but that Alma had known immediately.

"Look at the return," Alma said.

" 'The Bauer Property,' " he read out, " 'Star Route 9, Roulette, Pennsylvania.' It is from the twins. ... Or one of them," he amended.

The sheet inside was tissue-thin and crackled like vellum—some of the drafting paper Alma had left after that first geometry lesson. It was folded so small that the tiny envelope bulged at the corners. Alma suspected that the envelope, as well as the stamp, had been taken from Emily Bauer's writing desk without her knowledge.

"Read it," Alma said grimly.

"Dear Frau-Doctor-Professor," he began in a light voice, suitable for a message from a child. "We hope you are well. We are both well here, although we are very sad for Papa and miss him terribly. Trude and I miss you, too. We have only good memories of you.

"Our Mama is sad as well. She does not yell at us anymore, as she used to. We do not see her so much. She stays in her bedroom all day long and is very quiet."

Here the handwriting changed slightly. Alma perceived that Trude had taken the pencil from Hannah—although neither hand showed the grace of the note left for her at the farm on the day Ernst Bauer died.

"There is a question we must ask you, dear Frau Riesenberg.

"On Monday Mr. Maires came into the house to live with us. He eats at our table now, three meals a day. And he sleeps upstairs, in Mother's bedroom. So, please, tell us what is correct. Must we now call him 'Father'?"

The letter was signed, "Your friends, Hannah and Trude," with each name in a different handwriting.

"P.S. We are working steadily on the geometry that you taught us and wish we could have you back as our teacher."

Klaus absorbed this in one reading, then handed it to his wife.

"That is a bad woman," Alma said finally, summing up everything she had been thinking during the afternoon.

"Weak perhaps," Klaus said. "Emotionally confused. She had a great shock."

"*Feh!*" She made as if to spit. "A widow keeps her bed to herself for at least a year. That is the custom—even in this country."

Alma Riesenberg hesitated for a moment. Then she told her husband what she saw the last time she was in that house to teach the girls: how Lance Maires had come down the back stairs, picked up his hat, and gone out the back door; how Emily had come down a few minutes later and seemed flustered and angry.

"I told you," she said. "A bad woman."

"Maires always struck me as a hard man," he said. "One who gets his way."

"Hard enough to kill Herr Bauer in order to take his woman?"

"I don't know. I suppose that is a possibility."

"What about those girls?" Alma asked.

" 'Call him *Vater*,' indeed!" Klaus said.

"Well, what are we going to do about this?"

"I suppose we should ask Herr Wheelock."

"That is a good idea," Alma said.

"The Judge always knows what to do."

12. Naming a Suspect

ROBERT WHEELOCK WAS sitting at his desk in chambers, reading the Harrisburg *Bulletin*, which he did methodically, first page to last, every morning that court was not in session. Because it was not a court day, he was in shirtsleeves instead of his judge's robes. The coffee at his right hand was cold, and he was just thinking of getting himself a fresh cup when there was a knock at the door.

"Come in," he called.

"Judge, it is I, Riesenberg," Klaus said from beyond the door.

"Well, in that case then, come in," Robert said with a smile.

The man came through the door sideways, as if he didn't want to be seen. After a pause, his wife Alma followed. They walked up to Robert's desk and stood awkwardly. Riesenberg was turning a piece of paper over and over in his hands.

"Won't you sit down, Klaus? Alma?"

"I don't think—here." He put the paper on Robert's desk and stepped back.

"What is it?" Robert could see it was a piece of translucent drafting paper, folded too many times, and smudged at the corners.

"Please," Riesenberg said. "Open and read."

Robert took up the paper and did so. It was not until he reached the end, coming to the names Hannah and Trude, and remembering that these were the Bauer twins, that he understood some of what he was reading.

"When did you receive this?"

"Yesterday," Klaus said.

"Is this the girls' handwriting?"

"I'd swear to it," Alma said.

"How did it come to you?"

"By post."

"Do you still have the envelope?"

"Yes, here." Klaus pulled it from his pocket and offered it.

Robert took the envelope, read the address and return. Then he went back to the letter and re-read certain phrases. He suddenly became cautious: this could all be nothing. "Why did you bring it to me, Klaus?"

"Is it not obvious?" he said. "The hired hand, that Lance Maires, has taken up with the mother."

"So it would appear. And?"

"It …" Klaus took his lower lip between his teeth.

"It is not the first time," Alma Riesenberg said. "When I was at the Bauer farm, before that day, I saw the two of them together. Well, not together exactly. We were in the kitchen, the girls and I, starting lessons in geometry. Then Maires came down the back stairs. He did not expect to see us, I think. A few minutes later Emily Bauer came down. She was not … composed."

"Where was Ernst Bauer at the time?"

"Out in the fields. Away in town. I do not know."

"But you did not see him?"

"Not that day. Not around."

"Would you testify to this liaison in court?" Robert asked.

"Yes! Just so much as I have said here."

Robert considered for a moment more. Then he picked up the telephone and called for Sheriff Cobb and Prosecutor Twombley to come to his chambers.

Fifteen minutes later, with the court stenographer installed in one corner and Robert wearing his robes again, he read the Bauer girls' letter aloud for the record and recommenced the interrogation of Alma Riesenberg. When the woman had finished her story, Cobb whistled.

"It sure sounds suspicious," he said. "Maires and Emily Bauer."

"You said your deputies were looking for Lance Maires that day?" Robert noted for the record.

"Not looking. I just asked if they'd seen him. Emily said he was in town."

"And had they?" Robert asked.

"Nobody saw him," the sheriff said.

"Were you suspicious of Maires at the time?"

"Not suspicious. Just trying to figure out where everyone was."

Robert recalled the facts of the case as he knew them.

"You worked out the gauge of the shotgun?" he asked Cobb.

"Twelve gauge. Possibly an over-and-under," Cobb said.

"You asked about the guns on the farm, I take it?"

"Emily denied that Ernst ever owned a shotgun. She didn't know about Lance. When I asked him later, he said twelve-gauge. But he couldn't lay his hands on it right then. Said he hadn't used it in a couple of years."

"You and your deputies searched the farm," Robert pressed.

Cobb nodded. "We looked everywhere. Every cabinet and cupboard on the place. Even the crawlspace under the house. No sign of the murder weapon."

"But Lance Maires admitted to having such a gun," Robert summed up.

"I'd like to point out," said Twombley, "that a shotgun of that gauge is probably the most popular in the county. I'd hate to try to convict a man on that evidence alone."

"Objection noted," Robert said. Then he turned to Cobb, "Can you describe the wounds caused by the shots?"

"Two close patterns," the man said. "Neck and face, from about six feet or so. Pretty level firing angle. Doc Ramsey would be better to testify to this, of course."

" 'Level firing angle,' " Robert repeated. "What does that mean?"

"At that range, whoever was holding the gun had it same height as the deceased's face. Someone just about as big as Ernst."

Robert thought back over the years, to his brief contacts with Ernst Bauer's hired man. Maires had sold him a gun once, an antique fowling piece that Robert had restored. Maires was a big man, taller than Robert himself, maybe even as tall as Bauer.

Then there was the evidence of the children's letter. That might constitute motive, if a man's sexual urges were strong enough to cloud his judgment and erode his loyalties to an employer.

And still no one could say, for sure, that Maires had not been on the farmstead that day. The opportunity for murder was all around.

"From the way Bauer fell," Cobb went on, "bang, bang, and over backwards—it's pretty clear that whoever did it wasn't scared of Ernst. He faced up to his victim, didn't feel the need to waylay him."

Robert looked up at Peter Twombley. "Would you call that a case, Counselor?"

The county prosecutor grimaced. "It's thin enough. But who else have we got? Farm out in the country, and no trace of anyone else on the property."

Robert thought for a moment. "I'd have to agree with you on that point."

"Do you want me to arrest Lance Maires?" Cobb asked quietly. "We can at least see how he reacts."

"Yes," Robert said finally. "I'll make out the warrant this morning."

He dismissed the court recorder, as the formal proceedings were now completed. He thanked Klaus and Alma Riesenberg, and the couple left his chambers behind the stenographer. Robert set to tidying up the papers on his desk. The prosecutor and sheriff hung back. Robert put the unfolded letter and envelope in a manila envelope and handed it to Twombley, for evidence.

The prosecutor took it, then hesitated. "Who do you think will defend Maires?" he asked. "Not that I'm worried, mind you."

"For a sensational murder in a town this size?" Robert said. "Harris will break a leg rushing to offer his services. He'd take the case for free, too."

"That's right," Cobb said. "With the election coming up, word is Jim Harris plans to run against you again, Judge."

"So I heard," Robert said.

"Then I'll try not to lose this case for you," Twombley said.

"You'll put Maires away only because he's guilty, hear?"

"Yes, Your Honor," the man said. "Guilty as sin."

13. Jane Dobray

Alfreda Burke had accepted Jane as a boarder on her husband's say-so. But as Jane was carrying her suitcase up the stairs, she heard the woman make a telephone call. From the one side of the conversation she could catch, Jane guessed the woman was confirming details of her meeting with Harold Burke earlier in the afternoon. After the name Margot Dobray was mentioned, all Jane could hear was hissing whispers.

Well, she did not expect to stay in town longer than a day or two, until she cleared up the matter of her mother's two hundred dollars with Judge Wheelock. The weekly rate Mrs. Burke had quoted for room and board, twenty-five dollars, would cut into a big part of that, along with what Jane had already spent on a bus ticket to get to Roulette and what she would have to spend to leave. But if you took that room rate day by day—figuring three dollars and fifty-seven cents a day—it wasn't so much. And there was no other way to get her money.

"Really nothing else," Jane said to herself as she closed the door behind her to confront a small room with a painted iron bed frame, made up with sheets and blanket on a thin mattress, one upholstered chair, a dressing table that doubled as a bureau, and behind it a mirror whose silver backing ran in dark streaks of tarnish. The bathroom was down the hall, please knock before entering.

Jane suddenly understood that this room and others like it— barren, pinch-penny, featureless rooms—would be her lot for the foreseeable future, whether here in Roulette, back in New York, or wherever she went. Maybe for the rest of her life. "Really nothing more," she repeated sadly and began unpacking her suitcase into the bureau drawers.

Dinner at six o'clock was pot roast, boiled potatoes, and stewed greens, shared with three strangers and Mrs. Burke. The strangers were men, clean enough considering their cuffs and collars, salesmen traveling along the "Northern Tier" according to their mumbled talk. Jane asked Alfreda Burke about her husband and learned he usually stayed late when court was in session.

After dinner, the other boarders repaired to their rooms or went to look for a bar, leaving Jane alone in the parlor with her landlady and, after an hour or so, Harold Burke. The couple sat reading—he the newspaper, she a magazine—feeling no need to entertain their boarder. Jane wished she had brought a book.

When Burke made the slightest movement to lay aside his paper, Jane pounced.

"How long has Mr. Wheelock been judge?" she asked.

"Since before the war," he said. "Going on ten years."

"So I guess he's a pretty important man here in town."

"You could say that. He's well set up. Got a big house over on the river. His daddy was judge before him, you know, along with he owned the electric company and the branch-line railroad. And Judge Wheelock himself probably owns half the—"

"Now, Harold," his wife warned. "Don't get into gossip she doesn't need to hear."

"You said the judge is in the middle of a trial?" Jane prompted.

"Oh, yes," Burke said, giving Alfreda a look. "About the biggest thing to happen around here since the repeal of Prohibition, I guess. One of the local farmers got himself gunned down by his own hired man, who then took up with his wife, bold as brass. Case came to trial two days ago, and the prosecution just rested this afternoon. That's why you can't get in to see the judge for a bit. Not until this one goes to the jury.

"Tomorrow our Mr. James Harris will open for the defense," Burke went on. "I don't see as how he's got much to work with, though. The defendant, Maires, had plenty of opportunity and the only motive. He benefits from the deed if he marries the widow. The only thing that would lock it up is the murder weapon, and they never found that. But, hell—"

"Harold!" his wife exclaimed.

"Sorry, m'dear. But that shotgun could be at the bottom of the river, any river or creek, or down a well, anywhere within a hundred miles of here. Don't see what's so hard to figure out. The man's got to be guilty."

"I think that's about enough," Alfreda Burke said. "Our guest is bored to tears."

"Sorry, m'dear. … But since Miss Dobray's got nothing else to do the next day or two, she ought to drop by the courthouse. It's the best show in town right now, and the seats are free."

"Thank you," Jane said. "I might just plan to attend, at that."

It would be one way to see who this man Wheelock was.

14. Incident at the A&P

Libby Wheelock did not usually do the family grocery shopping. Alma Riesenberg had long ago assumed that chore as housekeeper. Alma would make out her own weekly list, check for anything special Libby might want, collect the money from Libby's desk, and drive Robert's big, black Chrysler down the five blocks to the Great Atlantic & Pacific Tea Company store in town. But this morning Alma had called up from the house at the end of the lane complaining of a headache, so Libby had urged her to stay in bed and undertook the trip herself.

Because she had a busy day ahead, Libby had gotten an early start and arrived at the market shortly after eight o'clock. Clearly, she was not the only busy person, as the small parking lot was already full of cars. She was forced off to one side, along the fence, where cars were required to park in parallel, rather than pull in diagonally in front of the store.

Libby was an inexperienced driver and admitted as much. She had taken lessons once, years ago, but she never traveled far. Her only need for a car was attending social functions around town, and she found she could walk to most of those. At one time, when he had served as Robert's groundsman, Libby had asked Klaus Riesenberg to drive as her chauffeur. But since he had taken the job as librarian, she was reduced to driving herself. She could maneuver a big car like the Chrysler safely enough along the streets, of course. But the procedures for backing and filling, and the mysterious sense one was supposed to acquire for locating bumpers and fenders without actually seeing them, all of it was hazy in her mind.

However, she managed to position the car well enough in the one available space without hearing the screech of tortured metal. Libby went about her business in the store and then brought out her bags of groceries with the help of a clerk, who packed them into the trunk. She meant to ask the young man to stay and guide her in extracting the car from the space, to stand in the narrow lane alongside her window and tell her when she was clear both front and rear, but he was already headed back into the market before she could speak.

Well, if she could get the car into this box by herself, that implied she could get it out again, didn't it?

Libby sat at the steering wheel with the engine running and experimented briefly to find which way her front tires were pointing. Satisfied with the results, she put the car into gear and moved forward gently.

Thump!

The noise from in front told her she had touched bumpers with the car ahead. She turned the wheel a quarter turn and backed off.

Thunk! This time from the rear.

Libby turned the wheel again and tried moving forward.

THUNK! Even faster and louder from the front bumper now.

The car was locked in place on a diagonal in a parallel space. Further trials with wheel and gas pedal showed she had just inches of room to spare.

Libby felt like crying. She thought about going back into the market and calling for a tow truck. She considered walking over to the library and asking Klaus to come and remove her from this humiliating predicament. Other than that, she was stuck.

"Can I help you, ma'am?" came a voice from beyond the driver's window.

Libby turned in her seat to see a young woman with a pretty face, short auburn hair, and a belted raincoat standing beside the car. Libby turned off the engine and rolled down the window.

"I seem to be stuck," she said.

"It doesn't look too bad." The girl walked to the front of the car, then to the rear, and returned to the window. "We can do this," she said.

"Do you want to get in and drive?" Libby asked.

"No, ma'am. I don't have a license. But I've seen plenty of taxicabs get out of squeakers a lot tighter than you're in and not lose a fleck of paint."

Libby did not find this reassuring, but she was in no position to argue.

"Now, ma'am, your front tires are about thirty degrees left. You want to get them straight. Turn right until I tell you to stop."

Libby followed along obediently.

"Whoa!" said the girl. "Good. Now start the car and put it in reverse. Ease back as far as you can, and don't mind touching the car behind you. You've got a big old bumper with a lot of chrome on it and so does he."

Libby complied and tried not to blush at the resulting *thump*.

"Okay, now. Turn your wheels all the way left. More. More. … More."

Libby turned the steering wheel until her arms ached. She could hear the front tires crunching the gravel of the parking lot.

"Good. Now a little bit of gas and go until you just tap the front bumper."

Libby drove forward and didn't mind the sound so much this time.

"Now turn the wheels all the way right," the girl said. "Turn. Turn. Turn."

Libby was actually grinning as she complied and the gravel complained.

The girl talked her through two more cycles of backwards and forwards, turn left, turn right. Then she walked to the front of Libby's car, studied the resulting clearance, and called for her to drive out.

Libby held her breath and moved the car forward.

The tires rolled softly across gravel. No bump. No thump. No screech.

The girl gave her a big grin and a thumbs up. "I knew you could do it."

"How can I ever thank you?" Libby asked. She reached across the seat for her purse.

The girl tossed her head. "No thanks necessary, ma'am. It's what people are supposed to do for each other."

Before Libby could embarrass herself by offering money, the girl had turned and walked off, disappearing out of the lot.

15. Case for the Defense

By the time Jane Dobray got to the courthouse it was going on nine o'clock, which was the time Harold Burke had said the trial would reconvene that morning. A crowd was waiting to go up the stairs to the gallery where members of the public could observe the proceedings. They were mostly men in cleaned-up farm clothes and baggy suits—what Jane thought of as their "Sunday best"—plus a few women in print dresses and hats. For anyone else, the chances of getting a seat up there would have been slight, but years on the New York subway had taught Jane the value of sharp elbows, and when that didn't work she relied on a feminine smile and flash of eyes. She ended up with a seat right up against the railing and overlooking the whole courtroom.

Jane was curious about this man Robert Wheelock, because he was the one solid link she had to her mother's past. Apparently, before Margot came to New York City, she had worked for him—although Jane could not imagine what as, because she didn't think he had any concert hall tickets for her to sell or steel to weld.

"All rise," ordered a uniformed bailiff down by the judge's raised desk.

Jane and everyone else stood up. A door opened at the back of the room, and the judge entered. He was a nice-enough looking man, middle-aged with light brown hair thinning on top and going to gray around the sides. He was tall and looked taller because of the long black robes he wore. He looked scholarly, but that could just be the glasses perched halfway down his nose.

Judge Wheelock took his seat and nodded genially to the room.

"Oyez, oyez, oyez," the bailiff called. "The Honorable Court of Sylvan County, Commonwealth of Pennsylvania, the Honorable Robert Wheelock presiding, is now in session. All who have business before this court come forward and you shall be heard. God save the United States and this honorable court. ... Be seated."

There was a general rustle as everyone in the room sat down.

"Thank you," Wheelock said quietly. "Last night Mr. Twombley rested his case for the prosecution. Do I hear any motions in this trial?"

"No, Your Honor," chorused two voices. Jane guessed they came from the two men in reasonably good suits seated at parallel tables inside the courtroom railing. The man sitting alone at the table on the right, whom she guessed was Twombley, would be the prosecutor. The man on the left was accompanied by another person, a big fellow dressed in khaki pants and a plaid workshirt. That would be the defense table, the lawyer and his client. What had Harold Burke said about the trial? A farmhand, supposed to have murdered his employer. Meers? Mayers? Something like that. With a shotgun nobody had found.

"Then, Mr. Harris, you may proceed," Wheelock said and settled back in his high, leather-covered chair. The judge seemed totally at ease, running his court like a family business, which from Burke's description Jane guessed it was.

It suddenly occurred to Jane, from the fact Wheelock had written a large check to her mother—and, from the lack of any cover note, he had probably been writing those checks for years—that this man might actually be Jane's natural father. When she was growing up, other girls always seemed to have fathers but Jane had none. And when she asked Margot about this, her mother had told Jane many stories. Once, her father was a cowboy from Colorado. Another time he was from Pennsylvania, some kind of miner. There was even one story where he worked the oil fields out in California. He was supposed to have died in a fire. Or a terrible explosion. And once Margot told Jane her father had died to make a lazy man rich—perhaps accidentally, or maybe he had been killed on purpose, to hush things up. Jane did not know what to believe.

While Robert Wheelock was from Pennsylvania, he obviously was not dead. Jane tried to fit this man's presence with any image built up from Margot's stories. Nothing fit. And besides, when she looked at Wheelock now, Jane felt no spark. She had always imagined that if she ever found her father—despite the condition that he was supposed to have died before she was born—she would recognize him instantly, that the psychic bond, the call of the blood, would lead her to him. This man touched nothing in Jane.

Perhaps then he was the lazy rich man, still paying Margot to hush things up.

"Thank you, Your Honor," said the attorney from the table on the left. He was a handsome, dapper man with, from what Jane could see of his face, a smile meant to be confident and at the same time trustworthy. She had seen a lot like him coming and going from the commercial buildings along Fifth Avenue.

"Call as my first witness Elias Bordon," Harris said.

That caused a murmur to go through the courtroom. Jane gathered that none of the spectators had ever heard of any Elias Bordon. It turned out when the man who came to the witness stand was sworn and Harris had walked him through preliminary questioning, that he was a detective, one of several, with an agency in Scranton, Pennsylvania. He had been retained by the defense to search the Bauer farm where the murder took place.

Here the prosecutor raised an objection about the propriety of a separate search. Harris stated that he had a warrant made out for it by Judge Wheelock. And Wheelock overruled the prosecutor. "Proceed with your questions, Counselor."

"Thank you, Your Honor," Harris said. Then to the detective, "and what did you discover in your search?"

"We found a twelve-gauge, over-and-under shotgun."

That caused another murmur, much louder this time.

"And where did you find the weapon?" Harris asked.

"It was concealed inside a bale of straw, in the barn."

Harris reached into a duffle bag behind the defense table and removed a shotgun wrapped in a transparent protective sheeting. A white card was tied to the trigger guard. Two expended cartridges, brass bases on red paper tubes, were visible inside the sheeting. He carried the gun to the witness stand. "Is this the weapon?"

Bordon checked the card. "It is. This is my tag."

Harris presented the object to the bailiff. "I enter this as Defense Exhibit A."

The prosecutor, Twombley, made a half-movement as if he was going to object. The judge looked directly at him. Twombley subsided. "Nothing, Your Honor."

Harris turned back to his witness.

"Did you inspect and test the weapon?"

"We did," Bordon said. "From dissipation of the volatile substances in the powder residue inside the barrel and in the cartridges there, we determined that the gun had been fired within the past month to six weeks."

"Did you run any other tests?"

"We recovered seven separate fingerprints from the gun," he said. "Two matched thumb and index finger of the defendant. However, those prints were partially obscured by two of the other five prints we recovered. We also recovered three prints from the cartridges, none of them the defendant's."

"Could you identify those other prints?"

"We obtained several common household objects from the farm, also under the warrant," Bordon said. "Among them were a hair brush, perfume bottles, lipstick, and other items from Emily Bauer's dressing table. The prints on these items match the prints on the gun and cartridges."

An extended murmur, this time punctuated by several small cries, went through the courtroom. To Jane's ear, the entire build-up of defense counsel's story had been near-perfect, leading to this climax and release of feeling. Judge Wheelock tapped his gavel for order.

Jane leaned over the balcony to study the spectators behind the railing on the main floor. If this was trial for the murder of Ernst Bauer, then Emily would be his wife. Jane expected the woman to be in attendance, seeking justice. And now she would be in a state of shock and collapse. But nobody down there was stricken with guilt or anxiety. Jane noticed other people in the gallery and on the floor similarly looking around.

"Good thing the widow's not in court," the man next to Jane whispered to his companion.

"Supposed to be prostrate with grief," the companion snickered.

During this pause, Harris had produced a number of items including the hair brush from his bag and entered them as exhibits.

"Did you find anything else at the farm?" he asked his witness.

"By the time we arrived, more than a week after the event, the crime scene had been examined, photographed, and cleaned up by the local deputies," Bordon said. "But I should mention that, for some unknown reason, they did not move or examine the hay bale, evident in the photograph marked People's Exhibit J, where we found the gun and cartridges. We did study those photographs, Exhibits J through M, and noted a curious feature."

Harris had the bailiff retrieve blowups of the photos and mount them on an easel. He handed Bordon a pointer.

"You see these drifts of straw?" Bordon indicated several low clumps. "They're scattered around the bale and in a general line leading back to the barn door. What we found, when we examined these photos, is that none of the straws show blood spatters on their upper surfaces. And those touching the puddles of blood from the victim are soaked only on their undersides."

"What does that tell you?" Harris asked.

"That the straw was laid down after the shots were fired and the victim fell."

"Now, Mr. Bordon, you've heard Doctor Ramsey's testimony about the victim's wounds and the angle at which the shots were fired. It's the doctor's contention that the person who fired them was a large man, at least as tall as Ernst Bauer—in fact, about the defendant's size. What would you say if I told you that Emily Bauer, whose prints are on the gun, was a small woman, barely more than five feet tall?"

"I'd say she could have stood on the hay bale to fire the shots. We measured the height of that bale and other bales in the barn, and it's consistent with raising a person of her stature to the firing height. The sides of the bale in the photo were run down enough for someone to have climbed all over it. In fact, if the straw had not been so loosened, no one could have pushed the gun inside, where we found it."

"Objection," said the prosecutor. "This is mere speculation."

Judge Wheelock looked at the defense attorney. "Well, Counselor?"

"It's an informed hypothesis, Your Honor, based on the physical evidence."

"Overruled," the judge said.

The courtroom let out a collective sigh, and Wheelock used his gavel again.

Harris continued. "Did you examine the note, marked People's Exhibit Q, that was written by the two Bauer girls to their tutor, Mrs. Riesenberg, about a week after the shooting?"

"We did," Bordon agreed.

"Did you further see the note, marked People's A, that Sheriff Cobb originally found in the farmhouse door, also addressed to Mrs. Riesenberg?"

"Of course, we did."

"Did anything strike you as curious about these two notes?"

"They were obviously not written by the same person or even, in the case of twin girls, by persons of the same approximate age and facility with penmanship."

"Did you obtain writing samples in your search of the farm?"

"Yes, several, from all members of the household."

"And what did comparison of these samples tell you?"

"Our handwriting experts place a very high probability on the note in the door having been written by Emily Bauer."

"Did you have a chance to interview the girls?" Harris asked.

"Under the terms of our warrant, we interviewed them in the presence of the prosecutor and a court stenographer."

"Did you ask about their visiting Thorvald's farm, as described in the note?"

"We did," Bordon said. "Each of the twins stated that the suggestion for the visit came from Emily Bauer and that she wrote the note to Mrs. Riesenberg."

"Thank you. No further questions, Your Honor."

"The witness may step down," Wheelock said. "Considering the hour, I think we'll take an hour's recess for lunch."

———

Robert could only sit high on the bench and watch as Harris and his Scranton detective demolished the prosecution's case. Of course he remembered signing the search warrant that Harris requested for the Bauer farm. At the time Robert had been fairly certain there was nothing more to find. He had trusted Cobb's deputies to make a thorough search and had not questioned when they failed to recover the murder weapon.

Now it was clear that they had not searched in any scientific, or even imaginative, fashion. The murder weapon had been practically in plain sight all the time. Only the fact that the average farm boy—which the county's deputies mostly were—considered a hay bale to be a solid thing and not a place of concealment had kept them from probing and taking apart that slipshod bale. Anyone who expected them to do that would want them to tear apart the hundred or so other bales in the barn as well.

The further revelation, about the blood on the straw, showed the deputies' simple lack of detective skills. Rafe Cobb had a lot of work ahead of him, to train someone from his department in current forensic procedure.

In the moment before he called for recess, Robert looked around at faces in his courtroom. Harris, of course, was quietly triumphant. Twombley was crestfallen. Lance Maires simply looked grim. And the spectators showed mixed emotions: admiration for Harris and his skill, relief if they were friends of the defendant, and concern as common citizens that the crime everyone had thought was so neatly solved turned out to be even more complex. Many of the men in town would sleep more lightly tonight, in their new awareness of what an unhappy wife was capable.

One face, up on the balcony, caught Robert's attention. It was a young woman who seemed neither relieved nor concerned. She seemed untouched by the proceedings altogether. But she shared down at Robert with an intensity that he could not interpret.

She was short, compared to the men around her, and had reddish-blonde hair. Her face was pretty enough, and the set of her eyes reminded him of someone. Robert tried to think if he remembered her from around town. But he could not place her.

In any event, he had a decision to make as judge, and that would direct the course of the afternoon. Based on the evidence now at hand and the obvious failure of police work supporting the prosecution, Robert could declare a mistrial at this point. In fact, he would welcome such a motion if Twombley would make it. But if not, Robert decided to let the case proceed. Jim Harris deserved his moment of glory with his closing argument. Sheriff Cobb deserved to eat some crow, if it would inspire him to do a better job next time—always presuming another such spectacular case might come along in the next ten years or so.

And Robert trusted that the jury, when the case went to them, would make the sensible choice and declare Lance Maires not guilty. He had that much faith in his fellow citizens.

16. Love at First Sight

Willie had taken his lunch hour at the automobile dealership early so that he could go downtown to Morton's Pharmacy and buy himself a bar of shaving soap, a new tooth brush, and sundries. The store always made him feel vaguely uneasy, with its shelves of wrapped bandages and its smells of camphorated salve and rubbing alcohol. It reminded him of an aid station, during the war—except for the blood. There was no stain of blood on the floorboards in Morton's.

He was looking at a display of Gillette safety blades, trying to decide if he needed any, when a young woman walked in. She passed right behind him, so close that he felt the breeze of her passage and smelled the faint spice of lemon verbena from her perfume. Willie looked after her and saw, from the back, a bell-shaped coiffure of glossy, reddish blonde hair, almost the color of raw honey, above a tan trench coat belted around a tiny, twenty-inch waist. Below that were a pair of shapely calves in nylon stockings, and then slender ankles that tapered into the heels of black patent leather pumps. This lovely manifestation did not suggest to him any of the women Willie knew from around town.

Roulette did not have many young women his own age, and not many of any age that were available. Willie found that he was holding his breath against the moment when she would turn and reveal a face, even a profile, that he recognized. He watched, one hand on the razor blades, to see what she did.

The woman went up to the counter at the back of the store, where Fred Morton dispensed his prescriptions and offered advice. Willie strained to hear the woman's voice, conscious also that anything she might say to Morton would probably be of a medical nature and so confidential—if not positively embarrassing. But he listened anyway.

All he heard was a velvety murmur.

Morton nodded and murmured back.

Then the pharmacist looked up and pointed back down the aisle, straight at Willie. The young woman turned to follow his gesture, and Willie was caught staring. He got the barest glimpse of her face before he had to look away to demonstrate that he was not—no, ma'am, not at all—staring at her.

Of course, she caught him at it. And surprisingly, in the instant before he diverted his eyes, she nodded to him and smiled.

Willie gazed out the drug store's front window, pretending to study the traffic but actually reveling in the afterimage of a sweet, oval face with wide-set dark-gray eyes that had a confident, glad light in them. The woman's mouth was painted red, of course, but it was a natural color that simply defined her lips—not the garish shades that women in the magazines seemed to be wearing these days. She was beautiful. And she knew it, too, from the way she had stared back at him—although that did not appear to make her haughty. Unlike so many American girls, she did not seem to be angry at him for looking at her. Instead, her smile suggested a European woman's pleasure at being appreciated. Perhaps—or so he imagined—she felt some kind of affinity for Willie and saw him as a kindred spirit. Best of all, she was nobody he recognized.

While Willie was engaged in these musings, he heard the click of her heels coming down the aisle. Within ten seconds he was once again aware of her perfume.

"Excuse me?" Her voice was contralto, pleasantly modulated, a singer's voice.

"Yes?" He turned to face her. "Can I help you?"

"You're standing in front of the razors," she said, pointing. "I need to buy one."

William Henry's heart sank. "For your husband?" he said, not bothering to hide his disappointment.

She laughed. "Now why would you think that?"

"These are men's razors," he said with a shrug.

"Don't the women in this town shave their legs?"

"I'm sure they do—but usually not where I can see."

"See what? The act of shaving—or the places they shave?"

"Sometimes the one," he said with a grin. "And sometimes the other."

"But you did say 'usually,' didn't you. So, do you have a wife or what?"

"At present, the young lady in question has not even become an 'or what.' "

"Poor you," she said with a sad little moue.

God, it was pleasant trading quips with an alert woman. It was something Willie had not done since his college days.

Keeping eye contact with him, she reached around Willie for the item she sought. He moved aside and, glancing down, saw that her hand was bare, ungloved, which seemed strange in a woman who was otherwise so stylishly dressed, because his mother would never think of going downtown without gloves. It was also a hand without rings. Then Willie noticed that she was touching not the blades but the item next to them, a bar of soap. He reached down, gently lifted her hand, moved it in the right direction. The bones of her hand were small and fragile, the exposed skin warm and dry.

She herself looked down then and discovered her error. "Why, thank you."

With a deft twist she removed her hand from his grasp and took the package of razor blades. She looked up into his eyes again. There was still that sense of recognition, of a mysterious gladness. Willie realized that within two seconds she was going to turn around and walk away. Their moment of contact would be lost forever.

"Can I buy you an ice cream?" he asked suddenly.

She looked startled. "But it's forty degrees outside!"

"I know, but that's what Mr. Morton serves here."

"Then it has to be ice cream," she agreed. "Chocolate, please."

Willie walked her to the counter and ordered two dishes of Morton's chocolate ice cream, then two cups of coffee because of the cold weather. The young woman put her purse on the counter, hiked herself onto one of the stools, and patted the other for him to sit beside her.

"This is good," she said, after tasting the lump on her spoon. "You clearly know where to get the best ice cream."

"Morton's does a good job," he said. "Or rather, his wife makes it for the store."

"Do you have a name? Or are you going to remain my knight of ice cream?"

"I'm Willie—William Henry—Wheelock. But Willie to my friends."

She gave him an appraising look. "My name is Jane Dobray."

"That's a nice name. Is it French?" He was guessing.

"So they tell me." She gave him the same quizzical look, with a slight squint. "I saw another man named Wheelock today. The judge over at the courthouse."

"That's my father. Then I guess you saw him at the trial?"

She nodded. "I wanted to meet him, and he was in court."

"You went looking for him?" Willie wondered. "Why?"

"Oh … just some business," she said.

"Oh."

Jane Dobray finished her ice cream, scraped across the bottom of the bowl in neat, parallel lines, and licked her spoon clean. Everything she did was compact and graceful. "Well, thank you for the ice cream," she said, meeting his eyes one final time.

"Are you staying here in town?" Willie asked, knowing it sounded desperate.

"I don't know how that's any of your business," she said—but with a smile.

"I'd like to see you again," he said simply. "To call on you … if I might."

She slid off the stool, put her purse under her arm, and started out of the store. Halfway to the door she turned back to him. "Then call at Mrs. Burke's," she said. The woman whirled, and in a heartbeat she was gone.

Willie turned to Morton behind the counter. "Do you know her?"

"Never saw her in my life," the pharmacist said.

"Jane Dobray," Willie murmured, half in love already.

"The name rings a bell," Morton said. "But I can't think why."

Willie barely heard the comment, because he was trying to remember why he had come into the pharmacy in the first place. Then he remembered. He bought his shaving soap, toothbrush, and a package of razor blades and went back to work at the Chrysler dealership.

17. THE LIBRARY CARD

MOST WEEKDAYS, THE Roulette library was deserted in the early afternoon, leaving Klaus Riesenberg alone with his books. He understood the reasons for this: the local people were mostly farmers, laborers, and shopkeepers—people whose days were filled with work and commerce, or housewives who had their own ways to keep busy. His regular readers came in the morning, and the school children came by to study and do research in the late afternoon. The time at midday was for himself, and Klaus usually settled in the office with a book and a cup of tea.

This year he was improving his understanding of his adopted country's culture through mystery stories. He had started with Edgar Allan Poe in January, and by October he had worked his way up to Melville Davisson Post and the "Uncle Abner" stories set in the hills of Virginia, a place that Klaus imagined was not unlike Sylvan County. For the remainder of the year he had set aside the urbane mysteries of Raymond Chandler and Dashiell Hammett for his future enjoyment.

"Ding!" The bell at the front desk caught him deep into "The House of the Dead Man." Klaus closed the book, straightened his vest, and went out into the library.

The pretty young woman standing there was no one he had ever seen before. She was bronze-haired, clear-eyed, and smartly dressed. He sensed she was a heroine more in the Chandler or Hammett mode than anyone out of Post's mysteries.

"I desperately need a book to read," she told him.

"I know the feeling," he replied with a smile. "What kind of stories do you like?"

"Got any Rider Haggard?"

"Have you read *She*?" Klaus asked.

"And *King Solomon's Mines* and *Return of She*. Does that exhaust your shelves?"

"Mostly, but not quite. We've got *People of the Mist*. Have you read it?"

"No." She brightened. "Thank God for that. I'm going nuts in this town."

"I know that feeling, too." Klaus laughed, then turned serious. "I don't suppose it's any good asking if you have a library card?"

"I just got into town yesterday," she admitted.

"There's a residency requirement." He bit his lip. "Are you staying with friends?"

"No, afraid not." She was disappointed. "I'm at Mrs. Burke's boardinghouse."

"Well, that's almost like a friend. Will you be in town for a while?"

"I doubt it," she said. "I'm just here for a ... business transaction. But I promise to return your book before I leave. Is that good enough?"

"I think I'm authorized to take your word on that," he said.

Klaus went over to the elderly Underwood and cranked in a blank library card. "Name?"

"Jane Dobray." And she spelled it for him.

"That's interesting," he said. "Did you know that, phonetically, in both Polish and Russian, your name means 'Good day'—as in greeting?"

"That would explain some of the funny looks I got at the Russian Tea Room."

"So you know New York City?"

"I was born there," she replied.

"Pretty fancy, to be hanging out with the ballet crowd."

"Oh, the Tea Room? I waited tables there once, is all."

"Still very sophisticated." He nodded. "And my name is Riesenberg, Niklaus," he said, remembering his manners. "Welcome to Roulette."

Jane Dobray nodded and extended her hand across the counter.

He shook hands gravely with her. Then he filled in the rest of the card with the date and her address at the boardinghouse and handed it to her with a pen. "It's not official until you sign it."

As Jane Dobray bent her head to sign the card, something in the shape of her face caught his attention. While the young woman was pretty enough, the corner of her jaw stuck out on one side, forming a sharp angle. This deformity—if that it was— appeared only when she turned her head or stood face-on to him; it disappeared at other angles or in profile. Normally, he would dismiss the feature as an accident of birth, but something about it seemed familiar. Klaus knew for a fact that he had never seen this woman before, but he had certainly seen this distinguishing mark. It bothered him that he could not recall where.

"Is that it?" she asked, holding up the card.

"That is it," he agreed. "I'll get your book for you."

18. Ruby's Café

On the morning after the attorneys had presented closing arguments in *People* v. *Maires,* after Judge Wheelock had sent the case to the jury, and the jury had returned an acquittal inside of fifteen minutes, the crowd at Ruby's Café found much to discuss.

"I always said that Lance's shooting Ernst down in his own barn never made any sense," said Walter Dufour.

"Oh? And when did you say this?" asked Doc Ramsey.

Dufour waved his comment away, because Ramsey was not a breakfast regular. "A lot more practical to do it when Lance and Ernst were out hunting together. Two men, all alone, out in the woods, and a .30-30 round through the back. That would make a terrible accident, and no one could blame him afterward. Not really."

"Kill him while hunting?" said the doctor. "You're talking sacrilege there, friend. Hunting creates a bond between men stronger than any lust for a woman. ... No offense there, Ruby."

"Just keep it clean, gentlemen," she said from behind the counter.

"Besides which," said Clarence, "everyone knew Ernst Bauer wasn't a hunter."

"Not to mention the fact," said Reverend Stevens, "that Jim Harris just showed Maires didn't kill Bauer at all."

"Yeah, his wife did it," Clarence added. "Churchy la femme."

"Do you think they'll charge her?" Leonard Kingston asked.

"I guess that's up to Pete Twombley," Dufour said. "Of course, after what Harris just put him through, Twombley might be having second thoughts about doing anything more with this case."

"Going to take Rafe Cobb a while to live that one down," said Ezra Stills.

Everyone looked around quickly, but the sheriff had not come in this morning.

"Rafe's not a big city detective and never claimed he was," Dufour replied.

"Just the point," said Stills. "He must have walked past that hay bale ten times in going over the crime scene. Anyone lives in the country could tell you it didn't look right, all torn apart like that. It was the biggest clue he had."

"They still have to try Emily to get justice done for Ernst," Clarence said.

"Oh, fine!" exclaimed Reverend Stevens. "And orphan those two girls?"

"Emily may not be able to stand trial," said Doc Ramsey. "Not the state she's in."

"They say her nerves are broken," said Kingston.

"I guess getting caught will do that to you," said Clarence.

"Well … I can't comment professionally," Ramsey suddenly backpedalled.

At this point Harold Burke came into the diner. It was a couple of days since the regulars had seen him, given his duties at the courthouse during the trial. "Guess who just blew into town?"

"Santa Claus!" one voice called out.

"Superman?" someone else guessed.

"Margot Dobray's grown-up daughter," Burke said.

"Who?"

"Girl named Jane Dobray," Burke supplied.

"How do you know she's related to Margot?" Clarence asked.

"Who the hell's Margot Dobray?" Walter Dufour demanded.

"She was before your time," Burke answered Dufour. "Because she had a check from Margot," he said to Clarence.

"Margot wrote her daughter a check?" Clarence was bewildered.

"It was not 'from Margot,' " said Theodore Burns, who worked over at the bank. "The check in question was made out to one Margaret Dobray." As the transaction had never been completed, he apparently did not think it was covered by the bank's policy of confidentiality. "The young lady came to my window trying to cash it. She said that it was for her mother, who had died."

"Margot Dobray is dead!" said Clarence. "And she was so pretty, too!"

"In a hard-bitten kind of way," said Reverend Stevens, "if I remember correctly."

"But *pretty*," Clarence insisted. "She had spunk."

"Well, what's the daughter like?" Dufour asked.

"Prettier," Burke said dreamily, then caught himself.

"Wasn't Margot before your time, too?" Dufour asked.

"Sure, but I've heard the stories," Burke replied. "This gal, her daughter, is no flapper or floozy. She dresses nice enough—no war paint or anything like that. She seems like a sensible, old-fashioned girl."

"Ain't it pitiful to see an old man in love?" Dufour said sourly.

The crowd greeted this with jeers and catcalls. "Lo-ove!"

"Gentlemen, please!" Ruby said, flapping her dish towel.

Suddenly Morton the pharmacist, who had been preoccupied with his eggs, sat up straight. "That's the girl! I *saw* her yesterday in my store."

"And is she pretty?" asked Clarence.

"I know one young man who certainly thinks so," the pharmacist said. "William Henry met her and ended up buying her an ice cream. Right on the spot, he asked her out for a date."

"The Judge's son?" asked Burke.

"Just as plain as day," Morton replied.

"Well, imagine that," said Reverend Stevens.

"I always said that boy was a fast worker," Dufour said.

"Well, who made out the check?" Kingston asked them.

"What check?" Burke asked, distracted.

"The check to Margot Dobray."

"Oh, it was the Judge's check."

"He was sending Margot money?" Clarence asked.

"She worked for him, didn't she?" Burke said.

"Was it a *recent* check?" Dufour asked.

"First of this month," Burns affirmed.

"I'll bet there's a story behind that," Dufour said.

19. Meeting the Judge

Jane Dobray finally got in to meet Judge Wheelock in person on the day after she had sat as an observer at the murder trial. As he led her up the stairs to the judge's chambers, Mr. Burke told her about the outcome later in the afternoon, in case she'd missed it: the jury had acquitted the man Maires in record time. Well, Jane could have predicted that before she left the courthouse.

The county clerk knocked on a solid oak door with the nameplate "Hon. Robt. Wheelock" on it and got a muffled response from inside. He opened it a crack. "Got that young lady I mentioned, Judge," he said. "Margot Dobray's daughter?"

The response was, to Jane's ear, still muffled.

After all this time, she was not about to be turned away. So she slid under Burke's arm, pushed the door open, and strode quickly forward, putting out her hand. "Hello, I'm Jane Dobray," she said brightly.

Wheelock was sitting behind his desk, still in his judge's robes, which ballooned at the sleeves to make the man look about four feet wide. Jane's gesture caught him off guard, and he scrambled to his feet. He was taller than she remembered from court. He came halfway around the desk and reached over the end to return the handshake.

"Oh, yes?" he said, looking over the top of his reading glasses. Jane detected a flash of recognition that he hid immediately. "Yes. … Harold told me about you."

"I came to see you, day before last, but you were busy with that trial."

He nodded. "I saw you in the gallery yesterday."

"Best show in town," she agreed.

"I guess I'll just leave you to it," Burke said stiffly, closing the door.

"Thank you, Mr. Burke," Jane called after him, then said to Wheelock: "Anyway, to business."

She sat in the chair facing the desk and took Margot's check out of her purse. By now it was limp along the fold and curling

340 · Thomas T. Thomas

at the corners. "This came in the mail last week. I understand that it's yours."

He barely glanced at it. "Yes."

The judge seemed distant, almost distracted.

"Well, Mother died recently," she explained. "As I'm her daughter and sole heir, I'd like to get the money. In cash, if you would."

He nodded slowly. "I don't have that much at hand." He frowned vaguely. "But I suppose we could work something out."

Jane realized that his apparent indifference was a veneer. Beneath it, the man was giving her sly, sidelong looks.

As a young woman with a face and figure that wouldn't exactly stop a clock, she was accustomed to getting such looks from men when they thought she didn't notice. In other circumstances, Jane might have said he was weighing the possibility of a romantic encounter, undressing her in his imagination, or mentally feeling her up. But in this case, with this man, the motivation seemed different. Jane sensed Wheelock was searching for something. And, if she was any judge of men, whatever he had found was scaring the crap out of him.

"Mr. Burke says Mother worked for you," she ventured.

"Yes, but … only for a short while."

Now he was acting downright nervous.

"What work did she do?" Jane asked.

"She was secretary in my law office."

"Margot? A legal secretary? She had a lot of jobs when I was growing up, but she never did anything like that. That's a really good job!"

"Well, not to speak ill, she wasn't particularly qualified."

"Yeah but, see, that must have been years ago," Jane said. "So why, now, did you write her this check?"

"Because …" He looked dumbfounded. "Well, I …" He stopped.

"That wasn't the only check you wrote for her, was it?"

"No, there were others," he admitted.

Since her first guess was right, Jane doubled down. "Regular checks, too, weren't they?"

"Yes, every month."

Now they had come to the question. "Why?"

"Your mother never told you?" Again, he gave her that side-long look.

Jane had already considered and rejected the notion that, of all the missing fathers she might have had, this man was among the candidates. As she had discovered in the courtroom, she felt no spark of connection on seeing him. And now meeting Whee-lock up close, she could not believe Margot would have been attracted to him. Not that he was at all bad looking, but the judge was too educated, too obviously intelligent, too much the patri-cian. And because he was a judge, an official of the courts and representative of the law, Margot would naturally have tended to put a safe distance between herself and him.

All of which was not to say that Wheelock himself might not have been attracted to Margot. She was too much the chorus girl. And maybe the sideways glances he was giving Jane now were the echoes of leers he had once given her mother.

Perhaps, then, Robert Wheelock was the rich man who, in her mother's stories, had caused her father's death. That would explain not only the glances but the money as well. Whee-lock might have a guilty conscience. The two hundred dollars might be blood money. And again, perhaps, it was none of these things—because, as Jane had found out over the years, Margot's stories were not always to be trusted.

Finally she said, "Until that check came, I never even heard of you."

"Then I don't believe I am at liberty to tell you the story myself."

"That's a lawyerly thing to say, sir. I'd like to have an answer."

"I'm sorry, but I can't say any more. There's a ... confidence involved."

"Well then, I guess I'll have to settle for a note to the bank," Jane said. And when shock registered on his face, she pointed to the check. "So they can release that money to me."

"Oh. Yes. Of course."

Judge Wheelock pulled a sheet of white paper out of his desk drawer, took the fountain pen from its holder, and wrote a note to the bank manager. He used black ink in a large, sweeping hand. When she took the paper and fanned it to dry the ink, she noted the two men were on a first-name basis, as big frogs in a little pond would be.

"Does that satisfy you?" he asked stonily.

On the face of it, yes. Jane's mission to the Pennsylvania back country would be complete when she had the two hundred dollars in her purse. But then what? Get on the next eastbound bus and back to New York? To do what? Live under a bridge and starve quickly on the money from the check. Margot's last days had already proved to Jane that the city had no future for people like them. Could she do better in a town like Roulette? Here, at least, if she got hungry she could go out in the fields and dig up a potato or something.

"If I think of anything else, I'll surely let you know." Jane told him flippantly.

Unexpectedly, Wheelock nodded at that. He did not look happy at all.

"Don't bother getting up," she said. "I know the way out."

It took two seconds for Jane to go through the door and out of the room. But she had a feeling her presence would stick in the mind of Robert W. Wheelock, Esquire for a lot longer.

———

After Jane Dobray left his chambers, Robert continued to sit at his desk for a long while. There were papers he had to read and sign, documents to be perused, writs and warrants to consider. He ignored them. They did not matter. Now that Margot Dobray's daughter had come to town, had come back from the mists of time and distance to which Robert had consigned her twenty years ago and sealed her existence away with a monthly check for two hundred dollars, nothing might matter anymore.

Clearly, Margot had never told the girl whose daughter she was. And it was clear from this encounter that Robert lacked the courage to tell her now. To acknowledge Jane Dobray as his own natural child would destroy everything he had built over the years. It would end his marriage, because Libby had said more than once, in conversation about the troubles of other couples, that she could not abide a philandering husband. It would ruin his reputation in the town, because Margot had been too obviously the *femme fatale* and Robert had taken her into his office too quickly. Wise heads had been wagging over that for years, but in the end they had nothing to show for their speculations. Not until Jane Dobray arrived in town.

It suddenly occurred to him that Jane Dobray might not simply leave town. The meeting just concluded might be only the opening skirmish in a much longer chess game. She might know exactly who Robert was and how she was related to him, having been told long ago by her mother. So this meeting was not just about the money, or not only about the money, but also a kind of test. She wanted to see if he would act the gentleman and acknowledge her parentage, or if … if what? If she could blackmail him for a lot more than two hundred dollars? Suddenly, that last "if I think of anything else," took on a much darker meaning. Jane knew who she was. She knew who he was and what their unspoken relationship would do to him. She was playing with him.

He thought back to the face he had seen in the courtroom gallery the day before. Jane's face, of course. The intent look. The searching look. She had known him then, of course. She had come to court only to see him. So she must have known something. But what? And how much?

Robert's whole future wavered before his eyes like a vision in a mirage, appearing and disappearing in waves of uncertainty. And there was nothing he could do—nothing he dared to do—about the situation. He was in agony. And all he could do was sit there—and not *know!*

20. THE LAST SHACKLE

WILLIE HAD ALREADY arranged to have dinner with Barbara Eccles for the day after the day on which he met Jane Dobray. The gentleman in him ruled against seeing one girl while he was courting another, and so he put off calling on Jane until he settled things with his fiancé.

Barbara spent her daylight hours doing chores on her father's farm and liked to come into Roulette in the evening. Since the murder trial started, she was avid for news of that too. The thought of a man killing his rival in love excited her immensely. She imagined Willie had unique knowledge of the crime, being the Judge's son, while in truth all he could tell her was gossip from customers at the automobile dealership. The trial's end would close off this topic between them. And, Willie was certain by now, that wasn't the only thing finished.

Willie drove to the farm in a blue Buick sedan. His employer, Leonard Kingston, believed the cars he sold were better for being driven occasionally. He said engines and transmissions, if they were not used, would gum up with sludge and quickly fall apart. So Kingston, knowing that Willie was a careful driver, let him use whatever he wanted off the lot.

He parked in front of the Eccles's two-story frame house and stepped out into the growing dusk. As he went up to the door, it opened immediately and Barbara hurried out. She turned to say something to her father, then came down to meet him, take his arm, and pull him to the car.

"Tell me what happened at the trial yesterday," she said breathlessly.

"Maires was acquitted," Willie said. "By unanimous verdict."

"How could that happen? Everyone knew he was guilty."

"Apparently twelve people didn't know it," he said.

"So now Maires just goes free?" She pouted.

"That's the way it works," he said.

Willie installed her in the front seat and went around to the driver's side. When he got in, she scooted across and snuggled next to him, pinning the arm he would need for turning the ignition and shifting gears. Not wanting to disturb her—not tonight, not yet—Willie did his best to get the car started.

"Are you hungry?" he asked.

"You know me—always!"

As he drove back into town, Willie couldn't find a thing to say. Barbara more than made up for that by chattering about the triangle involving Maires and Emily Bauer, the potato crop her father had just got in and the market price, her mother's rheumatism and whether she herself would be so afflicted one day, and everything else that seemed so inconsequential. Willie parked in front of Ruby's Café and they went inside. Barbara turned immediately for one of the two tables in the front, each tucked into one of the shallow alcoves made by the restaurant's store-front windows. It was her favorite spot—"for showing off my beau," she always said.

For once, Willie did not follow her. "I think a back table would be better tonight," he suggested.

Barbara looked at him directly. "Oh? And why is that?"

"We have things to discuss," he said in a low voice.

"You mean," she said, "you have *us* to discuss."

"Look, this probably isn't the time or place."

"Oh, it's time, all right. You've been real quiet tonight, Willie, like you're going to make an announcement. And I know what's going to be. She finally got to you, didn't she?"

"Who has?" he asked, appalled. For an instant, Willie thought she had found out about Jane Dobray. But there was no way Barbara could know about her.

"Your mother, that's who!" Probably her voice was still in its normal register, but Barbara's remark seemed to cut across the restaurant chatter. Several of diners glanced up at them.

"I don't want to make a scene," he replied quietly.

"No, that would be wrong, wouldn't it?" she said. "Your mother has made it so very clear to me what is *right* and *wrong*. Are you going to start in now too?"

"I'm sorry if I seemed to be lecturing you."

"That's right, *Professor*. No lectures from the college boy."

Now she *was* raising her voice. Willie saw Ruby coming toward them between the tables with a strange look on her face. From several feet away, she asked, "Everything all right, folks?"

Barbara turned on her. "It's none of your business."

"Please," Willie said, "let's keep this civilized."

"Oh, yes, we have to be civil. Your family always keeps things *civil*."

"I'm sorry, Ruby," he said to the proprietor.

Barbara wheeled on him then. "Don't you apologize for me, buster!"

"Why don't you folks take it outside," Ruby said evenly. "Please. Now."

"Take me home!" Barbara said, suddenly near to tears.

"All right," he said. "I'll—"

"Just take me home."

On the drive out to the farm, Barbara huddled silently against the passenger door, as far from Willie as she could get. He thought she was crying silently in the darkness. Although he felt guilty, he was also relieved. There was no chance now for a final good-night kiss, a hopeful farewell, and possibly a last-minute reconciliation. Ever since his lunch hour the day before, he had been thinking up excuses, rehearsing things to say, planning to ease the evening toward this moment. Now, he found, he needed none of these stratagems. The affair had fallen apart on its own, borne down by the differences between him and Barbara. And somehow Libby had a hand in that.

Willie knew he must kiss his mother when he got in tonight.

It was full dark but not too late when he arrived back in town. Jane had told him to call at the boardinghouse, and Willie could not think of any reason to wait. He had the evening, he had the car—and he had no idea how long the young lady would be in town, once she had completed her mysterious "business" with his father.

Of course, Willie couldn't take her out to Ruby's, not after the scene he had just made. But it was likely Jane had already eaten;

Alfreda Burke set an early table for her boarders. Maybe Jane would like to go to the new movie in town—and then maybe more ice cream!

———

After visiting the bank that afternoon—and enduring anxious huffing and puffing from first the bank manager and then the teller over Robert Wheelock's note and the propriety of the whole transaction—Jane now had her money safely tucked into the zippered pocket of her purse. She tried to think of a reason to stay another day in Roulette, and she couldn't. Only the fact that the next eastbound bus didn't come through until ten o'clock the following morning kept her in town for the night.

She had her suitcase open on the bed and was folding her clothes into it when she heard a knock on her door. "Miss Dobray?" came her landlady's voice.

Jane crossed the room and opened it. "Yes, Mrs. Burke?"

"Normally, I won't carry such a message, because I run a respectable house, but there's a gentleman asking for you at the front door."

Jane tried to think who this might be. Not the Judge, certainly, as she had a pretty clear notion he never wanted to see her again. It wouldn't be any of the shopkeepers or townspeople she had met, because no one knew where she lived.

"I make an exception, in this case," Mrs. Burke went on, "because the young man is known to me and he claims to know you."

The words "young man" struck an instant chord. "Is it Judge Wheelock's son?"

"It is, and only because—"

"Please tell him I'll be right down."

Jane closed the door, ran to the mirror, and passed a comb through her hair. A quick inspection of her blouse and skirt showed she had nothing better in her suitcase that was clean. She left the room, with the case still open on her bed, and locked the door behind her.

Willie was waiting in the parlor, standing nervously and fiddling with the switch on one of Mrs. Burke's lamps. He turned and smiled as Jane came over to him.

"I wasn't sure you'd agree to see me," he began. "Mrs. Burke said—"

"I always see the men who buy me ice cream," Jane assured him.

"If you're free this evening, there's a new picture in town, *The Treasure of the Sierra Madre,* with Humphrey Bogart. He's always good."

"Gee, I saw *Sierra Madre* in New York when it came out last winter." It crossed Jane's mind that, given the difference between her status and his, a film about digging for gold was somehow inappropriate.

Willie sagged a bit, and she knew immediately her words sounded like a rejection. She went on quickly, "But it's good enough see twice. I'd really like to watch it again."

He checked his watch. "We can just make the opening reel."

She patted his arm. "Let me get my coat and purse."

21. Accomplice to Murder

Robert was working in his chambers, writing letters in longhand on a yellow tablet, when the phone rang. He picked up the receiver while still writing and started to say, "Hello—"

"Judge Wheelock, is that you?" said an almost-familiar voice.

"Yes, of course. Who is this please?"

"Lance Maires, sir."

Robert paused.

The trial was less than two days in the past, hardly long enough for the talk in town to have died down. Maires had been acquitted and released, certainly, but he was still in a legally precarious position. If Emily Bauer were brought to trial, double jeopardy would not protect him from possibly being named as accessory to murder—which would be a different charge from the one he had faced. So the propriety of Robert meeting with or even speaking to Maires was questionable.

It then occurred to Robert that Maires might want to bring suit on grounds of false arrest. But then his own lawyer, Jim Harris, could advise him better than the judge—although Robert would bet long odds against Harris moving forward with such a case. He too clearly wanted to be judge in Robert's place. And not even Harris would have the gall to initiate a suit against Sheriff Cobb and Prosecutor Twombley, officers of the court in his future jurisdiction.

"What can I do for you, Mr. Maires?"

"Are you alone, sir?" the man asked urgently.

"Why do you ask that?" Robert was suddenly wary.

"I have to see you, but it's got to be private."

"Where are you now?"

"Across the square, at the café."

"Well, come on over then."

While he waited, Robert thought of the .38 Smith & Wesson he kept in the bottom drawer of his desk. If Maires were armed, or suddenly turned violent, could he reach it in time? And then do what? Shoot the man? Better the weapon stayed buried.

A few minutes later Harold Burke knocked on his door and, with eyebrows raised, admitted the man.

Robert stood up to meet him. He did not offer to shake hands. "Have a seat, Mr. Maires."

"Thank you, Your Honor."

"What's all this about?"

The man sighed. "I got to unburden my soul."

Robert sat down behind the desk. "Go ahead, please."

"The night after Ernst was found dead, me and Emily got into a fight. I'd been drinking, and she was wanting it, and when I couldn't get it up, she turned nasty. Said, 'You don't know the things I've done for you.' And that, sir, is when I knew."

"Knew ... what?" Robert said cautiously.

"That Emily had killed Ernst that day."

"You should have come forward then."

"I didn't have any proof. Just the suspicion."

"You could have used it to clear your name."

"Mr. Harris didn't want me to testify. He said Emily and me screwing provided a motive. And after his detectives found the gun and all, it was better we didn't get into the personal stuff."

"It makes you an accomplice," Robert summed up.

He knew that by saying this, he had impermissibly involved himself in a potential case. Now, if Emily were charged, and Maires were included in the indictment, Robert would have to recuse himself and send the trial out of the county. Or perhaps, after the November election, it wouldn't matter.

Maires looked at him blankly. " 'A comp'—what? What are you saying?"

"It means you took part in the act and benefitted from it."

"But I never did! If I'd known what that gal was going to do, I wouldn't of let her. I know there's talk around town I must've given her my gun, but I swear I hain't seen or touched it in years. Hell, I *liked* Ernst. He was a *good* employer."

"That didn't keep you from sleeping with his wife," Robert said drily.

"Oh, well, that's just fair game, if a man can't control his woman."

Robert grimaced but said nothing. It was the sort of remark Margot Dobray would have made—and Libby despised.

"So, why do you come forward now?" Robert asked.

"I love her, Emily, you understand, but …"

"But not at the expense of another man's life?"

"Yeah, that and, well, the farm really takes two people to work … Two men, you understand … And I kind of figured I might be next."

"Not a bad assumption," Robert concluded.

"No, sir. I mean, yes, sir."

"They'll have to arrest her, you know. She'll go on trial, just like you did. Will you testify to what you've told me?"

"I guess I got to, seeing as I came here. But it's a shame."

"What? Your testifying against Emily?"

"No, those two little girls. If they 'lectrocute her, the girls won't have a mama."

"I seriously doubt that Emily would get the death penalty," Robert said. "But she might go away for a long time."

"I can't take care of them," Maires went on gloomily. "They'll end up in the state home, won't they?"

"If it comes to that, I'll see what can be arranged."

"Thanks, Judge. Now my mind's at ease."

"You don't—don't mention it."

22. THE HOUSE ACROSS THE PARK

AFTER SITTING THROUGH the movie with Willie and bidding him a chaste good night on the boardinghouse porch, Jane had still finished packing her suitcase. But then she lay awake until the small hours, unable to decide whether to take the bus in the morning or not. She only fell asleep after she figured out that spending one more day in town wouldn't break the bank. Anyway, she still had to return her library book.

Jane was not such a fool that she would try to build a whole relationship, a future, a change in her life's course, on the basis of one date with a man. But she was interested. And she certainly could tell that he was interested.

She already knew Willie was a paid-up member of the gentility: it was obvious from his manner of speaking, the little courtesies he showed, the way he held himself and observed the world. And she had known from Burke's confidences on her first night in town that his father, Judge Wheelock, was well off: any man who sent two hundred dollars in the mail every month to virtual strangers was, by Jane's standards, rich. Since it appeared that, one way or another, she was going to be involved with the Wheelock family, she decided the next morning that she should get to know them better. At least she could see where they hung their hats.

"If I wanted to visit Judge Wheelock," she said to Alfreda Burke after breakfast, when her landlady was putting lemon oil on the front stairs banister, "where would I go?"

Mrs. Burke hesitated. "The courthouse?"

"No, I mean when he's at home," Jane said.

"Why would you want to visit him at home?"

"Oh, just to see where he lives. I'll bet he has a fancy house."

"Well, you're right there," Alfreda said. "Probably the biggest house in town."

"Gee, I'd sure like to see that."

Jane got directions and—after waiting half an hour, so as not to seem too eager—went out for her morning walk. Along Main

Street, on the other side of the wide bridge with concrete parapets over the river, she came to a screen of dense evergreen trees, exactly as Mrs. Burke described. There were a couple of pokey little houses stuck on lots cut into the side of the road, but Jane went right past them. She found the entrance to the white-gravel driveway and started walking up it.

Beyond the evergreens she came out into an open park, with broad lawns and clumps of spreading trees—maybe maples or chestnuts, Jane thought, although as a city girl she knew little about trees. Anyway, they had now lost most of their leaves. Above the treetops rose the round towers of a fairytale castle. One had square cutouts, like a fort, and the other a cone-shaped roof of black slate. Three days ago, coming into town on the bus, Jane had seen those towers and fantasized about the people who might live in such a mansion. They would be old money, of course, and have good china, starched white linen, and perfect manners—people such as Margot Dobray's daughter could never hope to meet. And now here she was!

Suddenly, Jane had the feeling of eyes watching her. She could not see anyone in the tower windows, but she felt exposed just the same.

Without appearing to hurry, she withdrew under the overhang of the nearest tree, although she was still exposed through the thin cover of brown leaves. She worked her way around and headed sideways, across the lawn, keeping one tree or another between herself and the house. Every so often, she came upon wide, flat plots of turned earth that was ridged and brown in the golden, autumnal sunlight. It looked like a patch of land lifted from a farm.

After a long walk, always keeping her attention turned sideways on the house, Jane came to the bank of the river. Or rather, the edge of a cement canyon with vertical walls and a sheer drop of fifteen or twenty feet. The river flowed as a slow, greenish trickle along one side of the canyon's flat bottom. Jane could look upstream and see, maybe half a mile away, where the river ran freely over rocks between grassy banks. She wondered why the townspeople would turn it into such a sterile, ugly thing. Maybe Wheelock had a hand in that—after all, the canyon ran right by his property. She could see it curve outward, along the edge of his lawns, to a point where another stream flowed into it, and that stream, too, was encased in gray concrete. This mechanical treatment of the river left her feeling sad.

Jane followed the broad, squared-off top of the canyon wall down toward the point. After a moment, the house came into view again, this time from the west side. The mansion was built of red brick with a peaked roof of black slates, like the nearer of the two towers. The windows all had lintels and sills of thick, gray stone, and the glass was bordered with small, diamond-shaped panes, like a church—except they were clear, not stained. Immediately below the house was a double row of six black trees, now leafless, planted in a small orchard.

If Robert Wheelock wasn't a rich man, then he was certainly doing a good job of faking it. The house and grounds were well cared for: Jane's eye could trace in the grass the track of a large mowing machine that followed the edge of the canyon, sweep upon sweep, until a trapezoidal pattern came together in the center of the lawn. The orchard trees were pruned back for the coming winter. Someone was hoeing and weeding those patches of turned earth—and it wasn't Robert Wheelock or Willie, either.

Jane decided she liked what she saw. And if, as she suspected, Wheelock was the "rich man" who had a hand in her father's death so long ago, then what better way to get back at him than by stealing his son's affections? That would not be hard for Jane, either, because Willie was so obviously sweet on her. It would be a pleasure, in fact, because he was also smart and good looking.

When Willie came to call again, Jane knew what her answer would be.

23. A Son's Confession

In the two weeks after the murder trial, Willie had virtually absented himself from the family dinner table. Accustomed to his son's occasional dates with the Eccles girl, Robert could not imagine their relationship had suddenly grown so intense. Willie might also be expected to make a weekly night out with the young men from his place of employment, but this was every night in a row.

Characteristically, Willie did not make excuses or offer explanations, just said he was going out. He returned later and later in the evenings, until he was coming home well after Robert and Libby had gone to bed. Robert wondered what might have happened, to make his son so preoccupied, but Willie was no longer a boy. He was grown now, with a good job, his own income, and a right to control his own time—much as Robert had been when he lived on the third floor of this house with his father and stepmother.

That whole floor was blocked off these days. During the war Robert had workmen erect a false wall of raw plywood inside the banisters on the stairs leading up from the second floor as a fuel-conservation measure. One that Robert had never found a reason to dismantle. His old apartment up there was used as a lumber room, and it had been years since anyone visited the place. Instead, Willie occupied the bedroom he had as a child, in the back of the house over the kitchen, next to the communal bathroom.

When Willie came in at night and went down the hall, Robert was usually lying in bed reading. He listened now for clues to his son's nocturnal activities: the cadence of a drunken footfall, although Willie never publicly took a drink; the rustle of paper and clink of coins as he counted his winnings, except that Willie was the only soldier Robert had ever heard of who did not gamble; or the giggle of a girl he might be taking into his room, although Barbara had never gone further than the foot of the front stairs.

No, Willie crept across the floor like a considerate son not wanting to wake his father.

And then one evening Willie took his usual place at the dinner table with no more explanation than he had ever given.

"You've decided to join us?" Robert could not help commenting.

"Yes, sir," Willie said, picking up his napkin.

"Did Miss Eccles have other plans tonight?" Robert probed.

"Barbara?" his son asked. "I'm not seeing her anymore, Father."

Robert shot a look at Libby, who was following the conversation from her end of the table. He saw a light of triumph flash in her eyes.

"Then whoever it is you've been spending time with," he suggested.

"Sir?" Willie said, confused.

"Did *they* have other plans?"

"Oh, no—that is, yes, Father." And Willie ducked his head to a forkful of roast beef. "Mrs. Riesenberg's done really well tonight," he said to Libby, gesturing toward the platter.

"I'll tell her you said so, dear," Libby replied.

"I guess we're not going to have the satisfaction—" Robert began.

"Oh, hush!" his wife said. "Of course, Willie's been seeing a new girl."

"Well, I'm certainly happy to hear it," Robert said. "Do we know her?"

Willie looked up, meeting his father's eyes, then his mother's. "Not really."

Robert was concerned. "I can't forbid you keeping secrets, Willie."

"It's not a secret," his son said. "I mean, she's a decent person. There's nothing inappropriate going on. I know you would approve of her."

"Are you in love with this girl?" Libby asked gently. It was a question that Robert knew she had never dared to ask concerning Barbara Eccles.

Willie thought about that a moment. "Yes, I believe I am."

"Then we should meet her, don't you think?" Libby said.

Willie hesitated. "It's just … I don't know where things stand between us right now," he said at last.

"Well, what do you expect?" Libby said. "It would appear you've been occupying a lot of her time—every night this past week, if I'm not mistaken. That doesn't give a girl much chance to think."

"Funny, that's what she said."

"Then she sounds wise to me."

"I think she is," Willie said. "She has her own mind, you know, not like the girls from around here. For one thing, she reads lots of books—and not just novels. She's gone to plays, but she also likes the movies. She has even attended concerts, in New York City, where she grew up. So I can talk to her about things."

As his son spoke, a warning siren began to sound in Robert's head.

"Is she pretty?" Libby asked quietly.

"Oh, she's beautiful, Mother!"

"Then it's certainly time we met her," Libby said decisively. "I will visit her people and extend an invitation to dinner. This Sunday, I think."

"She doesn't have people here in town," Willie said.

"I don't know that's such a good idea," Robert said suddenly.

"Why ever not!" Libby said to Robert. "Where is she staying?" to her son.

Willie answered first. "She's a guest at Mrs. Burke's boardinghouse."

"Well, that's respectable enough," Libby said. "And what is her name?"

"Jane Dobray," Willie replied.

Libby stopped and looked quickly at Robert. "Dobray?"

Robert looked down at his plate. "Her daughter," was all he could think to say. Of course, Libby would not know about the daughter. No one knew about a daughter. Best to leave it that way.

But Robert remembered that morning after the Maires trial and the encounter he had with the girl. It had been a shock, seeing a pastiche of his own features—the face he confronted every morning in the mirror—looking back at him. He could see in her face the same mouth, the same long jaw, the light-brown hair.

Because she did not contact him again, Robert had assumed the Dobray girl took her money and went away—back to New York, or off to more pleasing prospects. But apparently not. And now his son was falling in love with his own half-sister. That was disastrous, the stuff of Greek tragedy and Roman farce. Robert had to do something—and quickly—to discourage this consanguineous, this incestuous match. But what could he say that would not reveal his own shameful part in the secret?

"Whose daughter?" Willie asked. "When I first saw Jane, she mentioned meeting you on business. Did you know her family?"

"We knew her mother, dear," Libby said. "She worked in your father's office."

"Not for very long," Robert said.

"No, not long at all," Libby said.

Robert listened for any hint of anger, or jealousy, or criticism in his wife's voice, but her tone was perfectly neutral. And that could be just as bad.

"How did you meet her?" Libby asked their son.

"Just by chance, in Morton's Pharmacy. She let me buy her an ice cream."

"How can you think that's not inappropriate?" Robert burst in. "A girl who would let herself be picked up like that? In a drug store? And now you're content to court her? She doesn't sound at all suitable to me. In fact, it's shameful."

"Come on, Dad! This is the twentieth century. And Roulette is not some big city full of strangers," Willie said. Then he brightened. "Besides, you've met Jane already, and you say you knew her mother. So that makes her almost like family. I'll ask Jane to dinner here on Sunday, and you'll see what a great person she is."

"I'd prefer to invite her," Libby said.

Robert looked up to meet her eyes.

"It's my home," his wife said evenly.

"Yes, of course," Robert replied quickly.

"That's swell, Mother," Willie said.

24. The Invitation

Alfreda Burke answered the front door to Libby's ring, showed her into the parlor, then went upstairs to announce her to the Dobray girl. Libby knew the Burkes, of course, from the courthouse if not exactly socially, and she was curious to see the inside of their home. Chintz and waxed pine, Libby noted as she perched on the edge of the settee, with a braided rug in front of the hearth. She examined a bouquet of bright-red china roses on an end table and saw dust in the crevices. So Mrs. Burke's local reputation as a housekeeper was slightly exaggerated. Libby filed that item away for future consideration.

"Here she is," said Alfreda from the hallway.

Libby rose to her feet and watched as the girl came down the stairs.

She immediately recognized the brisk and capable young woman who had helped her in the parking lot of the A&P. On reflection, Libby realized she should have put two-and-two together when Willie first mentioned concerts in New York. Where else would a young woman become familiar with the driving exploits of taxicabs?

At the time of their first encounter, Libby had been deeply embarrassed by her own inability to maneuver the big Chrysler. Now she expected to feel resentment against the girl because of it. But she surprised herself by feeling only relief. Whatever Libby had imagined Margot Dobray's daughter might be, this cheerful and helpful young person was something quite different.

As she descended the stairs, Jane Dobray showed poise—one hand comfortably down at her side, the other resting lightly on the railing. Also, she dressed appropriately for the middle of the afternoon: a full skirt, nylons and heels, sweater set, and beads.

Or were those pearls?

No, tiny white beads.

"I'm so pleased to meet you, Mrs. Wheelock," Jane said, coming into the room with her hand out in greeting. "Or should I say, meet you again?"

Libby took the hand and felt a gentle squeeze in return. Jane's hand was small and warm, like a bird pressing against her fingers.

"You certainly didn't catch me at my best, that morning."

"Oh, don't think of it! I'm scared to death of driving myself."

"My son speaks very highly of you," Libby went on, after they had positioned themselves on the settee.

"Willie? He's a charming man," Jane Dobray said.

"I understand you've been seeing quite a bit of each other."

"I hope you don't mind. He keeps asking me out. What's a girl to say?"

"Don't you have any other beaux?"

"Not at the moment," Jane said casually.

Libby studied her face, looking for traces of the mother, whom Libby had known only by reputation and from a single glimpse one day from the other side of the street. Margot Dobray had been as bright and brassy as a chorus girl. Her skirts were an outrage around town and, if you could believe the stories, her behavior had been worse. The girl who sat beside her now was different. She seemed softer, more natural, and she certainly was prettier. She had something of Margot's reputed audacity and confidence, but where in the mother it had been like a shard of cold iron, with this girl it was a vein of warm gold.

Still, Libby sensed something else going on with Jane Dobray. It was something familiar—something that almost touched Libby's memory—but she could not put her finger on exactly what it was.

"You and Willie seem to be serious," she said cautiously.

"What's serious? He's taken me to a movie and dinner, and out to the Stateline a few times. That's all."

Libby recognized the latter as a roadhouse north of town. It once had a reputation as a speakeasy but now was known only for cheap food and fast dancing. Well, if her son could be seen there, Libby supposed, a modern young woman might respectably join him.

"I understand your mother died recently. My condolences, of course—"

"Thank you." The girl gave her a small, rueful smile.

"But I wonder, do you plan to stay on here? Are you looking for a job?"

"I don't know about that yet," Jane said. "I'm still sizing things up."

"Then may I ask how you manage to support yourself?"

"I have a bit of money. Mother left it to me."

"I'm so glad to hear Margot managed to leave you comfortably situated."

"She had her resources," Jane said with an enigmatic smile.

Libby felt obscurely that the comment was meant to work against her. "At any rate," she went on, "I do think it's time you met the family."

"I'm looking forward to it," Jane replied soberly.

"Sunday then? We dine at one."

"I'll be there."

"Shall I have Willie fetch you?"

"That would be so kind of you."

With her purpose accomplished, Libby bid good-bye and showed herself out into the hall, leaving the Dobray girl standing in the center of the parlor. Jane had her weight on one foot and the other turned out, the back of one hand pressed against her hip with the elbow stuck out to the side. Libby could see something defiant in that stance. Something old-fashioned and somehow ... western. It was the way stockmen and miners stood, in the old pictures. And then, as she closed the front door and went down the steps to the sidewalk, it hit her.

Libby knew what had seemed familiar about the girl.

And it told her volumes about Jane Dobray's origins.

25. RUBY'S CAFÉ

WHEN WALTER DUFOUR entered the café for breakfast on Thursday, he found the regulars strangely subdued. The men were uniformly distracted and thoughtful in their eating. Forks cut sausage and shoveled up their eggs with the tiniest clink of silverware. Knives buttered toast with the barest crunch. Occasionally a chair scraped. Finally the mayor couldn't stand it.

"Well then, who died?" he asked aloud.

"I guess you hadn't heard," Clarence began.

"Let me tell it," the sheriff said and then shut up.

Dufour turned to Cobb. "So tell it."

"We got a call from the Bauer farm about four o'clock yesterday afternoon. One of the twins—Hannah or Trude, I honestly don't know which—after they got dropped off from school by a neighbor."

An old, sour sadness, a kind of loathing, was rising in Dufour's chest.

"We went out there right away," Cobb went on. "Emily Bauer had hung herself from the second-floor banister. She was in her housecoat and slippers—well, one slipper anyway—and hadn't washed herself in days, I guess. And those little girls had to find her that way. To think they'll take that memory of their mother with them forever …"

"Oh, God," Dufour whispered.

"It's a terrible thing," said Reverend Stevens.

"Where are the girls now?" the mayor asked.

Harold Burke seemed to come awake. "Judge Wheelock took them. He and Libby put them up for the night, over at the big house. The Judge knows the Bauer family, of course. He says there's no else living, not since Ernst's father passed on."

"Is he going to keep them?" someone in back asked. "Raise them?"

"Be a shame if they had to go to the orphanage down in Emporium."

"I got a call from Klaus Riesenberg this morning," Burke said. "He couldn't even wait for me to get to the courthouse and open up. He was asking about adoption forms, and what kind of references he and the missus will need, and can they do it even though they're immigrants."

Dufour thought of Alma Riesenberg. "She was teaching the girls, wasn't she?"

"They trusted her with that letter," Cobb said, "when the hanky-panky started."

"Klaus and Alma certainly can speak German to them," Clarence observed.

"Polish," Leonard Kingston said. "It's Polish the Riesenbergs speak."

"They speak German, too. They speak all kinds of languages."

"Sounds like those girls will be cared for," Dufour said.

"Terrible things to have happen," said the reverend.

"But it seems something good always comes."

26. Sunday Dinner

Jane's preparations for Sunday dinner with the Wheelocks—her audition, as she called it privately—turned out to be a lot of work. She started on Saturday morning by dying her shoes.

When she opened the waxy preparation she obtained at the drug store, she found a thick liquid, more like brown paint. So she had to go back downtown again to the feed store and buy a brush, and the only one they had was about three inches wide, really more suitable to painting a barn. Jane ended up using just a corner of it to spread the goop all over her second best—second only, really—pair of shoes, being careful not to stain her hands or anything else in her room at the boardinghouse.

All of this effort was because the only clothes she had that were appropriate for the occasion, not to mention the weather, was a brown wool suit: a tailored jacket with slashed lapels and a pleated skirt once belonging to Margot that Jane had cut down for herself. A high-necked white blouse with ruffles across the front, which she had bought in what passed for a clothing store in Roulette with some of the Judge's money, made the ensemble almost work. Except that neither her black pumps nor the gray really went with the suit, and so she was sacrificing the gray shoes to her sense of style. She only hoped the paint would dry by the time Willie came to pick her up.

Just after noon on Sunday, as Jane was pulling on her stockings, Alfreda Burke called up from downstairs, "Your young man's here!" That way, the whole house would know that Jane was going out again. But then, in a town this small, everyone would know anyway, and who he was, and where they were going, and what the mother thought of her, and, for all Jane knew, what price she had paid for the chicken to be served at dinner.

Ah, the mother!

Jane touched the instep of her right shoe lightly, down low where a smear would go unnoticed, to test the paint. It felt dry enough, so long as she didn't rub her foot against anything.

Libby Wheelock was a formidable presence. Jane had found out her actual first name was Elizabeth, but the whole town knew her as Libby. As luck would have it, Jane just happened to have fallen under the stern gaze of Sylvan County's doyenne of taste and propriety. Like hens in a barnyard, all the women within a thirty-mile radius looked to Mrs. Wheelock to discover what they thought and felt about anything new in etiquette, dress, and manners. And Jane, being courted by this woman's only son, was definitely in the realm of the new.

The encounter in the parlor downstairs earlier in the week had been a tactical draw, Jane decided. She had countered a frontal attack on the grounds of "seriousness" with an insouciance that bordered on denial. That had been a lie, of course, because William Henry Wheelock was the likeliest prospect on Jane's radar screens, for right now, and probably for all time. Miraculously, despite Jane's pertness, the woman had still asked Jane to her home.

The one thing Margot had managed to teach her daughter was an appreciation of human character. After that encounter in the parlor, Jane decided she could grow to like and trust Libby Wheelock, perhaps even to love her. Jane already admired her. The older woman exhibited a grace, a sense of purpose, an emotional balance and, she suspected, a fairness that was uncommon in small-town matrons. Libby was her own woman and knew it. She had what Margot would have called genuine style. And, for all that Jane had loved her mother, that was the one thing Margot had lacked.

When Jane went down the stairs—slowly, so as not to scuff her shoes—she found Willie waiting inside the front door.

"Oh, hello," he said, looking up.

Jane bathed in the warmth of his gaze. "Hello!"

He offered his arm like a perfect gentleman and showed her out the door. Down at the end of the walkway, taking up most of the curb, was the biggest, blackest car Jane had ever seen. "Is that yours, too?" she gasped.

"My father's—but I picked it out for him."

Willie opened the passenger door. Jane sat down and swung her legs inside. As soon as she straightened on the plush upholstery, she sank deep into the seat cushions and backrest. She had to brace with her feet against the floor's thick carpeting to hold herself upright.

He got in the other side, started the nearly silent engine, and made a U-turn in the street. Jane knew exactly where the Judge's mansion was located, of course, and that they could have walked the distance from the boardinghouse. But she let Willie drive her as if it was her first time.

When he turned into the gravel driveway that disappeared under the trees and they came in sight of the fairytale towers, Jane exclaimed for his benefit, "You live *here?*"

"Of course," he said. "My grandfather built that house."

"It's beautiful …"

As the drive passed the broad lawns with those wide plots of turned earth which had piqued Jane's curiosity on her clandestine visit, she pointed and said, "It looks like a farm."

"Those are the glad beds," Willie replied.

"What are they glad about?"

"No … for gladiolus bulbs. My father raises them as a hobby. Each plant has a long spike with frilly flowers up and down the sides. You should see this place in the springtime, with the colors all sorted by rows, like a rainbow. Then he gives them out all over town."

"It must be beautiful."

The drive curved again to approach the house along a stone terrace built into the eastern side—opposite from the direction Jane had walked on that first visit. Stuck in the center of the red-brick house's eastern wall was a funny little porch with a flat roof and white columns, like a Greek temple. The driveway seemed to go right through it, and she could glimpse more lawn and gardens at the back of the house. But Willie parked the car out in front, in the middle of the driveway by the left-hand tower, the one with the archer cutouts.

He came around to get Jane, took her arm, and led her up the steps to the front door, with its carved oak leaves and leaded-glass insets. Jane knew she was about to meet old money at home.

———

By Sunday morning, with Margot Dobray's daughter due to arrive at—to invade, and to establish herself in—his home within just a few hours, Robert's state of paralysis and fear had reached the point of emotional collapse.

While getting ready for church, he cut himself shaving, which was not supposed to happen with a safety razor. Then he missed a button on his shirt—ending up with the collar and tails at odd angles—and had to start over. He put his left cufflink through the holes backward, so that the clasp showed on the outside of his wrist. Then he dropped the other link, so that he had to get down on hands and knees and grope under the bed.

Being down on his knees already, he thought about praying for guidance. Given his various duties as church usher, he knew he would not be able to organize his thoughts in the confines of First Methodist. But then, Robert knew exactly what the good Lord wanted of him: to do the right thing. That would be go down the hall this minute, take Libby aside, and confess everything—his liaison with Margot, his responsibility for Jane, the reasons why their son and this girl cannot be together. To confess his sin now would be to lance a boil that was only going to grow larger and angrier.

Perhaps it was already too late. Libby had known nothing about Jane until Willie mentioned her at dinner, early in the past week. By that time, Robert had already seen and dealt with the girl, so Libby knew by implication that he was keeping secrets. And now that Libby had met Jane too, she must have noted the strong physical resemblance between him and his natural child. That his wife had not remarked on any of this, Robert found ominous.

And the relationship between Willie and Jane had already gone too far. To oppose it now with sufficient force would require explanations that jeopardized not only Robert's marriage but the respect of his son and his position in town. He was willing to bear those burdens if the act prevented a greater wrong, which the incestuous relationship certainly was. Not to tell would spread the stain to two young souls who were still innocent.

And yet, Robert lacked the courage to plunge into confession. He knew it would put the household in an uproar. He suddenly realized that, up until now, his path in life had always sought balance and peace, usually at the cost of other considerations. He had avoided conflict—with Lydia over rights to this house, with Margot over her laziness and obvious deceits, with Harris over his ambitions for the bench. Robert's life-long choice was to wait and see what developments time and patience might bring.

Now it was simply too hard to grasp the thistle.

Robert finally found the cufflink under the bed and stood up. He fastened it with care, then took his suit jacket off the valet stand and put it on. He would go down to the front hall, join Libby while Willie went around for the car, and go to church as always, as if nothing at all was about to happen.

After church—which included a sermon on faith and Daniel's ordeal in the lion's den, which Robert found no help at all—the family returned to the house and then went in different directions. Libby headed upstairs to change out of her hat and gloves so she could supervise in the kitchen. Willie stopped to brush his hair in the front hall mirror and prepared to drive over and pick up Jane. Robert had nothing to do but wait in the library, across from the parlor, and console himself with a book and a small scotch—neither of which he consumed.

As one o'clock approached, he heard gravel crunching in the driveway opposite the front door. Robert looked out and saw Willie park there, in the middle of the curve, and retrieve Jane from the passenger-side door. Robert noted how his son's face beamed as he stood near the girl and how lightly his hand touched the back of her elbow.

Robert felt his insides curl up.

———

After church, Libby went back to the kitchen to check with Alma Riesenberg, who was preparing this day's special meal. The joke in the family was that Libby supervised the cooking, when what she actually did was taste this and that while making happy noises. Alma was serving one of her *mitteleuropean* specialties: roast duck with dill sauce, pan-roasted potatoes, baby carrots, and red cabbage. It was duck season, of course, and she had her sources among the county's hunters. Bending to peer into the oven, Libby could see that the woman had acquired four fat specimens and dressed them perfectly. The skins were already turning a rich, dark brown.

"How are the twins doing?" Libby asked.

"They are very happy," Alma replied. "Considering."

"Why didn't you bring them up to the house?"

"Today Klaus is taking them on a nature walk along the river. Those girls know everything about a farm and nothing about the wildlife."

Libby smiled. "Does Klaus know anything about wildlife?"

Alma returned the smile. "He has read about it. I think he knows the difference between a fox and a bear—but only if it shows both ears and tail."

"Lord preserve the children!"

"Amen, madam!"

At this point Willie pushed into the kitchen with Jane in tow. Robert came trailing behind. "Hello, Mother! We're all here now."

Libby came forward and took Jane's hand. "So good of you to come."

"My pleasure, Mrs. Wheelock."

"Please! Call me Libby."

"Why, thank you."

Robert Wheelock stepped up beside his wife. "When we met before," he said to Jane. "I'm afraid we didn't get off on exactly the right foot. I must apologize. Chalk it up to a difficult trial … and then the shock of hearing that Margot had died."

"All right," Jane replied. To Libby's ear, she sounded cautious.

"And Jane," Willie said, "this is our housekeeper, Mrs. Riesenberg."

"Riesen—?" Jane started. "I met the librarian in town. His name—"

"My husband, Niklaus." Alma said.

"Of course," Jane said. "Gee, something sure smells good."

"You like ducklings?" Alma asked.

"I'll try anything once," the girl replied.

"Ah! Then you'll come back, I think."

Libby glanced around the kitchen. "I think it's time we stopped interrupting Mrs. Riesenberg."

Alma took the cue. "Soup course in five minutes, madam? If you'll take seats at table, I'll bring it out."

Libby guided her family and guest through the pantry and into the formal dining room. Everything was arranged to perfection. After she seated them—with Jane across from Willie and facing out the windows toward the yard and the trees—Libby lighted the candles and took her place at the foot of the table.

As Alma Riesenberg brought out and placed the soup dishes, and then the other courses, Libby guided the conversation. She told her family the story of how she and Jane first met, putting herself in the role of helpless female behind the wheel. Then she asked Jane about living in New York, and shared her own memories of her and Robert's visits there. Willie told a funny story about going to a Broadway show when he was on leave, before the army shipped him overseas.

Still, there was tension in the air. Willie was oblivious to it, as he alternately hung on Jane's words and made fun of his own experiences. But Libby noticed that Robert, at the head of the table, barely spoke. From the way he sat, with his shoulders down and his head slightly forward, she thought he was merely preoccupied. Then she saw how his eyes moved, half hidden under his brows. He was watching the children—and in that moment Libby was stunned to discover she thought of Willie and this girl as "children" together.

But Robert was seeing something else. His eyes went from Jane to Willie, then back to Jane. Whatever he was thinking he did not share by so much as a glance down the table toward Libby. He just watched the two young people. His attention twitched from one to the other, as if he feared they would suddenly explode, either into argument or a fight, although to Libby the conversation seemed totally innocuous. At one point, Willie tried to interest his father in a discussion of the newest automotive technology, something called "hydraulically assisted steering," and Robert simply brushed him off—then looked at Jane.

Libby knew her husband had been out of sorts ever since Willie mentioned he was seeing Jane Dobray. At first, Libby thought it was the shadow of her mother Margot that he resented. Now Libby sensed it was something about Jane herself. But what it might be was a mystery, because Libby could find no fault with the young woman. That surprised her, of course, but there it was.

She liked Jane.

And Robert did not.

Libby just hoped he wasn't going to be difficult about it.

———

As Sunday afternoon progressed, Jane recalled the remark the housekeeper had made, early on in the kitchen, about Jane coming back. Now she was feeling less and less sure about that. During the dinner, she sensed strain in the family. Perhaps, for all the kind words given to Jane in greeting, these people were simply mannered and stiff after all. And too aware of Jane's lowly station in the world.

Not Willie, of course. He was as attentive as ever, laughing like a schoolboy.

And not Elizabeth Wheelock, either. "Libby," as she insisted Jane call her, was bright and talkative. She told the story about the parking lot with good humor. She praised the color and cut of Jane's hand-me-down jacket, even though her own clothes were better made. Libby paid attention to the amount of food on Jane's plate and twice asked whether she was enjoying her duck. And she followed Jane and Willie's discussion of a movie they had seen, although Jane could guess Willie's mother cared nothing for film as an art form. But once Jane caught the woman looking directly up the length of the table at her husband and scowling fiercely. Neither the Judge nor Willie appeared to notice.

Throughout the meal, Robert Wheelock himself sat quietly, staring down at the tablecloth, never once meeting his wife's eyes. He was obviously distracted, as if he knew a secret and could not share it. And that made Jane nervous.

Finally she decided that the judgment had already gone against her. Without Willie's knowing it, his parents had rejected her out of hand. Libby was being so very cordial and attentive only in order to hide her true feelings. Like a great lady, she was being especially kind to the thing that caused her the most pain and distress.

So it came as a shock—but also a relief—when the Judge and his wife finally made direct eye contact.

The table had been cleared and a bottle of port was put at the Judge's elbow with four glasses. He poured out the thick, ruby-colored wine and passed the glasses around. Jane lifted hers and was about to take a gulp, just to ease her nerves, when Libby spoke up.

"Robert, would you propose the toast?" she asked quietly, in a neutral tone, and with a voice so cold that, if Jane's own mother had been using it, she would have hidden under the bed.

The Judge nodded to his wife, seemingly oblivious to her manner, and looked narrowly across the table at Jane. He raised his glass.

"To our guest, Miss Dobray," he intoned. "May she ... be ever in our thoughts."

"Hear, hear!" Willie said enthusiastically. "And in our hearts!"

Robert and Libby silently held their glasses up to one another before drinking.

Jane did not know what passed between them, but she seemed to be off the hook for now. As the subject of the toast, she knew she ought not to join in, but she could not help herself. She discreetly put the glass to her mouth and took a long swallow.

Then she noticed that, while the glass touched Robert's Whee-lock's lips, he did not drink.

27. The Father Confesses

Niklaus Riesenberg routinely opened the library at nine o'clock each morning, for which he arrived fifteen minutes early to collect returned books from the depository, turn on the building's heat if necessary, and straighten chairs at the reading tables. When he arrived on Monday morning at the end of October, he was surprised to find Robert Wheelock waiting on the library steps. The man looked gray and ill.

"Good morning, Your Honor."

"Klaus, I must talk with you."

"Indeed? Is there trouble?"

"Yes … I am in trouble."

"Then please, this way."

Klaus unlocked the front door and led his former employer into the building and behind the counter to his office. He offered the man a seat, took his hat and coat, and excused himself while he made the minimal preparations for opening and started a pot of tea. When he had seated himself behind the desk—noting how different it was to have the Judge across from him, in the chair reserved for guests and library patrons with difficult questions—he studied the man. "You do not look well, my friend."

"I've had a bad week—bad couple of weeks," Wheelock stared down at the hands hanging between his knees. "I have done a terrible thing."

The librarian smiled. "I have known you for ten years, through peace and war, then peace again. I cannot imagine you doing anything so very wrong, even by accident or neglect."

Robert Wheelock merely shook his head. "Do you know about the young woman who came to town recently? Jane Dobray?"

"She borrowed a book from the library the first day she was here." Klaus nodded. "And Alma said she went up to your house for dinner yesterday."

"She's my daughter," Wheelock said bleakly.

"Ah! I did not know you had another child."

"No one knows. She is illegitimate. Her mother lived here for a time, twenty years ago. She worked in my office."

"In town one hears of the fabulous Margot Dobray. She disappeared suddenly."

"As soon as Margot told me she was with child I sent her away. I've been mailing her checks ever since. It was to cash one of those checks, after her mother died, that the girl came here."

Klaus nodded in agreement, then shook his head. "To give her money takes only a minute. If you do not acknowledge her as your daughter, then why is she still here? Why is she in your house?"

Wheelock sighed. "Willie met her in town. I knew nothing about it at first. Now he's fallen in love with the girl, and she permits it. And Libby, who knows nothing about her, encourages it."

"Why does Jane entertain the affections of her brother?"

"I can't say. Perhaps she does not know. Perhaps Margot did not tell her."

From the utility room at the back of the building, where Klaus kept a hot plate, the tea water started whistling. "Excuse me," he said.

Tending the kettle, measuring black tea into cups, pouring water gave him time to think. His first reaction was one of sadness. Every man carries sin, he realized, even one whose life was as careful and self-examined as Judge Wheelock's. A fragment from the Christian Bible floated through his mind: "Every sin that a man does is without the body; but he that commits fornication sins against his own body." As a churchgoer, Wheelock would know this. It would be part of his agony.

But what could Klaus do for him now? The Judge had turned to him as a friend and unburdened his soul. What response could he offer?

He returned to the office with two cups on a tray that included a can of condensed milk and bowl of sugar. He prolonged the moment by fussing about with the milk and sugar. When Robert was finally sipping his tea and looking at Klaus hopefully, he knew he could delay no longer. He placed his palms flat on the desk blotter.

"You know this situation cannot continue," he said.

Robert nodded and said nothing.

"Too many people already remember Margot Dobray. I assume she did not leave town with a wedding ring or other excuse for her condition."

"Hardly."

Klaus took a breath. "And I assume you have good reason for believing the child is yours?"

Robert glared at him. "Of course! We had … a liaison. The child came after."

"From the gossip I hear, or the fraction from around town that comes through that door—" He waved toward the front of the library. "—no one is yet aware of your relation to the girl. Or the reason for it. Perhaps no one will ever figure it out."

"And perhaps they will. There's still the sin of incest between the children."

"Willie has fallen in love. Perhaps he will fall out of love."

Robert grunted. "Why do you tempt me with these possibilities?"

"To dismiss them, of course. You have to tell the truth. You know that."

"It will destroy my marriage."

"Libby is a strong woman."

"She will never forgive me."

"That's not the woman I know."

"Willie will hate me for this."

"Experience disappointment, I think."

"It will destroy my reputation."

"Tarnish it—if the matter ever became public," Klaus said. "Not that is has to. You must talk to Libby. You talk to the children. And you set Jane up with a proper start in life—a dowry if she wants it—and she moves on. The rest is no one else's business."

Robert stayed silent and motionless for a long moment. His gaze was fixed in the librarian's eyes, and Klaus would not blink. Finally, Robert looked away. "You're right, of course."

"It's the only way," Klaus agreed.

28. From Beyond the Grave

JANE WENT TO the library on Tuesday morning to return the Rider Haggard book and see what else the librarian, Mr. Riesenberg, might have to suggest for her. As she approached the check-out counter, the man looked up and his eyes widened—in recognition perhaps, but to Jane it also felt like shock—before he actually smiled at her.

"Good morning, Miss Dobray."

"Good morning, sir. I brought back your book. I thought I might see if you had another, or something similar."

"We have many books," he replied. "So then … you are staying on in town?"

"It appears so. I still don't have fixed plans yet."

She had the uncomfortable feeling he was studying her. Given her sudden arrival in town and her more or less open attachment to the Wheelocks' son, she knew tongues were wagging. But this man's interest seemed deeper, more focused. His stare was driven by more than plain curiosity.

He suddenly looked around the library, and she followed his gaze. The building was empty, except for the two of them.

"Do you have time for a short drive?" Riesenberg asked.

"Can you do that? Just lock up and leave?"

"I can in emergency. This qualifies, I think."

Riesenberg disappeared into a back room for his hat and coat. He took her out the front door, where he posted a prepared notice that said "Temporarily Closed" and locked it with a key from his ring. "The Judge parks his car over at the courthouse," he said. "It's just a short walk."

"And you can just drive it away?"

"In this case, I doubt he'll mind."

They settled in the big, black car—for which Riesenberg also had a key on his ring—and headed west out of town on Main Street. "So …" he began slowly, "everyone here seems to know about your mother, Margot. But no one ever mentions your father. Tell me about him."

379

Jane sensed enough of the man's apparently good intentions to put down her first impulse, which was to declare the matter none of his or anyone else's business. It was clear Riesenberg meant to tell her or show her something important. She decided to tell him the truth.

"I never knew my father. Mother told me many stories about her past, before she came to New York, and they changed around quite a bit as I was growing up. There were a lot of men in those stories, so one of them must have been my father. But she never told me his name or anything definite about him. I guess he traveled around, because she mentioned California and Colorado—and Louisiana, I think. He did something with the earth, like mining or oil drilling. But once he was a cowboy. If I think hard about it, I can probably come up with an Indian story, too."

Riesenberg nodded as she spoke, but he kept his eyes on the road. After a few minutes he turned off at an iron gate set into a stone wall. Beyond it were the markers of a cemetery, receding in ordered rows and groupings up the hill among clumps of trees. He followed the entry road as it wound among the plots and parked halfway up.

He led her over the autumn-brown grass to a headstone standing by itself. It was a big, handsome stone cut from rough granite with deeply incised letters: "John Loring, 1904-1938." Beside the words was an oval bas-relief of a young man's face, staring straight at Jane out of the stone. He had smooth cheeks and boyishly smiling eyes.

"I believe this is your father," Riesenberg said. "I can't be certain, of course. But the first day I saw you, I noticed the angle of your jaw on the right side." He touched his own face in the place where Jane's jawbone stuck out lopsidedly. "I knew I had seen a jaw like that somewhere." He touched the bas-relief in the same place. Loring's jawbone made the same angle.

Jane touched her own jaw.

"When I first saw this," he continued, "I thought maybe an accident. But then I remembered that facial bones can be reliable hereditary markers. The Hapsburg royal line had a prominent jaw structure. So does the Barrymore family. You have your father's."

"How do you know all this?" Jane asked.

"When I was the Judge's groundsman in town—my first job after immigrating—he asked me to come out here and tend the family burial plot." Riesenberg pointed to an upright stone some way up the hill with the inscription "Wheelock" and a number of flat markers around it. "He also wanted me to take care of this grave."

"So Judge Wheelock knew this man Loring?"

"Yes, he brought Loring to Pennsylvania to drill for natural gas."

Jane looked around the cemetery at the other headstones. She saw carved angels in various poses. A few macabre death's heads. But no faces that were meant to resemble the actual people buried here.

"Why is his face on the stone?" she asked.

"When Loring died, they couldn't find any papers showing a family connection. No one, no place to send the body. They did find a photograph of Loring, though, taken in New Orleans. Robert thought it would make the grave seem less impersonal to carve his face here. Help people remember the man."

"Did Robert Wheelock kill my father?"

"Good heavens, no!" Riesenberg was shocked. "Why do you ask?"

"Mother once said my father died to make a lazy man rich."

"A drilling accident killed John Loring. I've seen the newspaper clippings. It was an explosion as the drill bit broke into a pocket of natural gas. The death was a terrible thing. Robert was certainly affected by it, enough so that he rendered this tribute to the man."

Jane nodded. She was not entirely convinced. But she had nothing more than one of Margot's stories to support the notion that Robert Wheelock might have wronged her.

"Thank you for showing me this, Mr. Riesenberg."

"That's why it's here—to keep Loring's memory."

29. WHAT EVERYONE BELIEVES

ON MONDAY AFTERNOON his father had used the telephone in chambers to call Willie at the automobile dealership—a personal use of resources, rare for the Judge—and ask him to a meeting at the courthouse during the noon hour on Tuesday. Willie asked what was the matter and couldn't they talk over lunch in town. His father was adamant: it had to be a private meeting, because it affected the future of the family. Willie held his peace and quietly agreed, even though he knew he would see his father at dinner that evening.

On Tuesday he arrived at noon on the dot. Harold Burke took him up to the Judge's chambers. The man rapped twice, opened the door a crack, and said, "Your son's here." Then he swung open the door for Willie to enter and closed it behind him.

Inside he found his mother and Jane Dobray already seated in front of the Judge's desk. As he took his seat, Willie exchanged glances with each in turn. His mother shook her head. Jane simply shrugged. His father saw these responses and bowed his head briefly.

"This is very difficult for me," Robert said quietly. "I am a proud man. Perhaps made too proud, because of the good fortune that has graced my life. When every wish is granted, and every prospect is pleasing, it's easy to forget your faults as a man."

"Father ..." Willie began.

"Let him speak, please," Libby said.

"I had hoped to remain silent, and so escape," Robert went on. "I thought I could have my way right to the end. But now I see that is not possible. I had never thought you would come here, Jane. And, for a fact, I did not know your name until two weeks ago. I never imagined that you, Libby, would have occasion meet this young person or, meeting her, give her more than a moment's thought. And I could never have dreamed that you, my son, would see Jane and become so ... attached to her. But there it is. All of this has come to pass."

"Sir," Jane said coldly, "if you feel my social background—"

Robert put up a hand. "My dear Jane." He smiled at the words. "Your social status has nothing to do with this. As my wife has told me on several occasions now, you are a charming young lady with both sense and wit as well as taste and style. She approves of you. In other circumstances, I might approve. But my wife is not in full possession of the facts—as I am. It is simply impossible for you and Willie to continue seeing each other."

"Really, Father!" Willie said.

"That's our business," Jane said.

"Please explain yourself," said Libby.

"When Margot Dobray came to Roulette," Robert continued, "she worked for a time as my secretary. I have explained that to you, Jane. What you do not know, what no one knows, is that Margot and I had a ... dalliance. It wasn't love, I'm ashamed to say. It was not even pleasure. It was a ... collision of bodies. But the result was that Margot had to leave town because she was with child. No one knew about it. I paid her to go and then paid to support you over the years. You are my natural daughter, Jane. And Willie is your half-brother. So you both can see how impossible it is for you to remain together."

The three of them sat in a state of shock for a heartbeat. Willie felt a dark cloud come over his heart and a coldness settle in his chest.

Jane broke the silence. "You are not my father," she said with conviction. "I saw my father's grave this morning. The librarian, Mr. Riesenberg, drove me out there, to the cemetery, and showed me John Loring's headstone. From the image that was carved on it, I saw that I have his face, his jawbone. And when Mr. Riesenberg told me the story of how Loring died, I knew the truth, because it matches all the stories my mother told me. John Loring was my father, not you."

"Loring was a fine young man," Robert said, "but he never knew Margot."

Willie listened in blank silence. He did not know what to believe.

His mother gave a small, cold laugh. "Oh, you men!"

"Libby, please!" Robert dismissed his wife.

"No, you let me speak this time," his wife replied. "Of course Margot Dobray was pregnant when she left. She and Loring were seen together in all sorts of places that year, but I guess you were stuck in your office and too preoccupied to notice. And a lot of women were jealous of Margot, too, I can tell you. Then he had that terrible accident, and she left right away. All of us could sympathize, of course. And not a few wondered if there might be more to it than simple grief, given Margot's reputation. Ten minutes after I met Jane, I knew those stories were true.

"You never knew that I met Loring once, did you?" Libby went on. "It was when he came looking for you after that first brine well. Loring was a very attractive man. And his relationship to Jane is obvious from the shape of her face, the set of her hands, her coloring, the way she holds herself, even the way she stands. I never saw resemblance so clear between a father and daughter."

Willie heard what his mother was saying, but it took his heart a moment to begin beating again.

"Jane is Loring's daughter," Robert said in a daze.

"Not a doubt in the world," his wife replied.

"But then, it's ... I mean, there's no ..."

"Father," Willie said, "if you'll excuse us, I'm taking Jane to lunch now."

"Yes, please," Jane said. "Let's get out of here."

———

When the two young people had gone, Libby sat looking at her husband. He was still bewildered and uncertain. She, on the other hand, experienced a moment of great clarity. The cloud that hung over Robert for the past two weeks was now cleared away. He had been living with shame and fear for twenty years, then suddenly the old wound had come to life and shed fresh blood. It had threatened to destroy him emotionally. Now the fear was gone, the shame evaporated, and he was required to adjust to a totally different view of the world and his situation.

But not quite yet.

"You and Margot had a 'collision of bodies,' eh?"

Robert met her eyes and nodded. "Yes. It was like, I don't know … I never meant to hurt you, Libby. And I never fell out of love with you. But just, one day …"

"Margot would have that effect on people," Libby said coldly. After a pause she corrected herself. "On men, anyway."

"I know that nothing I do will ever be enough for you," he said quietly.

"You took a vow, Robert. Cleave only to me. So did that mean nothing?"

"It meant everything. I've been faithful to you for thirty years. It's just—"

"One day you jumped the fence with a good-looking woman, is that it?"

"You make it sound so tawdry. It *is* tawdry. I am deeply ashamed," he said. "But you must believe me it was just the once."

"Just once with Margot?" Libby asked, her voice hardening. "Or that Margot was the only one?"

"Both. I never betrayed you—except the one time."

"And you expect me to take your word on that?"

"I suppose, yes, you'll just have to," he said.

Libby felt herself relenting. "I can't believe you would be attracted to a tramp like Margot. I thought you had more taste than that. You should have seen her coming a mile away."

"It wasn't something I planned. Or wanted. It just happened."

"You'll have to make your peace with Willie. He looks up to you."

"I know. Every child's parent starts out as a kind of subsidiary god," he said. "It turns out I'm not even a very good person."

"Oh, well … good enough," Libby said.

"Thank you for that." He met her eyes briefly.

"And then there's Jane. Lord knows what she thinks."

"The family hasn't made a very good impression. Except for Willie."

"Hm-mm-mm?"

"And you too!"

"In other words, then?"

"*I'll* have to make it up with Jane."

"We'll see where things go between them."

"Willie's fallen out of love before," Robert said.

"That's not the way to bet," she replied. "Not this time."

"No, I suppose not."

Libby gathered up her purse and coat. "Dinner's at six."

"Thank you, dear."

"Don't mention it."

30. Election Night

At eight o'clock in the evening of the first Tuesday in November, Robert closed the book he was reading and cracked a yawn. He turned to his wife. "I think I'm for bed," he said.

Libby closed her own book. She was frowning. "Don't you want to stay up and hear the election results? Harold said he'd call."

"I already know the result."

"But you can't be sure."

"Of course I can," he said. "A bungled investigation, with no conviction, and then the murderer has to help us all by hanging herself. That doesn't look good for the county or the bench. By comparison, Harris did a brilliant piece of legal work."

"You've done a fine job for ten years, Robert. People will remember that."

"Individuals, maybe. But people want a winner, Libby. The electorate remembers the last thing they hear. And that was Jim Harris winning acquittal for an innocent man—making a fool of me in my own courtroom."

"Then what will you do?" she asked quietly.

"What I've always done. Practice the law. Grow my garden. I've become pretty good at copper work, and I was thinking of trying my hand at casting in bronze. The post office could use a pair of lamps like the courthouse." He stood up and turned off the light by his chair. "And how will you get on, not being the judge's wife?"

"That's not important." Libby smiled with the half of her face still lit by the table lamp at her side. "Besides, it never was an official position."

"But you enjoyed the notice," he suggested quietly.

"We're still the same people," she said with a shrug.

"Thank Heaven for that."

"What will bother me more is," she continued, "that I don't think Jim Harris will be half as good a judge as you are."

Robert gave that a moment's consideration. When he spoke, he knew he was trying to be brave, a good sport, and "philosophical" about the pending election results. "If Jim stays within the law, he'll be all right. It's like learning to swim in a fast river. You have to find the right current and stay with it. Nothing hard about that, really."

"Harris is not as good with people."

"He will learn." Robert's lips lifted in a wicked grin. "Or I'll take the job away from him, next time."

On his way to the front stairs, however, Robert changed his mind about going up to bed and went into the kitchen instead. He took a tumbler out of the cupboard and filled it a third full with his favorite whiskey. Then he carried it out the back door and down the flagstone path to the garage. The keen night air cut through the cotton weave of his shirt and made him shiver, so that he took a large swallow as soon as he entered his workshop and switched on the lights.

The gas in the stove was turned low, but the place was still warmer than outside. Robert made his way around the Gravely tractor's mower disk and the sacks of peat moss to turn up the flame until the mica panes inset in the iron door were glowing cheerfully.

He thought a session pounding on a sheet of copper would be good for his nerves. Perhaps he would make another ashtray. He went to his metal bin and picked out a scrap that was more square than oblong and had only a few odd corners that needed to be cut off. When that was done, he smoothed out the metal and laid it on his bench.

To find the center of the irregular shape, he used the compass with a pair of sharp scribing points. Working from the trimmed edges, he located the center with two faint, short arcs, marked it with a punch, and put one leg of the compass in the resulting dimple. He set the other leg for the maximum possible circle and started around what would be the edge of the ashtray. Somewhere in the curve, however, the pressure of his fingers must have changed the angle of the compass legs, because the last part of the line was outside the first part by an eighth of an inch.

Robert looked at the gap. "Damn!"

He tried to correct the angle on the legs by taking off from a point halfway back around the circle, but his eyeball judgment was off. He ended up making a third line somewhere between the two ends of the circle.

Robert closed his eyes. He picked up his drink and took a large swig.

Then he closed the compass, grasped the two legs like a thick pencil, and made scribble marks all over the marred face of the copper sheet. The scratches were deep and, unlike his other traces, would not pound out in working the metal. He made a last stab with the tool and broke off one of the finely ground compass points.

"There," he said to himself with venom. "Does that make it better?"

He looked at the ruined sheet and the broken tool.

"No," he decided. "It makes it worse."

31. Proposing to Jane

All through dinner, Willie was conscious of the lump in his vest pocket pressing against the soft spot below his ribs. This was the third Sunday dinner that had Jane as a guest of the family. After the first time, when his mother had made the formal invitation, Willie had done the asking and Jane always accepted. In the weeks between, the two of them went out on dates at the picture show, lunch at Ruby's Café, dinner in the fancy dining room of the Allegheny Hotel, and dancing at the Stateline. Once, Willie had borrowed a convertible from his employer and driven Jane out into the country, to a wide spot in the road along the river, where they could park and, with the heater roaring, watch the moon come up over the mountains.

This Sunday, however, was more than just another social occasion, although only he knew it. When Jane put her fork down after the last bite, Willie stood up. "Father. Mother. Will you please excuse Jane and me?"

His father looked puzzled but nodded.

"Jane," Willie said. "I have something to show you in the library."

"All right." She smiled uncertainly, dabbed her lips, and put aside her napkin.

He took her hand in his as they passed into the front hall. At the entry to his father's study, Willie released the hand only to turn and pull the sliding paneled doors out of their recesses, giving the two of them complete privacy.

"You know I went down to Emporium this week," he said.

"And what business did you have there?" she asked.

"Something that you can't buy in Roulette."

"And what is it you can't get here?"

For answer, Willie went down on one knee before her.

"What!" she exclaimed. "Get up, you fool!"

"You can't get this," he said simply.

Willie dug the small, square box out of his pocket and opened it. Nestled in the black velvet inside was a ring of white gold with a one-carat blue-white diamond that the jeweler in Emporium had described as flawless. It had cost Willie three months' salary, but he was sure there was nothing better he could do with his money.

"Oh my God!" she cried, covering her mouth.

"Jane, we've only known each other a few weeks—"

"Is that a diamond?"

"It's a token, Jane."

The words he had prepared, the excellent phrases describing his love for her and his wishes for their future, flew right out of his head. "I love you, Jane, and I want to marry you," was all he could manage.

"Let me see it!" she said. In her excitement, her hands were opening and closing like mechanical things.

Willie pried the ring loose from its hidden clip. He set the box on the desk and took her left hand, intending to slip the ring onto her third finger. Instead, she twisted the ring out of his grip, took it from him, and put it on herself. He had the feeling, just for an instant, that he had vanished into the air in front of her.

Jane held her hand up to the yellowed light from the desk lamp. The diamond blazed like a star in the evening sky and threw its rays around the room.

"It's perfect," she whispered.

"Will you, Jane? Will you marry me?"

She took her eyes off the ring and looked deep into his. "Of course I will. I've been expecting you to ask me for a week now. And the answer has always been yes."

He stood up then and pulled her against him, kissing her on the mouth.

It was Jane who broke off the kiss. "There's just one condition."

"Anything," he said breathlessly. "Ask and it's yours."

"I want you to leave Roulette. Your life—our life together—must be more than selling cars in a small town like this."

"Yes," he said.

"It doesn't matter where we go," she went on. "You can go back to school. You should study something worthwhile. Possibly the law, like your father, or medicine or engineering."

"I said yes," he repeated. He did not tell her he was more interested in the classics or maybe philosophy, instead of the more lucrative professions she was describing so enthusiastically. They could argue about that another day. "I'm ready to go back to the university," he explained. "But we'll have to live somehow. So— just for practicality's sake—I might continue selling cars, just at first. We'll need the money."

"There are lots of ways to get money," she said breezily. "We'll borrow it from your father, if necessary. Or I can get a job. Don't worry about the money."

"And this would make you happy?"

"No, it would make *you* happy," she said. "And *that* would make me happy."

Willie held her tight and kissed her again. He thought his life was complete.

32. Ruby's Café

Walter Dufour finally returned to the breakfast regulars in the second week of November. He had kept away mostly from hurt feelings, having lost the mayor's race to Clarence Jaspers. To Clarence, who ran the feed store and never showed an interest in the town's political life. To Clarence, who was pleasant natured, sometimes a bit simple minded, and usually became the butt of every joke told here of a morning, but was no administrator. Once again Dufour wondered at how strangely the horses ran in local politics. But he also knew from experience there weren't too many ways Clarence could get into trouble. The mayor's job was really more a social perk than an administrative or fiscal chore. Dufour had been able to do it and still keep his post with the electric company. Jaspers would do the job and keep his store open.

Dufour's race wasn't the only surprise upset that November. No one had thought James Harris had a chance against Robert Wheelock for county judge. While Harris had pulled off a neat trick in the Maires trial, Dufour would not have said that anyone in town really liked or trusted the man. But maybe people were just ready for something new.

Of course, it wasn't political restlessness that had lost Rafe Cobb the sheriff's job. Although he was a decent man and well liked, everyone knew the Maires investigation had been bumbled. And since the war a lot of smart young men with military experience and good heads on their shoulders had been coming back into the area. Jimmy Teague, who hired on as deputy just a year ago, was one of them. He ran against old Rafe and won easily.

As Dufour entered the café this morning, he looked around to see if Cobb was showing his face yet. And he wasn't. Neither was Wheelock, although he had never been a regular. Dufour expected he might become one, now that he had to drum up business for his new law practice on Main Street.

"Hello, Walt," Ruby said, a bit shyly, from behind the counter.

"Hi there," he replied. "Eggs over easy and hash browns, please."

"Did you hear the news from over at Wheelocks?" asked Ezra Stills.

Dufour had a sudden apprehension. Maybe the Judge had taken his election loss badly after all. "No, I don't think I did."

"Willie proposed to the Dobray girl," the farmer said.

"She's sporting a rock big as a hailstone," Clarence added.

"Well, good for them," Dufour said. "He's a smart lad, that one."

"I don't know how I'll replace him," said Leonard Kingston. "He's given notice at the dealership, as of the end of the year. Says he wants to go back to school."

"I guess that was going to happen one day," Dufour said. "He's too bright to stay around here."

"His father had an ivy league education," said the Reverend Stevens. "That didn't keep him from making a life in Roulette."

"Times change, Reverend," Dufour said. "Willie's seen the world."

"I guess they'll ask you to perform the wedding, too," Clarence said.

"It's something of a tradition," Stevens said. "I married Robert and Libby."

"I remember. Be good to have another celebration at the house across the park."

"We have a lot to look forward to."

33. DEARLY BELOVED

SOMETHING OLD WAS one of Jane's stockings, which had a runner up the calf and little balls of nylon clinging to the sole of the foot. Something new was the rest of her ensemble—underwear, shoes, gloves, veil, the bouquet of silk flowers—all picked out and paid for by Libby. Something borrowed was the wedding dress that Libby herself had worn, which was so old-fashioned and heavy with lace that Jane had laughed out loud on first seeing it and quickly turned it into a laugh of joy to keep from hurting the older woman's feelings. Something blue was the diamond on Jane's hand, which flashed coldly in the sunlight coming through the windows. Other colors for the day were the pure, chaste, arctic white of the snow that blanketed the house and grounds and piled up three inches deep on the windowsills, and the pale green silk of the dresses that Libby had bought for all the women in the wedding party—"in the hope of an early spring," she had explained. Jane herself stood apart in her silver-colored wedding dress.

When they heard the first bars of the processional march from *Lohengren* coming up from the rosewood piano downstairs in the parlor, Libby leaned in close to Jane's veil and whispered, "Are you nervous?"

"N-no," Jane said, surprised to find herself shaking.

"Then let's go." Libby picked up the long train that swept behind the dress and guided Jane out into the hallway. The other women in the party followed her out of the bedroom, quickly passed her, and took up their positions on the stairs. On Libby's cue, they started moving, until Jane herself was standing on the top step.

"Slowly now," Libby whispered in her ear, "and in time to the music. Let yourself float down."

Holding the bouquet in front of her, Jane floated. She went down the short three steps that led to the intermediate landing, passed the dark old grandfather clock that stood in the corner there, then turned to the long flight down to the front hall. She kept her eyes on the frosted-glass globe that topped the tall brass lamp built into the newel post at the bottom of the staircase and let the toes of her shoes find the risers.

A crowd of townspeople was waiting for her below in the hall. Jane recognized Walter Dufour, who ran the electric company and had been mayor of Roulette; Leonard Kingston, from the auto dealership where Willie worked; Theodore Burns, the teller at the bank, who was the first person Jane had met on coming to town; Harold Burke, from the courthouse, who had been the second; Fred Morton, the pharmacist, in whose store she had first met Willie; and Clarence Jaspers, from the feed and grain, where she had bought her paintbrush, who was now mayor. Jane smiled at them all and glided past them down the hall.

At the arched entryway into the parlor stood the Judge. It had been agreed that, since she had no living father, Mr. Wheelock would give her away. He offered his arm, and Jane laid her gloved hand across it. He led her up the aisle between the folding chairs arranged across the parlor, to the circular niche at the far end. This curious extension of the room, Jane had figured out, was the base of the tower with the conical cap that had been her first glimpse of the house. They had hung this enclosed space with white draperies to represent a chapel. Inside it stood Reverend Stevens, looking severe in his dark robes with the starched white collar. Waiting in front of him, hands behind his back, half turned to see her, was Willie. He was grinning like a kid.

The reverend cleared his throat. "Dearly beloved …"

The rest of the service flowed over Jane without actually registering on her brain. Even the part about speaking now or forever holding one's peace passed by her. She stared at the reverend as in a trance, seeing in his lined old face the image of a benevolent if slightly demanding God. The words "I do" came out of her mouth as in a dream. The gold band appeared on her third finger alongside the diamond as if produced by magic.

It actually came as a shock to her when Willie lifted her veil and kissed her.

Suddenly, without a thought, she was Mrs. William Henry Wheelock.

And there was nothing in the world Jane could do about it now.

34. The Copper Bracelet

After the ceremony and the wedding feast that extended from the dining room throughout the house on tray tables and trolleys, Robert took his wife aside into the pantry at a quiet moment and produced his own gift.

Libby accepted the box wrapped in silver-colored paper. "What is this?"

"Open it and see."

"It's not Christmas."

"Just something I made."

She peeled back the wrapping paper, opened the box, and rustled through the wadded tissue paper Robert had used for packing. She pulled out the copper bracelet, which was polished to a warm red glow, with the three dimes arranged across the center of the band, the Liberty heads facing left with Mercury's wings sprouting from behind their ears. They shone like full moons in the evening sky.

"It's beautiful, Robert. But I have so much—"

"You can have more."

"Of your jewelry, I mean."

"Of whatever you want, my dear."

She slipped the bracelet onto her wrist.

"But why three dimes?" she asked.

"Look at the dates," he suggested.

"Nineteen-eighteen ..."

"The year we were married."

"And all the decades in between."

"But now that I think of it," he continued, "those dimes could also represent our children."

"I don't understand," Libby said.

"One for our son Willie," he explained. "One for Genie, the daughter we lost. And one for the daughter we found today."

Acknowledgements

This is a work of fiction. The characters and their lives are wholly my own invention. However, several of the story elements originated with the history of my grandparents in a small town in central Pennsylvania. If this book has any flavor and richness, it is due to the stories about them passed along by my family. The book would not have the structure it does without the critical reading and advice of Patrick Larkin, who is a best-selling author of military and historical fiction. And the text would suffer without the fine polish given by his wife, an able editor in her own right, Mennette Larkin. Finally, my dear wife, Irene Moran, made a gift of her patience and gave me the confidence that made this book possible.

ABOUT THE AUTHOR

Thomas T. Thomas is a writer with a career spanning forty years in book editing, technical writing, public relations, and popular fiction writing. Among his various careers, he has worked at a university press, a trade-book publisher, an engineering and construction company, a public utility, an oil refinery, a pharmaceutical company, and a supplier of biotechnology instruments and reagents. He published eight novels and

Photo by Robert L. Thomas

collaborations in science fiction with Baen Books and is now working on more general and speculative fiction. When he's not working and writing, he may be out riding his motorcycle, practicing karate, or wargaming with friends. Catch up with him at www.thomastthomas.com.

eBooks and Paperbacks:
Coming of Age, Volume 1: Eternal Life
Coming of Age, Volume 2: Endless Conflict
The Children of Possibility
The Professor's Mistress
eBooks:
Sunflowers
Trojan Horse
Baen Books and eBooks:
The Doomsday Effect (as by "Thomas Wren")
First Citizen
ME: A Novel of Self-Discovery
Crygender
Baen Books in Collaboration:
An Honorable Defense (with David Drake)
The Mask of Loki (with Roger Zelazny)
Flare (with Roger Zelazny)
Mars Plus (with Frederik Pohl)